THE

ASSASSIN's

WIFE

THE ASSASSIN's WIFE

A 5TH REPUBLIC Novel

Dan Daines

ISBN 978-0-9986610-0-1

First Edition – Trade Paperback

Episode●Media

Produced in the United States of America

Dedication

To my wife and progeny

Characters: (alphabetic by first name)

Andie Madsen—Secret Service agent on Madison's detail

Arthur Messanger—President-Elect Sarnoff's Chief of Staff

Bertrand Pinkney—Sarnoff's Lawyer, next Attorney General

David Maxtell—Technology wizard

Don Verde—DeCourcy operative

Eddie Smyth—computer consultant for Arthur Messanger

Garrett Miller—DeCourcy operative

Gene Artel—Chief of DeCourcy Security

Harlan Roscoe—Senate Majority Leader

Jason Southwick—Secret Service agent on Madison's detail

John Hancock—Mystery man behind the scenes

Karen Waldron—President-Elect Sarnoff's personal assistant

Kate Covington—Federal Appellate Justice, Talbot's wife

Keener B. Cluff—Sitting U.S. President

Landan Moss—Hancock's right-hand man

Larry Radisson—FBI Special Agent

Leon Fuller—President Cluff's Deputy Chief of Staff

Linda Liengford—President Cluff's personal assistant

Luau (Bob) Landau—uber-geek on Transition Committee

Lucy Hemsley-Tarlton—Madison's nine-year-old daughter

Lydia Covington-DeCourcy—15-year-old DeCourcy daughter

Madison Hemsley-Tarlton—Vice President-Elect

Meredith and Brian Lubneski (The Barbies)—DeCourcy operatives

Olivia Covington-DeCourcy—19-yr-old DeCourcy daughter

Palmer—FBI Special Agent

Preston Knight—Secret Service, head of protection detail

Renae Hinckley—Madison's personal assistant

Roger Burgad—Career Foreign Service, next Secretary of State

Sheila Lance—DeCourcy law partner

Talbot Tristan Thomas DeCourcy X—Enigmatic Billionaire

Thomas Carlyle—Wall Street financier, next Secretary of Treasury

Tristan Thomas Covington-DeCourcy XI—13-yr-old DeCourcy son

Wilson Able Sarnoff—President-Elect

Take a breath - take stock - take action - and move on
—Tom Hemsley

Chapter 1

January 7

Just before the shot, 8:04 AM

The assassin sat calmly and comfortably in his keyhole sniper-blind fourteen stories above ground level in an old downtown Chicago skyscraper. He was ready to take the shot. His target, surrounded by a massive entourage, would momentarily mount the open-stair approach to the building 586 yards away. The elevation difference between the rifle muzzle and the target was 113 feet—a tricky business. But the assassin had fired over a thousand rounds with this rifle, and with this exact profile. The wind could act like a cyclone between buildings, creating another accuracy problem. But he felt he was as prepared as humanly possible. The lake effect was light on this clear, freezing morning, and the air between him and the target's position was almost still. He was using a .270 caliber, 140 grain, Nosler-tipped boat tail round to counteract wind effects. He was cool and confident. *I've prepped the ballistics as well as any shooter in the world.*

He saw movement at the lower edge of his scope apprising him that the target's party was heading up the granite steps. As the group ascended, he could just see some of the heads in the peripheral area of his Leupold optics. His effective range of vision was limited by a keyhole alignment: he was set up in a storage room with his rifle muzzle positioned six feet back from an old-fashioned flagpole portal on the corner of the building. He could see a slim wedge of the target site as he focused past the corner of the building next door. His bullet would pass within eighteen inches of the neighboring skyscraper's edge and within twenty-four inches of the corner of the building down the block on the opposite side of the street. A very narrow line of fire. He could clearly see the top half of those stairs a third of a mile away.

The assassin had made dozens of kill shots over the last twelve years in Afghanistan, Iraq, and other combat hellholes around the world. But this would be his first American on American soil—his first kill that even approached the personal. He could see the heads of the distant humans as they slowly climbed up the broad steps.

All other shots this expert killer had taken were done with magnificently manufactured, military-grade weapons, all perfectly crafted and calibrated for the express purpose of blowing away bad guys. This time, however, he was using a commercially produced Winchester XPR 270, based on the model 70 bolt-action hunting rifle. It was tuned perfectly. The .270 ammunition was very fast and packed massive foot-pounds of energy at the point of impact. At 586 yards, it could take down an Alaskan brown bear with relative ease. The assassin was certain it would disintegrate the human head about to appear in the center of his scope.

There would be less than three seconds to acquire and fire, given the angle and the travel direction of the target. He was ready, breathing steadily as he again visualized the elegant simplicity of the Winchester's zero-creep trigger mechanism. There would be no subtle jerk as he smoothly squeezed the trigger between breaths.

The first view of his target appeared in the scope-reticle at 8:06 AM CST on this clear January morning.

Second one: he took in a slow breath and settled the crosshairs on the center of the moving target's head and tracked it.

Second two: he moved the center of his firing line exactly one-half second ahead of his target's forward movement. This had become instinctive during twenty years of serious shooting in the hunting grounds of Montana and the killing fields of combat.

Second three: he squeezed the trigger with a grace defined by the amazing sensitivity of the human nervous system as it translated thought into the movement of one finger. The same system that could give a surgeon the dexterity to perform a miracle on a child's spine in the operating room would contribute fantastic accuracy to this destroyer. As the trigger was in midpoint of its explosive energy release, the assassin felt, for a fraction of a second, emotional recognition and moral doubt—the first and only time in his shooting experience.

Second four: he felt the weapon's recoil and recovery. Still sighting down the scope, he saw a scene of pandemonium—sprawling, falling bodies, blood, chaos. Steep stairs were challenging to protect and defend, and bodyguards catapulted down the steps as the two high-value protectees lay helter-skelter in their own blood and gore, tangled up with two other persons who would soon be dead.

The assassin gave no more thought to the scene down the street. He packed his gear and sanitized the room. The world was now changed. History had started down a brand-new track. The American Republic would never be quite the same after a careful shot by a lone assassin.

Chapter 2

The shot, 8:06 AM

Moments before the rifle shot ruined so many lives, shouting and cheering crowds had watched President-Elect Wilson Able Sarnoff and Vice President-Elect Madison Hemsley-Tarlton mount the stairs, waving to the throngs on this beautiful January morning. They had come to Chicago for a prayer breakfast—the last stop on the party's victory lap thirteen days before the inauguration of the new administration. The protection detail hadn't liked the open approach to the building. Especially Secret Service Agent Arnold, who had argued vigorously against the exposure. He was proven correct—but it was his skull that finally captured the misshapen 140 grain bullet after it struck both the president-elect and vice president-elect and severed the carotid artery of another agent as it blasted through the minimal resistance of human bone and tissue.

The screaming of the crowds came after a few beats of stunned hesitation and sense of unreality. No further sound of a rifle shot followed the devastation on the steps, but stampeding began that soon overwhelmed police barriers and Secret Service agents.

Agents Jason Southwick and Andie Madsen had been at the bottom of the protective wedge as the party moved up the steps. Now they managed to keep their balance and stay on their feet as others careened by, tripping and rolling down the stairs. They lowered their centers of gravity and practically crawled up the steps to their protectee, the vice president-elect. They reached Madison Hemsley-Tarlton at the same moment. Andie unceremoniously pulled an agent's limp form off Madison, the agent still spouting an arterial spray from his neck as Andie let him roll down the steps. Jason lifted Madison onto his shoulder in a modified fireman's carry.

Circumstances didn't allow the usual protocol of two agents lifting the principle from under the arms and rushing forward to safety. As per training, Jason gave no thought of a second bullet finding his back. Andie, glancing down the steps and calculating their chances in the melee, shouted, "*Up! We go up!*" Jason stayed low and ape-walked up the remaining six steps.

Andie saw blood pouring from Madison's neck and head. She clamped her hand on the wound to staunch what bleeding she could, and the two agents raced with their charge up the stairs toward additional agents who were waiting at the entrance doors with guns drawn, scanning for threats. As an ambulance gurney wheeled out of a side room off the lobby, agents shouted commands and pushed dignitaries out of the way.

Through his ear piece Jason heard someone, he couldn't tell who, shouting, "We have Dolly on slats evacuating to Beta. *Roll the bus!*" He heard someone else shouting on the secure net, "*Top Hat is down…Top Hat is down! Move to recover. Move to recover!*" It took two long minutes for other agents to extract President-Elect Sarnoff's body from the dead and injured and get his mostly headless form up the top of the stairs and onto the gurney. All agents had done their jobs, but it was shockingly obvious that Sarnoff's brains and skull had literally exploded on impact.

The vice president-elect was carefully but expeditiously crammed into a black, unmarked ambulance where medics took charge of her. The driver pulled away from the back doors of the building, nearly riding the bumper of the agents' lead car. Jason climbed into the follow car as it practically pushed the ambulance. The vehicles cleared the alley, turned, and powered down the street.

Andie, her hand still clamping down on the oozing blood, had jostled into the ambulance and would only release her grip on Madison when a no-nonsense medic used two hands to slide a compress under Andie's hands, convincing her to let go. After wiping her bloody hands on a white jacket hanging close by, Andie tried to find an out-of-the-way place in the cramped wagon but finally climbed upfront beside the driver. She listened to traffic on the secure radio net for call-codes telling her what was happening back at the scene, even as she scanned the streets for threats.

Chapter 3

Seconds after the shot, 8:06 AM

In the plaza at the base of the building's steps, chaos spread unchecked after the shot took down Sarnoff. Guns appeared and people scattered as they trampled over each other with elbows flying. A veteran Chicago PD officer drew his weapon but was clipped from behind by a large woman as she spun around looking for her sister. His accidental discharge blew out the face of a man standing ten feet away. Two Secret Service agents turned at the sound of the gunshot and collectively hit the officer with eight rounds to his protective vest. One heavy-caliber slug got past the kevlar and carbon fiber, entering under the officer's left arm. Because the agents were standing on the steps two feet higher than the officer, the trajectory of the .40 caliber round reached the top half of the policeman's heart. It carried the momentum of a small SUV, and the supersonic contact of lead against tissue disintegrated the thirty-nine-year-old blood pump.

Nearly everyone in the crowd carried a cell phone with a high definition camera—each person was a potential Abraham Zapruder, (the man who caught the JFK assassination on his home movie camera.) Hundreds of views from every angle of the cascading tragedies were captured and launched to the world within moments via the Internet and instant messaging. All major broadcast networks had video crews on site capturing this national horror show with dual 8K, 4320P ultra-high-definition cameras at 120-frames-per-second. Never had a man's death been recorded with such perfect resolution and with such amazing detail in 3D. The zoomed-in, slow-motion images would soon leave even jaded journalists vomiting in the editing suites back at their stations.

First responders tended to the injured and covered the two dead Secret Service agents on the stairs where they had fallen. They reluctantly left the bodies in place for the forensic teams. After five minutes the screaming of the panicked mob ebbed; people milled about aimlessly in shock and fear. Many bystanders, suddenly finding themselves witnesses to an American catastrophe, slumped to the ground in tears, emotionally overwrought by the mayhem.

The protection infrastructure had been impressive but not up to the level accorded the sitting president. No one on the detail had heard the first shot, and the nine following shots from the plaza confused things further. A consensus quickly coalesced on the vague direction of the first shot's origin. The Secret Service rooftop snipers had seen nothing, and after rescanning the area, still saw nothing. The frantic search for the shooter moved up the street. Agents assumed the elevation of the shot was very high. Somehow a killer had struck from outside the protective perimeter.

Streets in every direction were blocked off, and no one was allowed to leave—other than the dozens who had already bolted in the initial confusion after the shot. FBI Special Agent Lars Hansen had originally been stationed at the very edge of "the outer ring," as they stylized it, for the morning's festivities. Now, he calculated as he jogged in the direction he assumed the shot had come from outside the protective ring. *Finding the shooter in this mess is like tracking down a single hair on a shaggy dog,* he thought with frustration. There were too many buildings outside the ring and too many escape routes with ways to disappear. It would take FBI, Secret Service, and every local cop in the city scrambling to lock the area down. *They'll be tripping all over each other trying to cast a net over the whole area.*

As Agent Hansen paused to look back at the plaza and the stairs where the kill had taken place, he realized that a sniper must have threaded an extremely narrow sightline between the corners of two buildings a full block apart. If that was true, the shot must have come from the Macon-Roberts Building halfway down the next block.

What an amazing shot! he thought, then shouted into his rover: "This is Special Agent Hansen, FBI. I think the shot came from the Macon-Roberts on the corner. I'm moving in that direction." He went to pull his weapon—but realized he was already holding it. He had no memory of drawing it.

Cars and SUVs with oscillating blue and red lights poured into the streets, racing to the Macon-Roberts.

Chapter 4

One minute after taking his shot, the assassin had his gear zipped up and ready to go. He slipped the rifle into a 48-inch triangle shipping box and dropped the pull strip from the self-sealing lid inside the box. The spent cartridge was still in the rifle. The shooter hadn't ejected it, eliminating the need to search the floor for the brass afterward. This was a one-shot deal. Taking a last look around his erstwhile shooting blind, the assassin exited the nondescript closet on the 14th floor. He drew a handgun, made his way to the opposite corner of the building, and ducked into a restroom to remove his gray Tyvec suit. He was convinced he had left no DNA in the blind, even after three hours in the hole. He came out of the restroom in a respectable business suit carrying a small bag and the shipping package. He went through the stairway door to descend downstairs.

Four minutes had elapsed since the shot.

Fourteen floors below, FBI Special Agent Hansen approached the Macon-Roberts Building. He spotted a man-door to the left of a large roll-up door. As he made the transition from bright daylight to the gloom of the loading dock overhang, he reported in: "I have eyes on the Macon-Roberts loading dock."

Six minutes had passed since the shot.

Suddenly, before his pupils adjusted to the lower light level, he saw the man-door crash open and a handgun emerge from the dark interior. As the gun fired, Agent Hansen returned fire and then felt his chest implode.

Several more shots fired in both directions, but Hansen would never see them.

Moments later, the loading dock was a madhouse of uniforms, plain clothes detectives, federal agents, and medical personnel. The damage was done; it was time for the sorting out.

Chapter 5

Ten minutes after the shot, 9:16 AM EST

The White House Situation Room buzzed with National Security Council members and staff arriving in frenetic urgency. President Cluff connected via secure video link from his office aboard Air Force One. The sitting president was on his way home from visiting other world leaders in a post-election *I'm-Still-Relevant* grand tour. He'd lost the presidential office in a squeaker of an election and was still seething about it. Every day he plotted his comeback. *In four years, I'm going to smoke those damn Republicans!*

Reports streamed into the White House, hopefully more reliable than the lunatic rumors wheeling from the web and broadcast networks. Eleven minutes had passed since the shot took down the winner of the recent election. Deceased President-Elect Sarnoff was a much-hated man by some of the players in the situation room — and especially by the loser on the big jet. *But, dammit, they will see Keener B. Cluff going out of office in style, deftly managing a great national crisis,* he mused. Secretly he was ecstatic. *Even though...sure, it's a tragedy and all that. Stuff happens, and now my comeback is more realistic than ever!*

"Mr. President," said Deputy Chief of Staff Leon Fuller, who was riding herd in the White House while the top bosses were out of town. "We have the latest status confirmation. As before, it's confirmed that the president-elect is unresponsive and unrecoverable.

I saw the video. His head's just gone. Vice President-Elect Tarlton reached the ER seven minutes after the shooting and has a bleeding neck wound. But it was a vein that got grazed, so she's really not in much danger. She's sedated and stable. The Secret Service has everything locked down. Two agents died at the scene, presumably from the same bullet that killed Sarnoff, and a Chicago PD officer was also killed in error by the Secret Service. Several people were trampled, and there may have been fatalities in the crowd. We haven't focused on civilians yet because those reports are confused."

"What about the assassin, Leon?" President Cluff snapped. Nothing about losing the election had helped to soften his nasty personality.

"Again, we have now confirmed that a Caucasian male was killed by gunfire in the stairwell near the loading dock of the Macon-Roberts Building. He shot it out with an FBI agent on the scene. The agent was pronounced DOA at the hospital. There's no ID yet on the shooter in the stairwell, but he was using a Glock. A floor-by-floor, room-by-room search is being conducted in the building, and it'll take time to secure the scene and clear the twenty-three-story building."

"Okay, Leon. Has this triggered anything in foreign parts that looks troublesome?"

"Not yet, Sir."

"Well, keep the Council on site and watch the threat boards carefully. Keep me informed as needed. I'll need to make a statement to the nation on this grave day." Once off speaker, he added to Leon, "But first I think I'll take a quick nap. Hell, why couldn't this have happened a week ago before Congress certified the election results?"

Ames knew that a quick nap was code for a romp with Cluff's personal assistant, Linda Liengford. Maybe the president thought tiring himself out in bed would disguise his glee when he went on the air to confirm the sad news to the nation.

Ames Fuller smiled to himself. *Cluff has to realize the conspiracy nuts out there will target him as the most likely suspect in this modern Greek tragedy. He probably would've liked to shoot Sarnoff himself if he thought he could get away with it!*

Chapter 6

First few hours after the shot, 10:00 AM CST

Television news coverage was mildly repetitive as wild rumors dissipated and a few facts became clear, but the alleged assassin's lack of identity still gave plenty of fodder for speculation. The endless parade of constitutional experts on every TV news program, radio talk show, and internet podcast spelled out the exciting first-time implementation of the Twentieth Amendment—the succession of a vice president-elect.

The closest the country had ever come to the vice president-elect succeeding the president-elect occurred when an assassin tried to kill Franklin Roosevelt after his first presidential win. Twenty-two days prior to that event, on January 23, 1933, the Twentieth Amendment had been ratified by state legislatures. Then on February 15th an anarchist from Italy, Giuseppe Zangara, aimed at Roosevelt but instead shot Anton Cermak, the Chicago Mayor, and four others. Cermak died two days after Roosevelt took office on March 4th. If Zangara had been successful, VP-Elect John Garner would have become president under the brand-new Twentieth Amendment.

And today, because this recent election was set in stone, first by the presidential electors voting in December, and second by Congress certifying the election one day prior to the shooting, the law stated clearly what must happen next. It was dawning on Americans and the worldwide community that in less than two weeks the United States would have a thirty-six-year-old single mother as their new president. Cries of foul ball came from all over the country, especially from hardcore far-right Republicans who had reluctantly gone along with the party's selection of the moderate Republican California governor as the presidential running mate. She was a compromise intended to bring in those California electoral votes—especially the female vote. Which she'd done. Sarnoff was a strong and healthy died-in-the-wool bull elephant who, they thought, would have put the country back on the proper track. Many party hacks bemoaned the lack of efficiency of the assassin's bullet: *Couldn't it have nicked a Tarlton artery instead of a vein? Then, at least, the speaker of the house would be next in line. He was the right kind of right-wing guy.*

The good old boys had tossed lots of sour grapes around during the campaign: *one of them* should have been the VP nominee. Now they were livid. Any one of them might be the new president-elect right now, with a little neck scar for added character. These same old boys began gathering their confidants around to scheme—someone could make hay out of this debacle, and every one of them wanted to be the one winning all the bales.

Chapter 7

As Vice President-Elect Madison Hemsley-Tarlton slowly rose from the deep fog of unconsciousness, she saw Jason Southwick and Andie Madsen watching her. She blinked a few times, willing herself awake and noticing she was in a hospital room. Her head felt terrible and her mouth was dry. Looking around the room, she saw several people in scrubs she didn't know and some graceful lilies in a green vase adorning the windowsill, and she noticed, outside the window, the vague silhouettes of Secret Service snipers stationed on the rooftop of a neighboring building across the hospital courtyard. Her eyes rested on her own form lying under white bedclothes. *I sure don't want to look in a mirror yet,* she thought inconsequentially.

"It seems something went bad," she croaked as she looked searchingly at her Secret Service detail. An energetic woman, tall and athletic, Madison was now worn and pale as she lay in a drab hospital room. Only her penetrating gray-blue eyes exhibited her inner strength.

Andie came to her right side and took her hand. "What's the last thing you remember before you woke up just now?"

"I was going up the steps to breakfast with Wilson Sarnoff—and then a lot of noise—and then I was spinning down. The last thing I saw was blue sky and wispy clouds—then you, here, now. Did I fall down?"

A doctor cleared his throat and stepped close to her bed to gently examine her neck wound. "I'm happy to say that I don't think there's any concussion, and you should be well very soon. Your vitals are good, but you need rest." He held a water glass with a bent straw to her lips, allowing her to sip. "My staff and I will leave you with your agents."

"Thank you," she whispered.

After the medical team left the room, Jason approached the left side of the bed. Looking up at both agents, she said, "Okay, you two. I'm not a fragile teacup. The doc said I'm sound, so what exactly happened?"

"Madison, there's no easy way to put this—three hours ago an assassin struck," Andie said. "Sarnoff is dead, and so are agents Arnold and Higgins. You are in Cook County Memorial under heavy guard, and you are now the president-elect."

"Damn!" Madison exclaimed.

After the agents filled her in on what they knew, Jason called Renae Hinckley, Madison's longtime executive assistant and chief of staff who was waiting in the lobby with the other staffers. "Time to come up to Ms. Tarlton's room, Renae."

Madison smiled reassuringly at her closest friend as she entered the room. Pulling a chair close to the bed, Renae reached for Madison's hand. They sat quietly for a few moments while Renae stroked the dark, straying strands away from her friend's forehead.

"You've had quite a day, huh?" Renae said softly.

"I need you to help me with something. I'd like to send condolences to the families of the victims." Madison was weak and tired, but true to her nature, she insisted on getting down to business. Renae—much better at the touchy-feely things—wrote the messages. Madison's forceful personality often needed airbrushing—and Renae was good at that, too. Madison signed the notes in her bold signature and didn't neglect anyone known to have died in the tumult that day, including a woman and child who had been trampled.

She was heartsick over the senseless loss of life and suffering set in motion by the killing, and memories of her own combat experience in Iraq came flooding back, ratcheting up her sadness. She shuddered as the tug of feelings pulled her back into past battles, past grief. Seeing the signs of Madison's drift, Renae gripped her hand again, squeezing to reassure and reconnect her to *now.*

After Madison asked the Secret Service agents to leave the room to give them privacy, her personal assistant didn't press with non-essentials and asked only what else she could do. Madison responded with a few instructions, while Renae took notes.

"You should get some more rest now, and I need to leave soon to collect Lucy at the airport," Renae said. Lucy, Madison's nine-year-old daughter, was being escorted to Chicago by the Secret Service from Madison's home in Woodside, California.

"Tell her I love her. I assume Tally called you or sent a text?"

"Yes, of course. He called me before you got to the hospital, and I've been texting him about your progress. He knows he has to stay away, but he wishes he could come. You'll see him in Georgetown when you get back to the city."

"Poor guy, he doesn't do helpless very well. I'm sure he'd like to wring a few Secret Service necks by now."

"I'm sure that's the case, but he looked over the trajectory and the supposed ballistics, and he doesn't fault the Service. He said that whoever did this planned very well but took a huge gamble on the wind conditions. He's pretty sure that if there'd been any wind, the shot would've been postponed for a later opportunity."

"Calculating as ever. Here, give me your phone. Let me talk to him a minute," she said, reaching out.

Renae handed her the phone and left. The Secret Service had cleared several rooms adjacent to the president-elect's room (still officially the vice president-elect until inauguration day), and Renae entered the one set up for her use, which was closest to Madison's. She made a few calls from her second phone before heading to

O'Hare. Long experience with her friend had taught her to have two phones in her possession at all times.

*   *   *

"Tally, it was pretty bad, I think," Madison whispered into the phone, her closely guarded vulnerability rising to the surface.

"Yes, it was. There's no way to pad this into a softer landing. You and Sarnoff were shot and several people died. But thank God you survived with so little injury. I was worried for a minute," Tally said in a lighter tone than the grave circumstances warranted. He was a man accustomed to extraordinary stresses and pain; his griefs had hardened his emotional reserve like obsidian cast from the furnaces of the earth. At times he seemed impenetrable.

"I'm fairly certain I learned profound understatement from you."

"I tried to teach you better things than that," he responded with mock defensiveness.

"Yes, you taught me lots of good stuff," she teased, regaining a portion of emotional control. The terrors of the shooting would stay with her for a long time, but she willed them to the back of her consciousness for now. "Stay steady in Rough and Ready," she said, smiling. It was one of their old maxims from the beginning of her connection to him back in her hometown of Rough and Ready, California. "I'm okay, Tally. Lucy's coming and I need to get past this so I can reassure her that Mommy's not going away."

"No, she is *not*," he said firmly.

Chapter 8

The Secret Service required those who had helped plan the event—Sarnoff staffers and local Republican Party officials—to remain in the banquet room where the prayer breakfast would have occurred. Most other guests were allowed to leave. While some agents still searched the Macon-Roberts Building, the most intensive investigation was centered around the people in this room who knew all the details, including *when* the president-elect's party would mount the steps leading to the building.

The investigation also extended to the Capital. The majority of Sarnoff's staff had remained in D.C., busily hammering out the last transition issues before Inauguration Day—until the awful news broke. More Secret Service agents, desperate to get a handle on the tragedy before their FBI antagonists ripped it out of their hands, descended on the transition team offices; some of the rank and file *here* might have supplied the shooter with the information on today's events.

Four hours after the shot, the Chicago banquet-room doors swung open, and a contingent of FBI big-brains swaggered into the room, heading straight for Preston Knight, the lead Secret Service agent on site. After brief pro forma back and forth and mutual condolences for their fallen agents, the turf battle and pissing contest began in earnest.

"I don't care *what* your director wants, Radisson. Until *my* director says otherwise, we stay lead on the scene," Secret Service Agent Knight pushed back on Special Agent Radisson's opening salvo.

"The AG and homeland director will get their heads together, and the gods of all things political will tip the ball—but right here and right now, we just want to talk to one person in this building, and we are taking her to the Chicago Field Office, ASAP," Radisson hissed back. "You can keep the party going with everybody else as long as you like."

"Who do you want to talk to?"

"We want to talk to Karen Waldron. Right now!" Radisson took a breath. "We identified the man shot in the stairwell by Agent Hansen. It was Douglas Waldron, Mrs. Waldron's estranged husband."

"That's not good," Preston said, shocked. "Agent Beale and I will come with you to keep us all on the same page. It's your lead…so lead on."

"I agree, Knight." They shook hands and sought out the woman whose world was about to collapse for the second time that morning.

They escorted Ms. Waldron out of the building and away from everyone, explaining only that they needed to escort her to the local FBI field office. She went along, not by choice, wondering why she was being singled out—even though, as Sarnoff's assistant, she was one of the people closest to the assassinated president-elect.

Karen Waldron had no inkling that she would soon be labeled *the Assassin's Wife* for all time.

Chapter 9

Eleven hours after the shot, 7:00 PM CST

"You don't want to go there, kids!" Bertrand Pinkney scoffed as he pushed brusquely past the FBI agents barring him from the interview room. "Ladies and gentlemen, I'm Mrs. Waldron's attorney, and I *will* talk to my client." Heads in the room jerked at the sound of his voice. "*Right now!*" The assembled agents had anticipated Bertrand's arrival and showed him a measure of deference. Closely associated with Wilson Sarnoff for twenty-five years, he had been on track to become attorney general in the new administration and hoped he still would be under a Tarlton administration. Fifty years old, he was extremely tall and stately, with steel-gray sidewalls and piercing blue eyes that made lesser mortals uncomfortable.

"Why don't you fellas take a little time out," he said, shaking hands with Preston Knight and Larry Radisson. The agents responded by leaving the room for a break.

"First, Karen, I'm so sorry for your profound losses. Both of them." Bert's tone simulated sincerity. He put his arm on her quivering shoulders to steady her as she began sobbing again. "How are you holding up, dear?"

Karen Waldron was exhausted. At thirty-seven years old, she normally operated at a high-energy level, but the extraordinary stresses of the day had left her depleted and drawn as she cried her tear ducts to dehydration. Her doe-eyes were mascara-streaked and swollen, her usually perfect hair a mess—she wasn't aware she'd been tugging at tawny forelocks as she endured relentless questioning. The murder of her boss and the shock of her husband's apparent role in this craziness had worn her down to doll-rags.

She felt so weak she could barely lift her head as she listened to Bertrand's attempts at comfort. They spoke quietly for several minutes, his head close to hers so the Feds wouldn't pick up their conversation.

When the Secret Service and FBI agents reconverged, Bertrand took command of the room, announcing, "I'll be taking my client to her hotel now."

"Now wait here!" Radisson stood to object. "We're not done with our interview yet."

"Yes…you are. You've been interrogating Ms. Waldron for seven hours now without a substantial break. She has fully cooperated with you, and she had no part in this horrific crime. There's nothing new you can ask her. You've asked every question at least ten times, Agent Radisson, and you've been treating her like a suspect rather than a potential witness. If by some amazing coincidence you think of something else to ask, she'll make herself available."

Preston Knight interjected, "Look, we're not finished, and we have an investigation to conduct. It's a terrible quirk of fate that Mrs. Waldron is married to the man who allegedly assassinated President-Elect Sarnoff," he paused, then added, "which also makes this a national security issue."

"Preston, I know you well and I like you, but I'll tell you where you're wrong. First, there's no national security element here, so don't try to make it into one. My good friend, Wilson Sarnoff, was receiving intelligence briefings, certainly; but Karen wasn't read in on any classified material. You are claiming that a deranged and jealous husband took revenge and killed Wilson Sarnoff. And if that's so, this is murder, plain and simple—not a national security threat. Second, you have a dead man, a gun with proximity to the crime, *and* an alleged letter from Mr. Waldron addressed to the Transition Office indicating his plan to harm the president-elect. You do *not* have witnesses to the murder; you do *not* have absolute proof of Mr. Waldron's guilt; and…you surely do *not* have anything hinting that Karen had foreknowledge of the act."

"I understand what you're saying, Bertrand, but we have to get every piece of information we can from Karen. We can't let her go yet," Agent Radisson exclaimed, his cheeks reddening.

"Karen has cooperated exhaustively with you, and now you are abusing that cooperation. If you try to hold her as a material witness, or anything else, I'll be back in thirty minutes with a writ of habeas corpus from a federal judge, who, by-the-way, is in his office upstairs waiting for me. And don't even think of trying for a temporary restraint to the writ. I have a federal appellate court justice waiting by the phone to slap that down, if you try."

"We have an investigation to conduct."

"Yes, you do, so go do it and stop harassing my client. Go find the truth. Without fail and within twenty-four hours, gentlemen, I want a complete copy of any and all audio, video, transcriptions, and contemporary notes from this entire interview."

"Absolutely not." Radisson's voice was strained; he was feeling the stress effects of both the assassination itself and the seven hours of intense interviewing. But he rallied his energy, feeling he'd been bullied long enough: "You will not get copies of this interview. The investigation is ongoing!"

"Oh, did I forget to mention? Here is a court order from a federal district judge—he is still sitting upstairs. Same rules apply if you try to get a TRO. I'll have an associate stay here in Chicago to be at your complete disposal, should you have further *appropriate* questions. And, Special Agent Radisson, let me be very clear on this final point. You've been pressing Karen to sign your statement. That absolutely will not happen. In my presence, she will produce and sign a truthful statement. That statement will unequivocally declare that

Karen Waldron had no foreknowledge of her late husband's plans—or anyone else's—to harm the president-elect, or those attending him. Further, the statement will declare that there was never, at any time, a romantic or sexual relationship between Karen Waldron and Wilson Sarnoff. And this is with regard to your salacious accusations toward both my client and my late friend during this interview. We'll be releasing said statement to the public at the same time we provide it to you. Karen, let's go." He nodded his head dismissively.

"He rose and gently helped Karen from her chair and out the door.

The agents had no way to effectively resist—especially since most of them were FBI, and they assumed Bertrand would be the next AG, and their uber-boss, in two or three weeks. They also knew that if they made too much noise, good old Bert would be on every morning news show tomorrow wringing them out by name in front of the whole country. Bertrand Pinkney had a well-deserved reputation for serving up *vengeance with a smile.*

Chapter 10

"Yes, Art, you heard me correctly," Bertrand said impatiently. "She's out from under the bright lights of the Feds. I sent her to the hotel to rest up, and I'll get her on the jet to D.C. first thing in the morning."

"How's she holding up?"

"Arty, this is me. Don't try to sound like you care about her well-being. You sound like a crooked club hitting a hollow mahogany tree."

"What? Never mind, your similes are so tiresome," Arthur Messanger said, frustrated and feeling the ubiquitous stress that had spread over the nation since the assassination. As Sarnoff's Chief of Staff, he had been the leading force in the presidential transition process—and that was how he liked it. *But now this travesty*, he thought savagely.

"So, enough about Karen; she's secure and under wraps. What about moving forward? Will Miss Pocahontas stay with the plan and keep the line-up that we laid out?" Bertrand asked.

"Don't worry about her. She's been so far out of the loop that she'll come back to the team shell-shocked and ready to take every recommendation I feed her. I'm in charge of this—not the prima donna, surfer girl."

"She was only out of the loop because you locked her out and told her to go sit on the bench and look pretty. You're always underestimating her. That could blow up in your face, Art."

"I have her under control. I'll make nice-nice so we can bury the hatchet for the good of the administration…and all that crap. She'll come along."

"You, nice? Forget that—you're a rattail and you know it."

"What the hell is that? Another metaphor from your bottomless well of wisdom?"

"Didn't you ever take woodshop in school way back when? There were these rasps, files for scraping wood. My favorite was the rattail bastard. That's you, Art. You're a rat-bastard and that's as nice as you get. The whole diplomacy gene was squeezed out of you at birth. It happens to a lot of sociopaths."

"So unlike *you*, the charming win-at-all-costs, smile-as-you-plunge-the-knife-in-the-back sociopath," Art said.

"Ah…we are what we are, and we're good at it. I'm just saying, you may want to bury the hatchet, but don't be surprised if Mad Tarlton spins around and buries her tomahawk in your forehead."

"I'm not a kid in his first schoolyard scrap, Bert."

"You just make sure we stay on track. If she wants to make any lineup changes, there are plenty of others to kick off the bench. But let's just be sure *I* get the AG slot," Bert said with intensity.

Chapter 11

Twelve hours had passed since the president-elect was killed. Much of the public mourned, but for television networks, the tragedy sprouted stunning TV news theatre and spectacular ratings. Before January 7th, broadcasters had been dreading the new administration's quiet honeymoon period, with mainstream journalists probing for story angles to torpedo the new president. They weren't on board with the right-wing Sarnoff holding power: he hadn't really *won* the election. As they saw it, their guy—the incumbent President Cluff— had *thrown* the match through stubbornness and stupidity.

At the Chicago Marriott, a numbed Karen Waldron went to her room, got undressed, and curled up on the shower floor under the hot water's heavy flow. She soon fell exhausted into bed but awoke from troubled dreams a dozen times. Finally at 2:12 AM, knowing sleep wouldn't return, she got out of bed, dressed, and scrounged up anything edible from the mini-bar and her fruit basket. *Thank you, Mr. Marriott, for chocolates in the mini bar.*

Donning hat, coat, and gloves and intending to go outside for fresh air, she went down to the lobby, but two men wearing the FBI shine approached her. The shorter of the two spoke as he displayed his credentials, "Where are you going, Ms. Waldron?"

"Out for air," she snapped.

"We don't think that's a good idea. We'd like you to stay here at the hotel for now."

"I'm not at all concerned with what you think, Agent Whoever- you-are. I'll do whatever the hell I want!" She was overtired, grumpy as a bear, and stressed to the point of wishing she had a very sharp object in each hand. Pushing past the pair of officious-minders, she headed out and asked the uniformed bellman to whistle for a cab. The Feds scrambled after her, one taking the next cab and the other hustling for the bureau car.

The confrontation and freezing night air worked to clear Karen's head, and she began to think rationally for the first time since they had dropped the assassin's identity-bomb on her at the FBI field office. During the long hours of interrogation, all the suspicion and innuendo had added to her trauma, and toward the end before Bertrand Pinkney arrived, her perception of the ghastly event had unraveled. While in her state of shock, she hadn't said anything of importance to Bert, but now she was thinking in hyperdrive and was completely sure of one thing—nothing was what it seemed.

As the cab rolled through the quiet Illinois night, Karen sent a text to Renae Hinckley, assuming she wouldn't hear back until later in the morning. She and Renae filled similar roles for their respective bosses.

> *Renae, I'm devastated by all that has happened and am very grateful that Madison was not more seriously hurt. I really need to talk to you for a couple minutes. Please get back to me when you can. Thanks. KW*

She sat back in the cab, stretching her neck and feeling the stiffness and aches brought on by the crazy events. In a moment or two, her phone chimed and she read the reply text from Renae arriving at 3:03 AM. Obviously, someone else was not sleeping.

> *Oh, Karen, I'm so sorry for all that you've gone through and for the great losses you've suffered. I'm here for you. We can talk as soon as you like. Where are you now? R*

> *Thank you, Renae. That means a great deal coming from you. I'm in a cab somewhere downtown, clearing my head. Can't sleep. K*

Come to the hospital, and ping me when you get here. I'll have an agent meet you in the lobby. See you soon. R

Thank you. See you in about 15 minutes. K

The FBI agents in the cab and bureau car kept a running communication between them as they followed Karen's cab. They were surprised when the cab dropped Ms. Waldron off at the hospital. Focusing on their own duties, they were at first unaware that it was the hospital where Madison Tarlton was staying for observation.

Karen was nowhere to be seen when the first agent arrived in the lobby, but he did notice the tall, hard-to-miss and hard-looking African-American male standing watch. Secret Service Agent Jason Southwick was back on duty after only a few hours of restless sleep. Hailed as heroes, he and Andie Madsen were back at the job doing what they did—nothing more, nothing less.

Chapter 12

January 8

3:15 AM CST - Nineteen hours after the shot

Secret Service Agent Andie Madsen showed Karen into a small private chapel, or *reflection zone*. She gave Karen a warm handshake and expressed her heartfelt sympathies. Moments later, Renae swept into the chapel looking fresh and ready to go for the day; she hadn't slept at all, but she was a dynamo that a few more hours without sleep wouldn't diminish. Feeling the Red-Bull buzz behind her eyes, she realized that stress would crash her sooner rather than later, but for now, she was still *on* all the way. Madison needed her, and she had a job to do.

The two women hugged fiercely with a shared grief. "Karen, I'm so sorry for what's happened and for your incredible loss." Tears flowed from the normally controlled Renae, and her weeping matched Karen's tear for tear. It took a minute of silent grieving before either could speak again.

"I can't believe that Doug could do something like this!" Karen said, her face cupped in her hands.

Renae agreed. She knew a lot about Doug and Karen Waldron and their problems. They had once been a happy couple, even with Doug—a highly decorated Army Ranger sniper specialist—continually deployed for years and Karen working as Wilson Sarnoff's assistant on Capitol Hill for nine years. Then Doug came home from the sandbox damaged; his physical wounds were minor, but his PTSD symptoms were escalated. Unable to cope with normal life in D.C., he retreated to the family ranch near Bozeman, Montana two years ago, where his depression became an abyss. The couple saw little of each other for a year and then effectively called it quits. While not yet ready for divorce, Karen doubted that Doug would make it back to the surface from the depths anytime soon—if ever.

Doug reverted to his inner mountain man: hunting, fishing, and camping in the wild for weeks at a time. Always a taciturn guy, he stopped communicating with people entirely. The family's lawyer kept his few bills paid and his taxes filed on time, but Doug was unplugged from society. Karen hadn't spoken to him in thirteen months, although she chatted occasionally with the neighbor living on the ranch nearest the "// W" (Double-Slash W), as the old Waldron place was called. The neighbor would fill Karen in on the rare bits of news and gossip she knew about Doug. There were never rumors of another woman—or of any interest in human beings whatsoever.

Karen confided to Renae: "You know, one of the glorious little ironies in all this disaster is that *I bought him that rifle*. I gave it to him for his birthday when he was home on rotation six years ago. Can you grasp that? I can't. I was the one who purchased the weapon that killed my boss, Wilson Sarnoff!"

"Oh Karen, no one would see that as a hint of guilt," Renae said.

"Of course not, but the FBI pointed it out at least sixteen times during our cozy little conversation yesterday. And something *finally* occurred to me while I was talking to them because I wasn't thinking clearly at first…."

"Of course you weren't."

"They were showing me the twenty different views of the gun with the fingerprint locations on the stock and trigger guard." Karen paused and sighed. "And I saw something very distinctly. But then that ass, Bertrand Pinkney, barged into the room with his white-knight routine and dragged me out of there." She closed her eyes and rubbed her temples at the memory. "Actually, for the first time ever, I was glad to see that bombastic jerk. He got me away from the inquisition, but I don't know why he came or who asked him to. He pulled the *this is my client card* and slapped it in their faces like he always does. It was news to me that I was his client. I guess he figured that I'm 'Sarnoff-property,' so naturally he's in charge. I really have no idea why he even showed up."

"That surprised us, also," Renae remarked thoughtfully.

"Bertrand thinks I'm getting on the campaign jet back to D.C. this morning, but it's not happening. I'm going home to Portland as quickly as possible. I'm not even going back to the hotel for my clothes and suitcase. I'm just done."

"I don't blame you, Karen. Go home. Barricade yourself in your house for a while. Ignore the press, turn off the phone, and rest."

"I will, but I need one small favor."

"Of course, what?"

"I know Madison probably loathes everything about me, but I really, really need to see her in person for a minute." Karen suddenly looked desperate, grasping for reassurance that she indeed bore no guilt. "I only need a moment to tell her how sorry I am."

"That'll be fine. We've already talked about that. She certainly doesn't blame you for anything, Karen." Renae stood to leave the room. "Madison's awake. She slept a long time yesterday, so I'll go check with her and send one of the gun-guys for you." She smiled.

"Thank you...so much." They briefly hugged again and Renae left the room.

Chapter 13

Andie reluctantly took Karen into Madison's hospital room. She thought eyebrows would twitch if people knew the accused assassin's widow was secretly visiting the VP-elect, who was also one of the victims, in the wee hours. Andie had lost two colleagues in that awful moment of tragedy, and although she knew Karen had nothing to do with it, she still saw her as a symbol of what had gone so terribly wrong. But always the pro, she kept her cool detachment as she escorted the widow—the assassin's wife—into the presence of the next President of the United States. The room was bathed in subdued, warm light, and Madison was sitting upright in bed, papers spread across her lap. Harboring no ill-will for the woman standing in her room, Madison was genuinely warm and unreserved.

After a delicate hug, mutual tears, and murmured condolences, Karen leaned in close and whispered, "People may be listening, Madison. This is not over. Please read my note." She pressed a bit of tissue into Madison's palm and stood back to watch her open it. Madison stared at her and then opened the crumpled paper Karen had brought from the chapel. She read it silently.

> *I'm not a delusional widow in denial. I have proof that Doug was not physically capable of taking the shot. Send someone you trust completely—I mean life and death trust—to see me, and please be careful. You are not secure.*

When Madison was sure she understood the note, she looked up and nodded slightly to Karen. "Thank you for coming, Karen. If you wait for a moment in the hall, Renae will walk you down to the lobby."

Renae reappeared and the two women made their way to the lobby in silence. A cab was waiting for Karen at the curb; Andie had seen to that. As they hugged in departure, Renae kissed Karen on the cheek in pure empathy for her plight.

Before they ended their embrace, Renae whispered, "A man will come to see you. He will say that he was asked to come by Jeemie. Please remember, Jeemie."

"Thank you!" Karen Waldron whispered before turning toward the exit door.

Chapter 14

4:20 AM CST - Twenty hours after the shot

The two FBI minders had no choice but to hang around the hospital lobby hoping Waldron would come back. Their supervisor, Radisson, had already chewed them out three times for their stupidity, negligence, and carelessness—finally ending his tirade when he couldn't come up with any more snappy descriptives.

As Karen Waldron returned to the lobby area, the agents smiled in relief and prepared to follow her, one going for the Bureau car, the other keeping eyes on the subject. Karen moved through the exit toward the waiting taxi with the FBI stud in the lobby walking behind her. Suddenly two Secret Service agents blocked his way.

"Get out of my way," he barked.

"Sir, please tell us why you are following Ms. Waldron."

"Leave it alone, boys. I'm FBI. Don't interfere." He tried to push past but was bumped back—on orders from Jason Southwick.

"Okay, then let's see some creds," one of the lobby Secret Service agents demanded.

"Yeah, well, show me yours, hot stuff."

They compared dual agency credentials, and the frustrated FBI agent continued to clench his jaw. After logging onto the federal agency database and verifying that Agent Brady's credentials were official FBI issue, the Secret Service let him pass.

"Now, Special Agent Brady, you're free to go. Have a nice morning."

The agent who had gone for the car, Palmer, pulled up to the hospital entrance. He saw Agent Brady rushing out to him and angrily snapped, "You let her go. What were you thinking? Get in!"

After Brady's explanation and a near collision as they tried unsuccessfully to catch Karen's cab, Agent Palmer cooled off a bit and added: "Okay, I got the cab number and license plate. Call it in. Let's find out where the dispatcher is sending this clown."

They were incensed when the cab company claimed that there hadn't *been* a hospital pick-up, and the driver with that cab medallion had gone off duty several minutes before. The Feds had no choice but to return to the hotel, assuming wrongly that Karen was headed back to her room. The bosses at the field office, Radisson in particular, were unhappy with that unlucky pair for a long time.

Speculations mushroomed throughout FBI Headquarters. Why would Karen Waldron visit Cook County Memorial where Madison Tarlton was hospitalized? No evidence for a case had emerged against Karen, but her visit appeared unseemly to conservative FBI minds.

After several hours, the chagrined FBI agents learned that Karen Waldron was on a plane out of Midway heading to Portland, Oregon. Although not inept, the Bureau simply hadn't considered she would roll that way. Her room was paid for two more nights, and she would later checkout online. It took only minutes for the Portland FBI Field Office to put a full surveillance package together on Waldron and her house, twenty-four seven, starting now, without the formality of a warrant, of course. This was merely keeping track of the woman, not gathering case evidence.

At 9:30 AM CST, Special Agent Lawrence Radisson called his boss at Headquarters to report. Larry was not a Chicago guy; he usually worked out of the D.C. Field Office. He had been assigned to Chicago on temporary duty the previous week to ensure that the FBI's part in the security arrangements for the prayer breakfast went off without a hitch. Some hitch!

Moments after he called his direct supervisor, Larry was packing for Portland.

Chapter 15

11:00 AM EST - Twenty-six hours after the shot

Because of an insatiable appetite for the 24-hour news cycle, tidbits filled the public slop trough every few hours. The story was too enormous, and leaks were seeping from every joint in the body of federal law enforcement. Many networks aired graphic video simulations demonstrating how the shooter had set up, sighted his target, and taken the kill shot—along with simulated photos showing the right-handed Waldron's fingerprint placement on the gun. The

Winchester XBR 270 was absolutely the murder weapon. The ballistics were a solid match.

However, pundits tossed around wildly differing versions of the shootout between FBI Agent Lars Hansen and the assassin in the Macon-Roberts stairwell—since no one alive actually knew. The scene had been contaminated by the onrush of federal and local crime fighters.

To the public's mind, the mounting evidence seemed overwhelming: the fingerprints, the rifle, a dead man holding the gun that killed the FBI agent. Even some national news commentators sometimes dropped the word *alleged* from their prattle, solidifying the assumption that Doug Waldron was indeed the killer.

Waldron's motive, while a little murky, was attributed to the note that no one in the public had seen. Nevertheless, the letter's existence enthralled the continuously opinion-polled audience because they were already convinced that Waldron *was* the crazed killer of the president-elect. The networks constantly alluded to the infamous note, while an unnamed source close to the investigation claimed that Waldron blamed the U.S. Government for taking away his normal life and sanity and equally blamed Wilson Sarnoff for taking away his wife—he supposedly accused Sarnoff of a long-running affair with Karen Waldron that destroyed their marriage. It made for great TV.

The blogosphere ran wild with conspiracy chatter of every conceivable stripe, but there was no real evidence—not even a grassy knoll.

The Secret Service possessed the actual letter that had been delivered to the Presidential Transition Office *minutes* before the fatal shooting. It had arrived via FedEx and was treated like all mail received by the transition team. Regular mail, express letters, and packages were delivered to an offsite processing center where they were bomb-sniffed, checked, and scanned for dangerous objects or poisons. All cleared mail and packages then went to the various addressees.

A staffer pulled said letter out of an overnight express envelope addressed to Sarnoff's Chief of Staff, Art Messanger. After reading it three times to make sense of it, the staffer ran screaming to Art. He instantly grasped the import and called the Secret Service detail in Chicago, but because Jason Southwick didn't answer his phone, Art began trying to reach another agent—when the shouting in the office started.

Live news coverage of the tragedy was exploding.

Chapter 16

11:00 AM EST - Twenty-six hours after the shot

Twenty-six hours after the devastation to the nation, three men met secretly in Culpeper, Virginia. They only *ever* met in secret. They could not be seen together, and one of them could not be seen in public *at all*.

"Obviously, it's an understatement to say that plans are awry at the moment." The first speaker was the youngest of the three and the most prone to worry.

"Certainly, losing our president is upsetting after our enormous investment in getting him groomed and elected, but we knew there could be problems. Plans can be adjusted." The oldest, the Mentor, soothed. "The machinery is still in place; it won't be difficult to adjust the calendar to meet current conditions. Our long-term commitment for the country isn't seriously harmed."

"I see huge problems with the stand-in," said the first speaker. "She was a tool for the election. I don't think she'll play ball like we want her to."

"Why do you say that? She's a babe in the woods—with no Washington constituency. She'll need help getting anything done, and *we'll* be the ones to provide it," the third member of the group said.

"She's a complete outsider! She doesn't have personal support from most movers in the party. As we chew the fat here, knives are being sharpened in many dingy backrooms," the first speaker chimed back.

"So many people are underestimating her. I think that's a mistake. Remember that *our knives* are the sharpest, and we never hesitate to use them," said the Mentor.

"She was supposed to be a replaceable consumable. We need to think very carefully about our next steps," the third member said.

"Agreed, my friends, agreed." The older man paused several seconds for emphasis. "This is an unusual moment in our long history. I think we should bring the whole body together to make sure we are united on the path forward. There's no time for errors after the tortuous road we've traveled," he pontificated.

"Of course, you're right, John. When should we call the council together?" number three asked.

"As soon as practical, my boy, certainly before January 20th."

The three left the old building by different exits, a few minutes apart. No one in the public world had seen these three famous and powerful men talking together in almost thirty years, and back then, they would have been three unknowns.

Chapter 17

An important man in New York received a phone call from a trusted D.C. contact telling him of a call-sequence that had happened a few minutes before. The sequence went like this: a call was made from Missoula to Seattle—from Seattle to San Diego—from San Diego to Washington D.C.—and then from San Diego back to Missoula.

"I want to look into this…call me back in a few minutes," the important man said.

When the D.C. contact called back, the New York man gave him crystal clear instructions: "You've got to take urgent action—stop this problem from expanding in scope. Tie off the loose threads in each of the call locations—immediately and without fail!"

A rare black swan had appeared: a detail that should have been uncovered in the original research. No getting around this. Bad things would happen if word got out and people believed it. In New York, the important man didn't have time to consult with his compatriots because their careful security measures, while valuable, were a bit cumbersome and would slow things down. He would take unilateral action using his own team, and the others would certainly ratify his course when he briefed them. Obviously, San Diego must be first.

Airplane tickets were purchased and skilled professionals hustled to the airport.

Chapter 18

January 9

6:00 AM CST - Forty-six hours after the shot

Madison Hemsley-Tarlton was released from her Chicago medical stay at 6:00 AM on January 9th. She boarded the campaign jet, a Gulfstream V, at 8:04 AM CST—exactly forty-eight hours after the shot that killed the president-elect of the United States. Renae, Jason, Andie, and many additional Secret Service agents accompanied her back to the Capital. Because she was the new president-elect, she received more than twice the number of agents as her previous detail and privately thought of them as the late-barn-door-closers. A couple of not so friendly FBI agents also came along for the ride.

Renae knew that Maddy was not feeling talkative and allowed her some peace to review the large binder of work-product she had requested. Watching her boss carefully, Renae could sense the strain emanating from this woman. The immense load Madison would carry for the next four years and perhaps beyond rested like a shipping container on her shoulders.

The new chief executive needed to speak to the nation sometime today and should strike the perfect tone, sounding *in-charge-without-doubts* about her ability to govern, to carry on. She also bore an additional weighty challenge: getting control of the transition process. The binder on her lap was a full workup of items finalized by the transition team and those still needing decisions. Arthur Messanger, President-Elect Sarnoff's Chief of Staff and longtime buddy, had pushed Madison away from the process. He considered her "election-chaff" used merely to get votes and counter Democrats. After the election, she'd been disappointed at the sidelining but accepted her role, seeing it as the required toll for entering the gate leading to higher career ground.

The one big blowout between Madison and Messanger was over comments she had made on a Sunday news show. She was asked about the new administration's legislative agenda, and the discussion led to one of Madison's hot button topics. She explained that when she was governor, her ability to eliminate useless pork-barrel items from legislative bills was crucial in getting her state financially on track. She emphasized that Congress should be subject to the same oversite.

Art went nut-balls over the comment, lecturing her loudly and publicly. "You don't set the policy agenda, and so you need to shut up!" Madison held her quick temper in check. Although hyper-competitive, she was also controlled, carefully choosing the correct time and place for battle.

Renae knew Madison's feelings about the snub and had acquired a secret weapon—an I.T. geek inside the transition committee's tech team who blind-copied her on every email and correspondence. Renae kept detailed logs of their proceedings without Art's knowledge, who would have come unglued if he'd known. Having read all the committee rules and establishing memoranda, Renae knew the VP-elect must be informed of all processes and decisions; consequently, she briefed Madison daily.

Now her boss must cram, getting ready for the first big battle of her coming administration.

Renae watched Madison, who was idly flipping an iconic Winston Churchill bookmark as she read. The words printed on it brought the hint of a smile to Renae's lips: *Keep Calm and Carry On.*

Chapter 19

At the request of the Portland FBI Field Office, local cops were keeping the press vultures off Karen Waldron's street in Tigard, Oregon—a town slightly southwest of Portland proper. For the first 24 hours, satellite vans and local news SUVs had frequently come and gone, sniffing out revelations about the Waldrons—especially Doug. Karen's prominent role in the national election had been well-known in the Portland area; she was the local girl with big dreams and a big career, *and* she was the right-hand assistant to President-Elect Wilson Sarnoff. Until suddenly she wasn't. Now she was bigger: she was the *wife of the assassin,* and everybody wanted a glimpse and a sound bite.

Before the roadblocks went up a day ago, media denizens had inundated Karen's quiet neighborhood, shooting B-roll of the Waldron home and interviewing every housewife or kid over 12 they could find. Disappointingly, all they got was the usual *"He seemed like such a quiet guy."* Out of dozens of on-camera chats, there was never *"I always knew there was something off about Doug."*

Network producers dispatched their most photogenic faces and articulate voices to the dismal city on the river. One exceptionally pretty CNN anchor with just the right length of blonde hair argued: *"Nobody* with a decent complexion goes to Portland in January, so send a *nobody!"* Her boss assumed that she was afraid her hair extensions weren't insured against Oregon weather. But go she must. With this compelling story and eleven days remaining before the most unusual inauguration ever, stories must be filed, and segments must be produced in the right locales. And unfortunately for all piranhas of the press, the presidential transition headquarters had gone silent as King Munmu's underwater tomb.

A day ago, the cops had pushed the journalists back a full block from Karen's house—not for her privacy but to keep news trucks from blocking the FBI surveillance cameras. The Bureau had appropriated a vacant house for sale directly across the street from Waldron's house and trained a video camera on the front entrance. Another camera, perched atop a cell tower a quarter of a mile away, targeted the back of her house. They put audio mics throughout her house and tiny video cameras in most of the important rooms. It didn't bother them in the least that they had no legal justification. They were the FBI.

Karen, using the house in the downtime immediately after the election, had decided to put it on the market due to the overly busy schedule of the next four years. But now traumatized and wanting to stay away from D.C., she assumed this place would be home again. Her mother called repeatedly, but Karen couldn't bring herself to talk. "Just let me rest for a couple of days," she pled with her mother. "I don't want to see anyone or talk to anyone." She planned to retreat into the isolating turtle shell of her sea-green sitting room.

Air brakes hissed loudly outside her house. Glancing out the second story window, Karen was momentarily struck by the beauty of Mount Hood. It was partially shrouded by clouds, but she felt a sudden pang realizing how much she had missed her own personal volcano. The sound of slamming truck doors brought her back to the cares of the moment; a giant moving van had pulled up across the street, blocking her view of the house she assumed the FBI was using to spy on her. She had seen agents coming and going all morning before they started using the back entrance. The moving truck also blocked the FBI's view of *her* house.

A vacant house stood next to the FBI's surveillance hideout. As the movers started opening the doors of the big trailer, a car with a realtor's logo on the side also pulled up. A woman and man got out, heading toward the door of the vacant house. It seemed someone was moving in; she noticed a *sold* banner attached to the *For-Sale* sign. But the sign wasn't there last night. She was sure of it.

Now, for the first time since arriving home, Karen saw her personal bad penny emerge from behind the truck. Special Agent Larry Radisson was waving his arms and arguing with the movers. The senior moving guy pointed to the real estate agent and the man with the keys, and shrugging, went back to work. Radisson disappeared behind the truck again to track down his new nemesis, the real estate agent.

Just as these antics piqued her interest, Karen heard gentle chiming from an electronic device. Renae had given her a small, flat phone as they rode down the elevator of the Chicago hospital and instructed her to keep it with her and wait for it to chime. The thing had silently existed with no hint of electronic life until now. She picked it up and the screen came to life with this text:

> *I'm a friend of Jeemie. Please do not startle or look around. The FBI are observing you inside your house. Casually gather your wallet, phone, and any essentials, medicine, etc. I will knock quietly on your door in five minutes. Open it but don't say anything. Come with me to the car.*

She smiled quizzically at the perplexing instructions, relieved that Madison and Renae had come through. She got the items she needed and went to her bookshelf, pulling a small envelope from between the pages of *All the Light We Cannot See* and putting it in her purse. After reaching the front door, she heard an almost indistinct knock. She opened the door, stepped out, and quickly closed it. A tall, broad-shouldered man with dark hair stood before her. He was wearing sunglasses on this cloudy day.

Without a word, they walked quickly to a nondescript sedan and got inside. Karen noticed the garage door of the FBI house rising and Radisson running out to the driveway—the dash to follow was apparently on. Inside the car, she opened her mouth to speak, but the man put a finger to his lips, pointing to her purse with his other hand. She thought she understood. He then pointed to the small black phone containing this text:

> *The FBI is following us to keep an eye on you as they have been ordered. They will not stop us yet. There are electrostatic bags in the glove box. Put your purse and anything in your pockets into the larger one and seal it. Put your own phone and this device into the smaller bag. This device will clone your phone. When I signal you, take this device back out and seal your phone in the small bag.*

Karen nodded at him and followed his instructions. Two minutes later he nodded, and she took the device back out. A new message showed up:

> *Your shoes and clothes could be compromised, so no talking yet. We will stop at a mini-mart gas station in a few minutes. Go into the store and quickly change into the clothes in the restroom cabinet. I will come in without knocking, so dress quickly if you're shy.*

Chapter 20

"I don't know what they're doing, but stay with them. Is her signal still good?" Radisson shouted into his phone. His was the second of a three-car federal parade keeping eyes on their subject. "And anything back on the plate yet?"

"Her signal's pretty good, but they're not talking. The phone's a little intermittent, and the shoes are five-by-five. The plate came back belonging to a local rental outfit, not a national chain, and it's a franchise that only operates on the west coast," Agent Palmer responded back at the surveillance house.

"Who's renting the car?"

"We don't know. They won't say."

"What? You did mention that you're a federal agent, right?" Radisson said snidely. He was getting fed up with Palmer's screwups.

"Of course, boss; but the woman I spoke to said she couldn't tell I was FBI—I was just a demanding voice on the phone and she wouldn't do business that way. Then she hung up. I called back and told her to call the local field office and ask for me," Palmer reported.

"And?"

"Yeah, well, she said it wasn't her job to call the FBI."

"What happened to respect?" Radisson was certain he was pumping a pretty high blood pressure. "Send a local agent over there ASAP—nobody from our own team."

"Already on the way."

"Good." Radisson saw the subject vehicle turn into a large gas station mini-mart on the next corner. Over the car radio he told the first car to go on past and circle back around the block while he pulled to the curb about a hundred feet from the entrance of the store. The third car followed the subject car and went to the pumps, posing as a regular customer.

"Can we see anything at all?" Radisson asked.

"Yeah, looks like Waldron walked into the store, and the guy is pumping gas," a voice from the radio crackled. (Unaware that Oregon prohibited self-serve fueling, the D.C.-based agents didn't question why the man was pumping his own gas.)

"No kidding," he said sarcastically. "Anything on the guy? Do we know him?"

"Nothing distinctive on the man…looks fit, forty to fifty… shades, so no eyes…head down, avoiding security cams."

After a short delay, the unknown man replaced the pump handle and got back into the car, pulling up to a parking space in front of the store. He got out again after tossing the keys onto the floor mat and locking the door.

"He went into the mini-mart, probably picking up a few things. Waldron hasn't reappeared yet," the voice from the radio said.

Eight minutes went by. Neither the unknown male subject nor Karen Waldron came out of the store. Radisson was getting antsy. Palmer called him with news that both the phone-location ping and tracking signals from Waldron's shoes had gone silent at the same time. Radisson wheeled into the mini-mart parking lot with lights flashing, shouting into his rover.

"We're going in! Everybody but Clawson; you stay at the back."

"Welcome to Northwest Talbot Mini-Mart. Let me know if I can help you find anything," a young man barely out of his teens said, smiling at the agents as they came through the door. Radisson went right up in his face and showed his creds with his left hand.

"Eight minutes ago a woman came in here; six minutes ago a man came in here. Where are they?" he demanded.

"Well, sir, Agent Radisson, is it? Eighteen people have come in here in the last ten minutes, which ones do you mean?" The boy was unnaturally calm for a kid at a minimart confronted by an aggressive FBI agent. Radisson couldn't have known that all Talbot employees took courses in counter-intimidation training; even young employees developed excellent skills for dealing with the hostile public.

"Here's a photo of the woman." Radisson showed the kid his phone with a headshot of Karen.

"Yeah, I saw her; she had no coat on," the young man stated matter-of-factly.

"Where did she go?" Radisson didn't realize he was shouting at the kid, but the kid didn't react.

"I believe she went into the restroom," he said, pointing to the restroom sign.

"And the man?" Radisson pushed.

"Which man would that be, sir? Do you have a photo of him, also?"

"No." Radisson and the other agents barged into the women's restroom. No sign of either subject. They scoured the store and pushed open the back door with the *Alarm Will Sound* sign on it. No alarm sounded.

"Hey, why isn't the alarm working on this door?" Radisson shouted.

"It works. I got a signal that you opened the door. It's silenced during daytime operating hours."

"Did you get a signal that it opened anytime in the eight minutes before I came in here?"

"None at all, sir. But if someone had the right key, they could open the door and not set off the alarm. It would reset when it closed again."

The agents went outside, looked around, saw nothing helpful, and marched back in. They assumed the man had another car stashed in the parking garage next door, twenty feet from the back door of the station.

"Let's see the security footage for the last ten minutes, smart-boy. You have cameras all over the place," Radisson said.

"With regrets, sir, I can't show you that footage." The boy gave a slight shrug and watched the agents take menacing stances.

"Show me the footage right now. If you refuse again, I *will* arrest you for obstruction!"

"Um, Special Agent Radisson, I didn't say I wouldn't show you. I said I couldn't show you. We have the cameras, but the video is compressed onboard, encrypted, and sent up to servers on the corporate cloud. There's no way to access the feeds from here. Corporate security has to display it from their end onto one of the screens behind the counter."

Agent Radisson stared hard at the arrogant little pissant for a couple of long seconds, trying to gauge if he was telling the truth. "Well then, Justin," Radisson read his name tag for the first time. "Get your security chumps on the phone so we can get a look at the footage!"

"I don't need to call anyone. They're on the way and should be here momentarily."

"When did you call them?"

"I didn't need to. The local area team is monitoring the store all the time. They saw and heard your harassment. I saw a message on my screen saying, *'Security team on the way.'*" Radisson's eyes narrowed as the boy said "harassment."

Three men cruised into the store. They were big guys, and armed, wearing body armor and carrying batons. The first of the three spoke up. "Agent Radisson, step back from my employee."

"Look here, rent-a-cop…" he said, but then recognized it was his former boss, whom he had never liked, confronting him. "Neven, what are you doing here?"

"I run corporate security for 682 stores in this chain," Neven Haltz said, smiling and reaching out to shake Radisson's hand. Haltz had retired six years previously after thirty years with the FBI and had moved into the private sector. "Now what seems to be the problem? Why are you giving this young man such a hard time?"

Radisson pulled a face as though the young man in question smelled badly. "We have two subjects who entered this store, and we didn't see them exit. They left a car parked in front of your store. We have the identity of the female, and we need to get a handle on who the man is, and we need to look at the security video from your cameras, Neven."

"Perhaps they'll be back for their car."

"I seriously doubt it; these guys are on the run. We really need to track where they're going."

"Certainly, Larry. Glad to help. Bring a warrant on over to the corporate office downtown. We'll fix you right up." Neven smiled at Radisson.

"A warrant? We don't have time for that kind of formality. Let's do this off the record. I only want a quick peek. Surely you can do that from here—with a little slice of professional courtesy?"

"Well, Rad, even though I'm a 'rent-a-cop,' I'm stuck with my old habits, and I'm still a by-the-book guy, as much as that always chapped you. So get out of my store, Larry. You and your tag-alongs, Darryl and Darryl, are trespassing."

Glaring, Radisson and his merry band stormed out of the mini-mart and hurried back to the surveillance location.

Chapter 21

As Radisson drove back to the surveillance house, Palmer called with details about the suspicious coincidence of the moving van blocking their view of Karen's house just as the mysterious stranger arrived and skirted her away. "The buyer purchased the house yesterday on the condition that he could move in immediately while he waited for escrow to close," Palmer said. "He was happy to pay rent against the escrow amount."

"A timely coincidence for somebody," Radisson said.

"No, the story checks out. His name is Ralston Westbury, and he's been down here house-hunting for a month. He's a high-level scientist working for a Seattle-based tech firm, T3-DC-Tech. They opened a new facility in Beaverton eighteen months back," Palmer said, satisfied he'd dug deep enough.

He didn't know that the entire house purchase and move-in had been concocted the morning before. A crew had worked through the night loading the moving van with a large selection of furniture purchased from rent-to-own shops in Oregon. Palmer's coincidence-conclusion was exactly what Karen's mysterious benefactor wanted to convey.

If Palmer could be faulted for his shallow research efforts, Radisson was also taking shortcuts. He didn't pause to wonder why his old boss, Neven Haltz, was close at hand to the store where Waldron and her companion vanished. A brief check would have revealed that good old Neven Haltz usually worked at the Talbot Corporate Headquarters in Seattle—quite a distance from the Tigard, Oregon store. Radisson and Palmer's shared problem was their tight focus on pursuing Waldron; they were not examining the larger canvas of possibilities.

"What about the car, Palmer?" Radisson asked.

"One of the Portland agents, Mary Ramsey, drove to the rental lot, but the rental agent was not cooperative and said Mary needed to bring a subpoena in order to get the renter's name."

"Everybody wants a warrant or subpoena," Radisson moaned.

"But Ramsey got tough, and the girl finally coughed up the fact that the car isn't on a current rental agreement and is supposed to be at a body shop getting minor repairs. I'll text you the address of the body shop," Palmer said.

"Listen—have one of our guys follow-up with Mary Ramsey and meet her at the body shop. Find out how one of their cars went on a joy ride." Radisson rang off.

Inside the surveillance house, Palmer heard Agent Benjamin Terrel shouting from somewhere outside: "What's that gray van doing in Waldron's driveway?"

Terrel and another agent ran across the street toward a gray van, labeled TTT Security Co., that had just parked in Karen's driveway. A four-person crew got out and headed to the door.

"Hey, hold up there!" Agent Terrel shouted. "What are you doing?"

One of them turned around to face the agents while the others proceeded to the door. "How can I help you, gentlemen?" The speaker held a clipboard in his left hand, but his right was out of sight under his coat resting on the butt of a handgun at the small of his back.

"FBI! Why are you here today?" The two agents pulled their creds and held them up as they slowed to a stop.

"We're processing a work order to upgrade the security system for the owner, Karen Waldron," the crew supervisor stated in a level tone.

"She's not home right now, so you'll have to come back later," the agent said impatiently.

"We know that Ms. Waldron's not home. She's left town for a while, but we have a signed work order and the house keys because she wants us to beef up her security system. Seems like she had a little break-in here a couple of days ago that spooked her pretty bad. Her old alarm company didn't even detect it...so here we are—nothing but the best!"

"You *cannot* go in there right now."

"Oh, and why would that be, Agent Terrel?"

"How do you know my name?" Terrel started for his gun.

"I can read. You held up your creds, remember?"

"Sure, but that's a long way for you to read such small print."

"I see pretty well, Special Agent Benjamin Terrel."

"Still, you can't go in there. We have an investigative operation going."

"Is that right? Well, show me a court order that puts this house under restrictive surveillance. If you don't have one, I suggest you back off—and *stay off* the grass, gentlemen. This is private property."

"You're not going into that house!"

"Really? I was with Portland PD for twenty-five years, so I have a pretty good idea what the rules are. Show me a writ, big boy." The local cops and FBI rarely got along in Portland: the cops didn't like the feebies' arrogant attitude. The retired police officer turned and followed his crew into the house.

When the agents reported the episode back to Lawrence Radisson, he swore a blue-streak-and-a-half, and then muttered, "Who's *helping* this woman?"

Two hours later as the TTT van was leaving, a knock came on the door of the vacant house, the FBI surveillance house. Palmer opened the door and saw a cardboard box on the stoop. It contained all the FBI's surveillance gear—mics and cameras—in individual antistatic plastic bags.

Chapter 22

1:00 PM PST - Two days after the shot

Karen Waldron and her new friend—whom she knew nothing about except that Madison trusted him—drove east along the Columbia River. They pulled into the parking lot of Multnomah Falls, thirty miles east of Portland. The scenery here was spectacular on a clear day, but even with the cold wind and mist, it was a stunning place and Karen appreciated nature's calming grace. They got out of the car and walked to the visitors' area. She was wearing the clothes, shoes, and warm coat her new traveling companion had supplied. Everything was exactly her size…although two sizes larger than she wished she were.

"We're clear of your groupies, so can you explain what you meant about your husband not being physically capable of taking the shot that killed Sarnoff," he said.

"Yes, but I don't know if you or anyone else will believe me."

"Go ahead. I'm here to listen."

"My husband was a very skilled sniper in the Army Rangers, as everybody knows, then he developed terrible PTSD symptoms that caused our marriage to fall apart, and for the last two years, he's lived on his family's ranch near Bozeman, Montana trying to get his head straight." She shook her head but wasn't able to shake off the sad memories.

He waited patiently for her to continue as they walked along in silence. She resumed, "Then thirteen months ago, he was over near Missoula and had an accident. He snapped a bungy-cord hook into his right eye and nearly blinded himself, so he was treated by an ophthalmologist in Missoula and paid for it privately. He's so private and reclusive now…I mean *was.*" She paused again, unable to gain control.

"Here you go." He handed her a tissue and she wiped away the tears that came.

"Thank you…He had virtually no friends left in his life. The doctor forwarded copies of his test results to my home here in Oregon because it was the only address Doug gave when he was treated, and I doubt he told anybody but me about it. In fact, it was one of the last real conversations we ever had."

"What was the result of the injury?"

"After he healed up as much as possible, he wasn't blind in his right eye, but his sight was really damaged. The doctor called it 'severe macular compression.' One of the things Doug said was that he would never be able to shoot again using his right eye. He would have to learn to shoot left-handed if he was going to hunt anymore."

"Did he learn to shoot left-handed?"

"Probably, but not at the level of a skilled sniper. He wasn't out shooting a thousand rounds every day for years like he did in the army. But that's beside the point. When the FBI was grilling me for *seven* hours, Agent Radisson kept shoving photos of the rifle in my face to show me where Doug's fingerprints were on the gun. I couldn't focus on it at first…but then I saw it all at once. The fingerprints were positioned for right-handed shooting. Doug *couldn't* have shot Wilson Sarnoff right-handed! Suddenly, nothing was making any sense. If he didn't take the shot, then who did? *And who killed him?* I got very scared. That's why I went to see Madison. She needed to know."

"Can this be proven—about the eye injury?"

"Yes. Take this and check it out yourself." Karen handed him the envelope that she had brought from her house. Inside was a detailed medical report and an old-fashioned, 35mm color slide with an orange/red image on it that looked like a picture of the sun. On the side of the slide was a date from the previous year and the words "D. Waldron, right-eye."

"Show that to any ophthalmologist, and see what you find out."

"Ms. Waldron, as I told you before, I'm very sorry for your loss, but now we have much more to be concerned about." He looked down, deep in concentration.

"What do mean?" Karen was getting a bad feeling about all this—that is, a much *worse* feeling; she'd already been through so much.

"The FBI is keeping an eye on you, seemingly because they think you may be a material witness. If that's all there is to it, then you could go home now and be fine…" he paused.

"But you don't think I can go home and be fine?"

"Let's walk through this. No matter how unlikely you believe it is, the most logical explanation is that your husband took the shot left-handed. Then he wiped the gun down before stashing it. Remember, it took the Feds hours to find the rifle and identify it as belonging to the man killed in the stairwell, your husband. If someone at the Bureau thought they needed a stronger case with no doubts about the gun and who used it—because *one of their own* was killed—they might have tampered with the evidence. Suppose they got Doug and the weapon together postmortem and added the fingerprints to the gun to give strength to their case. They wouldn't have known that they needed to fake a left-hand print pattern. Slimy and illegal, but still within the realm of possibility."

"I don't believe Doug…" Karen started.

"The big problem with this scenario is the time frame. Your husband's body was transported long before the gun was found. To get his prints on the rifle after the fact would've required a conspiracy of several sworn law enforcement personnel, and jerks like Radisson aside, most of the FBI are upstanding and dedicated folks. I don't believe the agents on this investigation would be party to something like that."

"What do you think really happened, then?"

"Okay, theory two: if your husband didn't take the shot, then someone else did. Which means that between the moment of the assassination shot and six minutes later when your husband was killed, someone placed Doug's prints on the gun. Then they put him in position to be killed in the stairwell, and they killed the FBI agent who supposedly shot it out with your husband."

"Can we prove any of this?"

"Right now proof is not the critical item."

"What is, then?"

"Keeping you safe, Ms. Waldron."

"What do you mean, keeping me safe?"

"You're the only person right now who believes your husband didn't kill Sarnoff." He inhaled and added quietly, "And perhaps I believe it, too." His words quickened. "If some unknown person killed Sarnoff, then he wasn't working alone. The shootings—manipulating your husband—getting the prints on the gun—sending the note blaming Sarnoff for your ruined marriage—it all smacks of a very deep and carefully planned conspiracy."

"That note is another stupid thing."

"What do you mean?"

"Doug never spoke a sentence with more than seven words in it. And that was before he got bad with PTSD. After that he was really terse, more like an adolescent boy in the grunting stage. He was almost monosyllabic, if he spoke at all. That note sounded nothing like Doug, depressed or not."

"If there is a group, a force, behind this assassination, then Doug is merely part of the elaborate setup. The setup is really about *you*—Doug is just part of the details."

"Me? I've got nothing to do with this!" Even as she spoke she realized the logic behind his statement. "Ah…so because I was close to Sarnoff, my husband's PTSD gives plausibility to a motive."

"Yes, it does." He continued to stare at the famous waterfall as they spoke. "This leads to more problems. The conspirators are obviously unaware of your husband's recent medical condition. I doubt the pathologist will examine the right eye, even if he can. But you're not the only one who knows. The doctor who treated Doug and perhaps some of his staff—they are the likely ones to put together the same fallacy that you did."

"But that's good, right? If the doctor goes public, then the cat will be out of the bag, and I won't be alone on the hot seat anymore." She brightened for a moment.

"It depends on how the doctor breaks the news, and *who* he tells the news to first." He pulled out his phone and activated a call feature. Seconds later he was speaking to someone through an all but invisible earpiece and the phone was back in his pocket. "There is an ophthalmologist named Robins in Missoula who has dangerous information rolling around in his head. He may not even know that he has it, yet. He could be in grave danger, and his staff also, so lock him down with a protection package, and find out who was working in his office a year ago in December. Call him and tell him that someone is coming to help him. Is anybody in Missoula today?" He finished the call and looked over at Karen.

"This could be really bad for the doctor, right?" Karen said, reaching for something to say.

"It could be. Let's go back to the car. I have a delightful couple for you to meet."

Chapter 23

2:00 PM PST - Two days after the shot

Twenty minutes later, Karen was on her way to a safe house with the "delightful couple." The man, she still didn't know his name, said he was leaving her in good hands as they parted ways and he drove back to the Portland Airport.

As he drove he discovered the tragedy had already escalated. He listened through his earpiece as an operative explained: "That's all we know right now. The doctor and his wife went off the road in very icy conditions, six miles southeast of Missoula on Interstate 90. They hit a concrete overpass abutment and both were pronounced dead at the scene. The highway patrol thinks it happened about 6:00 AM MST. The call to 911 came in at 6:04 AM, and the investigation is ongoing," the Missoula operative said.

"Anything untoward at the medical office?" He could imagine the gears of a relentless machine stamping out any trace of evidence.

"Yes, absolutely. Very coincidental. The alarm company reported an open-door alarm at the doctor's office at 6:25 AM. Police showed up in eleven minutes—not much of a priority at that time of day. They believe it was a false alarm, since everything was locked up tight when they arrived."

"Chances are a patient record will be missing if they look carefully."

"Should we give Missoula's finest a heads-up?" the operative asked.

"No, better not. Doing that may get more innocents killed. They'll put the break-in and the accident together soon enough. Without the thread of a patient's name, they'll remain blissfully ignorant and a bit safer for a bit longer."

"Someone out there is a brutally efficient clean-up guy."

"You're right about that. So be careful as you get ahold of the doctor's phone records and emails. Look at everything since the moment the assassination news broke. The late doctor obviously told someone, but it didn't get out to the public, so he must've told the wrong someone."

"Or that someone told the wrong someone. There may be more bodies in this tidy-up trail," the Missoula operative finished.

"I suspect you're right about that." The man visiting Oregon was now certain the scope of this little conspiracy had far more targets than he had supposed—and a much broader range.

Chapter 24

Even though the nationwide press conference was hastily assembled, it still took hours to prepare after Madison had arrived in D.C. All the major networks and news outlets were set up and ready to go, and everyone was aware of the historic implications of this moment. As word spread about the event, tens of thousands of spectators braved the chill, flooding onto the Washington Mall to witness "a great moment in history," as the news outlets promoted it. D.C. Metro police responded with a huge overtime call. No one except properly vetted and badged VIPs were allowed to be close to the viewing stand—along with members of the sacred fourth estate. The press always got the great seats.

Madison had personally chosen the venue. As she stepped to the microphone array, a hush seemed to smother all sound from the Lincoln Memorial to the Washington Monument and beyond. Police had blocked traffic on both sides of the National Mall, and loud speakers and massive portable jumbo-trons were quickly set up to accommodate the growing crowd of Americans. Network producers expected this to be the largest audience in television history, and the online audience would be most of the entire world.

The Honorable Madison Hemsley-Tarlton *took a breath* and looked straight into the cameras. "My fellow Americans and citizens of the worldwide community, I feel it is necessary and proper that I address you tonight. This occasion is a solemn one as we collectively mourn. As everyone is aware, two-and-a-half days ago the president-elect of the United States, Wilson A. Sarnoff, was struck down by an assassin's bullet. Perhaps many have asked, 'how could this happen?' Living in a free society, indeed, living in any society has risks that we all share. But for those who stand to take leadership roles, the risks are much greater.

"I will not comment further on the cowardly act that destroyed one of the great lights in our country. Law enforcement officials are expertly investigating this horrendous crime. They need to have latitude to do their jobs without me commenting prematurely. There will be an appropriate time for me to speak publicly about this subject.

"Eleven days from now, Wilson Sarnoff would have mounted the steps at the *other* end of this historic mall to humbly and honorably take the oath of office. Now, he will be mourned instead. We continue to grieve as a people and as individuals, as friends and family of Wilson Sarnoff. I will climb those steps in his stead, as the law provides, and take the oath of office as the next president of the United States.

"Now I stand on *these* steps, at the feet of this remarkable statue of Abraham Lincoln. I chose to stand here—to feel of his strength and hear the echo of his greatness. Lincoln entered the executive office during very trying times. I will enter that same office, also during trying times. The severe economic troubles many nations face and the growing threats of fanatical terrorists continue to weigh heavily across the world stage.

"Our nation will continue to exert a leadership role in seeking peace and economic stability. We will continue our efforts to assist all our allies and economic partners. There are forces in the world that would try to break down our form of democratic government and end this great social experiment. Lincoln commented on this same challenge at Gettysburg: '[Can] any nation so conceived, and so dedicated,…long endure.' My simple answer is *yes!* With his same words, I echo his resolve: 'that government of the people, by the people, for the people, shall not perish from the earth.' *Yes!* To the best of my ability, I will faithfully execute the office of president and do all I can to preserve and defend the Constitution of the United States."

Madison paused, accepting the outpouring of shouts and applause. When calm resumed, she continued, "Our Constitution is not a static or a dead document. It has endured many monumental tests and trials. It has provisions for change and adaptations to meet the needs of this people. We have ratified amendments to this great foundation of our society. When I take the oath of office, a provision of the Twentieth Amendment will be employed for the first time since it became law. Our nation has enjoyed a peaceful transfer of power in every case since the Constitution was first ratified. This is one of the aspects of that document's genius."

After another long set of applause: "My parents loved and honored our founding documents and the men and women who brought them forth. They so admired the Father of the Constitution that they burdened me with his name." Laughter rippled through the vast congregation. "I say *burdened* because who could ever live up to the great mind that was James Madison? Nevertheless, I have born this burden with both pride and humility.

"Many have been called upon to stand up, enter the breach, and defend this Constitution and this country. As you have heard — perhaps too many times during the recent election — I proudly chose to don the uniform of my country. I did my small part in the defense of Constitution and country." The audience voiced boisterous recognition of Madison Hemsley-Tarlton's past military service as a Marine pilot. Everyone knew she was only the second woman, and the *only* woman since the American Civil War, to be awarded the Congressional Medal of Honor for her amazing valor in the Middle East conflicts.

"I swear to you, whether we agree or disagree on policy and politics, I will continue to defend this country with all that I have in me. I will not shrink from my duty. As others much greater than I have said in times past: *To this I pledge my life and my sacred honor.* Thank you."

The audience would not let her leave their sight for many minutes as they poured out mixed emotions of grief and elation. They were, for a brief time, a non-partisan body of fellow citizens experiencing a truly great moment. The bickering could begin again tomorrow.

One pundit summed it up best: "Whatever she says in her inaugural address will only be an afterthought."

Chapter 25

January 10

8:30 AM EST - Ten days before inauguration

Disquiet spread among many Washington D.C. kingmakers; the Tarlton coming out speech put them on notice that the "Republican window dressing" was stepping up to take charge. Opinions about Madison needed to be modified and past backroom deals renegotiated. The control that a few thought they exerted over the political process was turning into slippery mercury, hard to grasp.

The entire transition committee and all the staffers stood and politely applauded as Madison entered the Presidential Transition Committee Office. Fresh out of the hospital, she walked under her own steam—if a bit slower than her usual power stride—and was flanked by her Secret Service detail and Renae. When she received expressions of good will, she smiled, accepting their acknowledgement. She shook hands with almost everyone. The shocking trauma of losing President-Elect Sarnoff was still an open, emotional wound for most everyone, and the collective mood was subdued. But those who were complicit in excluding her from the transition proceedings were considerably chagrined.

Madison had not been a regular at the Transition Office before the assassination. Art Messanger, Sarnoff's Chief of Staff and transition committee chairman, had made it clear that Madison's input was not needed for the transition process. He had affected a veneer of cool cordiality during the campaign, which soon froze to a solid block of arrogant ice. Clearly, he didn't want to engage with the vice president-elect on any level. He had too much important work to do.

On the morning after the election, when the extended adrenaline surge was over and had sapped the good humor from exhausted campaigners, Art confronted Madison in the hallway of the victory-party hotel. He told her without preamble that she was purely a hood ornament, and now the election was over, she should keep her head down and her nose out of big boy business. She could enjoy the next four years of being number two without much to do. Madison did not even blanch at his rebuff. She knew the score—painfully obvious by the way she had been treated while campaigning. But she also kept a scorecard—privately taking names and having Renae keep a record of everything. She was well aware that Messanger underestimated both her force of will and the fact that *she* was elected, while *he* was merely an appointee. Understanding this gave her a platform and a position of strength.

She was not a vengeful person by nature, but she knew how the dynamics of loyalty operated—and would not hesitate to use them.

Madison anticipated that Art Messanger, bless his tiny titanium heart, was about to truly meet her for the first time. He didn't understand the depth of Madison's leadership training in her young life. Both her mother and father had taken great pains to develop her abilities and augment her natural gifts with real world experience. She had developed world-class skills through thousands of hours of practice—in education, military service, business, and politics. And although she had become governor of California at thirty years old and vice president-elect of the United States at thirty-six through the vagaries of political fate, she was eminently qualified and prepared. She had fully earned her accolades, and she never felt entitled.

Madison often remembered her father's mantra drummed into her consciousness from age seven on. It always guided her when she took a significant action:

Take a breath, take stock, take action, and move on.

*   *   *

After the bustle of Madison's entrance quieted down, Renae announced, "Madison will conduct a brief discussion in-camera with the executive staff and then will address the entire group." Madison was escorted into the conference room and was followed by Bertrand Pinckney, Art Messanger, two from her own V.P. staff, and a few others. Secret Service Agents Jason and Andie also followed.

As soon as everyone was in the room, Art stepped forward to welcome Madison with all the graciousness he could muster; he knew she needed him and his organization. Everything for the transition was set in motion under *his* tight control, not Wilson Sarnoff's. *He* was the big brain here and he knew it. He now assumed he would have to soften his approach a bit to mend fences with Ms. Tarlton—but no harm, no foul.

"Ms. Tarlton, welcome to the party," Art said. "We've a lot to go over, as you know. We've already completed a lot, but, *of course*, there are a myriad of small details to finalize before we can put confirmation packages before Congress. And, *of course*, we've established some strategies to win confirmations for some of the more controversial nominations." Expectant ears waited for Madison's response.

She stood military straight as she said, "*Of course*, Art, I have gone over all of the proposed appointments, and I have several changes to make immediately..."

"No, Madison, you can't be serious," Art interrupted. "That would be going against Wilson's wishes. He was the one elected president; you are only taking over. You should consider yourself his successor and carry out his intentions." He was adamant and combative right off the mark. Even though Art operated under the Sarnoff aegis, his blunt approach to the new boss caught the transition committee members off guard.

Madison responded: "Everyone, listen carefully. The concept of the vice president succeeding to the presidential office and being considered *only* an acting-president was settled by the Harrison-Tyler succession. You all know this. I will not be an acting-president."

"But Madison, all these names have already been cleared and the FBI is almost finished vetting them," Art came back forcefully. "You weren't in on these choices; you can't arbitrarily undo promises we've made. It was my job to orchestrate all this. I will not allow it."

"Art, I'm pretty sure you would like to let bygones be bygones and not rehash the past. Remember what you said to me as the transition committee began to assemble? You told me to basically enjoy the ride for the next four years. You said something like 'If we need your pretty face for a photo-op, we'll call—we don't need your help right now.'"

Art went beet red as sweat formed on his upper lip and above his bushy brows. He cleared his throat to speak again, taking an aggressive step forward. "But..."

"Don't bother to say anything, Art. *Of course*, I don't hold a grudge; however, old buddy," she paused for dramatic effect, "you're fired. Furthermore, anyone, I mean *anyone*, who works for our committee and communicates with you about transition business will be fired and prosecuted for breach of his or her non-disclosure agreement."

The room's occupants were stunned. Jason and Andie took Arthur's arms to guide him from the room and out of the building. Other agents supervised Art's assistant as she cleared out the personal items from his office. The phone, tablet, computer, credit cards, and ID badge belonging to the committee were confiscated. IT geeks busily changed passwords and protocols while Art was led to the sidewalk.

*   *   *

Murmurs bubbled through the room. Madison waited while Renae gathered the committee's focus: "Ladies and gentlemen, your attention please. Vice President-Elect Tarlton will now speak to you."

"Folks, thank you for welcoming me. I'm very cognizant of the deep emotions and sorrow we all feel, and I thank you for continuing to work diligently on this transition in the face of such terrible national and personal losses. We all know that this has never happened before, and having the vice president-elect step in as president-elect is both challenging and historic in scope. So, to echo Churchill, 'We will keep calm and soldier on.'" She chuckled and the room erupted in applause now that they had permission to celebrate the new administration soldiering on.

"To all you loyal folks who remain to complete the huge task of a difficult transition, let me officially introduce Renae Hinckley. Ms. Hinckley will now take the reins of the transition committee. In addition, she will serve as the White House Chief of Staff. Please give her your support and cooperation. Although the outgoing administration has been uncooperative and obstructive, we will be ready to start running the government at noon on January 20th.

"Thank you, I will see you all again this afternoon. The clock is running and time is short, as you are all very aware." With that, she swept out of the room, giving the team time to process the dramatic changes and allowing Renae freedom to take charge.

Renae was a short, slender, dark-haired woman with a pixie-like face. Soft-spoken and often underestimated, she was forceful when she needed to be, and her eyes flashed heat when she was riled. No one dared cross her a second time. Renae coached the entire group on the changes and the reasons for the leadership shakeup. Seven other staffers and four committee members were escorted out of the building and reminded of their obligations to their non-disclosure agreements. They would be given modest severance packages out of the transition funds but not the cushy West Wing jobs they had expected.

Art Messanger was booted out—and there was a new sheriff in town. Renae Hinckley was the chief of staff now, the excellent leader who would corral the herd and drive it forward.

Chapter 26

11:00 AM EST - Ten days before inauguration

"I was asked to tell you that Tally is in town. He needs to speak to you, but he suggests it should be in person." Renae spoke quietly to Madison in her new Transition Office. It had been a hectic day so far, and all nerves were taught, but the troops were reassured knowing who was in charge and feeling confident in her.

"Are we sure it's safe to talk in here?" Madison half-whispered. Renae shrugged in response and left the room, soon returning with her geek-in-chief, Bob Landau. He was a very large, half-Hawaiian surfer dude with the obligatory aloha shirt turned inside out, the baggy board shorts, and the flip-flops.

His appearance was a cliché straight out of a young adult novel, but he was the real deal out of the original package. He had recently been invited onto the transition team by one of the IT guys who had set up the committee's computer and data systems. Bob Landau, known as "Luau" and famous as a wizard of the IT industry, wanted a change of scene from Seattle and was quickly snapped up by the power brokers in the U.S. government, with no problems in his background checks.

Luau had been working for Seattle-based DeCourcy Security Technologies—the premiere cyber security firm in the nation—which gave him a huge cachet with propeller-heads across the online community. The firm's prestige was built on phenomenal performance: for one thing, none of their client companies had ever been hacked; for another, the slacker-hackers who tried were bug trapped, pinned down, and prosecuted without mercy. At DeCourcy Technologies there was none of that mythical stuff about enterprising kids getting offered jobs for being good hackers. They were burned

right down—and Luau had the reputation of being the guy who
torched them.

"Madison Tarlton, this is Bob Landau. 'Luau' is what they call
him. I call him Bob," Renae introduced a surprisingly polite Luau.

"Pleasure to meet you, Ms. Tarlton, your Honor. I really admire
the companies you built; I owned stock in both of your IPO's."

"Madison will do, and thank you." She smiled with a touch of
deference at this brash millennial who exuded supreme confidence.
"Is it safe to have private conversations in this office?"

"Have I got some stories to tell you…" he began.

"Bob," Renae prodded firmly; he often wandered off track.

"Okay. Yeah, you're free to talk in this room, and the conference
room is also fine," he said. "Art Messanger had this place swept for
bugs, the listening type, twice every day. He used a contractor, Eddie
Smyth, who he completely controlled. The guy did a good job, but
then he also inserted a ton of listening devices all over the offices, and
who knows why he did that! He can activate them remotely and
catch the audio with a receiver not far away, and he aggregates the
signals and sends them out to a repeater for distance transmission.
The Secret Service is clueless about all the bugs. I left them in place
because it was Messanger's team and his bugs. But now, of course,
things have changed."

"So if they're still in place, how are we safe to speak openly?"
Madison asked.

"In here and in the conference room, I've installed little white
noise generators right on top of the bugs. When I activate them, the
listening snoops only hear static noise." He pointed at the badges
hanging on lanyards around Renae and Madison's necks. "The RFID
chips in your badges activate the noise generators anywhere you go
in the office area. The snoopy dudes will hear what's going on until

you or Renae walk into an area. Then squuuueeeeessssk is all they'll hear," he said, grinning proudly.

"Won't that make them a bit suspicious that they've been discovered?" Madison asked.

"Well, yeah, but it is intermittent enough that they'll wonder for a while. Renae cancelled Eddie Smyth's access, and so tomorrow when he shows up, he's not getting in."

"What about the computers?" Renae followed up.

"Oh, that's worse. Every keystroke on every computer except mine is logged and sent via a secret backdoor in the network to Messanger's servers somewhere offsite."

"We changed the passwords and rebuilt the firewall, right?" Madison asked.

"Oh yeah, but the backdoor is still in place." Luau sat down. "Here's the thing. We have more spies peering into our documents and data than you can imagine. There are foreign governments, tech companies, and Wall Street traders who are looking at everything the team is doing."

Madison was shocked. "Why haven't you shut this down?"

"Um, well, until Renae showed up, I wasn't actually in charge of anything. But I've been busy making plans to shut them down, and…" he paused.

"And what?" Renae broke in.

"Look, let me lay out a narrative here, okay? There's a mean machine here, and it has a lot of moving parts. Can I use your white board?" Luau scratched out a diagram showing his brilliant maneuvering. It explained how he had installed a data trap to watch the net traffic in and out of the transition team's office, and how he had examined all the computers and virtual machines on the servers. In general terms, he explained how he had smeared digital cheese on the rattails and followed the data rodents back to their nests. The upshot was that Messanger was porting copies of everything offsite to his own secret servers. Luau also identified four other foreign government intrusions by Russia, Israel, France, and Pakistan, as well as four U.S. based companies, who were hacking in and routinely harvesting confidential information. He finished by mentioning a strong possibility that China, in turn, had hacked into one of the intruding companies and was also downloading data.

"Tell me, Bob, why hasn't this been reported?" Madison queried with keen interest.

"Ah, well, here's the thing. I laid some traps in each of the nests I found."

"Meaning?" Renae pushed.

"Before I go on, I gotta say here that I may need a presidential pardon-thingy in a couple of weeks, kinda like right after you become president officially." For the first time he looked a little sheepish.

"A pardon, Bob, how so?" Madison could not help smiling. She had employed hundreds of bright engineers like Bob in her technology companies and was used to their odd thought processes. "Have you been engaging in a little bit of counter-hacking, Bob? Have you been spying on four governments, a couple of companies, some stockbrokers, and maybe a former chief of staff?" Madison pointed a mockingly accusing finger at her new favorite staffer. "I sure hope DeCourcy Security Technologies isn't expecting you back anytime soon."

Chapter 27

After Luau left the room, Madison and Renae sat down at the desk to *take stock*.

"We need to decide quickly when to cut off the hackers. Having the committee's servers penetrated is dangerous, but I can see how it could be useful later," Renae said. She was a superb political operator good at projecting possible adversarial reactions to their defensive actions. Madison was an exceptional strategist, and when she combined her gifts with Renae's tactical brilliance, they made a fabulous team.

Years before, while on a summer internship with a major Silicon Valley company before her senior year at Berkeley, Renae had run into Madison, freshly returned from Iraq and recovering from her wounds—both physical and emotional. At a late summer industry reception, they struck up a conversation that began their lasting friendship. Renae was maid of honor at the Hemsley-Tarlton wedding. At the time of her wedding, Madison had earned a political science major / business minor from Stanford, was polishing off an MBA, and was contemplating starting a company in the tech space.

"Count me in when you're ready to crank up a company," Renae had told her.

When Madison *was* ready to launch her first internet appliance and software company, Renae had just finished her MBA and was ready to hit the bricks, also. Madison brought her in as executive admin., giving her plenty of latitude to hone her natural skillsets into razor-sharp business tools. Renae, as Madison's most important advisor, soon became assistant CEO, participating closely in decision-making. Renae was diplomatic but never equivocated when Maddy needed to hear a contrary opinion. Such moments were called *Renae-Reality-Reads*. She was the second most trusted person in Madison's life.

Renae was compensated with a top-end salary and generous stock options—Madison's financial success was Renae's success. After Madison's stunning IPO and millions of dollars in personal gain, Renae also became independently wealthy. But instead of thinking she had learned enough from the master to move on, Renae stuck with her friend and mentor. They built a second highly successful company in the valley of software and silicon chips, and the second IPO was almost as big as the first.

Madison's success story was legendary: she was born at home in a tiny town high in California gold country, and her grandfather, the local doctor, delivered her into the world. It was a modern version of famous early presidents' log cabin stories. Young Madison's reclusive father occasionally took her and her mother into nearby Grass Valley. Only one photograph existed that included all three: father, mother, and daughter. She was homeschooled until high school; Mom and dad were her fulltime teachers.

Publicly, Madison seemed to live a charmed life. But her inner story was fraught with rigorous learning curves and painful mistakes. And when she suffered the loss of her husband, she relied on Renae to complete the second IPO—while she held her daughter close and mourned. After a time, she decided to throw herself back into the business game and *move on* as best she could, but almost incapacitated with grief, she doubted whether she could do all of this and still be a decent mother to Lucy, her daughter.

Eventually, Madison felt ready to go for a hat trick. *A third IPO would be amazing,* she thought. But surprise pounded at her door when the lieutenant governor of California was forced to leave office in disgrace, creating a vacancy she was asked to fill. Renae convinced her to accept the gubernatorial appointment. She was only lieutenant governor for six months when the governor stroked-out at his desk, and she filled his remaining two years as governor. She adapted to the rough-and-tumble, mud-wrestling of politics as if it were her natural environment; she discovered she had missed the feel of battle fury because business was too tame, too polite. Madison was a tough person, relishing confrontation if circumstances required it. Her style was to take charge and push the opposition until they were driven to their knees. Once she was clearly the winner of a clash, she would back off, show mercy, and reach out a conciliatory hand. Her California political foes began calling her "Mad Tarlton."

Many admirers flocked to her from both sides of the political divide, and she decided to go for a hat trick of a different kind this time. She ran for reelection. After winning in a cakewalk, she did bigger, better things with the state's economy, the energy crisis, and the water shortage. She was so popular she could have been crowned Queen of California. Again, the public didn't witness the struggles of the private woman off-camera: the loneliness and self-doubts of a single mother with a high-profile career. But she was brave and forceful, and although she knew her feet were made of clay, she could put on iron shoes and step forward.

Behind the scenes, Tally was encouraging and helpful. And her father, the biggest role model of her life, was always mentoring, comforting. But she was losing him. Plagued by many injuries, he was fading fast. Through it all, Renae—her gubernatorial chief of staff—was supportive and present and added her own personal strength to every meeting and decision.

Madison was in the middle of a reelection campaign, fifteen points ahead of her opponent, when the Sarnoff VP hunters came calling. Again, Renae encouraged her to meet with them. The two women analyzed scenarios for accepting a place on the ticket from every conceivable angle, and because the previous California

Governor had died in office, they talked through implications of the
same thing happening again on the bigger White House stage.

Madison had served heroically in combat, built great
companies, lost a husband, inherited a state with huge problems, and
come out on top of the heap. Inwardly, she knew she owed her
success to the adversities she had weathered, to her ability to *take a
breath, take stock, take action, and move on.* Those tempted to dismiss
her, thinking she had made it on her wealth and charm, were
frequently amazed when exposed to her political acumen.

She was now recognized by some as a brilliant and determined
street fighter. And no matter how the lesser pundits and detractors
droned on, Madison Hemsley-Tarlton was a woman well prepared to
sit at the presidential desk.

Chapter 28

8:35 PM EST - Ten days before inauguration

Madison Hemsley-Tarlton walked into her Georgetown
townhouse. Because her personal Secret Service detail was much
larger now and her protective perimeter widely expanded, the little
bit of privacy she had retained since the election was inevitably gone.
Her well-heeled neighbors, in turn, resented the greater dose of
inconvenience her heightened importance brought them. Madison
had purchased the townhouse when she was selected as the VP
nominee, and the Secret Service had searched, scoured, and secured
it. But now they did it all over again.

Art Messanger's goons were unable to breach her house to install listening devices, even though most homes were relatively easy to enter. But on a scale of one to ten in security integrity, this house was a twenty. The man she was about to see had arranged these security elements—and he had arranged the location of the house itself because of its proximity to his own extremely secure property at the other end of the block.

Ostensibly, an offshore real estate investment syndicate had previously purchased the house, along with *all* the homes on the block and dozens more in the neighborhood, upgrading the utilities and beautifying the structures, landscaping, and parkways. The supposed investors and developers had knocked down four houses in the center of the block not included in the Georgetown historic preservation codes of the 1960s. Because the lost value of those homes had been offset by the fabulous neighborhood park replacing them and the improvements to the remaining homes had shot home values sky-high, the neighbors were very pleased. Maybe enough to disregard all the security inconveniences.

The soon-to-be-president had glamorously dined on pizza and salad at Transition Headquarters before returning home. After the tiring day she craved the reclusive solitude of a hot bath, but knowing agents were in front of her house, in the back garden, and in her living room, she felt more like a well-protected claustrophobic tightly hemmed in.

She called her young daughter in California to revive both their spirits. Being separated was hard, but it was better for Lucy to continue her normal life with her Auntie Janine and her school friends until she moved into the White House in a few days. Once Madison had proved to her daughter during their short hospital visit that she really was not hurt and *would* stay alive, the little trooper was okay with going home to pack and say goodbye to her friends.

After a luxurious bath, Madison dressed casually and bid goodnight to the Secret Service agents. She invited Agent Andie Madsen into the study adjoining her bedroom.

Andie was tall and muscular, with ginger hair and freckles. A competent, courageous agent, she was less comfortable in social situations than in dangerous ones. Madison looked at her fondly as she said, "Andie, I know that you and Jason are doing your jobs, like all the other agents. But you and I have become friends over the last several months. I want you to know that I deeply appreciate your personal efforts to keep me safe, *and* I appreciate your friendship."

"Thank you, Madison," Andie said awkwardly. "Obviously, you're more than just a protectee to me. It's a pleasure to serve on your detail." She was gratified by Madison's words. She had tried to keep a professional detachment, but Madison's warmth and genuine nature had pulled Andie into the famous Hemsley-Tarlton orbit.

"So, I have something to say that you're probably not expecting. Please hear me out before you react," Madison said, her expression serious. "After I'm sworn in, I'll be making some changes in my security detail. I know that your director believes he's in charge, but he works for the secretary of Homeland Security—who will be working for me. I also know that you enjoy your career and want to move up." She paused to search Andie's face. "We've become close in our friendship, and I sense your strong devotion to me. Don't they call it 'emotional attachment to the protectee?' Well, the protectee is attached to you, too."

"Um, Madison…," Andie began to protest but stopped quickly in order to listen; she was nothing if not highly disciplined.

"I'm not worried that you will fail to protect me; you've already demonstrated that you're great at that. Here's what I'm proposing. With Renae moving into the chief of staff slot, I'll be losing the close minute-by-minute assistance I get from her. I'd like to take you off the detail's shift rotation and make you my personal assistant and advisor…who also carries a gun." A slight smile crossed her lips. "I'll raise your security clearance, so you'll be read-in on almost everything, which will put you inside the door rather than outside guarding it. You can stay with the Service if you want, but essentially, you'll be on loan to me. I need your helpful insight, not simply your body as a human shield protecting my life. I've made a career of spotting talent, and I want to use yours in my administration."

"Madison, I don't know what to say. This is a stunning honor and career move you're offering me." Andie was deeply moved by Madison's confidence in her.

"Think it over. It's your choice, of course. Talk it over with Jason if you like, but keep the discussion just between the two of you, Renae, and me." She shook Andie's hand. "Okay?"

"Yes, of course. Thank you." Andie left the room and waited until the end of her shift to call Jason. She asked him to meet her at the all-night diner they frequented when both were on the late shift. They had worked together for years and served as each other's sounding board and supplemental conscience, and so far, they had resisted any romantic entanglements—because agents weren't supposed to date each other. But it was a challenge sometimes.

Chapter 29

10:00 PM EST - Ten days before inauguration

Madison rose from her desk to turn on the sound machine she kept in her bedroom. Most of her life she hadn't needed help getting her usual six hours of sleep—until Marcus was killed. Even though seven years had passed, she felt the familiar ache every night as she tried to drift off. They had only been married three years when a terrorist bomb disintegrated the combat chopper carrying Marcus and seven other Marines in northern Afghanistan. Wahid Sayed was a trusted Afghani intelligence asset flying with them that day, but defense intelligence determined that he had carried the semtex explosives on board in his rucksack.

She pushed her old sorrows aside and took a moment to pray silently for strength. Her life was full of frenetic activity and massive accomplishments, but she would trade it all for a few more years with Marc. She took a couple of deep cleansing breaths to clear her thoughts—time to *move on* to the next moment of her future.

As Madison's Secret Service detail kept vigilant watch, assuming the next president of the United States was in bed buttoned up for the night, she crossed the room. This day still required more emotional effort from her. She entered her closet, enormous by the standards of this Georgetown neighborhood, and closing the door, activated a low-level safety light. She then used her thumb to activate the biometric-code on her phone and opened an obscure app that looked like a mindless game. In seconds, part of the wall and shoe rack slid aside, revealing a dim light coming from an opening. Following the light, she descended a spiral staircase to an alcove, then entered the unlock code on a keypad next to a nondescript door.

When the door slid open, Madison saw that the corridor lights were on; the air was fresh-smelling, but warm and comfortable. She had only been in this tunnel that passed under her neighbors' backyards one other time, shortly after accepting the vice-presidential nomination. Coming to a wide sitting area she knew lay directly underneath the neighborhood park, she was again struck by the other-worldly, spy-techy feel of the place—it was like she had stepped onto the set of a James Bond movie. She pressed a code on her silly game app and got an instant response.

A door opened a few yards down the hall. A man came out and walked toward her with outstretched arms. As he reached her, she put her arms around him and they hugged tightly.

"Hello, Jeemie, it's good to see you," he said.

"Tally, it's more than good to see you!" She gave him a peck on the cheek and squeezed a little tighter. "I so need to have you with me right now. Thanks for coming."

"It's been very hard to stay away. I had my white horse saddled and ready to ride the moment it happened."

"I know, but our lives are even more complicated now that I'm the next president...all of a sudden," she shook her head with a sigh.

As they broke their embrace and sat on the couch in the sitting room, he said, "How is Lucy handling all this?"

"She's as resilient as ever, but I miss my time with her. In the White House I'm going to find a way to get our mommy-daughter routines back on track."

They chatted inconsequentially for a bit longer, making the human connections that people separated by time and miles crave. For so long, they had spent little time together, yet their bond was forged in a time and place that couldn't be dimmed by physical separation.

"Well, let's get to the critical stuff. I have to fly out to Seattle soon, and you need your battle rest for another day." He smiled; she smiled. It was so good to see this man. Their last face-to-face visit had been shortly after the election, and they had talked only a few times on the phone since then. Now, they had to be more careful than ever to make sure no one associated them together.

"Okay, let's have it," Madison replied, noticing that he had called her Jeemie again, like the old days. Only two people on the planet ever called her that: one was her father and the other was this man sitting beside her. He was one of the few people she could trust unconditionally in all situations; he had proved that to her over and over again.

"Doug Waldron couldn't have shot you, Wilson Sarnoff, and the others," he stated without preamble.

"That sounds very definitive and conflicts with the consensus building among the FBI investigators," Maddy replied unemotionally.

"The investigation hasn't collected all the facts yet."

"What information did Karen share with you?"

Talbot explained the eye injury and its inevitable effect on Doug's ability to *be* the sniper. He told her about the sixteen eye doctors he had asked to examine the records and slide of Waldron's eye, with the patient's name redacted. All of the doctors agreed, with little variation, that given the severity and time of the injury, the patient couldn't have used his right eye to aim a weapon—for hunting or anything else. He rehearsed his discussion with Karen Waldron. Doug couldn't have taken that long, difficult shot left-handed, so person or persons unknown must have planted the right handprint on the gun next to the trigger.

"So, if Mr. Waldron wasn't the shooter, it'll have to be exposed at some point," she contemplated.

"That's not a foregone conclusion; both Doug's eyes were destroyed by gunfire in the Macon-Roberts stairwell, so there couldn't be a postmortem discovery of his medical condition. And there are even more problems to consider."

"Obviously, there's an *actual* elaborate conspiracy, pretty much like talk radio is claiming!"

"There's certainly a conspiracy, but I think it's worse than the conspiracy theorists are spouting."

"Tell me."

"Doug didn't shoot you or Wilson. He was the proverbial patsy."

"Is the FBI investigating Karen's information?" Madison was getting more animated because *she* had been shot, too. Her cool, analytical detachment could only stretch so far.

"This is where it gets very complicated and leads to some big questions," Talbot pressed on. He explained about Doctor and Mrs. Robins' murder in Montana and the break-in at the doctor's office.

"My security people tracked the ophthalmologist's phone calls from his office and cell phone. Presumably, he was reaching out to someone he trusted to tell them what he knew about the assassin. Given the short time frame, there were a limited number of phone calls to sort through. My people tracked the entire call-chain once they fit the initial puzzle pieces together."

Talbot DeCourcy, *Tally* to Madison, explained the call-chain: Doctor Robbins had called a Seattle lawyer, who then called FBI Agent Josiah Mathieson of the San Diego Field Office on his cell when he couldn't be reached at the FBI office. Agent Mathieson, in turn, made two calls: to Doctor Robbins and to FBI Headquarters in D.C. He was subsequently called back from a D.C. mobile ten minutes later. And that same mobile then called an unknown New York number.

"All the FBI calls were made on cell phones, by the way, so there's no official record on FBI logs," he said. "The call-chain was acted out in reverse order later that evening. But violently. Agent

Mathieson received several calls from a disposable phone in New York over the next several hours—they were obviously setting him up for his final call, which came to him at 6:15 PM PST while he was a few blocks away from the San Diego Airport. At 6:35, his body was discovered. It was crumpled beside his car on a small side street, shot with a nine-millimeter automatic weapon in what the local police are calling a gang-style hit. It'll be thoroughly investigated, as all law enforcement deaths are. *Suspects* will be found and later dismissed for lack of evidence," Talbot said with disdain.

"Four hours later, at about 11:00 PM PST, the lawyer's home was broken into and the entire family—including his wife and two young children—were slaughtered in an apparent home invasion robbery. At least three shooters participated—no suspects at last check."

Talbot was deeply distressed as he told about the lawyer's family, and Madison well understood why. It was too reminiscent of his own horrific losses. He stopped talking and cleared his throat, feeling the silent surge of righteous anger welling up inside him. He began to lose his edge and became that boy of fourteen again who wanted to claim justice for his murdered family. Tears oozed from the corners of his eyes as he closed them briefly. Madison had seen Talbot's full range of emotions, but his displays were a rare occurrence.

He swallowed back his feelings and went on. "Then six hours later, at around 6:00 AM MST, the good doctor and his wife ran into an overpass abutment, dying instantly. The timing all adds up to our glorious sequence—these guys are sick, brutal bastards."

"I agree with what you said earlier: there's no coincidence here. This is devastating." Madison spoke for the first time since Talbot had launched his narrative. "It sounds like one team is moving very fast, directed out of New York. The guy in New York sounds like the shot-caller who also kept Agent Mathieson on the hook until they could get to him."

"Yes..." Talbot paused. "So, it seems that the group—and it has to be a group of multiple persons who set up Doug Waldron and perpetrated the assassination—didn't know about the eye injury before the assassination."

"Then the FBI putting the screws to Karen probably had nothing to do with her knowing about Doug's handicap," Madison speculated.

"That seems right. They didn't seem to know about the eye injury at first, but someone was already very interested in Karen even before the sudden killing flurry out west. And we have to figure out *who*."

"Radisson. Do you think he's somehow involved?"

"I think that Special Agent Larry Radisson is just a convenient tool obeying what he thinks are lawful orders from on high. But someone up there is dirty."

"Are we sure someone in the FBI is involved?"

"Well, the someone who took a call at FBI Headquarters must have passed information on to the unknown party in New York. Then the murders started, or continued, actually. Normally, I would suggest that we turn what we know over to the FBI investigators who are looking at Sarnoff's assassination because otherwise we would be withholding evidence. But as it is, we know the FBI was informed by one of their *own agents*—who's now dead," Talbot concluded.

"This is a real mess, Tally."

"Well, I think it gets worse. Put aside the whole false-flag effort to make Sarnoff's killer look like a disturbed, jealous husband. If we accept the idea that Doug was a patsy, then he was only needed to make the motivation look plausible. We don't have to accept that Wilson Sarnoff was the actual target."

"What? Who then?"

"*You*, Maddy. You were hit first. The bullet was in flight for a nick over half-a-second. Heads moved, placing yours out of line and Sarnoff's in line. I reviewed the video that was shot at 120 frames per second. That means at least 60 frames of video captured the shot—from firing time to impact. Your head and Sarnoff's changed alignment."

"Are you serious? Why shoot me? I wasn't the one becoming president."

"Big questions, no answers. But either way, with you or Sarnoff as the target, the culpable parties are still out there—and they still have the same agenda they were working on when the assassin took the shot!"

Chapter 30

11:55 PM EST - Ten days before inauguration

Back in her bedroom, Madison took slow, deep breaths, trying to let go of her wildly jumbled thoughts. What Tally revealed was disturbing and the future seemed uncertain. If suddenly being thrust into the role as the next president was not crazy enough, now a shadowy something out there was killing people to squash even the hint of their plans. Clarity was now a rarity—and everything and most everyone was suspect.

She calmed herself and practiced her self-hypnosis drills to fade into sleep. She thought about her late father and his gentle, sweet ways. He had recognized early her precocious and extraordinary

mind. In honor of her namesake, he called her Jeemie—the pet name
Dolly Madison had given her brilliant husband. So many times when
she was still a small child, Madison's father would say: "Jeemie, you
will be a force of nature. You can change the world someday, but
never forget that love, goodness, and honor are more important than
anything else you can accomplish." In every case where she swam
with the sharks in business or in politics—and discovered her own
inadequacies—her father would calmly reassure her. His confidence
and faith spurred her on, supercharging her next effort to overcome a
mistake or weakness. Because of him then, she would take the
calming breaths and carry on now.

Madison's father had passed away two years ago. It still stung
every day. He hadn't been physically strong her whole life, and he
had lived in self-imposed isolation as a virtual exile, but she clung to
the memory of how his hands felt when he stroked the back of her
head and how his voice sounded when he sang her to sleep. He was
always melodically off-key. She could still hear his rendition of "Red
River Valley."

Also, she was not done grieving the loss of her husband,
Marcus. Yearning for her Marc and Maddy life, she allowed her
thoughts to drift back.

*   *   *

Marcus Tarlton had wrangled a two week break for R&R in
England, but it wasn't all relaxation. He had met with the British SAS
(Special Air Service) sniper-training unit to compare performance
data from their respective Afghanistan missions during the last year.
After three days of confab, Marcus caught a train north through
Manchester to Preston. He had been in country for six months and
needed the break, but mostly he needed to see his bride.

Madison waited in the same converted Victorian mansion turned Marriott Hotel that they had honeymooned in three years earlier on another R&R. She sat in the lobby in the early afternoon, attempting to be the patient war bride watching for her hero's return. When she saw Marcus drive up, she sprang from her seat and ran to push the elevator *up* button. She anchored herself there. As Marcus came into the hotel, he searched around and didn't see her at first.

"Over here, Marine—no time for pleasantries. Your presence is required, upstairs, forthwith, on the double, Captain Tarlton."

"Yes, ma'am, right away, ma'am," Marcus called as he trotted over. He knew his wife and wisely left his bag in the car. No encumbrances tolerated. *Probably should've left my shoes and belt in the vehicle as well.*

Hours later Marcus said, "I don't remember the grounds looking like this." The couple walked hand-in-hand as they took their evening stroll through the gardens beyond the hotel's patio.

"They're just as beautiful as last time, Marcus," Madison responded wistfully, more connected to the perfect evening sights than to conversation.

"Three years ago there was only one focus of beauty," he said, pulling her closer.

"Single-minded on your object of conquest, as I recall," she smiled.

"Oh yeah; truth is truth."

"Now that you've reconquered, let's absorb nature's beauty. I want to crystalize this midsummer moment." They sat on a decorative concrete bench watching the sunset.

Several minutes later, Marcus spoke quietly: "Maddy, my tour ends in two months, and I'll be posted stateside. We need to decide if I'm getting out for good."

Madison squeezed her husband's arm and pressed her face into his shoulder. A surge of joy enveloped her. *He's willing to give up his career to be home with me.*

"I love you, M.T.," Madison whispered.

"I love *you*, M.T., more than ever!"

It was a delightful rendezvous, and the trip went by much too quickly. Marcus went back to his combat zone, and Madison headed home to California.

When Madison landed in San Francisco, Marcus' father was at the airport bearing the tragic news. She tried to take it like a Marine, but could only manage to take it like a wife who was devastated — shattered — and suddenly alone. She could not even *take a breath.*

*   *   *

Marcus died honorably defending his country, but he is still dead…still gone, Madison thought as she drifted past conscious thought into sleep.

Chapter 31

January 11

9:00 AM EST - Nine days before inauguration

Nine men sat around a conference table in Reston, Virginia. It was not the whole group, but they had gathered enough for a quorum, enough to conduct business according to the bylaws in their charter and long tradition. They called themselves "The Brotherhood of the New America."

The Brothers took great precautions whenever they met, ensuring that the conference room was carefully selected, screened, and electronically scrubbed. They posted trusted guards about the office building and outside the doors of the conference room. These precautions existed because the group included a few famous faces. While a vigilant reporter could easily recognize all but one of the attendees, many members were familiar faces to the general public—familiar, but certainly not what they seemed. Only their mentor, their guiding light, was a complete enigma. Once a famous man himself, he had vanished into oblivion.

He called himself "John Hancock," the nom de guerre he had adopted thirty-eight years earlier before dropping out of the public eye. He was not in hiding per se but was working behind the scenes for *his* version of the greater good. His ego was large enough to fill the universe but small enough to compress into his cold heart. Somewhere in his past he came to believe that he was capable of ruling all he surveyed—that he could succeed where the Napoleons of the world had failed—that he alone deserved to write the destiny of the modern world—and he had worked to do exactly that for over fifty years.

He hated that his life sounded trite: the impatient heir not willing to wait for his destructive old man to die off so he could claim his fortune; the son of the twisted man who abused his mother and tortured everyone in the family. But he had to own it, and he did. Because his unfaithful father had beaten his mother, she, in turn, took lovers to compete with her husband and his many mistresses. John inherited not only the family fortune but its severe emotional dysfunctions. He reached adulthood despising his crazy parents but reflecting their lunacies. He considered women as biological conveniences, as temporary as any other meal eaten quickly, satisfying momentarily, and forgotten. He also learned the important lesson that one should not take chances on a random heir by birth but should create and manage that heir, chosen for his loyalty and talent.

As a much younger man, the mentor and founding member of the Brotherhood had attempted to build an earlier version of the Cabal. It had failed to match his vision because his chosen companions were too weak and self-absorbed. But in reading *"The Fifth Republic Treatise,"* he realized that his timing and tactics were wrong: he had unsuccessfully tried to gain his followers' loyalty by appealing to their lust for power. So, as he had done with his own family, he killed off those he felt were rivals or those who had glimpsed his plan. He was the only survivor of the previous Brotherhood generation.

Erasing the other members and their contributions to the effort, he started over. He also controlled the vast fortunes that the previous members had pledged on the altar of their cause.

He studied the great leaders and cults in history and cataloged their failures. First, he learned that trying to gather the public glory, like Napoleon and Adolf, simply sewed a target to one's back. It would be better to raise surrogates and demand fealty with mortal consequences, mentoring them to take the public-facing position. It was better to control the empire by controlling the emperor than to be the front man. He could rule the world with the right, compliant minions.

Second, in his exhaustive study of secret societies, he learned that the most successful ones shared three things in common: they wrapped themselves in pseudo-religious or sacred fervor; they were crafted with blood oaths and solemn ceremonies; and the blood oaths carried dire punishments for betrayal.

After designing a custom-sacred myth and its attendant falderal, he began seeking acolytes.

In the ensuing years, John Hancock recruited young men to be the tools of his plan, the arms and legs of his grand design. The dozen new members—his sons, as he thought of them—were all from the same age group, in their twenties back then, now in their fifties. All were extremely bright, ambitious, and filled with promise. He molded them into what they became. They were poised to be the masters of the New America—the next incarnation of the Great Republic.

Knowing all systems evolve, Hancock desired to control America's evolution, to make the nation more meaningful, powerful, and dominant. This evolution should not be left to the whims of chance or ignorant voters, and especially not to grasping, self-important politicians.

Hancock believed that the pronounced leftward drift of the American political machinery must be stopped. More and more, younger Americans were openly courting socialism—liking the prospect of free stuff and "a level playing field." It was a huge disaster in the making. He was dead set on turning the ship of state around and correcting its course. He didn't want America to become Venezuela or Sweden, and he was certain his own vision of a strong America would be the platform from which to successfully rule.

A wrinkle had recently developed in the master plan, as often happens in great adventures, and continual incremental adjustments were required to stay the course and reach the overriding goal. John was not overly worried by recent events, but since timing was critical at this juncture, he wanted a hands-on, face-to-face working session with his sons of the Brotherhood.

The mentor officially opened the meeting: "Gentlemen, brothers, thank you for making the time to meet on short notice. We need to bring you up to speed on some developments so we can make a few decisions. Thomas, would you please fill the rest of us in on the Waldron problem and how you dealt with it?" He turned the time over to fifty-three-year-old Thomas Carlyle, a very successful Wall Street hedge fund manager and investment banker. It was said that more people in power owed Carlyle money and favors than anybody else in the financial world.

"In summary, gentlemen, my highly placed asset at FBI Headquarters heard from another contact in the Bureau that a California agent possessed extremely compromising information. No time to call a meeting, so I dispatched a team to cauterize the leak. They were successful, and a potentially disastrous bit of knowledge was contained."

Thomas Carlyle explained how his team had taken out the FBI agent, the lawyer, and the doctor. The bottom line: no one could put the events together, and the "eyeball" issue wouldn't come out. Others asked a few clarifying questions and Thomas answered them. The victims were all connected: the doctor and the lawyer had been undergraduate roommates; the lawyer and the FBI agent had been in law school together.

"Now that you've heard Thomas explain the cause and effect of this issue, I would like a vote to ratify the actions taken." The mentor requested a hand vote, which went smoothly. "Now we must deal with the other Waldron problem. Thomas, please continue."

"My FBI source told me that Karen Waldron has vanished. An Agent Radisson had her under surveillance, but she slipped away with some sophisticated help."

"Is she really a big problem for us? I was under the impression that the FBI only wanted to keep an eye on her as a possible material witness," Leon Fuller said.

"That's our understanding, but she may have absorbed some of Sarnoff's knowledge about our plans and schedule," Thomas Carlyle answered. "They could've engaged in a little pillow talk, regardless of Wilson Sarnoff's claims otherwise. We put them together romantically in case we needed some blackmail leverage to keep Sarnoff in line," he continued. "Sarnoff didn't know much and was only aware of his own operational details; ergo, Karen Waldron might have a clue."

"I thought Bert went to get her away from the FBI anal-probes in Chicago," said Roger Burgad, a very hardened ex-CIA man, who, until recently, was serving on the President's National Security Council.

"Yes, I did," Bertrand Pinkney spoke up. "I got our dear heart away from that jackass Agent Radisson and dropped her at her hotel, but she was already gone in the morning when my driver called to take her to the airport. She didn't mention going home to Portland or wherever. It also seems that she went to the hospital and had a brief conversation—a condolence visit—with Madison Tarlton. We have no idea what they talked about."

David Maxtell, the group's technology wizard, spoke up. "Is it prudent to assume that Karen Waldron didn't know of her husband's eye injury? If she was aware of his problem, it could've spooked her more than anything Wilson Sarnoff might have hinted at."

"Questions and more questions. I suppose we had better get ahold of Karen and seal her lips," the mentor suggested. "All in favor of taking Karen off the playing board, please raise your hands."

The motion carried unanimously.

Chapter 32

8:00 AM PST - Nine days before inauguration

Karen Waldron was dressed and ready to go by 8:00 am. A pair of former Secret Service agents, the "good hands" the man had mentioned at Multnomah Falls, had driven her to Seattle the night before. They were both blond, tall, and handsome. The woman, Meredith Lubneski, was five feet eleven, lithe, and wondrously graceful. The man, Brian, was six feet four and powerfully built, yet moved with the ease of a dancer. They were an intelligent, striking couple who enjoyed everything and everyone. Life for them was a lark. They had met while in the Secret Service and had chosen each other over their government careers.

When they resigned from the service and wondered what would come next, they realized they eventually *would* need jobs. Upon returning from their thrilling Andes Mountains backpacking honeymoon, they got a call from their former boss, Preston Knight, assistant director at the Service. He told them that an interested party had requested a meeting with them and they ought to hear him out. The very next day, they sat with an enigmatic billionaire at a downtown D.C. coffee shop. "I have special security needs," he said, "both for myself and for the many companies I own. If you accept my offer, you'll work together doing what you love. In addition, you'll continually take advanced training—oh, and your salary will be more than twice your government pittance."

Because they respected Preston Knight's opinion absolutely, Brian answered, "Heck yeah, no need to think that one over. We're in!"

"The Barbies," as their coworkers affectionately called them, took charge of Karen Waldron at Multnomah Falls and quickly drove her to the legendary Edgewater Inn in Seattle, Washington. They avoided checking in and giving names; their suite was pre-rented. They went straight up to room 272, the same room the Beatles had famously fished out the window from during the Seattle leg of their 1964 world tour.

Karen was comfortable with her two protectors, although they were closemouthed about her benefactor. Brian would only say, "His name is Talbot DeCourcy, and he put you in our keeping."

"And you're the 'good hands' he told me about, and his name is Talbot DeCourcy?"

"We're moving you to a private location, but first we'll take a helicopter tour over Elliot Bay like regular tourists. The tour is a ruse, of course," Meredith explained in her breezy way.

Karen was grateful but extremely curious and found that her sense of deep dread was lessening with each passing hour because of the couple's comforting manner.

After the tour, a DeCourcy aid drove them to a small FBO (fixed based operation airfield) where they boarded a Gulfstream V private jet. "Karen, we plan to get you to the east coast by tonight, but we need to make a short stop beforehand. By the way, Talbot went to D.C. to meet with Madison and filled her in on the information you gave us," Meredith told her as they buckled into the luxurious leather chairs.

Karen was surprised to see Brian sit up front in the co-pilot's seat. She had a lot to learn about the advanced training of DeCourcy field agents: flying both rotor and fixed wing planes, driving cars at over two hundred miles per hour, and rappelling out of copters headfirst while shooting weapons and/or disarming bombs. "Where are we stopping?" she asked, not really expecting an answer.

"Oh, we need to make a quick visit to Talbot's house. His wife wants to meet you. Given your homewrecker reputation, she'll probably want to warn you to stay away from her husband. And, by the way, she shoots really well, so I would listen." Meredith's delivery was so dry that Karen wasn't sure how serious she was. After a couple of beats, Meredith grinned widely, adding, "Lighten up, Karen. The woman is really nice, and in her whole life she has shot and killed only three people. I mean… really…she actually has. But you don't need to worry." Karen laughed nervously at what she hoped was a joke.

After an hour-and-fifteen minutes of combined pre-flight and actual airtime, they descended through the thick January inversion layer and landed at a private airfield in the deep wooded hills north of Spokane, Washington. The vast estate covered sixteen square miles of land, bordered on the north by tracks of forest service land, on the south and west by sparse housing areas, and on the east by the Idaho border.

An associate had left an SUV running for them at the taxi apron. The three were happy to jump into the warm vehicle, with the outside temperature only thirteen degrees Fahrenheit. Karen glanced out the back window as they drove away and was startled to see a small building rising up from beneath the ground and a few silhouetted people exiting it and running toward the plane. She wondered if she was hallucinating and didn't comment on this strange sight—assuming she was probably in for many more.

Chapter 33

Karen and the Lubneskis traveled in what appeared to be a dark blue SUV, but she couldn't be sure of the color. Unaware that DeCourcy Industries created stealth-vehicle technology, she was amazed that the car's paint seemed to absorb the dim light of the day and its only noise came from its tires on the pavement. *The vehicle must be electric,* she thought. She also saw that the snow-cleared road was a dull brown rather than the gray-black of asphalt.

Looking at the icicles on the pines and the tire marks on the muddied, snow-covered side roads they passed, she silently recited her creation from high school English class, *"Triscuit tracks on the mocha snow, care for some crackling cream?"*

"Beautiful area," she said aloud.

"We like it a lot," Meredith answered.

Karen had only driven through Spokane on Interstate 90 while heading up to Bozeman, Montana from Portland. She knew nothing of the area except that it was a lot drier than Portland. East of the Cascades and central drylands and north of the rolling prairie called "the Palouse"—which stretched down to the Snake and Clearwater Rivers before they joined the Columbia—Spokane sat near the foot of the Rockies.

It took six minutes to get from the airfield to the architecturally remarkable manor house sitting atop a lovely hill, with grounds sloping gently on all sides and giving way to forest. Karen saw a lake off to the south and three separate roads leading to the driveway and garage, but she couldn't see a highway or major road anywhere that those roads might have come from. *One of those roads must connect to civilization,* she thought.

Another thought tickled the back of her brain as they drove toward the massive structure that was someone's home. Finally, it came to her: "defensible" was the word she remembered from discussions with her Army Ranger husband. Driving toward this estate felt like approaching a well-defended medieval castle.

"Defensible!" she blurted aloud. "Who built this place?"

"Someone who will never allow invaders or snipers to shatter the peace of *his* home and hearth," Brian responded with pride.

The thought of snipers brought her pain. She blinked away tears and focused on the meeting looming ahead.

The car pulled to a stop at the center of a circular, crushed gravel drive. A wide stairway rose to magnificent entry doors. Karen thought it was beautifully tasteful and not at all gaudy. This was not like so many of the tiresome "McMansions" she had visited on countless fundraising trips and parties during the recent campaign. The thought of the campaign and Wilson Sarnoff pinched at her emotions again.

Exiting the car, Meredith and Karen mounted the steps as Brian drove away. A housekeeper opened the door, and a lovely woman with a bright smile and sparkling eyes waited in the entry foyer. "Welcome to Courci Downs," she said, extending her hand to greet Karen and giving her a brief hug. "I know the name sounds pretentious, but my husband is a closet romantic and still reveres the Kentish lands of his people. Mind you, his 'people' left Kent, England for the wilds of America in the 1630s. I'm Kate DeCourcy. Welcome to our home."

Karen instantly liked this warm-hearted woman, who was probably a few years older than herself but didn't look it. *Well, money and good care can keep you young,* she supposed. Kate DeCourcy was in fact older by fifteen years and had never had "work done." She was from an enviable gene pool of ever-young-looking women. She had wide set, almond-shaped eyes, high cheekbones, and a wide mouth with perfect teeth.

Damn her anyway, Karen thought. *How fair is it that this woman is rich, beautiful, and probably smart, too, just to ice the cake?* The jealous thoughts were fleeting, but she internally argued that she would be a traitor to all womankind if she didn't resent Kate at least a little.

"Thank you, Kate, I guess you already know who I am—the infamous assassin's wife."

"Let's sit and talk for a few minutes. Do you need to freshen up first? And how about something to eat and drink?" Kate asked as she led them to the parlor.

"Yes, that would be nice. I mean both," Karen answered, and Meredith showed her to the guest bathroom. When she returned, she found Kate sitting in a gorgeous, yet simple parlor. A young girl was holding a tray with teas, hot cocoa, and warm chocolate croissants.

"This is my daughter, Lydia. Lydia, this is our guest, Karen Waldron. She's a friend of dad's."

"Nice to meet you, Ms. Waldron. Would you like tea or cocoa?"

"Lovely to meet you, Lydia, and yes, I would love some hot cocoa. Thank you." Lydia, a bright-eyed girl of fifteen, smiled, and setting the tray on the side table, bounced out of the room. Kate served Karen, Meredith, and herself.

After sitting down to chat, Kate said, "First, Karen, I want you to know how sorry I am about your husband and the great loss you must be feeling. You've obviously been through a horrible few days."

"Thank you, Kate. I'm a wreck, actually, and scared to death, besides." Karen began to open up. Although Meredith and Brian had given her assurances about her safety and she was relaxing more and more, she couldn't simply flip a mental switch to get over the kind of trauma she'd experienced—and she was still feeling exhausted from it.

"I don't want to be presumptuous," Karen said, "but I have a pretty good memory for faces, and you look familiar somehow. But I can't quite place your name yet."

"Perhaps you've seen my photo somewhere in your work. It's not relevant to our discussion, but you may be vaguely aware of me professionally."

"What Kate is not saying due to their family's absurd propensity for modesty—and outright reclusiveness—is that she is Federal Appellate Court Justice Kate Covington," Meredith cut in with her frank, animated style. "She's known as one of the most brilliant legal minds in the country. When your late boss had started putting together a list of possible Supreme Court nominees, Kate was on the list." She beamed like an adoring younger sister as she bragged about her boss; Kate frowned at the boasting.

"That's right; now I get it. But you're Kate Covington…not DeCourcy?" Karen asked, perplexed.

"Professionally, I've always used my own name, which suits me and my husband. Talbot is a very private man."

"Private!" Meredith blurted. "Howard Hughes was a raving socialite compared to Talbot!" Meredith chortled and Kate smiled.

"Well, there's a wide spectrum of privacy." Kate changed subjects. "Karen, I'm aware of your dilemma and the revelations you shared with Talbot. He met with Madison Tarlton last night, and they have worked out how to proceed. This is very delicate, as you might imagine."

"Yes, I certainly get that," Karen said, tracing the top of the warm cocoa mug with her finger. "I didn't know what to do. I was scared, and I thought Madison should be aware of what I know."

"All of us agree that you did the right thing. And just so you know, we're convinced you're absolutely correct. Your husband, even with his deep problems of depression and PTSD, couldn't have shot Wilson Sarnoff."

Karen finally broke down and sobbed. Both Meredith and Kate moved in to put their arms around her, silently letting her tears flow. Soon, Karen dried her eyes. "Thank you. It feels so good to release the burden. And to think I'm actually a phony—I'm not the assassin's wife after all." They all laughed as tension released its grip.

"Well, if you're going to be a fake, that's a good kind of fake to be," Meredith added jovially.

"Can I ask you what the connection is between your husband and Madison? I mean, I told Madison to have someone she absolutely trusted contact me, and then your husband appeared out of nowhere."

Kate's expression changed, not with anger or sadness but with an emotional wall long-honed to reveal no chinks or cracks.

"I'm sorry, but that story is out there on the privacy spectrum beyond the view of anyone but Tally and Maddy," Kate replied, unwilling to say more. "Now, I'm sorry, but I have to leave for work. I need to be in Seattle in a couple of hours for a committee hearing, and you need to be on your way to The Field. We've prepared a written statement expressing what you told Talbot. The statement is addressed to me as a sitting federal judge. Due to some bench vacancies, I fill in as a district court judge in Seattle and here in Spokane. So in that capacity, I'm accepting your sworn statement of the facts as you know them. Talbot will keep you hidden and protected because he's concerned about your personal safety. He's also willing to handle all of the legal issues you'll face, if you would like him to represent you."

"He's a lawyer?"

"Let me just say, if I want legal advice or clarification on any obscure Constitutional question, Tally's the expert I go to. He graduated first in his class from Stanford Law School at twenty-one. So yes, the man is a lawyer." Kate would not brag about herself but couldn't hide the pride she felt in her husband. For his own part, he never mentioned his successes to anyone.

"Certainly. I'd love to have Talbot as my attorney." Karen gushed a little. "What's his actual name?"

"You asked for it," Meredith answered ahead of Kate, laughing as she spilled it out. "The master of the house is affectionately known as Talbot Tristan Thomas DeCourcy the tenth, or Talbot-X. Some call him T-X or T3. Or it's Tally to his closest associates."

"Wow," was the only word that came out of Karen's mouth.

"Meredith is a notary, so she'll witness your signatures on your formal statement and the representation agreement. I've also issued a protective custody order. Brian and Meredith will see you to your destination—a place we call The Field. They'll tell you the whole story, I'm sure. Good luck, Karen."

Kate hugged her for a moment, and Karen left the room wondering about "The Field."

Chapter 34

Madison sat in the conference room with Renae and the indomitable Luau discussing the strategy to get control of their data.

"Okay, guys. I understand the ramifications of cutting the cord and locking out the hackers, and I agree with Renae that we'll only go public about the American companies hacking us. But in effect, we'll be shutting down the foreign players also, and since they hacked in through the U.S. companies, they'll think they're undetected," Madison recapped.

"Art Messanger will be fairly certain that he's being outed," Renae said. "But yes, the foreign governments will probably believe they got away with it," she agreed. "They may suspect the game we're playing, but they won't know for sure."

"That is, until I zing them with it in our first heads of state meeting in the Oval Office," Madison said. "I think I'll especially enjoy teasing the Israeli Prime Minister. We may be friends and allies, but boy, am I going to tweak his ear with this…to get what I want. As for the Russians and Pakistanis, we'll wait and see what comes up. These are nice chips to have in the game."

"The FBI cyber guys may figure out that the second company stealing data from us was also hacked by the Chinese, but that can't be helped," Luau interjected. "I have all the digital fingerprints partitioned. And we can claim privilege, so we don't have to give the Feds any more than we want to. Is that right, the privilege bit?"

"Yes, you've got that right," Madison answered. "So, what I'd like to do is time this exactly right. Renae has asked the FBI director over for a courtesy sit-and-sip, and he'll bring along his executive assistant director over cybercrime. While I have him in the room, I'll pass him the hacking-evidence package you've put together, and Renae will hit the press pool with the same information at the same time. The FBI will want to do their own forensics, and the director will likely try to get me to delay announcing this—but my agenda is not his agenda."

"When do we cop to knowing about the foreign intrusions?" Luau asked.

"We've looked into this, Bob. Even though it's a series of illegal hacks, we're not officially the government yet, so it's not a case of national security spying," Renae explained. "We're not legally required to air our exposure. And before we let anyone know about the rest of it, we'll need to cover you with that little pardon thingy to keep you out of prison if it comes to that."

"Yeah, like that's a really fine point there, Renae. I mean, I'd go for exile in a non-extradition country rather than get tossed in a supermax lockdown."

"Now, now, Bob, don't worry. Maddy will take care of you, sweetie, but you're not going back to DeCourcy as long as we need you. Agreed?"

"Oh sure, I think I'll like the whole West Wing gig—low light levels, whispered secrets in the halls, and all of that." Luau grinned.

"We were thinking more like a deep basement closet or something. You know, a reminder of where you *could* be. But we would shove cokes and pizza under the door twice a day if you play nice!" Renae wagged her finger for emphasis.

"Ouch, Miss Grouchy. I think I should get a bit-o-props for finding this and nailing it before it's too late."

"Of course, you did great!" Madison said. "Keep doing it and maybe we can draft that pardon sometime." She tilted her head and raised her eyebrows. Both women laughed, but Luau wasn't altogether sure where he stood.

Chapter 35

Arthur Messanger and the mentor called John Hancock sat down for lunch in a private club in Leesburg, Virginia. The main attraction was the absolute privacy that enabled John to order food and stay away from prying eyes and ears. He affected patience toward Art, who was dealing with the burgeoning anger and overwhelming sense of failure at being fired by Madison.

"Obviously, Art, we've suffered a logistical setback with Tarlton kicking you out of her administration. You must have really pissed her off!"

"I hope that's all it is. If Sarnoff slipped up and leaked anything to Karen and she passed it on, well, I'm going to strangle somebody," Art said truculently.

"Remember, son, there are elements we cannot control, but we can redirect assets." John calmly rehearsed the lecture he'd given for years. "The moment-by-moment steps we take are not crucial to the plan. They are just rocks in the streambed we climb; there are always several to gain our footing on, and we shouldn't be overly focused on any one rock. Remember…our goal is to subtly grasp the levers of power and slowly take total control…change the rules of government. We'll make the system much stronger and our power will be absolute. It really doesn't matter which president we own. Once we're in power, we'll redefine the government by creating a catastrophic event that'll allow us to build anew from the ashes. We'll eliminate the inefficient legislature and the vacillating courts. We'll have the strongest nation the world has ever known; and we, my brother, will hold it in our hands."

"Yes, of course I remember," Art said with undisguised peevishness.

"So, Arthur, my lad, here is what I suggest we do. There appears to be a vacancy in the Ohio Junior Senate seat. I want you to take that position and shore up our legislative efforts."

"I don't think I've heard of a vacancy in the Senate ranks," Arthur's expression was quizzical—with practiced control. He hadn't had a natural, honest facial expression in years.

"Oh, not yet, of course, but in a couple of days. I understand that the unfortunate senator's blood pressure is going to spike, and he'll suffer a serious coronary event. He's not likely to make it through the surgery."

"Very accommodating of him."

"Yes, quite! The governor and I have an arrangement that covers the next vacancy, and we'll exercise that option forthwith. Congratulations, Senator Messanger." They clinked their wine glasses and went on to other business.

"I'm worried that Mad Tarlton is going to unwind some of our work with the cabinet nominees." Art Messanger buttered his bread as he spoke; the crust was flakey and shattered a bit. He always left a mess when he ate, living up to his name.

"That *is* a problem. Without your inside guidance, we need to find another way to position the right person for the newly opened VP slot. Of course, the existing plan calls for six months of this congressional session to pass before we insert Harlan Roscoe as the new VP. All the cabinet positions and most of the judicial appointments will have been confirmed by then. This is really the stickiest wicket in our game plan. We'd better move cautiously and not let the Senate leadership get any self-directing ideas."

"Senator Roscoe may not stay in line."

"That boy has a lot of ambition and doesn't know what he's doing. He's taken suggestions fine as long as the dollars met his expectations. Now, though, I fear he may see an opening that he'll want to exploit. You'd better have a chat with him and keep him on the bus with us," Hancock said pensively, aware that the best-laid plans can be undone by small events.

"I'm meeting with him tomorrow," Art Messanger reassured him.

"Very good, Arthur. Carry on."

Chapter 36

6:30 PM EST - Nine days before inauguration

Renae sat in her office speaking to Talbot on her DeCourcy Technologies M3 device. She called it a phone for want of a better name, but it was light-years ahead of any device on the market. DeCourcy Technologies outfitted all their security personnel with these units and didn't sell them on the open market. These smart phones had a data and computing capacity a hundred times greater than any other handheld unit. They used existing mobile networks as carrier signals, but their DeCourcy proprietary transmission protocols would not be recognized by the telecom industry for several more years. While these protocols provided perfectly secure communications for the M3s, these devices additionally possessed astounding features too futuristic for Renae to comprehend.

All phone calls placed to or from a DeCourcy mobile M3 were voice-over-ip-based wireline, not mobile. Every few milliseconds, the phone would let a local network know its current location—but not in the traditional tower-ping way. Because each M3 could assume up to 2,048 alias-phone numbers on a random basis, the device's identity (SIM#) would be opaque to the local network—a veritable *ghost phone*. The closest commercial comparison was a secure, spread-spectrum, CIA-grade device on steroids.

Without DeCourcy Technology's inside knowledge, an outsider had no hope of tapping into a conversation or tracking the location of an M3. There wasn't even an on-or-off button. The unit was activated by thumb print, voice recognition, or command sent down from DeCourcy NOC (network operation center)—and conversely, could be turned into an internally melting chunk of plastic and silicon, if need be, via remote control from the NOC, or by a self-destruct timer. The self-destruct method was called *the dooms-phone code*. The user could set a timer commanding the device to implode if not properly accessed within regularly scheduled time increments. These methods prevented adversaries from prying out data or reverse-engineering the M3.

The M3s paired with tiny ear canal inserts that transmitted and received sound for the users. They operated similarly to traditional Bluetooth units but were much smaller—with better sound and batteries that lasted for days.

Renae listened intently to Talbot's update: "We're not positive who's behind the fatal chain of events, but we have a few leads. I've decided to smoke out some cave dwellers in D.C. and elsewhere by letting news filter out about Karen and her choice of lawyers—and that'll be happening soon. But your team has nothing to do with that and probably doesn't need any details about it."

"Got it. Is Karen's life in danger?"

"If she were on her own, absolutely! But she's in a safe place with good company, and she can communicate freely with anyone she wants. Her phone number is now connected to an M3, and she knows not to hint to anyone about her location."

"Good, thanks. I'll call her."

"Tell Maddy to keep kicking the troglodytes and she shouldn't worry about our investigation. I know you made some changes in the cabinet positions, but I suggest you be very cautious in your dealings with Bert Pinkney, Harlan Roscoe, Thomas Carlyle, and Roger Burgad. I can fill you in with more details later. Renae, I'm absolutely serious. These men are very dangerous."

"We didn't uncover any major concerns about Thomas Carlyle; we still have him on the list as the Treasury Secretary nominee." Renae sat back, waiting for what might be coming.

"You definitely need to find a new name to pop out at the last second, but keep it quiet for now. In fact, it might be good if Thomas thinks he's still keeping his nose under the tent."

"Okay, I'll talk to Maddy. Oh, and she wants to keep Luau for the duration."

"I thought she would. He seems a bit unorthodox, but he's amazing. It's up to him whether he stays with you or not. I'm using three very sharp people to keep up with his workload, and if they find out he's not coming back, they'll demand three *more* bodies." He laughed. "And maybe you should hold out on the pardon I heard might be coming for as long as you can. He could stand to sweat some more."

DeCourcy ended the call without a goodbye. It was one of his idiosyncrasies; he routinely ended calls abruptly. Renae had known him almost as long as she had known Madison but was in the dark about their relationship and had stopped speculating about it years ago. She only knew that Madison trusted Tally without reservation and obviously loved him on some deep level. She also knew that their connection was utterly unknown to the world—except for a small number of people.

Chapter 37

The man they called John Hancock read through the pages of the dispatch from New York. The note began: "We have Karen Waldron's location."

Hancock was ensconced in a luxurious cabin in the Blue Ridge Mountains overlooking the Shenandoah Valley, and he didn't take phone calls. Not ever. He'd gone into complete seclusion, exile really, two years earlier. The Brotherhood was extreme in their caution — and Hancock was by far the most cautious of all. He had twelve hideout locations, but other Brotherhood members only knew of three.

Landan Moss, Hancock's trusted personal aid and a man of profound loyalty, stood nearby. He was the only one able to physically reach Hancock and had delivered the dispatch concerning Karen Waldron a few minutes earlier.

Landan used a team of six highly skilled and carefully vetted security men, known to the Brotherhood only as "A-F." They took calls from the Brotherhood and moved around in public. If they received an urgent message, as they had several times in the last few days, they would contact Landan through an obscure "dead-drop" email account.

All of the "A-F" security team changed out their mobile phones on a seemingly random basis. But, in reality, a sophisticated algorithm told them when to make the switch using an endless supply of prepaid phones purchased all over the world. When one of the A-F operatives initiated a new phone, he would send texts to the private phones of the three Brotherhood members for whom he was the information conduit. This system allowed each Brotherhood member three points of contact to reach Hancock or another member.

They also used a blind email drop unique to each security man, and this email changed on a random basis.

Even David Maxtell—the reigning tech guru of the Brotherhood who had devised the system—didn't know which three contact operatives were assigned to which Brother. (Landan Moss had set it up this way.) It was cumbersome and necessitated delays, but the system was very secure. When circumstances required a face-to-face gathering of the Brotherhood, texts and emails would fly, bringing the members into proximity; however, Landan Moss wouldn't reveal the final destination until a few minutes before the appointed time.

Moss waited patiently while Hancock read the dispatch and then watched him burn it in the fireplace. "Landan, please communicate to Thomas Carlyle that he should proceed with all haste and secure Karen for a brief interrogation, if he can," John said. "If that's not feasible, then his men shouldn't leave her body behind. We want the opposition to have questions, not answers."

"I'll let him know. Because of the nature of the message, I'll get out of the mountains first and then relay the instructions to Thomas's contact in New York. There'll be about an hour delay before Thomas gets the message."

As a security precaution, Landan Moss never brought any electronic devices within thirty miles of the cabin. In case something happened to him, he put a dead man's switch in place, which was a timed-email trigger that would send out coded instructions to his six men if he didn't reset it once every twelve hours.

"Good enough," John said. "His team should be on standby. I assume this will be concluded before the sun comes up."

"Yes, it will. But there'll be some worry that the location was leaked intentionally as a trap," Landan said.

"I think the risk is low, given the sophisticated methods Thomas used to track Waldron down—but you'd better get a sniper to follow his team in and seal off any dripping remainders," Hancock said, finishing his instructions with a dismissive wave.

Chapter 38

9:20 PM EST - Nine days before inauguration

Thomas Carlyle's team was in the air heading to a small unmanned airstrip in the middle of Florida. The spotter and team leader, Glen Romano, had been onsite hours ahead of them to assess potential threats and map out the tactical assault parameters. His team of mercenaries was skilled and highly efficient. Glen was the Brotherhood underling who had set up the logistics for the kills in California, Washington and Montana, but was only personally present for the Washington kills where he had spotted for his shooters.

Glen had distinguished himself as a skilled shooter in the Army Rangers and Delta Force, and shortly after he was no longer killing for Uncle Sam, he'd been recruited privately by Thomas Carlyle—the chief financier for the Brotherhood. Glen was personally responsible for helping many of Carlyle's big Wall Street deals play out perfectly, and sometimes Glen needed to persuade the other side of the deal through elimination. Two years ago arthritis in his ankles had limited his field work and stopped him from performing the advanced stuff; he was no longer reliable when needing to move fast with accuracy. His second-in-command took over the active side. *I like the planning functions anyway—the head stuff. Anybody can crawl through the dirt and pull a trigger*, he would sooth.

Glen was oblivious of the larger brotherhood organization or its goals; he worked for Thomas Carlyle and that's all he needed to know. The pay was great and the missions were challenging and interesting. *People dying because of me doesn't mean anything. People die all the time.* But he didn't relish killing like some of his guys did.

After arriving in Palmdale, Florida at 9:20 PM, Glen was off scouting the landing zone, the locations, and the targets. The FBO airfield (fixed base operator) was only fifteen minutes from the house where Karen Waldron was hiding. He positioned an SUV at the airstrip for his team, then jacked the car of a road-warrior sales guy. *Good ole Billy Bob's body won't be found before the local fauna spread its pieces around the glades.* He parked his stolen car out of site, then crawled through the brush to get eyes on the target house.

He observed the silhouettes of Karen and two body guards, a man and a woman. The setup was sweet: the nearest occupied property was more than two miles away and the landscaping was sparse, granting good angles of fire from all directions. A car was parked in front of the run-down farmhouse, but there was little else around. The plates from the car came back as a rental checked out to a private security agency from Tampa. The elusive Ms. Waldron obviously chose the wrong agency. *Tough rocks for her.*

Unfortunately, because the surrounding ground was flat, there was no place for an overwatch sniper to set up. Glen needed a bucket truck and found one easily enough from a power company. He doubted anyone would notice it going missing in the middle of the night. *It will all work out. Six more hours and we'll all be heading home. A sizable bonus is riding on this for me and my team.*

He crawled back out of range and hustled to the stolen car. After writing a detailed operation plan and emailing it to his boys in flight, he returned to the scene two more times before infiltration.

Careful observation and attention to every detail were the lifeblood of all his black operations—always had been.

Chapter 39

9:00 PM PST - Nine days before inauguration

Talbot DeCourcy's plane landed at the airstrip south of Courci Downs late in the evening, and he was driven quickly to the house. Working in her study when he walked in, Kate stood to kiss and hug him, then began rubbing his shoulder blades.

"How's Madison holding up?" she asked.

"Fine, I think. I spoke to Renae this afternoon—they're getting it all sorted out in the transition committee. Maddy is going to have to thread a very narrow channel through the perilous straits of DC."

"No doubt. I assume she's getting some top-notch advice from the brilliant T-X!"

"She's the politician, not me. But yeah, I've given a few watch out and put-your-armor-on warnings."

"Have you figured out who's orchestrating all this?" Kate pulled Talbot down to her couch and thrust her feet out for a friendly foot rub. She'd been waiting for this all day, and she knew it relaxed them both. "The fate of the country and its new president-elect can wait. But foot rubs are the essential part of life," she said, smiling.

Talbot pulled off his wife's shoes and worked on her arches as he spoke. "Boy, is my conspiracy-detector clanging everywhere, but I think I've narrowed down a couple of things. We know that the FBI and other law enforcement agencies have some moles and bad actors, but there's no way to know exactly how deep and wide it goes yet. My guys are on it."

"What about Cluff? Would he stoop to this out of spite?"

"The sitting president is currently the world's biggest ass, but I can't see how he imagines this might get him back into office. You never know—destroying the new administration is undoubtedly a goal of his so he can stage a comeback in four years. Leon Fuller, on the other hand, really bothers me. I'm almost convinced he's in on this somehow, but not at the president's bidding."

"How so?" She had him switch to her right foot.

"Back when I finished at Stanford and you were starting law school, something happened that's never been settled for me."

"This is about that mystery man, John, and his band of brainy boys?"

"Yes. Although I never saw the guy after our few dinner discussions, I wondered who he was and never found out. He was trying to recruit me for his idiotic plan—change the world and remake democracy and all that crap."

"You think this ties all the way back to that, almost thirty years ago?" She wiggled her left foot for a re-do.

"He described a very long-term plan and was pretty disappointed when I told him I wasn't interested in his version of nation-shaping." Talbot rubbed continually as he talked. "It really set my alarms going when I found out that Bert Pinkney, Art Messanger, and Thomas Carlyle are deeply involved in the Sarnoff inner circle because all three, along with Leon Fuller, were also part of Mystery-John's inner circle back then. He'd hinted that he planned on a roundtable of twelve disciples—with himself as the architect and deity figure of the New America."

"Do you still think it was John who sent the killers after you back then?" She knew this topic had never been and probably never would be resolved.

Yeah. It was him, or one of his boys. That thought has never gone away… big mistake not letting one of those bastards live long enough to spill the details."

"As I recall, you were under a bit of proximate pressure at the time. *Extreme exigent circumstances*," she said in her most judicial voice.

"Well, there was that!"

"Okay, *my* brainy boy. You've done a passable job on my feet, and I know you're taking off soon to go save the country and make it safe for democracy. So, I suggest that my freshly massaged feet would like to have their toes curled a bit before you leave. Off to the shower with you, and meet me in the room at the end of the hall."

"You plan on me being rather pliable to your charms? Well then—democracy can wait. The order of the court is my command, Justice Covington."

Chapter 40

Talbot DeCourcy was again aboard his plane, heading east this time. Before he slept, he reviewed the strange swirlings of time and connections that, for him, never dissipated. He had been a twenty-two-year-old Stanford law graduate when John Hancock invited him to lunch at an Italian restaurant on University Avenue in Palo Alto. Talbot still remembered the delicious Sicilian pasta dish and green salad with basil olive oil.

The mystery man was supposedly an admirer of Talbot's recently published treatise, *The Fifth Republic, an Analysis of the Evolution of American Democracy.* The man extolled the merits of the work, but Talbot was cautious—this man he only knew as "John" seemed to gush in his flattery. Although a young man, Talbot possessed keen perceptions of human nature; the maneuverings and manipulations of others were blatantly transparent to him.

The mysterious stranger never revealed his last name, but in a subsequent lunch meeting, he introduced Bertrand Pinkney—a scion of the famous South Carolina family, and Thomas Carlyle—a young man destined for greatness on the stage of world finance. In the final meeting Talbot attended, John introduced Leon Fuller—a man with ego larger than his home state of Texas, and the infamous Arthur Messanger—a young leader already a master of Machiavellian methods.

John outlined a plan with details only hinted at, but he indicated that a very wealthy and powerful group, which included these future icons of the nation, would studiously prepare and someday usher in The New America. They would design a better government and save the doomed Constitution from the elected minions of the rabble. They had a broad, bold vision and knew that Talbot was the right kind of thinker capable of embracing their goals and helping to bring in the era of *The Fifth Republic*.

Talbot, thanking the man and his little cadre of sycophants for the entertaining lunch, told them bluntly that he was not interested in creating a New World Order. He stood, and before departing, said, "Please don't attempt to contact me again. I find your entire thought process despicable and assume that your narcissism will only bring disappointment. Leave me out." The faces at the table were incredulous as he walked away from the stunned group. Thomas Carlyle, recovering from his shock, chased Talbot to the door and swung a roundhouse punch at the back of his head. Detecting the assault, Talbot spun around and took counter measures.

Carlyle's arm was broken in three places and never healed quite right.

None of them tried to speak to Talbot again, but later that same summer thirty years ago, three former East German Stasi commandos sought to ambush him while he was backpacking through the Selway River Canyon of the Bitter Root Mountains in Idaho. None of the three Germans emerged from their mission alive.

He didn't know for certain but suspected that the Germans were hired by the New World Order-planners. He also assumed that whoever sent them became more cautious after that. The message must have been understood—Don't mess with DeCourcy.

Chapter 41

January 12

3:30 AM EST - Eight days before inauguration

Glen Romano reported to Thomas Carlyle that his team was in place and going in as soon as the overwatch sniper was up in the bucket truck 400 yards down the road. Even over the secure communication line, he used code phrases. Both Thomas and Glen were unaware that Hancock had sent a sniper of his own to clean up any mess left behind in case Glen's team screwed up. Landan Moss provided one of his own shooters for this task—his close personal friend named Hans Nielsen, nicknamed "Handy." Moss hoped all would go according to plan and his guy would remain invisible.

When the bucket-sniper was ready and the six guys on the ground checked in, Glen counted down. On his mark, the sniper shot twice through the window and watched the "babysitter" on shift go down. Men at the front and back doors attacked simultaneously while a shooter on either side of the house guarded the windows. From his observation spot a hundred yards out in the brush, Glen Romano monitored the action through his scope and saw multiple flashes, but he couldn't hear the suppressed rounds from that distance.

In seconds, all was dark and silent. He waited several more seconds for the all-clear notice to come over the secure radio link. It never came.

"Alpha, report!" Glen shouted. Nothing. "Bravo, damn it, what's the report?" These were all highly trained professionals. Something was wrong. Maybe the radios were out—some kind of interference. He tried again. He swung the scope to the three positions he could observe. Nothing. His men weren't visible.

"What the hell?" He began to rise from his prone position but was slammed back down by a heavy force. He turned his head in time to see a dark apparition swinging a riot baton at his face. Blackness was next.

Handy Nielsen scanned the infiltration site and looked for Glen's operators. He had seen the flashes, his optics compensating for the brightness. He had also seen the security guy inside the house go down, but now there was nothing else to see. All the heat signatures of Glen's men were suddenly gone. Even if they had been eliminated by the opposition, their heat signatures should take time to dissipate because bodies cool slowly. He couldn't figure out what had just happened. He had no targets. He scanned the area where he knew Glen had been watching his men. Glen was gone also. Nothing to see.

Handy pulled his phone from his shoulder pocket and started to dial. Before he got to the second digit, his head was cracked from behind. He was out instantly. He didn't feel the cold thermal-masking tarp being tossed over him. Even when he eventually woke up, his memory of that night—and other small pieces of his brain—would be gone. He had been hit a little too enthusiastically.

Chapter 42

"My team has gone dark, Landan. What the hell's going on?" Thomas Carlyle spat the words into his phone.

"I have no information on your team's actions." Landan Moss was guarded and deadpan. He, too, was agitated about losing communication with Handy Nielsen. The last thing he had heard from Handy was that Glen Romano's team was going in. Handy had his secret orders to either protect Glen's flank or take out the whole team as a cleanup measure.

"Don't shine me, buddy. I know you had your shooters down there as insurance, you always do. What just happened?"

"My last report said your team was ready to go. Since then, nothing." Moss sighed in failure mode. "I don't know any more than that, and I'm worried. Even if your guys got tagged in an ambush, my guy should've cauterized it or at least reported it."

Silence from the other end of the line—he heard Carlyle breathing.

After several seconds: "It had to be a trap. Somehow, they knew we were coming," Carlyle said, following with several more seconds of swearing before he calmed down.

"Ya' think, buddy?" said Moss.

"If any of them have been taken alive…I'm vulnerable…maybe. But then, Glen is the only one who knows who I am, and he'll clam up…no problem. But we need to know who did this." Carlyle started breathing more slowly, realizing he sounded panicked and paranoid. "Okay, I got this. I'll reach out to our friend at the FBI to get a read on *who* knows *what*. If Glen is still alive and in custody, we'll need to either spring him or put him down. Either way, this'll be closed out."

"We need to know about Karen Waldron. Did they get her? Was she even there? These are not good questions to have to ask."

"I'll let you know what I hear from the FBI. You'd better get in touch with Hancock and then get back to me," Carlyle said.

"My team will be rolling their phones as a precaution," Landan Moss said. He knew that his own sniper, Handy Nielsen, would have taken proper precautions: if the opposition had his phone, all they could retrieve from the phone company right away were anonymous calls and texts. It would take them twenty-four to forty-eight hours to get a warrant, get the phone company moving and get answers.

Landan rang off. He was disconcerted over this monumental screw up, and he had misplaced a very good operator and close friend. *Somebody is going to pay for this one*, he thought viciously.

Chapter 43

7:45 AM EST - Eight days before inauguration

Landan Moss was driving to an emergency early morning meeting with Hancock. The security protocols were extremely effective but imposed time gaps that couldn't be helped: the surveillance detection routes; the Mentor's twelve hideout locations; the electronics-dumping and car-switching thirty minutes before reaching John; and Landan as his one point of contact. *As clumsy as these rules are*, he thought, *they maintain valuable cover now more than ever*. Moss still had over an hour to drive before he could stop, shed his electronics, and drive the last half-hour to John's mountain hideaway.

Hancock and his Brethren had been working on their master plan for thirty years, and timeliness hadn't been urgent in those years. But now as the timetable was accelerating, they needed to speed up their ability to contact each Brotherhood member. In this urgent operational mode, how could they streamline the protection protocols while still maintaining their efficiency? *How to solve this dichotomy?* *Maybe I should get John to let me work autonomously from now on.*

Mr. Hancock was not going to be happy about the news from this morning's takedown attempt, but Landan knew his boss would receive the news without an emotional outburst. John was a disciplined, level guy. He dealt with each crisis like a naval battle-group commander, watching the movements of the entire fleet and looking at the big picture. No temper tantrums punctuated his leadership style.

The same could not be said for several others in the Brotherhood. In fact, at least half the men Moss served were prone to violent outbursts and vindictive behavior. They ranted and railed when things went wrong, but John always brought them back to a calmer state—seeming to hold some pied piper sway over them. He had been their mentor and guide for over thirty years, which must account for his deep influence. Still, Moss wondered if one or more of the boys was unraveling, moving toward a psychotic break. They had experienced a few big setbacks over the last year—and lately, more setbacks seemed to bring more hissy fits.

When Moss reached Hancock and apprised him of the situation, Hancock reacted predictably, philosophically. He asked Landan to set up a full meeting of the Brethren for the next evening in a small Pennsylvania town. "All precautions must be maintained," John reminded Landan for the hundredth time. "We are in the long game for the greatest stakes ever played," he said thoughtfully, closing the door softly behind Landan.

Chapter 44

DeCourcy Security Chief Gene Artel switched the phone to speaker. He spun around in his chair at Headquarter's Technical Operation Center (TOC), and held his hand up for quiet. The room went silent. His field team leader, Garrett Miller, was reporting about the Florida mission. "Go ahead, Garrett. We're all ears here."

"The Florida Op. went down textbook. It's a done deal. No friendly casualties." Garrett Miller's voice was strong over speaker phone.

A round of cheers and whoops erupted in the TOC—smiles, clapping, and fist-bumping everywhere.

After the shouting died down, Gene Artel said, "Give us the highlights, Garrett."

"The opposition used a sniper high up in a stolen bucket truck to start the party. He shot through the front window of the target house, and when the bullet slammed into the plexiglass barrier, our decoy dropped to the floor. Then our crew took out the sniper. He's wounded and in guarded condition. The enemy was completely taken in by the thermal decoys." Garrett spoke excitedly.

He continued explaining: when Glen Romano reported to Landan Moss that his team was ready to go, he was unaware that Garrett Miller's team was listening in and ready to intercept. The female decoy was standing behind the ballistic-resistant transparent shield, and the sniper's bullet created a spider web of cracks but didn't penetrate the shield. After dropping to the floor, the female decoy waited to receive the breaching teams with a warm, 9mm welcome.

When Glen Romano's guys burst through the door, they didn't expect much opposition since they were heavily armed and moving fast. But opposition they got. They slammed into the solid walls of transparent ballistic plastic, becoming shocked and disoriented. After Garret Miller's undetected shooters came out from behind infrared-shielding tents on either side of the entrance, Romano's men realized they were outgunned and outmatched. In seconds, the four mercenaries who had breached the doors were down, restrained.

Romano's pair of window watchers experienced a similar fate. Positioned outside both ends of the house, they were taken by Miller's operatives appearing out of nowhere. The operatives had hidden in trenches covered by thermal shields, and rising up behind the watchers, completely surprised and overtook them.

After Romano's six-man team was neutralized, a pair of DeCourcy operatives positioned near the cars—but unseen among the bushes and wearing thermal-blocking ghillie suits—stood up and slammed Glen Romano down on his stolen car, while another of Miller's team took out Handy, the backup sniper.

Sniper-shot to total containment took eighteen seconds.

Taking down motivated, hardcore shooters is not a tidy process. Of the nine-man team that had come to Florida to kill Karen Waldron, two were dead, bundled into body bags, and seven were trussed up, tossed into the back of a van that arrived on the scene after the all-clear signal.

As soon as the prisoners were on the road, a clean-up team in a second van pulled up and erased all traces of action—in less than thirty minutes. They sanitized the blood splatters, filled in the trenches, and removed the transparent shields. They replaced the front window glass and installed replacement doors and frames painted to match the ones shattered by Romano's breaching teams.

They removed the rented and stolen vehicles from the area and dropped them at least thirty-five miles away from each other.

Two hours after arriving in Florida, the clean-up team was wheels up and heading home. Five hours after the sniper shot, everyone involved was far away from the attack site. The seven surviving mercenaries sat ensconced in underground containment cells in West Virginia, and the two bodies lay on ice at the same location.

After Garrett Miller finished his narrative and received another round of applause, Gene Artel turned off speaker phone to privately conclude the conversation.

"So, boss, all is secure," Garret said. "Interrogations began on the plane, and the tangos are processed into the Quarry at MWV. I hope they enjoy their new digs."

The MWV was a facility built over a former granite quarry near Martinsburg, West Virginia. Because the construction costs of building deep, underground facilities were enormous, builders greatly reduced those costs by incorporating large pits already carved out of solid rock during decades of quarrying. Talbot DeCourcy owned dozens of these rock quarries around the country and had converted several into secure, high-tech underground facilities — many of which were on contract with various government agencies. Keeping a few for his own purposes, he had built Courci Downs on one of these rock quarries.

The underground facility in West Virginia now warmly welcomed the new enemy combatants captured by Garret Miller's team.

"Thanks for bringing in Romano's raiders," Gene chuckled. "Any issues from our guys on the KIA's?" he asked his field commander.

"No qualms, Chief. They knew the score and what was at stake. I allowed each one to say *yes* or *no* beforehand, and they all opted in;

they knew lives might be lost. Talbot made a pretty compelling case to my guys, so they're all in for the whole mission—whatever comes next." Garrett's men were experienced combat shooters in various military units and were deeply committed to honorable causes.

"It's not every day you get to save the country from evil-doers," Gene deadpanned.

"Roger that, Chief!"

"Excellent work, you and your team. Talbot will want to do a video-conference debrief sometime today after you all rest up. Thanks for your dedication, Miller."

"Aw shucks, Chief. I feel a blush coming."

Chapter 45

5:45 AM PST - Eight days before inauguration

Gene Artel called DeCourcy to report the mission's success with all the necessary details—including nine operators neutralized and contained. Talbot first asked if anyone on the team was hurt and then gave a heartfelt thanks. It was a terrible responsibility putting lives at risk, but both Talbot and Gene knew that if they didn't act, the United States government might not survive in its current form. Talbot had been predicting this fulcrum event for years, and Gene had been a believer from the beginning.

"Any backchatter on this from official channels?" Talbot asked.

"Not a peep, Tally. We have our ears open, but nobody seems to have caught a whiff. I expect an unknown someone will reach out to another unknown at the FBI, but I don't have a clue yet who the players are."

"We're going to dig till we find that particular bastard—or bastardess, as the case maybe."

"Is that even a word?" Gene teased his friend of many years.

"Not really, but it fits unless you want to use bastrix."

"Okay. Either way, we'll find out who it is and shut them down, one way or another."

"Keep working your magic and expect some activity once I've visited the Justice Department. Is the new Portland office ready to go?"

"Up and running! Sheila Lance is the office queen who gets to push the alphabet boys around," Gene said.

"Lucky kid. But she's earned it. I understand she's been teaching our new counter-intimidation training course."

"Oh yeah, and she's something to watch. I wouldn't want to go up against her, in court or out."

"Send me the overview on the intelligence yield from the Florida takedown. *Let the games begin!*" Talbot enthused.

"Thanks. Preliminary network diagram's on its way."

Chapter 46

Talbot opened Artel's intelligence file arriving through his secure intra-mail account. Traditional email systems were not used within DeCourcy global communications or its security apparatus. All messages remained tightly locked inside the private IT infrastructure and couldn't be gleaned by outsiders—no matter how sophisticated their methods. Moment by moment, the NSA notoriously scooped up vast amounts of voice, text, and email messages existing out on the web and public airwaves, but Talbot's information was never publicly exposed—unless he wanted it to be. If privacy advocates around the country became aware of his privacy provisions, they would declare him the zealot with no equal in the digital age. DeCourcy's people did not live off the grid—they had created their own grid.

He perused the intelligence file. Garrett Miller's team had secured the prisoner's phones and forwarded data dumps to Gene Artel's analysts. They, in turn, had put together a quick summary of all the phones used by Glen Romano's assault team, including all their contacts over the last several months and each call location. These facts told the unfolding story of hired killers in a deep conspiracy.

Romano's phone had only been active for two months and was used all over the country. Obviously, he was the guy who had set up the hits on the doctor, lawyer, and FBI agent in San Diego. He also had regularly called an anonymous New York number active for the last two years. The locations on that phone were interesting, with a high frequency use in Manhattan—especially on the Avenue of the Americas. Gene would narrow an address down soon.

The overwatch sniper's phone contained a narrow set of contacts with only nine other phones. In service for three weeks, it had originally been purchased in Belgium four years earlier. No name yet to go with the sniper, but Gene would get it eventually from the man they were interrogating, Glen Romano. Gene's security team also constructed a matrix showing that the phone of the additional sniper, Handy Nielson, belonged to a network of seven individuals located within the greater D.C. area and points up and down the east coast. Gene's techies determined that this phone network frequently shifted numbers as well as physical telephone units, but each phone within the core network never contacted phones outside the network—except for three numbers.

A clear pattern was emerging. Using DeCourcy technology tools, Gene Artel tracked all the phone activations and deactivations in the network going back two years. Not a bad intelligence yield in ninety minutes. Clearly, a seven-man team (known as A-F and now only six because of Handy Nielson's capture) functioned as the arms and legs of the Brotherhood big boys. Glen Romano and his mercenaries were apparently not connected to the seven-man team but were an appendage of the unknown Manhattan caller. Gene speculated that Thomas Carlyle might be the New York kingpin in this little techno-drama—and he would confirm it soon.

Talbot's M3 chimed and he answered Gene's call: "So you forgot to parlay your successful takedown into a request for a raise?"

"Are you kidding me? You already pay me at a level that makes my taxes a nightmare! Please, no more."

"Okay, what popped?"

"The New York number that you saw in the file called FBI Headquarters. We can't see who it was transferred to, but we have a place to start. There were no other calls from that phone to the FBI, so we're working on the theory that the New York person used a different phone to call the FBI after Karen went AWOL."

"Well done. Full steam ahead, Gene."

Chapter 47

11:45 AM EST - Eight days before inauguration

Talbot DeCourcy navigated security at the Robert F. Kennedy Department of Justice Building and handed over a manila envelope for inspection. The envelope was quickly bomb-sniffed, x-rayed, and shaken like a Christmas present. A guard, handing the thin packet back to Talbot and giving a curt nod, said, "Proceed straight down this hall and turn right at the first corridor. The door is on the right."

"Thank you," Talbot replied, accepting the envelope and walking away. When he entered through the door labeled *Legal Counsel Office,* he introduced himself to a woman at the intake desk. "My name is Talbot DeCourcy. I'm providing a copy of a legal representation agreement between counsel and client covering any and all potential federal proceedings and investigations."

The woman barely looked up and motioned for him to drop the envelope into her inbox. "What, y'all neva heard of the U.S. Postal service or ah messeng-aah service? Ah-mean, dude, y'alls re-turn address is Portland, Or-ee-gone."

"I seemed to be in the neighborhood, and there's a chance that some people may consider this particular communication time-sensitive." *White trash worthless bureaucrat* popped into Talbot's mind, but he smiled and pushed his prejudice down.

"Oh reeeally? I-aah'm she-ure that aah'll be eempressed when aah gits round ta lookun' to this eem-poor-tent com-mu-nee-cation's aa-dress. Now's that abouts all? Aah be ah-headun ta lunch an' y'all are ah-holdun' me the hells-bells up."

"Thank you, I hope you enjoy your lunch, but could I trouble you for an intake receipt and timestamp, please?"

With a disgusted huff, the woman stamped the envelope and document and printed a receipt for Talbot without glancing at the client's name. Unfortunately, at the same time she stamped her way to a quick termination for negligence of duty.

Talbot was out of the Justice Building for a full two hours before anyone with a professional level of competence laid eyes on the document, (complements of his bureaucrat friend.) He moved through his string of errands, stopping briefly at *The Washington Post* and *The Washington Times* to drop off a press release addressed to the national desk editors of each paper. He didn't stay to chat or give his name. The press release revealed that a Portland Law firm, T.T. Thomas P.C., intended to represent Ms. Karen Waldron in any and all legal proceedings arising from the recent unfortunate circumstances in Chicago, Illinois.

The press release also included a copy of the representation agreement, the Portland law office address, phone number, e-mail address, and website. It didn't mention that the office had only been operational for a few hours or that the firm had done no public business until now.

Located in the Portland high-rent district overlooking the Columbia River, the office was airy and open, with tall windows and a great city view. It was nestled among offices of accounting firms, investment bankers, and an essential oils sales group. Modern glass and titanium furniture gave off an edgy vibe—more like a design firm than a roost for vultures of the law. DeCourcy owned the building, but that fact was completely separate and might take investigators years to discover, if they ever tried.

Chapter 48

Karen Waldron sat in stunned silence watching multiple infrared views of the dreadful events in Florida. Brian and Meredith Lubneski explained the details of the takedown, including the fact that nine mercenaries had shown up to kill or capture her and her security detail—no doubt remaining now that Karen was in mortal danger. Clearly, these men were anxious to keep Doug Waldron's bad-eye issue quiet and were willing to kill to accomplish it.

"But why did they think I was in Florida?" Karen asked through fresh tears. "This makes me sick."

"Once we allowed you to use your M3 device, all the calls to your mother and friends looked like they were coming from that little house in the middle of *Nowhere, Florida*," Meredith answered soothingly. "We made it appear like a competent IT geek was bouncing the calls all around. The killers thought they were a lot smarter at tracking it all down."

"And it took longer than it should have. We left bread crumbs a blind bear could follow," Brian added. "But they got there—several hours after we figured they would."

"The surprise to us is that they didn't seem worried about a trap," Meredith continued. "We only gave them a fifty-fifty shot at falling for it."

"Guys like that are always arrogant and gung-ho to go shoot somebody," Brian put in.

"Are we sure that they're the same ones who killed those people in Washington, Montana, and California?" Karen asked.

"Dead sure. The exact same cell phones were on site at each killing and were used to communicate with the same band of dark lords in New York and DC," Brian reiterated for the third time.

"This is too hard to comprehend…I mean…to accept…as real. With all this going on, it's like something in a spy novel," Karen said bleakly.

"Let's go out on the deck and see if we can spot some of those cute beavers in the lake. The fresh air will be good." Meredith rose from her chair, attempting to distract Karen.

They put on coats and hats and went out into the crisp air. The winter marsh scene was lovely in its own way. To the southeast Karen could see Mt. Katahdin, the highest point in Maine, in the distance. Karen and the Barbies were staying in a massive lodge in Maine's northern wilderness. The property, adjoining Baxter State Park, was bordered by rugged country on one side and by Nesowadnehunk Lake on the other. During the winter, access choices were limited to either a helicopter flight or a snow-sled ride that took eight hours from the trailhead. DeCourcy people called the location "the Field," named after Nesowadnehunk Field Campground inside the nearby state park.

The scenery of this remote land comforted Karen's soul. Because she felt confident in Meredith and Brian's abilities to keep her safe from the beastly men trying to silence her, she could use this time to begin recuperating. And this was the first time she'd ever been in a place so distant from the signs of civilization. It helped her avoid thinking about her life in the future. *No need to worry about tomorrow. Right now, I only need to mourn my losses and survive one day at a time.*

Chapter 49

In addition to attending official intelligence briefings, Madison Tarlton dealt with a steady stream of dignitaries dropping in on her every day. They lobbied for status, sought personal positions, or tried to influence her decisions on cabinet choices. The brashest and boldest visitor came at 4:00 PM without an appointment demanding to see the new president-elect. Renae came into Madison's office to alert her that a VIP was sitting in the conference room.

"Senator Harlan Roscoe is here at last. No beating around the bush. He said, 'Get me in a room with Mad Tarlton right now or else!'"

"Well then, Renae, let's watch and see what the 'or else' turns out to be. Send somebody in with water, coffee, tarts, or whatever else about every seven minutes. Have them tell him that since he didn't call ahead for an appointment, I'll get to him as soon as possible."

"Okay, so we *dis* the Senate Majority Leader and piss him off?" Renae smiled at the prospect.

"Absolutely. Let's keep him on ice for a while, if he can stand it without walking out. He'll probably go hunting to find me once his patience collapses. Tell Jason Southwick to put him back in the conference room if he starts wandering around. Oh, and have Luau put the sound and video up on my screen. I want to observe the Senate boss man before we meet."

"Sure thing," Renae said as she left the office wearing a canary-eating grin.

Thirty-five minutes later, Madison entered the conference room and smelled the tang coming from Roscoe's anger sweat, his foul mood increasing as time ticked by. She was ready for this blowhard.

"So, Senator Roscoe, to what do I owe the pleasure?"

He was too angry to rise from his chair to greet her, his diplomacy skills—always at war with his person-in-charge narcissism—giving way to his intrinsic egomania. "Do you realize you've kept me waiting for over an hour? Is this the way you plan on relating to Senate leadership, especially to me?" he said, ready to boil over.

"Senator, thank you for coming and waiting to meet with me. I realize you arrived in the building exactly forty-seven minutes ago, and that after being screened through security, you've been in this room for thirty-six minutes. Perhaps your inability to tell time accurately helps explain your inefficiency in the Senate," she said, smiling. Talbot had warned her about him, and she didn't mind putting him on the defensive. Harlan Roscoe bolted from his chair, his face red with bluster. As he jumped up, both Jason and Andie moved toward him. He took the hint and raised both hands, palms out in conciliation, and sat back down.

"I'm busy and stressed, that's all. I don't understand why you kept me waiting for so long," he said, his tone moderating slightly.

"You didn't make an appointment, Senator. That type of courtesy is expected. We're on a tight schedule around here with a lot to get done in a short time." Madison had watched Roscoe's body language on camera and wanted him impatient and stressed when she arrived. She found this an effective way of getting clowns to reveal the true face hiding under the guise of civility. Like most people, Roscoe could fake it by wearing his game face whenever he cruised into an ad hoc meeting.

"I'm the Senate Majority Leader, young lady. I'm used to being treated with more respect than you've shown."

"All chit-chat aside, Senator, what would you like to discuss?" She used her stern voice, indicating intolerance of non-sequitur comments.

"First of all, you need to know that you won't get anything done in your presidency without my help. Second, you need to *earn* that help. Third, I'm the one who should be sitting in this office as the VP-elect. I should be the heir-apparent."

"*Really?*"

"Yes, really. I agreed to step aside as the presumed VP nominee in your favor for the good of the party and the election. Art Messanger and Wilson Sarnoff made a boatload of promises to get my cooperation, especially regarding my place and influence in the new administration. I granted extensive favors."

"Oh? You do realize that Mr. Messanger no longer has influence in this administration?"

"Of course I realize that—but firing him was your first big mistake." Roscoe could not resist smirking or saying too much. "You have no idea what's really going on here."

"Such as?"

"Look, you're young and very west coast. Things run a little differently over here where it matters. You'll need to come up to speed quickly; and that, my dear, will only happen if I say so. You need me. You'd do well to remember that," he said testily. "The deal is, Madison, you were just a tool for the election. Art was planning to scandal-you out of office by July. And then I was going to take my rightful place as VP. So, now we have a quandary of sorts."

"Which quandary is that?" Madison looked slightly amused, and it bothered Roscoe.

"What to do with you. And how to help you succeed, for the good of the party, of course! Here's how it's gonna work, carrot and stick. So listen up." He stood up and sat on the edge of the table to tower over her. "You have a whole cabinet to fill, and I promise you that not one name will get approved or even be brought to a vote unless I say so. Not a single judicial appointment will get to the floor without my nod. So here's your first big-boys-on-the-beltway lesson: I'll personally champion all of your nominations as long as I approve them first. We'll sweep them through confirmation in thirty days. Right after that, you will nominate me as the VP. I'll have no trouble in the Senate. Then you'll designate very substantive tasking for me, at my suggestion, of course. We'll make the Dick Cheney vice presidency look like he was a lady-in-waiting. I'll be the fist behind the throne! You got all that, Madison? This is non-negotiable."

Madison controlled her revulsion of this obnoxious windbag. "That's an audacious and bold plan, Senator, I must say. I have not even begun to consider who I'll nominate as the new VP, but you're certainly giving me a lot to think about. Let's talk again in a couple of weeks and see where everything stands, shall we?" Madison rose from her chair, turned and left the room without a backward glance at the shouting, swearing Senator from Missouri.

She caught something about, "How dare you turn your back...you'll regret..."

Jason ushered Roscoe to the door.

Chapter 50

5:00 PM EST - Eight days before inauguration

"*That* was something." Renae giggled as Madison re-entered her office and sat heavily in her chair.

"Oh yes. The good Senator from Missouri is determined to be a problem, and that 'scandal' me out statement was what I was looking for. Talbot warned me to watch out for the jerk, but I had no idea he might be part of something bigger. He's such a fool, after all; and no one could trust that monstrous ego very far."

"You said that just right." Renae shook her head.

"Please send Luau's recording of the whole exchange to Talbot, and also Roscoe's waiting room antics. Let's see what he can make of it. We'll have to pour some alkali on that pool of acid to get a neutral PH...mitigate the damage he'll do." Madison rubbed her temples. "Okay, scram. I want to call Lucy and see how tough school was today. Those are the real concerns."

"Okay, boss lady. But I have to say, that was the most entertaining thing I've seen in a long time. I mean, it was even better than booting Messanger out of here! You're so good at making lifetime enemies."

Madison sat back and reflected on the "scandal you out" statement. Maybe that had been the original plan, at least as far as Roscoe knew. Could it be that the same people pulling Roscoe's strings had stepped up the timetable and changed *scandal-out* to assassinate? Had she been the target after all as Talbot suggested? And if that was true, then the enemies were not just at the gates—they were inside the perimeter and everything just got a lot more dangerous. But if they had intended her to die instead of Sarnoff, how were they modifying their plan now? What was their contingency? How many contingencies?

One thing she could be certain of: Talbot was the best person on the planet to make sense of all this and construct a counter-plan. She really hoped she'd live long enough to get a plan going...This was way too much to comprehend in one sitting. It was time to be a mom again—for a few minutes.

Chapter 51

6:44 PM EST - Eight days before inauguration

"When in hell did this come in, noon?" The managing editor at *The Washington Post* was ranting. "We've had this information for almost seven hours about a woman the entire country is looking for, and we've not even confirmed it!"

"Don't shout at me, Ralphy! I got this from my minions thirty minutes ago," Betty Meese, the national desk editor, shot back. Referring to her notes, she said, "First I called the Justice Public Information Office and got the overnight guy. I'll dig up his name later, but he said he couldn't confirm or deny that an attorney representing Karen Waldron had contacted the Justice Department to inform them. Then I asked him if he was aware that we at *The Post* had a copy of the representation agreement presented to the Justice Department, along with a copy of the signed and stamped intake receipt. And he said, 'Crap, I didn't know that.' And just to be clear, he didn't request the 'crap' statement to be off the record. Also, I called the Oregon law office that was named in the press release. A very professional-sounding woman, Sheila Lance, confirmed that her firm was representing Ms. Waldron in any and all legal matters. Then I called the Justice Department Chief Public Information Officer on her cell phone. Her name is Prairie Patton, and she was having drinks with the head of the FBI Public Information Office. She said, 'What the hell are you going on about? You must be out of your mind. I would've heard about that before, you bitch.' I suspect she was on her third drink by then. You know she's a complete lush and about two minutes from dropping into rehab. So, Ralphy, you decide if we're confirmed or not."

"Okay, okay. Check out the law firm, and if they're real and the documents are real, run it as a 'claim.' But also mention that we have the documents. State clearly that Justice has not confirmed it." The editor smiled. "And use the two stupid Justice quotes. Prairie Patton is a witch, so burn her at the stake without mercy on this. I'll check with legal, but I think we're clean as is. Who else has it? How about *The New York Times* or *The Wall Street Journal*?"

"Don't know; but there isn't an indication of exclusivity."

"Run it, front page, below the fold. Use your own byline for gravitas. Done. Good work, Betty."

Chapter 52

"Okay, so you're turning the dogs loose on that poor little law firm in Portland." Kate Covington spoke into her M3 device as she flew home to Courci Downs from a judicial conference in Portland. "Radisson will be scratching at the door with a warrant by 8:00 AM. Then he'll be sniffing the countryside for Karen and following his nose right up to our house. Should I set lunch out for him?" she joked.

"I expect so. He'll meet Sheila Lance at the office. Poor guy, he may not get out of there with his manhood intact. Gene Artel has a complete profile on all the agents Radisson's using, if you want to review them; but he'll probably have trouble finding our house to serve a warrant."

"Most people can't find it on the first try." Kate yawned.

"Sounds like somebody got up too early after a vigorous night," Talbot said, grinning.

"Oh, stop bragging. I had a busy day. Trusts and environmental case reviews—very stimulating." She stifled another yawn. "I viewed the video of Roscoe and Madison going at it in DC. What's up with Roscoe? Did he go cold turkey off his meds or something?"

"Maddy let the big man stew in the conference room for thirty-six minutes before she went in to pull his chain around the floor."

"I saw that. What part in all this do you think he plays?"

"I suspect he's on the periphery of the Cabal. We're getting a clearer picture little by little, and it's as bad as I thought it would be. It appears that Sarnoff was just a soldier following orders, not really aware of the bigger plan; and Roscoe's just a tool—in more ways than one. Art Messanger is definitely on the inside and is one of the puppet masters."

"What can you do about Roscoe?"

"That, Your Honor, is something you do *not* want to hear about before the fact, shall we say. But Roscoe's public career is over." Talbot spoke slowly for emphasis.

"Seriously, Tally, people are getting killed. This is turning into a shooting war, not just an ideological exercise."

"They started the shooting and the killing, beginning with Sarnoff. At least now I'm fairly certain he was a friendly-fire casualty. Jeemie was the real target."

"You sure?"

"Yes, Roscoe admitted that they were going to get rid of her, although he probably doesn't know for sure what that means."

"Are Madison and Lucy safe?" Kate said, worried.

"Madison is safe as she can be, and the Secret Service is guarding Lucy at her Aunt Janine's home in California. I have a team backing them up, but we can't really determine what these guys' contingency plan is. At least not yet."

"You'll get it sorted out. You always do. What can I do from here?"

"To keep my profile low, would you mind setting up my lunch date with four of the Supremes, including the Chief Justice, for tomorrow, please? I want to talk to two from each side of the divide," Talbot said.

"You know them better than I do."

"Yes, but your call will seem less suspicious to the groveling clerks who gossip like old women in winter."

"Says the former clerk. You liked it so much you did it for two years."

"Well, I was too young to know any better."

"I should say. Not a lot of twenty-one-year-old Supreme Court clerks."

"Uh, that was a long time ago. Fly safe, sweetie. Give my love to the progeny and save some for yourself. I have to go to another clandestine basement meeting with the president-elect."

"Copy that. I'm going to nap for a few before we land. Good night, love."

Chapter 53

10:30 PM EST - Eight days before inauguration

Talbot and Madison met again in the underground hideaway in Georgetown. Madison vented her spleen about Roscoe and the other super egos she had entertained that day. California politics was brutal, but Washington was a slaughterhouse by comparison. And it stank commensurately. Her main concern was that she wouldn't have enough time to put together a functioning administration with Roscoe's interference looming. She didn't even ask about the investigation Talbot was conducting; she trusted he would do what it took to sort out all the craziness.

"I need to fill you in on just a few uncomfortable details and no more—because if anything goes sideways, you would have a duty to disclose. I'll keep it general." Talbot sat still and spoke solemnly. "This isn't just a matter of someone using violence to seize control of the presidency. It's much bigger—these monsters are aiming for a more fundamental shift in the universe."

"You're sure?" Madison fell back into her chair from her forward leaning position.

"Yeah, Jeemie. This looks like the real thing, a full blown *Fifth Republic* manipulation. This also means we've only seen the opening act. There must be more monumental events on the horizon shepherded by these people."

"Isn't it nice that I get the dubious honor of sitting smack dab in the nexus of this massive historic rift?"

"Actually, I can't think of anyone *better* than you to be at the center of this storm. You'll have to drive forward with your personal strength of will...like a Lincoln, or a Washington."

"Those are big knickers to fill!"

"Too bad you've kept yourself so trim and fit. You may have trouble keeping those knickers up."

"I'll use a belt."

Talbot smiled and began giving her the general outline of the Florida takedown and his move to reveal his role as Karen Waldron's attorney of record. He explained how Leon Fuller, Thomas Carlyle, Bertrand Pinkney, and Arthur Messanger were connected—he remembered them from the fated lunch meeting with Hancock thirty years ago. There were also others he suspected, and he was mounting heavy surveillance on each of them, hoping to find out where Hancock was hiding and who else was in the conspiracy of fools.

"I'm having lunch with some members of the High Court tomorrow," he added. "I believe they need to know that something is coming."

"Do you think they'll accept the idea of a real coup conspiracy? Won't they think you might be a little bit crazy?"

"We shall see what we shall see." He rose, hugged Madison, and kissed her on the forehead as he often did. "Jeemie, we *will* work through this, but there's no way to predict the future—no matter how much we think we know. Good night."

Chapter 54

January 13

7:30 AM EST - Seven days before inauguration

January 13th turned out to be a big news day…with headlines other than Doug Waldron's motivations. The press, losing interest in those motivations, had moved on to Mad Tarlton's inadequacy to ascend to the presidency. But even that was losing steam. Pundits, conceding that she *would* be president, started analyzing what few tea leaves and sheep livers they could get their hands on. Not a lot of rumors were coming out of the transition committee lately, and information leaks had completely dried up. Only official statements were getting airtime anymore.

Today's first big headline was about Karen Waldron, the suspected shooter's wife. *The Washington Post* placed the story of Karen hiring a lawyer on the front page, but *The Washington Times* buried it inside, citing lack of confirmation from Justice. *The Post* used blurt quotes from the Justice weenies, setting off a firestorm. And the AP spread the dirt far and wide. Cable news and network morning shows offered a wide variety of opinions on this little revelation. No one seemed to know what it actually meant, but plenty of TV time was used to speculate about it. Radio talk show hosts felt completely vindicated in their opinions now, chanting and ranting that Karen was somehow involved in the assassination, or at least had foreknowledge. Maybe even Madison Tarlton, the evil Moderate California Governor, had ordered the hit on her own boss.

More big headlines came at 9:00 AM. Word circulated about Senator Lewis's tragic early-morning heart attack while he was on the toilet—just like Elvis. The radio crowd thought they could connect Madison to this, too. She obviously wanted to get a new person in the Senate. But by 10:00 AM, the Ohio Governor announced that Art Messanger, the recently fired Sarnoff Chief of Staff, would assume that vacated Senate seat. Now it was difficult for even the most vitriolic talk show shouter to draw a plausible line from Madison to Art indicating a transition committee scheme—unless Art and Madison had faked their rift!

News frenzy was already in high clover when another salvo hit the web with newly released sex tapes and testimonials of victims. The audience of sleaze went crazy. Senate Majority Leader Roscoe and Senate Majority Whip Patterson were shown in compromising situations in secretly recorded HD videos. The videos were real, unedited, and depicted despicable men being entertained in a variety of third world countries. No comments came from the good senators' staffs. For an hour, the Democrats were drunk with glee.

The hour passed and then new videos and testimonials circulated showing leading Democratic senators and *their* antics: actual bribery transactions salted with drugs and sex. The minority leader and six of his cohorts cavorted unknowingly on camera. One of those senators committed suicide before the day was over.

The Democrats and Republicans alike sought to cast blame on the video-leakers, whoever they might be, but that line did not draw many takers. One of the most caustic left-wing TV-ranters suddenly left the air without explanation upon discovering that he was featured in the senate majority leader's internet video debut. A popular right-wing talk show host was similarly outed and disappeared from the airwaves in mid-segment.

Scandal drove wonderful TV ratings all day long, and pundits rolled in the glory of their commentary—as long as *they* weren't the ones starring in the newly released videos. Short of an assassination, scandal was the greatest numbers-booster for media outlets.

The president pro tempore of the Senate was not implicated in the scandals but was out of pocket having triple bypass surgery. The Senate, now under the dubious supervision of the sitting lame duck vice president acting as president of the Senate, voted to adjourn until the leadership could be sorted out; barely enough sitting senators gathered to say *yay* or *nay* in a voice vote. The House likewise voted to adjourn.

Because of this explosive news day, the Wall Street scaredy-cats were in a selloff frenzy.

Talbot sent a text to Madison on her M3: *"Interesting times."*

She responded with a single *"!"*

Chapter 55

8:01 AM PST - Seven days before inauguration

The office door at T.T. Thomas P.C. in Portland, Oregon was locked, so Special Agent Radisson and his gaggle of Feds knocked impatiently. They had known about this little law firm representing Waldron since 3:30 AM when an angry special agent in charge woke Radisson up and read him the riot act for not knowing about the firm before the newspapers did. Never mind that the Justice Department had received the information nearly a full day before the newspapers, (again, courtesy of Talbot's bureaucrat-friends at Justice).

Armed with a search warrant, the federal agents were after information leading to the location of one Karen Waldron, who was sought on a material witness warrant. After a few moments, the door opened and Sheila Lance stood before the FBI agents. Radisson handed her a copy of the search warrant; she motioned for the agents to sit while she read it.

"No, ma'am. We won't be sitting and waiting. You've been served—so please get out of the way and let us search the office. If you resist, we'll arrest you for obstruction," Radisson spouted with his characteristic bluster.

"No, Agent Radisson. You've presented a specific warrant for very specific evidence. This is a law office that may contain information on other cases not included in your search parameter and is therefore protected by attorney-client privilege. You will not be allowed access to *those* records, if they exist." Sheila Lance had been a feared and formidable federal prosecutor for eight years before moving to the private sector—Agent Radisson was in over his head.

"Are you resisting our official efforts?"

"Not at all, Agent Radisson. And before you do or say anything regrettable that may be outside the scope of your duties, be advised that everything occurring in this lobby is audio and video recorded for the security of the firm and its personnel." This revelation gave Radisson a moment's pause, but he tried to move past Sheila to the inner door. It was locked. "Before you get your hackles up, I'll get in touch with the federal court clerk and verify the legitimacy of this warrant. It won't take long, so relax," Sheila said, ignoring Radisson and activating her M3 device to call the clerk. After a minute she ended the call and looked at Radisson. "Ok, Agent Radisson, I'll entertain your little witch hunt. Please remember: this warrant is limited to records applying specifically to the current location of Karen Waldron and nothing else. You'll remove nothing from this office except what is expressly designated in the written warrant. I understand from the court clerk that you needed to produce four drafts of the warrant before the district judge would sign it."

Radisson's anger flared. "How do you propose to keep us from deciding what we deem relevant?"

"Good question. The answer is coming through the door right now." Radisson turned to see four armed men entering the room. He realized that the scumbag lawyers were way ahead of him and had played him from the beginning.

"Well, Larry, here we are again," said his former FBI boss. Neven Haltz entered with the same crew that had been with him at the convenience store.

"Neven, what the hell are *you* doing here?" He was starting to smell a really big rat—like the rodent of unusual size he remembered from…somewhere.

"Larry, we provide security for this law firm. We're here to observe and make sure you and your gang conduct yourselves within the legal parameters of your authorized warrant. In addition, I'll serve as legal counsel for the firm in this search. So, shall we proceed?" he said, reaching out a hand for the warrant Sheila was holding. He read it quickly and handed it back. "Okay, we'll open the door, and you'll be permitted to conduct a limited search as specified."

They filed into a large, sparsely but tastefully appointed office. Radisson and his agents peered around, seeing nothing to search. The desk was a modern glass-topped affair with a couple of trinkets on it. The room was devoid of filing cabinets and computer hardware.

"Where are your client files? Specifically, where are the files relating to Karen Waldron's current location?" Radisson said irascibly.

"We don't keep any paper files here in the office. Everything is digital," Sheila said politely, smiling as she spoke. "This is the modern age, Agent Radisson. We use computers and everything."

"Where's the computer? We'll take the hard drive."

"You're not authorized to take it, even if we *had* a hard drive for you to take." She stared him down with a look as intimidating as anything he'd experienced from his FBI superiors. "You're only permitted to see the information we *may* have on Ms. Waldron's location. Nothing else."

"Show me that information!"

"As it happens, Agent Radisson, we don't *have* any information at this office that pertains to Ms. Waldron's location." Sheila enjoyed toying with him a bit. "Her physical location is beyond the scope of our representation agreement. We can communicate with her by sending or receiving messages, but that's it. I'm afraid your search warrant is useless."

"Palmer, check the computer," Radisson ordered without responding to Sheila.

Agent Palmer was perplexed as he moved closer to the desk and saw only a smooth surface, no computer in sight. The desktop's center could hinge up at an angle. As he sat in the desk chair and touched the desk top, it came alive, showing a computer screen work surface with the T.T. Thomas Law Firm logo and a blinking curser. He touched the desk surface's edge and a virtual keyboard appeared. As he tapped the glowing *Enter Key*, a login window opened. He was stunned. No wires led to or from the desk. He had never seen anything like it. He pulled the tilted portion up for a better angle.

Radisson walked behind him to look over his shoulder. "What's the password, Ms. Lance?" Radisson growled.

"That, Special Agent Radisson, is not within the scope of your warrant." She was calm as could be, wearing a sly smile that obviously irritated the FBI boys. "Will there be anything else?"

"Palmer, grab the hard drive and let's go."

"Larry, there isn't any hard drive," Palmer said. "This seems to be some type of remote terminal, but no computer here per se. There's nothing to take." The feebs looked all around—no wire closet, no hiding places, nothing to confiscate. Palmer didn't know the particulars but guessed this was a terminal that wirelessly connected to a router and then connected via fiber to an offsite server.

"Okay. Let's do this another way. Ms. Lance, where is the attorney of record listed on this representation agreement," Radisson paused to glance at the document he carried, "Talbot DeCourcy?"

"I've no idea. He's never stepped foot in this office. He works remotely from his home office, I suppose."

"Where does he live?" Radisson assumed a calmer tone, seeing how badly he'd been outmaneuvered. Neven Haltz and company hadn't spoken again since first arriving. His security team stood at parade rest.

"Somewhere in Washington State, I believe. But, of course, I have no obligation under the auspices of your warrant to give you anything regarding his personal information. You can get access to that through legal channels."

Considering her work done, Sheila smiled and walked back through the lobby and out the front door. The agent guarding the door tried to prevent her from leaving, but her withering stare reminded him that he was legally groundless—he dared not bring down the wrath of her personal guardians and the gods. Neven Haltz and his men chuckled as the FBI contingent slunk out of the building and headed to their cars.

Within the hour, Agent Radisson received orders from D.C. to proceed with his team to Seattle, and Lawrence Radisson was like a mean dog with a rancid bone—no letting go until the job was done. He led his troops to a downtown Seattle office building, home to DeCourcy Technologies and other companies under Talbot's name. The security staff at this facility were all former federal law enforcement veterans, and when confronted by Larry's group, they were unflappable and unimpressed with the warrant he waved around. Since Talbot didn't practice law out of this corporate office, they denied the FBI entry — and the agents were powerless to do anything about it. No one was going to help them find Talbot DeCourcy.

Chapter 56

12:30 PM EST - Seven days before inauguration

The Brotherhood was meeting again, at least most of them, this time in a private lodge near Front Royal, Virginia. Thomas Carlyle couldn't attend, but it was just as well. Given the failure of his team in Florida, he would have suffered the subtle wrath of his comrades.

"Gentleman, our game has gotten a little more complicated. The opposition has reacted more swiftly than we gave them credit for," John Hancock opened the discussion.

"It's that S.O.B., DeCourcy," Leon Fuller said morosely. "He's responsible for all the damage to our schedule. First, he ruined the election and made us have to jump ahead two years, and now he's harboring Waldron. She's gotta know more than she should." He swore under his breath.

"I agree," Roger Burgad jumped in. "We have to assume that whatever she knows, DeCourcy knows. If that's the case, then he's put the pieces together. He must know about the eye doctor and how we cauterized the information leak."

"You're probably correct, but we shouldn't assume that he's made the other connections to the Seattle lawyer and the San Diego FBI agent," Hancock inserted.

"Why not?" Leon asked. "We already know he's one resourceful guy. He brought down a winning presidential re-election campaign! And I've no doubt that it was his men in Florida who took out Thomas's mercenaries." Leon stood and began pacing the large room, warming up for one of his typical rants. "Thomas sent former Special Forces operatives to silence DeCourcy thirty years ago, and those guys disappeared. No one knows for sure what happened, but I have a good idea. We can't underestimate this jerk again." Some of the men around the table had never heard about the attempt to kill DeCourcy with former German Stassi commandos in Idaho. They began to murmur. He continued, "I'm not sure why he hasn't brought in the FBI. If he'd contacted the authorities, we'd know."

"Please sit back down, Leon," John soothed. "Talbot DeCourcy is certainly a force to be confronted, and we'll plan carefully."

They spent an hour arguing about how to get Karen Waldron and how to take care of the thorny DeCourcy problem. Finally, John ended the debate, saying to Roger Burgad: "I want you to utilize your considerable field resources and get some leverage on DeCourcy. He will cough up Karen Waldron if he feels vulnerable about his family."

Roger Burgad was a former CIA heavyweight. "Happy to jump into the fray," he responded.

"Once you secure Ms. Waldron, I'll use my own agents to take down Talbot DeCourcy *once and for all*," John said with menace. There was silence as the group ruminated on that thought.

Arthur Messanger broke the silence, bringing up the Roscoe misfire: "The good senator made an appointment with Mad Tarlton and spent an hour in the Transition Committee Headquarters." He stood to emphasize his message. "My informants tell me that Roscoe made threats and tried to strike a deal. He went way off the reservation, the idiot. He tried to make his own grandiose play and demanded to be named the new vice president."

"Senator Roscoe was always a risky proposition for us. We had good material on him, but it seems someone else had better dirt," John stated matter-of-factly. "We need to consider who is the culprit that effectively closed the Senate. Without Roscoe cracking the whip, our ability to control the new administration is impaired, at least for a few weeks."

"Could Madison have orchestrated all the scandals after Roscoe threatened her?" Art asked. "Is it possible that she's in league with DeCourcy?"

"No way!" Leon Fuller blurted. "David Maxtell and I conducted extensive research, and there's no possible connection between them. It's much more likely that someone else is taking advantage of the assassination and chaos to make a power play."

"I agree," John responded. "We should not ascribe every act to a single adversary. We've always known that we can put things into action with our plans, but we can't control the enemy's reactions."

John motioned for Art to sit down. "The Senate problem is an irritant, but it should work itself out in a few weeks. The upside is that once Art gets seated as senator, he'll have fewer opponents for the influential positions with so many knocked out of the Senate. Maybe we should take out a few more senators," he chuckled. "Okay, we've done what we can with the situation on Capitol Hill, so let's turn to other operations. Dennis, what's the status in Mexico?"

"Everything's ready to go," said Roger Burgad, former CIA station chief for US Embassy operations in Mexico. He was tasked with coordinating the southern activities. "It turns out that moving the timetable up will help, based on the movements in the cartel's hierarchy."

"Good to know. I understand that we should hear something from news outlets very soon." John waited a moment, then nodded to Roger Burgad and moved on. "Before we break up, I want everyone to know that we will have a recommitment ceremony on our 30th anniversary!" He let the implications sink in. Some faces in the group smiled—a few showed signs of unease. Recommitment to the Brotherhood was serious and sobering.

These men had proven their loyalty to the cause thirty years ago and were tightly bound together by the terrible acts they had committed back then.

Chapter 57

1:00 PM EST - Seven days before inauguration

Lunch with four members of the Supreme Court was pleasant enough. Talbot had handled the restaurant owner, making sure he and the jurists dined privately. After the entree and usual catching up, Talbot was ready to present his case, as it were.

He had known these great legal minds for many years. After clerking for the Supreme Court, he had spent three years doing in-depth interviews with numerous federal judges of the United States, gathering a wide set of thoughtful opinions from the sitting jurists and later publishing his findings under the nom de plume, Tristan Thomas.

He had revisited many of those same judges for updates over the years. Some of them sat on the high court now—and beside him at lunch today.

With this frequent contact, they had picked his brain on trends and opinions. They recognized Tristan Thomas as one the great legal minds in the country—he had penned several constitutional treatises and books on legal theory. Many of the Supreme Court justices considered him a personal friend; the four he was dining with were tuned in to his *"Fifth Republic Theory."* They also knew that America sat on the cusp of a turning point; however, understanding that something was coming was not the same as knowing *what* it would be. No one could predict the future, and Talbot could only poke at the factors influencing its direction and outcome.

*   *   *

"The Fifth Republic Theory" postulated a regular cycle of fundamental shifts in America's form of government. Talbot had shown that after the collapse of *The First American Republic,* which only survived eight years under the Articles of Confederation, a new pattern emerged. Each succeeding "republic" lasted about three generations, or eighty years.

The Second Republic, born with the adoption of the Constitution in 1789, was an agrarian economy. Power resided in the state legislatures and the Congress. The American population grew dramatically, both from a healthy birth rate and from massive immigration. This era, lasting eighty years, extended from Washington's Presidency to Lincoln's.

The pressures of Civil War politics led to *The Third Republic Era,* with the Executive Branch emerging as the dominant power. This "Lincoln Period" saw a huge shift in Americans' perception of the role of government in an emerging industrial economy. State's rights and legislative power declined as the Union became the default concern. The Third Republic coincided with the rise of the third-generation of Americans since Washington's time, who took for granted the sacrifices which had formed the American legacy.

About eighty years and three generations later, *The Fourth Republic* arose, with a new generation looking to make changes and receive protection from the whims of economic upheaval, i.e., the Great Depression. These Americans accepted the dominance of a powerful executive branch in collusion with Congress, setting socialist-type wrappings upon the people and limiting the private ownership of property. Under President Roosevelt's New Deal, The State granted you the boon to keep some of your wealth, but only at the State's discretion. Roosevelt and Congress imposed massive tax rates to control wealth. (94 percent was the top bracket.) Private gold ownership, without the express permission of the government, was outlawed. While private ownership of property increased in later decades, the generations of the Fourth Republic widely accepted that they were the subjects of the government, rather than that the government was subject to them.

America traversed those eighty years, leading to the present time. The Supreme Court ascended in importance as a powerful hedge against overreaching presidents and legislators. Congress came to a gridlock halt. Presidents became petty politicians with no regard for the welfare of the Union. Something had to give. This generation demanded a fundamental remake, and past history had demonstrated that Americans, during a crisis, would ignorantly accept extreme changes.

With a growing groundswell of socialistic fervor, millennials' ideology diverged greatly from that of their parents, and they lacked understanding of socialist systems' manifest failures in other countries. But the concepts of "free" education and healthcare, guaranteed wages, and no-fail safety nets were seductive to the young.

The Fifth Republic change would either move in this radically liberal direction, or the reactionaries would fight back and pull America into a totalitarian morass. Change would inexorably come closer, while malevolent actors were moving to manipulate the direction.

*　　　*　　　*

Talbot informed his guests about the motivations behind the president-elect's assassination and the unknown player in upper FBI echelons involved in the cover up—and perhaps in the assassination itself. Distressed by this news, the justices peppered him with questions.

Chief Justice Marilyn Taft summarized: "So, Tristan, you've identified a domestic group trying to orchestrate a fundamental change in the government and bring in The Fifth Republic. The Article One branch of government is already sliding downhill fast, and you believe that this group is working to supercharge the Article Two branch of government to create an uber-executive. Okay, I see the logic in that. If they want to succeed at that game, they'll need to marginalize the Article Three branch of government, which puts us— the court system—in their crosshairs just as much as Congress."

"That's it in a nutshell," Talbot said, nodding. "They'll break down our checks and balances while maintaining the illusion of keeping the status quo, and they'll spout *for the greatest good* rhetoric as a cover."

"Our deliberative approach allows for thoughtful course corrections, but because everything happens slowly over time, regular Americans just don't see how we help align our laws with the realities of the modern world," said Marilyn.

"Feeling unappreciated, Madam Justice?" Talbot teased.

"They constantly attack the courts," Justice Rebecca Welch added, "claiming that we are activists on the one hand and

Neanderthal constructionists on the other. That probably plays into the narrative of your…what should I call them…*creepy* group."

"Well, for a nest of treasonous vipers, that's as good a term as any," Talbot said.

"Do you have any idea who's behind this latest bit of political machination?" Justice Jeffrey Hinton entered the conversation. They all looked at Talbot.

"I believe I do." This sharpened their interest quotient. "Thirty years ago, I was approached by a man who called himself John Hancock. Over the course of a few lunches, he flattered me and tried to sell me on joining his brilliant group of 'forward-thinkers.' He bragged that they were going to remake America and bring a better government into the future. He had read my *Fifth Republic* treatise and was convinced I'd want to help shape the new republic, not merely predict its inevitability." Talbot paused briefly. "He introduced me to four of his recruits and explained that he was building a group of twelve 'wise men'—as though they were disciples." He looked around the group intently. "Mr. Hancock hinted that he'd been part of a previous group striving to do the same thing, but the timing wasn't right, so they had disbanded." Talbot thought of the recent revelations from the Handy Nielson interrogations and grimaced. "I've recently come to understand that he had actually *eliminated* all the members of that former group and was its sole survivor."

"How?" Rebecca Welch asked.

"This same man had approached my father a few years earlier and tried to recruit *him*. I was unaware of that fact when I was being wined and dined. Not only did my father reject him, but he threatened to expose John and his Cabal." The bile rose in his throat as he pictured Handy Nielson glibly spilling this information at the Quarry. He continued, "This man called John, who thought of himself as the great founder of the new republic, was undoubtedly the same man who later ordered the murder of my entire family to cover his tracks and hide the plan that my dad had threatened to reveal."

Everyone sat in shocked silence. It took a moment before Talbot could go on. "The four up-and-coming young men Hancock introduced to me are all in their fifties now, and you surely know of each of them."

"Who?" came the almost comical chorus from four supreme court jurists.

Talbot said with emphasis: "Hang on to your robes—Leon Fuller, Arthur Messanger, Bertrand Pinkney, and Thomas Carlyle!" He sat back and let this revelation sink in.

"I can understand Art, Tom, and Bert possibly working together—but Leon, the disagreeable twerp, is on the opposite side of the political divide." Marilyn Taft voiced what many were thinking.

"Part of the ruse. This is not an ideological front working on a single-party agenda. This is a malicious masterplan using tools that they've sharpened in every conceivable corner," Talbot said. "I've identified four more players in the game and believe they are insiders, not just useful idiots on the outside like Senator Roscoe—and they span the political spectrum. They want to undermine the foundation of the whole political system.

"By the way, I believe President-Elect Sarnoff was a patsy, not an insider. They would have eventually pushed him out or killed him off because one of their *own* brotherhood members would be in place as vice president to be inserted into the presidency slot."

"Not Madison!" Marilyn said. "There's no way *she* could be part of this."

"No, in fact, she was the intended target of the sniper," Talbot said. He heard a few gasps.

"Let me backup. I'm fairly certain that the assassination was part of their *plan B*—to kill Madison and get a Brotherhood member in the vice president slot and then get rid of Sarnoff. But President Cluff was *plan A*. Originally, a Cluff win seemed like a certainty, but they didn't have the same level of control over him as they did Sarnoff. They'd been managing Wilson Sarnoff's career for twenty-five years, but they needed to make him bigger…larger than life. So they would wait through part of Cluff's second term, then destroy his term so badly that Sarnoff could run again next cycle. And because the contrast between Cluff's failure and Sarnoff's rock-star image would be monumental, Sarnoff could stroll into office with a *Reagan-esque* landside and an overwhelming mandate—giving him unprecedented latitude to act."

"Okay, that makes some kind of twisted sense," Marilyn said.

"When I went up against Cluff and revealed his scandal right before the election, it turned his sure win into a narrow loss. This messed up their *plan A* and altered their master timetable. They were forced to adapt and speed things up with *plan B*, which fell apart when they missed Madison, and now they're calling audible plays at this point…with some kind of *plan C*." Talbot was reluctant to go any further but felt he must. "I'm actively working to expose this group of would-be kings. I'm going to bring them down."

"You're going to destroy their *plan C*!" said Jeffrey Hinton.

"There'll be some information in the press soon that'll put them on the defensive. They'll have to scramble to save their plans, and because they're *ultimately* invested in this, I afraid they'll amp up the violence and murder…*all* options are acceptable means to them."

"Will they try to kill Madison Tarlton before the inauguration?" Rebecca asked.

"I don't think so. They influenced Sarnoff to choose a slate of executive-appointees, and they still need those individuals in key positions. Hopefully, they think Madison will go along with their picks. Then, after the swearing in, a sitting president is a nearly impossible target to reach. So, I think, I hope, she's safe."

The justices murmured ascent.

"I'm looking for them to create some ancillary movement among foreign governments that'll put pressure on the new administration—a strong attempt to keep Madison off-balance by forcing her into constant crisis management. But the current political blood bath in the Senate—and their adjournment—may work to her advantage. It'll be a while before that august body gets back into working order, and that'll give her some breathing room."

Talbot finished his comments and thanked them for coming. After handshaking and expressions of concern, the lunch companions left the restaurant with new burdens.

Chapter 58

3:00 PM EST - Seven days before inauguration

Roger Burgad sat with his fellow Brotherhood member, David Maxtell, at Tyson Tech Security. Maxtell was the owner and CEO of Tyson Tech. Following service in the Air Force Space Command and a stint at the NSA, Maxtell created one of the nation's premier tech-based security consulting firms in Tyson Corners, VA. The Department of Homeland Security and the FBI frequently outsourced some of their stickier electronic surveillance tasks to his firm. Recently he was disturbed by the loss of some key surveillance signals from the Presidential Transition Office; Madison's new people were locking things up tight, and his guy, Eddie Smyth, couldn't get back in to fix things.

"I have the muscle all cued up to get leverage on DeCourcy, but I need electronic stuff and some background real quick," Roger Burgad said, starting the business of their meeting. "My guys are already in the air heading to Washington and California."

After his time as a CIA operative, Roger Burgad had spent years in the State Department Foreign Service, then took a post on the National Security Council during President Cluff's first term, and resigned from the Council when Cluff failed to win re-election. Even though some considered him a little left-leaning, he'd been President-Elect Sarnoff's pick as the new secretary of state. Madison Tarlton was changing some of Sarnoff's intended appointments, but as far as anybody knew, Roger Burgad's appointment was still on track; his FBI vetting was continuing. In fact, he was scheduled to meet with Madison at 10:00 AM the following morning.

"No problem, Roger," David Maxtell said. "You can have Eddie Smyth since he's out of the loop at the transition committee now, and he can coordinate with the data researchers to get what you need almost instantly. As soon as we found out that DeCourcy has been hiding Karen Waldron, we got on him. But I gotta tell you, he's not an open book. We don't have a cell number for him or any of his family. Almost no online presence at all. Nothing on YouTwitFace..."

"What's that, the Twitface thing?"

"Oh, that's what Eddie Smyth calls the whole social media universe—you know, YouTube, Twitter, Facebook. We haven't been able to crack into his credit card records either. Usually when we get into a credit card provider's server, everything is wide open. But with DeCourcy's credit card company and his bank, it didn't work. Once we got past the main firewall, we found that every single account is encrypted separately. We could hit it with supercomputers for years, but my guys tell me that even the NSA couldn't break into those records. We can see that he owns a lot of companies, L.L.C.s, and

hundreds of properties, but there's absolutely no personal
information on him."

"What about pulling his tax records? You do that all the time."

"Eddie can fill you in on that. He's getting some data together
for Landan Moss." David chuckled. "Poor Eddie, that heavy of
Hancock's creeps him out. Good luck, Roger." They shook hands and
David left the conference room.

In a couple of minutes, Eddie Smyth, hacker and bug-planter,
slunk into the room. Everything about him looked sneaky. He wore
faded jeans and had long, scraggly hair. His dark brown eyes moved
quickly and constantly, refusing to settle on anyone. "Hey, so David
Maxtell wants me to help with your data needs."

"Thanks, Eddie. Let's go over a few things," Roger Burgad said.
They shook hands and sat opposite each other at the monstrous
conference table. "David mentioned that you pulled DeCourcy's tax
records."

"No way. We tried, but it blew up in seconds!" Eddie was
suddenly animated. "I never saw anything like it. I normally use three
different sources inside the IRS. We pay them really well and they've
never, ever failed. I gave one of them DeCourcy's name and asked for
the whole package. 'Sophie' is the code name I use to connect with
this source. She responded that she'd get it for me but then went
completely silent. That's never happened before. I contacted the
second source, who told me that the record was flagged and Sophie
had been arrested by US Marshals—in like fifteen minutes. 'Jasper,'
the second source, won't touch it!"

"Can it come back on you?"

"Nah, they think I'm a hacker in Romania selling data to Euro
creeps." Eddie was obviously awed by this strange event. "This guy,
DeCourcy, has some juice, bro. When I went after his driver's license
in Washington State, it turned out that they have a new program

there. If you try to pull a driver's record, you need to have a certified requestor ID and a bunch of other stuff. If you don't have the DL number or birthday and stuff, you're done. Those records are encrypted in a way that no other state's DMV records are. I looked into it and found out that DeCourcy Security Technologies created the encryption system and supplied all the new security protocols. And I have no way to hack in and hide the intrusion. Usually I can back out without leaving a trace, like a responsible backpacker in the woods. But no way!" This failure to produce usable information seemed to invigorate Eddie rather than depress him.

"How about the information I need to go after the leverage?"

"Oh, I got all that, pieced together from some ancillary public records that were unprotected. I put the items together in this file." He handed over a flash stick. "Please let me know if you need anything else, like access to cameras or stuff. Okay?"

"Thanks, Eddie. Big help." Roger Burgad stood up and left Tyson Tech Security.

Chapter 59

January 14

12:45 PM PST - Six days before the inauguration

"They call themselves the Brotherhood. I knew it would be some cheesy comic book name," Gene Artel said to Talbot over his M3 device as he reported highlights from the interrogations of the Florida bushwhackers. "With the names you've already got, we've now identified six Brotherhood members. This other guy, Handy Nielsen, is one of their praetorian guard—the ones identified as A-F."

"Sounds like Nielson spilled pretty easily," Talbot said.

"Once he figured out that we're not associated with law enforcement and there's no due process, he caved. He's a smart guy. He caught on that he's not gonna get a lawyer and none of his buddies know where he is or who took him. So he wants to stay useful—and alive."

"Anybody else willing to share?" Talbot asked.

"Yes, indeed! The leader of the hit-and-snatch squad, Glen Romano, has been doing nasty things for Thomas Carlyle for years, but he only knows about Carlyle's operations and seems ignorant of the bigger picture. He's never met Hancock or heard anything about him. In fact, he's firewalled out of the rest of the Brotherhood's business, so all our intel about them came from Handy Nielsen."

"I guess we need to get ahold of all the praetorian guard, and they'll lead us to Hancock," DeCourcy said.

"That sounds right. Handy Nielsen only knows the other five guys by the code names 'A—F,' except for the leader named Landan

Moss. And I get the feeling that Handy is betraying a good friend when it comes to Moss…But these dudes enjoy killing—they've killed dozens of people for the Brotherhood. We need to learn as much as we can about this Moss guy, who seems to be the only one in contact with Hancock."

"What about Thomas Carlyle's thugs? Any more of them lurking out in the woods somewhere?"

"I'm sure there are. The Brotherhood has access to billions of dollars. Each core member has his own army of mercenaries and contractors in his own separate silo, and each silo operates independently. But all the silos are coordinated by that clan of sociopaths because the Brotherhood always acts in concert. Along with their private armies, they seem to have lots of surrogates operating inside the system: folks like Roscoe in the Senate and our mystery guest at the FBI."

"Your people did a superb job, Artel. If it comes to it, their presidential pardons will be signed and ready to go. But that presupposes we keep Madison alive!"

"You got that right! By the way, since you've gone public about representing Karen Waldron, I've pushed up the security and *Threat-Alert-Level* for everyone connected to you personally. They're all required to wear their activated MW4s."

An MW4 was a wristband like a watch or a health recorder. It functioned as a geo-locator and a life-and-safety monitor and could not easily be removed by force. It was also a backup phone that would replace an M3 device if the M3 got out of range from the ear canal insert. The MW4 device allowed privacy when the wearer was unharmed and free to act but could be activated and controlled by DeCourcy Central Command at Security Headquarters, if need be. To an unauthorized observer, it looked and functioned like a stylish and expensive watch.

"Thanks, Chief, good idea," Talbot said.

"You'd better up your vigilance quotient, too, boss."

"Thanks, I will."

"Okay, here we go. Looks like your new best friend at the FBI is arriving at the gate. He should've been here an hour ago. This guy's losing steam. Talk to you later, boss." Artel rang off, happily anticipating pulling a few threads of wool over Radisson's arrogant features.

Chapter 60

1:00 PM PST - Six days before inauguration

Two fast-moving black SUVs with federal government license plates and four unmarked local law enforcement sedans moved along the scenic parkway. After taking a sweeping turn onto the 300-yard-long private drive, they were forced to slow down to navigate the "S" curve traffic-funnel leading to the target property. They stopped in front of a military style, hydraulically-actuated steel barrier that raised or lowered at the owner's discretion—the same type used at U.S. embassies and the White House.

The Feds idled, staring at the anti-vehicle barrier as it lowered. Beyond it a stone gatehouse connected to a tall, intricate wrought-iron gate. Rustic brick walls bordered both the gatehouse and the ironwork gate, extending away to the left and right. The brick walls were misleading. Viewed from the outside, they appeared to be twelve feet high but were actually a decorative facade covering high-density, reinforced concrete barricades. The walls were four feet thick at the top, widening to twelve feet at the base and extending to a depth of twenty-four feet below the earth. At the top of the walls, a hidden, razor-sharp steel shield could rise within five seconds, making the total personnel barrier fifteen feet high.

The gatehouse was deceptively quaint in appearance—it was designed to survive grenade, machine gun, and other heavy weapon attacks, thus protecting the security personnel within. The general appearance of the property was a throwback to rural Americana, but it sat atop the five-acre, underground DeCourcy Security Command Center. In addition to living quarters for security personnel, the Command Center contained spacious underground parking for a wide variety of vehicles: rapid ATVs, motorcycles, UAVs, snowmobiles, and 4x4 trucks.

All this was hidden from the Feds, who now viewed a non-threatening, silver-haired security guard sitting inside the gatehouse near an open window. The window allowed the guard to engage with drivers before he lowered the hydraulic barrier. The wrought-iron rollback gate standing a few feet inside the steel barrier was also deceiving. If the barrier was already in lowered position, the "decorative" gate could withstand an SUV slamming into it at sixty miles per hour without collapsing. But due to the shape of the curving entrance-drive, the only straight acceleration area was less than 100 feet long, and testing had shown that this prohibited approach speeds above forty miles per hour. Even this speed required extreme reckless driving.

In case of trouble, the friendly security guard in the gatehouse could instantly fall back through a fast-close blast door, putting him inside the protected area. If someone shot at him through the open window, other watchers would slam the blast door closed—even if the unfortunate guard's remaining body parts were left in the way. Nothing could prevent the door from sealing shut.

As Radisson and his Keystone contingent of FBI agents stared at these curiosities, they couldn't have guessed a fraction of the security elements in place. The driver, Special Agent Palmer, lowered his window and held out his credentials to a smiling Gene Artel.

"Open this gate. We're on official FBI business," he demanded.

"What's the nature of your business, agent?" Gene Artel replied evenly, without a hint of annoyance.

"Our business is none of your business, grandpa. Get this gate open before I arrest you for obstruction of a federal investigation!" Palmer favored Larry Radisson's moto: when in doubt, intimidate. This was standard practice for many of Radisson's fellow agents.

Gene, the self-assured former deputy director of the Secret Service, smiled calmly back and said: "Please present credentials for each occupant of the vehicles and provide a subpoena, court order, or warrant that allows you to gain access to the properties located beyond this gate."

"I said open the damn gate, old codger, or else," Palmer again commanded. "I'm not showing you anything but these creds and my handcuffs."

Gene, still smiling, hit a switch that closed the bulletproof window panel. He relaxed on a high-backed stool and picked up the latest Lee Child novel he'd been reading when the vehicles arrived. Having seen their approach on camera when they first entered the private parkway six miles away, he had waited patiently while the contingent stopped for a last-minute briefing two miles down the road. Then they came on fast, expecting to drive through in force with lights flashing and shock-n-FBI-inspired awe. They *didn't* expect the barrier, lacking intelligence on it because their surveillance team couldn't see past the curving, tree-lined approach. The driveway began 300 yards before the barrier, and from the FBI watchers' vantage point hidden among the trees facing the driveway, it looked like a long, winding drive leading to a country house atop a hill.

Agents and local law officers piled out of their vehicles. A couple of tactical-clad deputies hung back, smiling and whispering. Special Agent in Charge Larry Radisson rounded the front of the SUV, raising his credentials in his left hand as he reached the window. He stage-whispered to Palmer to shut his mouth, whose "old codger" remark and lack of diplomacy was getting them nowhere. As Radisson tapped his knuckles on the thick glass, Gene Artel looked up. The "lowly gate guard" didn't open the window but talked through an embedded microphone-speaker system and peered at a monitor showing a camera-generated magnification of Radisson and his credentials.

"How can I help you, Special Agent Radisson?" Gene intoned pleasantly.

"We're here to serve a search warrant on the house located at 11235813 Tight Squeeze Lane." He almost choked saying the silly address aloud. "You need to lower the barrier and open the gate so you don't impede the performance of our duty."

"As the duly appointed security supervisor for said Tight Squeeze address, I will need to examine the aforementioned search warrant," Gene said, mocking Radisson's official tone. He was the one who had chosen the Fibonacci numerical sequence as an address and had borrowed "Tight Squeeze Lane" from a narrow road running between natural granite walls near his hometown in Woodstock, Virginia.

"Certainly," Radisson said. "But I warn you, it's a federal violation to call the residence listed on this warrant to alert them of our presence."

"Nice try, Special Agent Radisson, but there's no section of Title 18 that makes such a communication a federal violation. Be assured I'll not call or attempt to communicate with anyone at the address you seek. As it happens, there's no one currently at the residence," Gene said politely.

Agent Radisson held the warrant out, and an almost invisible slot opened with a tray extended. He placed the folded pages onto the tray, the tray retracted, and he saw Gene's arm movements unfolding the document. To Radisson's surprise, the guard didn't hold up the pages to read them but quickly scanned them on a high-resolution, flatbed scanner. A minute later the tray extended again, and Radisson retrieved the warrant.

"Have each of the agents participating in the execution of the search warrant step up and scan their credentials on the pad below," the guard said. Palmer and Radisson hadn't noticed the LCD pad slide out of the wall. Palmer started to balk, but Radisson realized this was a well-planned security procedure, not a delay tactic. He restrained Palmer's snarking and told the other six agents to scan their creds while an obvious camera photographed the agents.

When a sheriff's deputy stepped up to the scanner, Gene said, "Sorry, Deputy Kintson. You and the other county deputies are not covered by the warrant, so I won't be letting you in. Nothing personal."

Overhearing this, Agent Palmer shouted, "What are you talking about? Of course they're going in with us!"

"Agent Palmer, this warrant only refers to federal law enforcement officers executing said federal search warrant." Gene was matter-of-fact and non-confrontational.

"That doesn't matter. You will permit them to enter; they are supporting us in our official duty." Agent Palmer snidely spat the words. "I'll arrest you for obstruction."

"I'm sure that Agent Radisson is aware of the numerous examples in the *FBI Warrant Authoring Manual* showing how to include local law officers in the enforcement of a federal warrant.

None of those excellent phrases are used in this specific warrant. After all, if one such local deputy found something that you wished to seize from the property based on the warrant, a moderately skilled attorney could have that item excluded from an evidentiary proceeding because it was improperly obtained." The condescension in Gene's tone was inevitable—he had taught warrant and subpoena-writing classes for federal and local law enforcement agencies many times through the years.

"You could get this revised and get a new signature from Judge Dolman in Seattle, and we could certainly wait right here for you." Artel didn't intend the last statement as a taunt, but for Radisson, there was no other way to take it. He felt a flush rise again, and attempting to regain his cool, stifled a cursing tirade. After conferring with Palmer, he signaled to the deputies to stay outside the gate.

Gene Artel knew many of the left-behind deputies well and had recommended some of them to the department when they first sought employment. He invited them into the gatehouse for coffee and pastries while the Feds went off crusading.

Chapter 61

The federal vehicles drove slowly over the galvanized grate of the inner courtyard, negotiated a sharp left-turn, and passed through another steel gate. After following a curve that led immediately through a right dogleg, they opened onto a long, upslope driveway. The driveway ended at a tastefully landscaped circular drive accentuating an attractive, three-story brick house.

Agent Radisson examined the three keys Gene had given him. Each was of a different kind, and Radisson recognized them as the hardest lock-types to pick. After Palmer sent agents to both sides of the house and around to the back, Radisson rang the bell. No one answered. He unlocked the front entrance door and drew his gun.

The group stepped inside. A few beats passed before a confused Larry Radisson muttered, "What the hell!" Inside the residence they met a massive sloping dome of reinforced concrete filling the entire interior of the house. "This is some sort of decoy house...a bunker!"

The agents marveled at the structure never intended for habitation. It would obviously withstand a heavy attack from all kinds of man-carried-weapons and probably from aerial missiles as well.

Radisson swore, adding: "This is meant to absorb a full-scale assault...while the human targets are somewhere else...safe." He swore again. "Who *is* this guy? I'm gonna ream whoever did the location research. Even if this address is the only property listed in DeCourcy's name, *someone* should've gone deeper to investigate the L.L.C.s and trusts tied to him."

After roaring back to the gatehouse, the agents were required to stop and wait while Gene opened the gate and allowed one vehicle to exit at a time. This was the only way he could do it; the wrought-iron gate would not open until the inner steel gate had closed behind one car. The extended process didn't lower anyone's blood pressure.

The agents and local law enforcement regrouped in the driveway outside the gated area. Special Agent in Charge Larry Radisson gesticulated as he paced along the road, yelling into his phone to cover his embarrassment. "This operation has gone completely sideways. Someone's gonna pay!...That's what I said. The address is a decoy built to withstand a bomb hit and heavy arms fire...and probably the zombie apocalypse," he reported to his boss. "You understand how humiliating it is to serve a search warrant on the decoy of some paranoid jackass. Worse yet, we've lost the element of surprise now, and it's unlikely we'll find anything, assuming we can even find the actual address." He listened briefly, then responded, "Yeah, we'll see what we can do." He switched off his phone, and after taking a few calming breaths, noticed a young deputy sheriff hanging close by.

"Larry, I think you should hear what Deputy Kintson here has to say," Special Agent Palmer said, pointing to one of the locals who had been smoking beside him while they waited for Radisson to report up the chain. "He has an interesting slant on things."

"Well, what've you got for me, deputy?"

"I mean, I was say'n ta Agent Palmer here that you ought'a get'a hold'a your buddies in the Secret Service."

"Why?" Radisson tried to be patient while he pulled the story out.

"Well, as I was asay'n, the Secret Service, they knows where'ta find the DeCourcy house. I mean, they could tell'ya, like, maybe give'ya fellas directions," Kintson said, playing up the bumpkin bit.

"And the Secret Service would know where this property is because why?" Radisson said, irritated with this local.

"They was here fir a visit like back in August, we was thinkin', about the 18th."

"A visit here, at this gatehouse? Why would the Secret Service visit here?"

"I mean, their job's like'ta protect the president, right? The president, he come out here fir a visit last summer. Like, they was here ta, like, keep'em safe an all a'that."

The ironic smirk on Kintson's face was subtle, but Radisson noticed. He chose to let it go and get on with it. Turning away from the deputy without further acknowledgement, he stomped back to Gene Artel's post and demanded to know where the real DeCourcy residence was located.

"Bring me a proper warrant and I'll be glad to show you the way. I think that would be elementary, Agent Radisson." Gene smiled at the allusion and went back to his Lee Child book. Radisson stormed off.

When the FBI vehicles reached the long driveway's end, the advanced surveillance team emerged from the trees and stepped onto the parkway to report. Palmer got out of the SUV to confront them.

"What, you couldn't tell this was a decoy?" Palmer rounded on them. "And where's your vehicle?"

They both hesitated until one of the agents cleared his throat to speak. "Someone towed it while we were on recon. We saw a sign warning that this was private property, but we never thought anyone would tow a government vehicle."

"Idiots," Agent Palmer sighed. He turned around as the sheriff deputies pulled up beside him.

Deputy Kintson unrolled his window to speak: "Gentlemen, I have a message from Mr. Artel up there. He says now that you're finished serving your warrant, figuratively speaking," he chuckled, "you are to vacate the property, or else he wants me to take you into custody for trespassing." His bumpkin act was gone.

"Can't you see we're off the property and we're now on the public thoroughfare?" Palmer retorted.

"Well, no. Sorry, you're not. The property line is at least three miles from here in any direction you choose, and what you're on now is the DeCourcy Parkway that runs six miles back to the public road. That's probably why one of your cars got towed. So-o-o, my professional advice is that you federal boys be on your way, or I'll arrest you. Got it, Agent Palmer? Tell Agent Radisson over there to take his condescending attitude out of my jurisdiction."

Chapter 62

2:30 PM PST - Six days before inauguration

Agents Radisson and Palmer stormed into the Thomas Foley Federal Building in downtown Spokane. Radisson knew he would get hit with blowback for bringing his special unit into the Spokane area without first contacting the hick, Woodruff, who ran the local Spokane Resident Office. Something about showing common courtesy. *Common courtesy, my ass.* And he was moving too fast to check with the Seattle Field Office. His boss could sort the fallout. *I'm on the job,* he thought.

The agents were directed to the FBI office and strode in arrogantly. After a brief verbal battle with an administrative assistant, they were ushered in to see Ron Woodruff, the Supervisory Resident Agent. Radisson had heard the download on him while traveling back from the decoy debacle. A twenty-two year FBI veteran, Woodruff stacked up as a very solid agent and carried a sterling reputation with other agents and management. Earning his choice of most any field office in the country, he had specifically requested the Spokane assignment.

"Agents Radisson and Palmer, I presume?" Rising to greet the unlucky duo, Woodruff shook their hands without an air of recrimination. "Please sit and tell me what I can do to help you." His gesture invited them to the visitors' chairs.

"Thanks. We came here to try and chase down Karen Waldron on a material witness warrant. And now we want to get to her attorney to find out where she's hiding." Radisson spoke rapidly.

"Waldron, the assassin's wife?" Woodruff smiled. "Do tell."

"I'm sure you've heard that Talbot DeCourcy publicly announced that he's her lawyer, but he's intentionally avoiding us," Radisson continued.

"Really? How is he avoiding you?"

"We went to his office of record in Portland, and he's never worked there," Palmer jumped in. "According to his partner, he works from home. We went up to his corporate office in Seattle, but they claimed he wasn't there either and doesn't do any private legal practice from the corporate office. So we obtained a warrant from Judge Dolman in Seattle and served it on the only house listed under DeCourcy's name, but it's some kind of concrete bunker—a fake house, like a decoy."

"What's that all about? This guy's some kind of paranoid oddball," Radisson said, warming up to the conversation. "I mean, *who has a bunker*? You don't see that every day."

"What are your plans now?" Woodruff asked.

"We heard that the Secret Service may have a line on his actual residence. Some local county-mountie claimed that POTUS visited

DeCourcy in August. I think the jerk was pulling our leg, but we put in a call to Homeland just the same to liaise on this."

"You would've been better off calling me in the first place. I could've given you directions easily enough. I was on the local protection call-up when POTUS came to see Talbot DeCourcy last year."

"Really?" Radisson was surprised. "POTUS came out to visit this clown?"

"Yeah, it was quite a presidential party. What'd you say happened when you tried to serve your warrant out there today?" Woodruff deftly changed the subject.

"First, we roll up to an enormous fortified gatehouse and meet some obstructionist rent-a-cop who thinks he's a sheriff in the wild, wild west. He scans our creds and refuses to let the locals join the search, and then we find a damn bunker that just looks like a house on the outside. It's crazy! Then the old yokel refuses to cooperate any further, so now we're going upstairs to get an updated warrant signed," Radisson finished.

"Who was manning the gate?" Woodruff asked.

"His name's Gene Artel, a complete self-righteous jerk," Palmer answered.

"Gene Artel was manning the gate? I guess they laid out the red carpet for you guys!"

"What do you mean?" Palmer asked quickly, not sure where this was going. "They had to know we were coming."

"Gene Artel is the Global Chief of Security for all DeCourcy companies and properties. I believe he has about two-thousand people working for him and probably earns north of two-million a year in salary and bonu…"

"No way!" Palmer interrupted.

"Yes, he does. Besides that, fifteen years ago, he was deputy director of the Secret Service. The president back then tried to appoint him director, but he declined the post and went to work for Talbot DeCourcy instead."

"That sounds nuts. Do you know this DeCourcy?" Radisson was becoming more convinced he'd been led down the garden path all along.

"Sure, I've known him for years. A very standup guy!"

"But he's a crazy-paranoid-entitled-jackass, right?" Palmer added.

"DeCourcy, an entitled jackass? Not at all. He's actually a great guy, very reserved and quiet. Really unassuming for a billionaire. As for paranoid, well, he *is* a target, if you want to know the truth. Also, if you understood his history, you might think his paranoia is reasonable caution."

"What do you mean?"

*   *   *

"For starters," Woodruff began, "his family used to spend summers in Idaho up in the Selway River country, and when he was fifteen, he came home from a weeklong Boy Scout river rafting trip and found his whole family murdered. Not just murdered—but assassinated."

"What the hell?" Radisson reacted with something approaching humanity.

"Terrible thing! According to the reports from the sheriff at the time, his father, mother, and two sisters were brutally killed. The dad put up a valiant fight, and three of the killers were also found dead. A fourth shooter got away, but he ran his Range Rover into the river and presumably drowned—probably severely wounded in the battle," Woodruff continued. "Young Talbot took over the family fortune and enterprises when he was just a teenager."

"Hard breaks," Palmer intoned.

"Yeah, but he was up to it. He graduated from Stanford law when he was twenty-one and clerked for two Supreme Court Justices. And he was a very young prosecutor in Seattle with the nickname, *No-deal-DeCourcy*. His rep was that he got the highest conviction rate and the longest sentences for the criminals he prosecuted. He wouldn't deal down to get somebody to testify against a bigger fish. His philosophy was 'keep taking away the little fish and you'll find the big fish.' Not only that, the guy has argued at least seventeen appeals cases before the high court and never lost!"

"So a tough guy?"

"Oh yeah! This is where the paranoia sets in. Years back, while he was prosecuting a bunch of Russian mob-types on conspiracy and murder charges, they tried to frame him on a bribery deal, which he turned around and added to their charges. During the trial, DeCourcy was at lunch in downtown Seattle when associates of the defendants came up on him. There were two in a car: a shooter and a driver, and two shooters on the sidewalk: one in front of him and one behind. It was a tightly coordinated attack. I've read everything on this."

"How'd he survive that?"

"He must've seen it coming, because he threw himself backwards to the ground as he drew a weapon from a paddle holster. He gave a double tap to the head of the guy coming from the front, and hit the one behind him by looking backwards over his shoulder and shooting him under the chin twice. Then without getting up, he took out the shooter and the driver as they started to open up on him. He was slightly wounded, but the mob-trial resumed with only a couple hours delay."

"I'll be damned!"

"That's not all. He left the county prosecutor's office, got married, and took a job as a federal prosecutor in Seattle. Three years later he was doing a RICO trial of Chinese Triad gang members. One night they put three rocket-propelled grenades into his house. He got more cautious after that. You can call it paranoid, but I doubt he sees it that way. Not only that, he interrupted a terrorist ambush on a bus in Israel a few years back on the road to the Dead Sea. He managed to kill all five gunmen."

"How'd he manage that?"

"He came from behind the bus as the attack was starting and drove his car up over two of the attackers, then retrieved one of their AK-47s and blew away the other three. The FBI agents helping with the Israelis' investigation came home with the impression that the whole ambush might've been a ruse to take out DeCourcy in the first place. But the Israelis had nobody left alive to waterboard, so the final report was inconclusive. So, yeah, you could say he seems paranoid. I say he's cautious."

"That's just crazy stuff," Palmer blurted.

Radisson remained thoughtful. "Sucks to be a billionaire, I guess. I heard there's only one judge available here right now," he said, moving on. He didn't care about DeCourcy's life or heroic past. "What can you tell us about this Judge Covington?"

"Because of vacancies and health issues, Spokane is short on federal judges. Kate Covington is a Ninth District Appellate Justice filling in as district court judge temporarily. She lives here, so she takes up the slack. She's tough as kukui nuts and doesn't take crap or nonsense from anybody. If you want to get an updated warrant from her, you'd better have a solid story. She's known as a conservative law-and-order type, a former US Attorney, but she also cares about individual rights and liberties."

Woodruff, not wanting to make it easy for this arrogant piece of work, didn't add that Kate Covington was DeCourcy's wife. He called up to the court clerk to check on availability. "She's in court and probably won't take a break again till the end of court business, say 4:30."

"Can't the clerk ask her to pause for a second and sign an urgent warrant?" Palmer asked incredulously.

Woodruff just laughed. "Go ahead and try that; see how far you get. The clerk is meaner than snakes."

Chapter 63

6:00 PM EST - Six days before inauguration

Renae Hinckley strode into Madison's office as Andie Madsen was getting up to leave. Renae was juggling a lot of tasks as the inauguration deadline loomed, and her stress was showing. Because the outgoing administration was acting more obstructionist than ever, the peaceful handover of power was proving to be like a slow slog through molasses.

"Cluff's people are being idiots. None of the sitting cabinet members will respond to a meeting request, but I have responses back from some deputies and assistant deputies. We have sixteen meetings stacked back to back for the next three days. Sorry!" Renae sighed.

"Okay. The folks in the number two and three slots probably know what's going on better than the secretaries do anyway. Are any of them keepers?" Madison asked.

"Yes, I think so. My analysts have been reviewing the records of their selection processes. Several seem to be straight up good folks trying to do the best they can for us."

"Well, don't tell me who until after I've met each of them and formed my own impression." This was the way Madison usually worked with Renae when potential employees were presented to her.

"Got it." Renae laid personnel files down on Madison's desk. "Everything is set for the FBI Director's visit and the press briefing tomorrow morning. We'll hit them in the regular 9:30 update instead of giving them an early warning."

"Very good. I sent Andie off to work things out with metro-police so they can act at the same time you notify the press. She has excellent contacts over there. It seems she dated one of the lead detectives for about five minutes, and they're still friends."

Renae switched topics. "What about the Tyson jerks? They'll try to purge the evidence once this goes public."

"Tyson Security keeps everything in backup storage outside the blast ring at their own unmanned secondary data center way out in the gaps. I understand that a very civic-minded group will be preventing that purge." Madison smiled.

"That's so cool!" Renae clapped her hands and they both laughed, anticipating the coming events. The laughter was a welcome release from extraordinary pressures.

"Cheers to those intrepid civic-minded folks, but too bad about poor Roscoe and his friends," Madison said, and they laughed again.

Real Estate maps of Virginia were often printed with concentric rings extending out from D.C. proper. Each ring showed the proposed blast zone for various levels of attack on Washington D.C. and revealed the likely distance for safety. This morbid view of greater D.C. allowed enterprising real estate agents to say, "See, build your data center out here in Manassas, and you'll be safe when the terrorists blow up the politicians." The Tyson Security Backup Data Center was way out in the fringes of Southern Virginia, nestled among one of the gaps in the granite walls of the Blue Ridge Mountains.

"I'm going home now—I'm so looking forward to a quiet early dinner with Lucy and Auntie Jan. They got settled in today. Being with Lucy melts some of this stress away. But I don't get enough time with her," she said wistfully. "I sure hope she'll be okay."

Chapter 64

7:00 PM EST - Six days before inauguration

"How'd you score this intel?" David Maxtell asked his best research operative, Eddie Smyth. They were sitting in David's corner office of Tyson Security.

"With extreme luck," Eddie answered. "There's nothing…I mean *nothing* out in the online world that relates to DeCourcy. We can't track his cell phone because we have no clue what his number is. I've hacked every phone carrier I can…and no dice. He doesn't use any known internet service provider—but it turns out he *owns* one. It's the first ISP I haven't been able to hack. But I know that he travels and meets with various people. So I started looking at Google calendars for anybody in the big companies that he could possibly meet with. And bingo! The CEO of Jarrick-Mantle Petroleum scheduled lunch with T.T. DeCourcy for tomorrow at 12:30 in New York."

"Fantastic! When did this pop up? How do we know it wasn't planted by DeCourcy to expose anybody who goes after him?" Maxtell asked, happy but hesitant after Thomas Carlyle's Florida disaster.

"I considered that kind of crap. I found out that DeCourcy has lunch with this New York guy about every quarter. The actual date varies each time, and over the last two years the guy has scheduled the lunch only one or two days beforehand each time. So my gut says this is a legitimate, routinely scheduled lunch. I'll bet DeCourcy is clueless that his name is on a public calendar." Eddie's body language displayed total confidence—chest puffed out and chin extended.

"Great, Eddie. I'll take it from here. You get back to your other research items. I'll hit you with a sizable bonus for this."

"Yes! Thanks, boss."

David Maxtell went out to his car and drove away from the office before using his alternate phone to contact Landan Moss with the actionable intelligence. It was highly time sensitive, and he hoped Landan could put an effective team in play on short notice. There wasn't a convenient way to coordinate Landan's actions with whatever Roger Burgad was doing about getting leverage on DeCourcy. It would be nice to know what Burgad was up to, but Maxtell understood how important compartmentalization was. Even so, because of his tech and intelligence apparatus, Maxtell felt he had a better window into the other Brotherhood activities than any of his fellow members, except for Hancock, of course.

*   *   *

Landan Moss was on his way to visit Hancock when he took the call from David Maxtell telling him of the DeCourcy lunch tomorrow and instructing him to "handle it." *It'll be a tight schedule, but I can handle it, and Hancock will be so pleased…what great news from Maxtell!*

Landan decided to hold off going to see Hancock and deal with the opportunity ASAP. He could fill him in later. John wanted *results* in the DeCourcy project—and Landan wanted payback for Handy Nielsen.

Chapter 65

"Tell me why you want a new warrant to search the home of Karen Waldron's attorney?" the Honorable Katherine Covington asked FBI Special Agents Radisson and Palmer when they came into her chambers presenting the printed search warrant and practically demanding a signature. The new warrant included the details of the previous warrant: the addresses of DeCourcy offices and the house on Tight Squeeze Lane.

"We consider Karen Waldron a material witness, and she's hiding from us."

"What makes you think she's hiding from you?"

"It's obvious that she's hiding from us! We had her under surveillance in Portland until she and the man we assume is her attorney, Talbot DeCourcy, snuck away from our surveillance."

"Was she somehow under a court order to remain within the purview of your surveillance?"

"No, of course not, but we want to interview her again, and she's not made herself available."

"Is she under an obligation mandated by a federal judge to be at your disposal?" Kate asked and didn't wait for an answer. "Has she been presented with a valid subpoena?"

"No. We can't contact her to present a subpoena!" Radisson said, exasperated again. "Look, Your Honor, with all due respect, we consider her a material witness in the assassination of the president-elect—a crime committed by her husband, and we have every right to require her to be available for additional questioning."

"Oh, and have the FBI and the Secret Service concluded their investigation of the assassination? And have they definitively determined that Douglas Waldron is the assassin? Because I have to say," she paused, "that according to all the reports I've seen, your agency continues to call Mr. Waldron a 'deceased *suspect*' in the ongoing investigation."

"Of course the investigation is ongoing, but we all know that Doug Waldron killed Wilson Sarnoff on January 7th. There is absolutely no doubt."

"Really?" Kate smiled a little. "So to my original question: why this extraordinary action of seeking a search warrant for the residence of Ms. Waldron's attorney?"

"We believe he's harboring her," Radisson raised his voice a little—not a good approach in a federal judge's chambers.

"Harboring? Is she a fugitive from justice?"

"We have a material witness warrant. She hasn't responded."

"Have you informed her of the warrant?"

"We can't!"

"Have you tried to speak to her attorney, rather than simply showing up at his offices and home with some thinly disguised pretext of a warrant?"

"What are you talking about?" Radisson barked.

"Did you forget something in that question, Agent Radisson?" she snapped.

"Your Honor," Radisson said after a few beats of hesitation. He realized he had to get this under control.

"Agent Radisson, surely you realize that once Ms. Waldron engaged counsel, the proper course would be to contact her lawyer and request a conference with her. But instead of that course, as I understand the events, you burst into her attorney's office with a search warrant planning to tear the place apart, and then made a beeline to his corporate offices and his legal residential address."

"He played us and he's avoiding us."

"How on God's green earth do you know that? Have you tried to call him and ask?"

Radisson was speechless. He had no reasonable answer; he was so invested in the hunt and so angered by Karen Waldron slipping away from him—twice—that he hadn't stopped to consider *why* he was pursuing her, except on principle and on orders from Washington.

"Your Honor, we need to ask her more questions."

"Why is that? I understand she signed a detailed statement after many hours of intense interrogation by you and others."

"We don't believe everything she told us."

"Really? Can you present me with evidence that demonstrates reasonable doubt about anything she told you? Do you have something that would create probable cause for considering her a material witness to the crime currently under investigation?"

Radisson could say nothing. He had nothing.

Palmer jumped in. "Your Honor, the fact that she is hiding from us creates enough suspicion that she is hiding *something* she doesn't want us to know."

"Really, Agent Palmer? Perhaps you should consider the possibility that she's avoiding what she considers gross abuse of her civil rights by investigating agents, including massive electronic surveillance of her home without a proper warrant." Both agents sat stunned in silence. They knew better than to argue with a federal judge who obviously was not going to be persuaded. The FBI mystique was not working here.

"Not only am I refusing to sign your completely groundless search warrant for the home of an officer of the court, Ms. Waldron's attorney, but I also want you to listen carefully to the following. I have signed a court order—my clerk will provide you a courtesy copy—and I will forward the original to the director of the FBI. This said order proscribes you from seeking to intimidate the attorney,

Talbot DeCourcy, or from seeking to obtain additional warrants relating to Ms. Waldron, until and in such case new evidence is presented to a federal judge showing actual probable cause to question any part of Ms. Waldron's previously sworn statement. This order is in effect until the FBI formally concludes the investigation of Douglas Waldron and the Justice Department makes a final determination."

"Your Honor, we'll get this order overturned!" Radisson stood to exert physical dominance.

"Good luck with that! You'll need the minimum of a three-judge panel in one of the federal districts, or the Supreme Court of the United States." Kate smiled and waved her hand to dismiss the pair.

Ten minutes later the agents listened to their boss shouting at them over speaker phone as they drove away from the Spokane Federal Building and headed to the airport.

Chapter 66

January 15

9:30 AM EST - Five days before inauguration

Madison Hemsley-Tarlton sat with the FBI director and his executive assistant director over cybercrime. Initially, the briefing covered the general status of the FBI and a preview of classified issues on their hotlist.

Presently, she asked Renae to bring Luau into the meeting to give them a rundown on the data-hacking intrusion perpetrated by several American companies. The news caught the FBI leadership by surprise.

The director insisted that Madison not release the information to the public, "…so we can begin an effective investigation. This is already bad, and we want to get out in front of it."

"Director Hamilton, we've provided you with all the information you need to launch your investigation," Madison said. "You'll find that one of the accomplices, or even the key perpetrator of the data-theft, may be Eddie Smyth—an IT specialist who was working for the committee before I arrived in this position. Also, you may find that Arthur Messanger copied confidential material to his personal data servers offsite in violation of the terms of his employment."

"I understand, but respectfully, we need to keep this quiet so we can do our work without the press hounding us too soon."

"Well, Director Hamilton, I disagree. I have always had a policy of 'go ugly early!' When you discover a serious error, you destroy it quickly—like a thistle weed you've got to pull out by the roots—to eliminate the negative effects as much as possible. If it is my error, I take full responsibility and *move on*. To that end, my chief of staff is briefing the press pool right now at the daily update, and this issue is included. And so now our meeting is concluded, gentlemen. Good to see you; thanks for coming."

The FBI director and assistant director were offended that she had acted boldly without consulting them, but there was nothing they could do—this formidable woman was going to be their boss in five days.

*   *   *

Madison knew that DeCourcy had a team in the field taking down the Tyson Security Backup Data Center at this very moment. They would be cutting all fiber-optic and copper-line connections into the Data Center and knocking down satellite and microwave antennas. She assumed the team would take the power lines and generators offline before they breached the building but wasn't sure whether they would simply suck the data out of the servers or actually unbolt and physically confiscate them.

Technically, the attack on Tyson was an illegal act of a private citizen, but David Maxtell was colluding with corrupt government officials, and the stakes were extremely high in this brutal game of capture the government flag. The niceties of due process would have to wait on the sidelines for this contest to play out.

She had never met David Maxtell, but if he truly was one of the Brotherhood, she didn't envy him or his cronies, knowing how rigid Talbot was about miscreants once he decided what to do with them.

Chapter 67

8:00 AM PST - Five days before inauguration

Tristan DeCourcy was walking the short two blocks to his middle school. At the halfway point, he walked past a man in a jogging suit holding the leash of a handsome Belgian shepherd named Kazan. The man made brief eye contact with Tristan, but there was no outward acknowledgement between them. To an observer, it was a dog walker and a schoolboy passing each other on the sidewalk—two strangers sharing the neighborhood. In reality, Tristan and Kazan were the best of friends. The man was someone Tristan knew well, and he relied on that man and dog to keep him safe during his daily walk to school.

Kate Covington wanted Tristan and the other DeCourcy children to have normal social lives and go to regular schools filled with regular kids. She *didn't* want them associating exclusively with the entitled brats of other billionaires. Certainly, the children had tutors and all the advantages of excellent education, but they also needed to be part of common society relating to real people. This created a logistical conundrum for the family: how to keep the children safe during their "normal living" exposure.

While all the children attended public school until college, each DeCourcy child got the chance to get closer to *life as usual* during the middle school years. Now it was Tristan's turn. He was out the door of Courci Downs early each morning in plenty of time to reach a seemingly regular house in middle-class suburbia, and he liked the cozy, yellow house located on Thornton Drive, the same street as his school.

The Seth Henry Middle School principal was the only school administrator or staff member aware of the unusual residency and security arrangements. Kate's first priority was not to hide Tristan's family identity—although that was kept under wraps—but to help him blend in with his classmates and be treated the same as everyone else. None of that *snobby rich-kid* name calling for him.

The so-called "normal house" was occupied by a married couple—security employees of DeCourcy. When Kate and Talbot were occasionally out of town, Tristan would stay over at the normal house in a modified boarding school experience. Each week day, Security staff would supervise him as he ate breakfast and headed to school. At about the halfway point on his walk—calculated to be the maximum point of vulnerability—he would pass his dog-and-handler team. The dog, Kazan, was perfectly trained not to respond to Tristan in this working scenario, even though they were lovingly bonded. The dog would sacrifice his life in a heartbeat to keep his charge safe.

Other security team members, from both directions of the road, would casually drive past Tristan on his way to school—one car dispatched out of a security safe house two blocks north of the school, and the other, two blocks south of the "normal house." Both safe houses were on the same street as Tristan's fake-home. Functionally, an invisible security net covered Tristan, moving along with him as he made his way to and from school.

The first trouble report came in to Gideon-Overwatch at 10:30 AM and wasn't earthshaking—but tremors would soon rock Tristan's world.

Among key DeCourcy personnel, panic never took over; cool professional skills ruled Gene Artel's security apparatus. Artel listened calmly to the report on the Command Center speaker phone: "Overwatch, this is Gideon-4 Team Leader. We have unusual movement at Tristan's school. A Fed car with GI plates rolled up, and two suits are walking to the entrance. Seems benign, but something guts me wrong. Doesn't look right."

"Copy that, Gideon-4 Leader. Roll Red-4 and Blue-4 now, silent running," said Artel, taking the call directly when he heard his Gideon-Overwatch call sign invoked. "Survey-one, mirror the G-4 views at the school. Bring up everything." He was telling one of his monitoring operators to bring up a display with surveillance images from inside and outside Tristan's middle school.

Gene would see the same display that the Gideon-4 Team Leader saw, who responded from the safe house four blocks south of the school: "I'm on my way, also." The other two team members from the north safe house, designated "Red" and "Blue," scrambled to a pair of cars and raced to the school two blocks away.

Another of Artel's operators ran the government license plates for identification. They came back as legitimate plates from the Seattle FBI motor pool, but the cars carrying those plates were officially located inside a parking storage lot in Seattle, Washington. The operator then put in a call to both the local Spokane FBI Resident Office and the Seattle Field Office asking for information about the FBI agents approaching the school of a DeCourcy Security protectee.

The Gideon-3 Team called in a similar trouble report three minutes after the initial Gideon-4 report had come in. A fed car was approaching Lydia DeCourcy's high school, also. The car's plates came back same as the first.

"Okay, people, let's be cautious," Gene Artel instructed. "This may only be FBI pressure coming from Radisson's bruised ego, and maybe he's trying to get at Talbot through his kids. But as a precaution, roll teams to all Gideon schools *now*. Let's see where this goes. Message-out a security warning *system-wide*. Raise the alert level one notch to *Level-Three*, and look lively."

Thirteen-year-old Tristan DeCourcy felt the MW4 vibrate on his wrist and heard a quick set of tones sounding quietly in his ear. A message came through the tiny hollow earpiece he wore, and a digital-sounding voice whispered: "Tristan, alert level is raised to *Status-Three*. Please acknowledge." The message repeated as he reached to his left wrist to tap the MW4. Security-alert had been raised to *Level-Two* the day before when the family and all key personnel were instructed to put on their MW4 wristbands. Tristan heard a three-note tone respond to his tactile acknowledgement of the warning message.

Everyone who used an M3 device or an MW4 also possessed a supply of tiny, transparent conical ear inserts that were capable of pairing with the M devices and were invisible because they fit snuggly into the ear canal. They were hollow so that ambient sound wasn't blocked or distorted. The internal battery and chipset were practically molecular in size—a product of a DeCourcy tech company in Seattle called T3-DC-Nano.

The DeCourcy security organization used a set of protocols called "the Gideon System." All family members and their security teams had Gideon designations based on their age position in the family. Tristan and his team were designated "Gideon-4," while his mother was "Gideon-1." The DeCourcy security measures were not passive. Tristan and the others had trained regularly with their teams, building deep, long-term, life-and-death trust with them. Tristan had run through countless emergency scenarios in all imaginable types of places and weather. He had dropped out of helicopters and engaged in weeklong survival and evasion exercises. Closely bonded to his team, he knew they would risk their lives for him—just as he would for them.

Chapter 68

10:32 AM PST - Five days before inauguration

Two stocky men in suits entered Seth Henry Middle School and went straight to the office. They displayed official looking credentials, made their request, and were shown into a conference room to wait.

"Tristan, this is White. This is not a drill. Please listen." Tristan could hear his security team leader in his ear. "We have eyes on you and see that you're headed to the office. Acknowledge, please."

"Got you five by five, Whitey," Tristan said quietly.

"Tanny, two tangos, possible federal agents, are in the office waiting for you. We have eyes and ears on them. This is a wait-and-see situation until we know what's going on. They are suspect at this time, but they could be legit. Keep your egress options open. Red and Blue are inbound, twenty seconds out." The Gideon-4 Team Leader was reassuring, but his words carried the solid impact the situation demanded. Tanny (Tristan's nickname among the team since he was four years old) responded perfectly in keeping with his many hours of rigorous life-safety training. He remained calm and collected in a crisis. He was his father's son.

"Copy that, Whitey. I'll be mindful of the playground rules." Tanny entered the office and was directed to the conference room. He saw the principal and assistant principal sitting at the conference table waiting for him: the two stern-faced men were on the far side of the table, away from the door so they could see him enter. *The Feds must be idiots if they expect to grab me.* Obviously, they were underestimating their quarry. He stopped inside the door and said nothing.

"Tristan, come in and sit down, please. These two gentlemen are from the FBI. They need to talk to you," the principal said in his usual, friendly manner. The assistant principal glared at Tristan, assuming he was probably guilty of some crime, which squared with his personal bias toward "Tristan the Troublemaker." Tristan had never made any trouble, but the assistant principal imagined that his least favorite student was secretly at the bottom of many misdeeds at the school.

"Hey guys. I'm fine standing. What's up?"

"Are you Tristan DeCourcy?" the redhead asked.

"Yes, I am Talbot Tristan Thomas DeCourcy," Tristan shot back at them. "And who are you?"

"Our names don't concern you, we are taking..." the same man started.

"Whoa, cowboy. Let's slow down here a bit." Tristan held his left hand up to make sure the MW4 was getting good video. He knew the overhead camera was also taking this in. "Before we have any conversation whatsoever, may I trouble you for a look at your federal credentials?" He did not talk or act like a thirteen-year-old boy. He was a well-trained DeCourcy and was not a kid to be intimidated.

"Tristan!" the assistant principal snapped. "Mind your manners." There was a pregnant silence. Tristan ignored the yapping assistant principal.

"If you're representing yourselves as federal agents, you're obligated to present your credentials. If not, we're done."

"Sure," the redheaded mouthpiece hesitated and then nodded to his partner, and they both held up their creds. Tristan noticed that they absently pulled them out with their right, or strong hands. Both had watches on their left wrists. That was enough to convince him they were not really FBI agents, who were trained always to display creds with their weak hand, keeping the strong hand ready to access their weapons.

"I don't really read small print from fifteen feet away, so please slide them across the table." After hesitating, each man slid his credential wallet down the length of the table.

Tristan heard White in his ear: "Good job, Tristan. We're scanning them now. Go ahead and pick them up and take a look. Read the names out loud."

"So, Special Agents Jesse Francis and Owen Higgins, you are obviously not from the Spokane office. Where are you from?"

"That's none of your concern. Are you satisfied?" Agent Francis said as he caught the wallet Tristan tossed back to him.

"Running them now, Tanny. Keep it up. Go slow," White instructed. "Red and Blue are out of their cars and checking out the third guy, the driver waiting with the vehicle."

"What do you want?" Tanny said.

"We're here to take you downtown to the federal building for a discussion about your father and a material witness issue."

"Well, guys, you do realize that I'm an un-emancipated minor child, and you can't transport me, question me, or otherwise engage with me without supervision by my parent or legal counsel or a court-appointed advocate." Tristan smiled as he spoke to them, not condescendingly, but firmly. "I suppose I should call my attorney since my parents aren't likely to be available."

"No, that's not the way this works, junior." Higgins spoke up. "You will come with us now. You can make a call from our car on the way."

"I'm an eleventh, not a junior." Tristan spoke casually.

"What?"

"I'm Talbot Tristan Thomas DeCourcy XI, not junior. Don't you do your homework at the FBI?"

"Enough of that backtalk, we're…"

"Agent Higgins, do you have a custody warrant?" Tristan grinned.

While Tristan stalled, security headquarters was buzzing with feverish activity. Gene Artel's staffers determined that these guys were definitely not FBI but didn't know if they were Feds of a different stripe. It didn't matter. Even if they were real federal agents, they were committing a series of felonies—and Artel would not let it pass. Job one right now: *keep Tanny safe.*

"Tristan, urgent egress—stat. Front door on my count. Move to my car for exfiltration!" White ordered sharply. "Mark, 3, 2, 1, *go-go-go!*"

Tristan spun out the door, racing from the office to the front entrance of the school. He pushed through the entrance door and saw two things at once. In his peripheral vision he detected Red and Blue, with weapons raised, positioned on each side of the school's entrance.

Ahead of him he noticed a fed car with a man lying on the ground — his hands and feet flexi-cuffed beside the vehicle. Tristan sprinted toward the DeCourcy SUV positioned in front of the fed car. Behind him he heard the fake-feds slamming into the breaker-bar of the entrance door and crashing it open again.

It required all of his discipline not to look back over his shoulder, but as he flung himself through the opened passenger door of the SUV, he heard the pop of Tasers taking down the mock-feds bolting after him. White, behind the wheel, accelerated out the driveway, ignoring the school speed zone as they began the race to Courci Downs. Red's car was still parked on the street ready for rapid egress. After Red and Blue secured the phonies alongside their cohort, they called 911 to report the incident. Red remained behind to deal with the police while Blue jumped into his vehicle and caught up to White as they continued the extraction.

*   *   *

At Lydia DeCourcy's school, Dale Arthur High, things were similarly different. The three pseudo-feds were slower to the party, and the G-3 Leader moved his team as soon as he heard of G-4's fakes. The DeCourcy Gideon-3 Team roared into the school drop-off area, taking down the tangos before they entered the school. The team trussed up three hogs and made another 911 call less than a minute after Tristan's G-4 team had called from Seth Henry Middle School.

At the Marion Nelson Elementary School where nine-year-old Eddy (Gideon-5) attended, G-5 White, Blue, and Red arrived before the faux-fed car showed up, extracting Eddy without incident.

The children were hustled back to the castle — no casualties.

Chapter 69

Kate Covington had just begun the drive to downtown when she felt the security-alert update on her MW4. Two minutes later as she exited the six-mile long private parkway, her earpiece came alive.

"Gideon-One, Kate, this is Gideon-Overwatch. Please return to Castle Keep, *stat*!" Gene's voice was calm but emphatic. Kate responded to training without question.

"Copy that, Overwatch. I'm turning around." She braked to a rapid stop and checked her mirrors, then spinning into a power reverse U-turn, headed for home. Suddenly, in her mirrors she noticed SUVs racing up behind her. "Overwatch, I'm on return, but I have multiple SUVs rolling fast on my six—no flashing lights, Gene."

"Copy that, Kate. Move with all safe haste. If they catch you, stay in control of the vehicle—don't let them PIT you—stop and defend in place. We're on the way."

Everything was happening at light speed. Overwatch (Gene Artel) didn't need to give the order to deploy. Three security cars were already rushing to intercept Kate—two came from the gatehouse three miles down the parkway, and one, currently patrolling the parkway, was a mile away from her.

"Launch the ballistic drone, Aero-One. Send Gideon-1 Team with double backup. *This is going down on the grounds!*" Gene ordered.

An operator immediately hit a red mushroom-button designated "Aero-One" on a console. It blasted a sabot-encased projectile shaped like an artillery shell out of a high-pressure, pneumatic launch tube. In less than a quarter second, the hydrazine jet in the projectile kicked in, accelerating the unit's speed to 210 miles per hour. It tracked the position of Gideon-One (Kate Covington) via

GPS and was over her location in seventeen seconds, even though she was three miles from Security Headquarters as the crow flies. The drone descended, shucking off its sabot encasement and unfolding, becoming a fast, stable camera platform guided by a DeCourcy team operator.

While Kate watched the SUVs in her mirrors, they sandwiched her in. She knew it was safer to come to a stop rather than possibly careen off the roadway. She took her foot off the accelerator and held the wheel steady as the car slowed down.

"Overwatch, I'm being forced to stop. Please advise," Kate said, trying not to sound panicked.

"Copy that, Kate. We're on the way. Follow defend-in-place protocols, and smile all the while."

Kate almost *wanted* to smile at Gene. She knew everyone was doing all they could to help her. She wondered about her family...but knew Gene wouldn't tell her anything because he wanted her full attention on her own dire situation right now. Once she was stopped, she saw men emerging from the other vehicles, pointing weapons and shouting for her to get out of the car. No worries. She knew that the windows and armored roof and doors would withstand moderately heavy-arms fire. This had to be a kidnapping, not a hit. She followed procedure.

"Good job, Kate. I see that you blacked-out the windows," Gene said in her ear. "Eye-in-the-sky is on its way. We'll see you from above in about six seconds. We have good views now from the car's cameras. We see six tangos, small arms only—nothing that will penetrate. Stay calm, boss. Put on your eyes and ears and hit the switch."

Calming herself, Kate reached into the center console. She extracted a pair of full-cover ear defenders with noise control and integrated eye shields. Once the ears were on snug and the eye covers tight, she hit the hot-switch inside the console and clamped her hands over her ears. She could feel Gene Artel with her, knowing he was seeing everything she was doing from his work station.

The men outside the car were suddenly hit with ear-shattering shrieking—at over two hundred decibels—and lights strobing at a frequency that would cause disorientation and possibly induce seizures. The effect was instant and devastating. The three men closest to the car went down trying to cover their ears. Two others went into grand mal seizures, and the sixth was far enough away that he almost maintained his equilibrium. As the first DeCourcy security team arrived, the last tango standing tried to open up on the superior force and was shot dead by Gene's operatives.

After the men on the ground were secured and handcuffed, Gene remotely killed the noise and lights, and Kate and her security team removed their eye/ear protectors. When told about the attempts to take her children, Kate swore a few fierce oaths before getting back into the car and asking to be driven immediately to the Command Center. She called her clerk to cancel court for the day. Although deeply shaken, she was grateful that the family's security forces were so well prepared and perfect at their jobs.

At the underground Security Command Center, Gene Artel called Special Agent Woodruff of the FBI Spokane Office, explaining details of the school attacks and the rescue of each DeCourcy. He did not mention, however, the attack on a sitting appellate court justice. That bit of business happened on DeCourcy property, and like the Florida escapade, would be handled without official notification. It had been a harrowing day, but on the bright side: Gene had five more prisoners to interview and one more body for the cooler—more guests for the Quarry.

Chapter 70

10:40 AM PST - Five days before inauguration

The crisis was not over. At the same moment Kate had come under attack, Gene had signaled a *Max-Gideon-Alert Condition*, which meant that DeCourcy Security personnel worldwide went on full defensive status and began reporting in to their section chiefs, who in turn boiled up reports to Artel.

Eight minutes earlier, Olivia Covington-DeCourcy, a junior at Stanford, had felt the vibration of the raised-alert level on her wristband and had heard three tones in her ear signaling *Alert-Level-Three*. She had acknowledged by tapping her MW4 as she exited the psych building and walked across the Stanford Oval with her friend, Lisa Tomlinson.

Now as the *Max-Gideon-Alert* came, Olivia stopped dead and spun around to take in her situation, aware that she was about one mile from her security safe house off campus. Through her earpiece she listened to her Gideon-2 Team Leader announcing the Aero-Two drone launch.

She heard White relay: "Red and Blue are on the fly, Overwatch. ETA two minutes. Do you copy that, Gideon-2?" *Obviously not a drill,* she thought, her pulse quickening.

"Copy that, White. I see three suits. Definitely out of place. They've locked on to me. Two are about 100 meters behind me in a thin crowd. The other one is straight ahead of me." She went instantly into Gideon mode, responding to years of training. She turned to her friend. "Lisa, listen to me. Three guys are coming to try and grab me."

"What are you…?" Lisa gaped in disbelief.

"Shut up, Lisa. No questions. This is real serious! They only want *me*, so you have to run. Now! See that crowd by Wallenberg Hall? Go! Just *run*. I mean it!"

"But, no, you can't..."

"Lisa, *go! Go now!*" She shouted at her and gave her a shove. Spinning around again, Olivia jogged in the direction of the one tango straight ahead. This was a public place, after all, and there was still time to be civil. She ran in the direction that would put her near the closest road. Suppressing her panic, she controlled her breathing. *I've trained my whole life for this.*

The ballistic drone slowed down to deploy the copter blades and stabilize the camera feeds. It was directly overhead, guided by Olivia's MW4 GPS signal. White could see Olivia and track the attackers coming her way.

"Gideon-2, Timber, do you copy?" White, the Gideon Two Team Leader, used her childhood nickname. All of her security team called her "Timber." They had been with her for eleven years and were a tight unit. She loved them intensely and they her.

"I copy, White." Timber spoke clearly. "I see three, and I'm moving in the direction of the lonely one."

"Copy that, Timber. We have eyes above you, and your MW4 is broadcasting five-by-five. Red and Blue are forty-five seconds out. They'll scream right up onto the Oval. Can you avoid this guy?"

"Negative, White. He's on my vector."

"Copy that, Timber. Do it by the numbers."

Timber moved toward the single attacker, putting greater distance between herself and the other two. As she approached the suit, he held aloft a badge wallet and shouted for her to stop.

"I'm a federal agent, and I just need to talk to you."

She slowed a little as she drew close, saying nothing and moving to pass him on his left. He lunged for her. He was bigger and stronger than she was, but she carried momentum. She seized his wrist while moving, spun under his arm, and hip-threw him without loosening her two-handed grip on his wrist. When she twisted his arm, she heard his pained scream and his shoulder pop as it dislocated. Taking him to the ground, she kicked him in the side of the head and the groin. *This is more than martial arts practice—this is my life!*

Her attacker tried to take his handgun out of the shoulder holster, but Olivia snatched it as she heard White shout in her ear, "Move to the right, Timber. *Move right!*" She dove over the man, heard a gunshot as she rolled, and came up on one knee. She saw the shooter behind her trying to reacquire his target as his companion also drew his weapon. Using the just-acquired weapon, she shot the gunman twice in the torso and then managed to hit the other one in the shoulder before he could fire, and he dove down to the ground. She jumped up, ran fifteen yards back to her attackers, and kicked their guns away.

Chest-shot-guy was wearing a vest and moaning. Without hesitation, she kicked him in the head and stomped on the other guy's wounded shoulder. He passed out. Fieldstripping all three weapons, she threw them far from the tangos and turned to see Blue slewing his car across the grass. When he pulled to a stop, the passenger door flew open and she dove in.

In the near distance, some onlookers were screaming, some were silently stunned, and many pointed camera phones at Olivia from all around the Oval. Lisa Tomlinson watched in horror. Blue and Timber spun out of there, bouncing over the curb and veering sharply onto the roadway. Red raced up, slowed down to check out the scene, then hot-footed it as he followed Blue back to the safe house.

From the safe house, White first reported the whole event series to Gene Artel, then called the local Police, FBI, and Stanford Campus Security, telling them that unknown assailants had made an attempt on Olivia Covington-DeCourcy's life and she was now in protective custody. DeCourcy lawyers were already on their way to the various agencies to get in front of any misunderstandings.

"But she can't leave the scene!" the local police captain said. "We've got three wounded men, two of them GSWs. They're assumed to be federal agents. In spite of the fact that you say otherwise, it hasn't been confirmed that they're imposters."

"If they're not imposters, then you've got an even bigger problem, because *if* they're really federal agents, they tried to kidnap my protectee at gunpoint. I'm sending you a video of the whole thing right now, and our lawyers will be there soon to cover the details. Ms. Covington-DeCourcy will provide a statement within the hour, and she'll fully cooperate with the official investigation," White explained patiently.

White then called the San Francisco Bay Area FBI. The special agent in charge said: "The local cops are hollering to have her in custody. Let me look at your video file. I'll call you back."

White relayed these conversations to Gene Artel while they waited for the local FBI to scramble and get a handle on things.

*   *   *

A thousand miles to the north at Courci Downs, Kate Covington was outwardly controlled but inwardly raging about the attacks on her children. Before going home she asked her driver to stop at the gatehouse, and as she made her way to the underground Command Center, she listened on her M3 to Gene Artel's full report of the attempts on each of her children and the security staff's responses.

"Everyone is completely secure," Gene reassured her. "Everybody did their jobs with precision, and the kids performed like machines. These guys took a huge risk, and they *100 percent* failed. Kate, our system worked. You're okay."

"Thank you, Gene. Thanks to everybody in your organization. No one could ask for better people. I would like to review the video."

"Of course, Kate."

"See you in a minute, Gene. There's going to be some serious fallout over this. I know that Tally wants to move carefully against these Brotherhood thugs, but I am personally going to castrate those bastards!"

Kate Covington was ready to wage war.

Chapter 71

10:44 AM PST - Five days before inauguration

Kate was anxious to reassure and comfort her children—to hold her babies. But because she was still in mother-lioness mode, she focused on her yoga breathing as she strode purposefully into the Command Center. Artel was on the line with Olivia, and looking up at Kate, he almost feared for the fate of the jackals who had attacked her cubs.

"Your mom's here. Just a second—she has to retract her claws," Gene said with a wink, holding the phone out to Kate.

"Mom, are you okay? Gene was telling me about your att…" Olivia began, speaking loud and fast, still amped up from the excitement.

"Olivia, honey, are *you* okay?" Kate cut in. "Forget about me. Gene said you had to shoot people! Are you hurt? Are you at the safe house?"

"Mom, it was so crazy; you should've seen it. They came at me so fast, but my training just kicked in. I never thought I'd ever use all that judo stuff."

"I'm so proud of you, Livy…and so relieved you're safe."

"Um, I just realized, you'll see it on the drone views, right?" Olivia wanted her mom to see her awesome moves.

"I'll see it in about two minutes after I speak to the other kids. Love you."

Kate understood what her daughter was feeling. When Olivia was three years old, Kate had also pulled the trigger on attackers: a Triad gang had come after Talbot by trying to kill his family. On that horrific night in Seattle when Talbot was out of town, she and her little ones—Lydia was just a baby—had escaped three RPGs fired into their house. The family was on the second floor when the rockets exploded, and because the structure was reinforced, they survived by going out a window and making a run for the backwoods. As two Chinese hitmen tried to grab her, Kate shot them both at point-blank range. She knew killing was a terrible act, even when justified, and it was hard to bear the emotional cost of it. She still felt that cost sometimes. The shooters of the rockets in the front yard had slipped away and survived three whole days before Talbot tracked them down. They put up enough struggle that they didn't live to face juris prudence.

Kate called Tanny next as he and his siblings were on their way back to Courci Downs. "Tristan, I hear you had some excitement. Gene tells me you're a rock star."

"It was so cool, Mom! Red wants to call me Captain America from now on!" He was thrilled and adrenalized. "I really got to use my training." One excited boy.

"Big rush, huh, Tanny?"

"Oh yeah!"

"I'm so proud of you, my man. Love you. Talk to you soon."

When she spoke to her husband, she was trembling with anger. And she was resolved. "The stakes are off the chart now, Tally." She was keenly aware of the risks to both her family and the country, and although the family had recently taken fifteen enemy soldiers off the field, she urgently wanted to go after the generals now. "It's time to step up our game—take the battle to the dirt-bags. Make them pay. I want some of their big boys to go down. *Nobody messes with my kids!*"

"You're right," Talbot agreed. "Whichever Brotherhood member ordered the attacks is going to be toast *very soon*. Uh, Gene has something to tell you. I'll call you back in a minute."

When Talbot said "something to tell you," she felt a mounting sense of dread. She knew it would be important.

*   *   *

Gene Artel's crew set to work getting information from the men captured on the road to Courci Downs. The interrogation began even as the combatants were strapped in on Talbot's jet flying to the Quarry in West Virginia. But these surviving combatants were tough and resisted spilling anything—they were confident, at least this early in the process, that their employer would rescue them. After all, they were positive that this DeCourcy guy was no match for the power of the man they served.

Gene's technical wizards tracked the calls from each of the six phones they'd retrieved from the counter-assault on Courci Downs Parkway. It became clear that the one man killed in the group was the team leader, and his phone was the only one showing recent calls to an individual outside the team. They quickly cross-referenced call locations and identified a primary location.

A name would soon emerge from their search.

Chapter 72

Before all the action out west, Talbot DeCourcy was enjoying a relaxing lunch with the CEO of Jarrick-Mantle Petroleum despite the hoity-toity climate of the nameless French restaurant half-a-block off Times Square. The exclusive establishment only allowed approved patrons with established billing accounts. No prices appeared on the menus, and the pretentious diners would never be crass enough to ask. One simply acknowledged the final bill—delivered in a Moroccan leather folder—and handed it back to the waiter. Even the tip was an assumed amount.

DeCourcy received the *Alert-Level-Three* notice as he stepped from the warmth of restaurant onto the sidewalk and into New York's frigid winter air. He appeared unconcerned as he walked but was hyperaware of everything around him. A dark-haired, olive-skinned young woman, dressed too skimpily for the weather, walked toward him. As she neared Talbot, she dropped her phone and bent over to retrieve it, displaying plenty of cleavage and thigh. He sensed threatening movement in his periphery, and as he smoothly took a step backward, two pairs of rough hands from behind his right and left shoulders shot out to grab his arms. Thrusting his arms forward, he windmilled the persons back over his head. The bodies attached to the grabbing hands continued moving forward when he stopped his own momentum and stepped further back. He caught both gorillas by the hair and slammed their faces hard into each other.

Because the two were not quick-thinkers, they couldn't understand, let alone prevent, what was happening. Pain paralyzed them. A sedan rolled up to the curb, and as the back-passenger door flew open, Talbot steered the attackers' forward motion toward the car, sending the two thugs sprawling into the back seat. He heard curses and shocked exclamations in Armenian. Three quick gun shots followed. The vehicle slowly rolled forward after the dead driver's foot came off the brake pedal, and the car nudged firmly to the curb but did not jump the sidewalk.

Talbot straightened his jacket and peered into the car. The shooter in the back seat had accidentally fired his automatic pistol at his own men, including the driver who was tangled among the bodies of his partners and was unable to extricate himself or his weapon in the moments before police officers converged on the car. As the cops were shouting and aiming weapons, the shooter raised his gun hand and dropped his weapon through the window onto the street. The girl, the distraction, was long gone. After scanning the milling crowd for additional active threats, Talbot quietly conversed with Gene Artel and his own local security team via his M3. He told Red and Blue to hold back and wait.

Within minutes, the crime scene became a complete zoo: coroner, medics, crime-scene techs, police captains, press vultures and FBI all present in the boisterous fray. Someone finally had the good sense to cut the car's engine. Talbot stood with his back to a building, his eyes moving over the assemblage while detectives incessantly asked questions and witnesses rendered confused and conflicting accounts of the attack.

DeCourcy kept his line open with Gene Artel. As soon as he was momentarily free of police questioning, he asked Gene for more details of the attacks on his family, then said: "Hey, is Kate right there? Please give her a minimal account of the Armenian attack after I've spoken to her."

Talbot conversed with his wife briefly, ending with: "Gene has something to tell you. I'll call you back in a minute." The police wanted to hammer him again.

The next time he called the Command Center, she came on the line, her voice shaky: "We're all safe, and I'm so proud of Tanny and Livy—they did everything perfectly. But they tried to get you, too? Tally, I'm mad as a grizzly!"

Talbot downplayed his own experience as a typical New York sidewalk misunderstanding: "You know, a little bump and shove among guys—no big deal, honey."

"What about the shooting?"

"The shooting? Uh, Armenians and guns—bad combination every time..."

"You sure you're alright?"

"Sure, I'm sure. The cops are back again."

"I'll see what I can do," Kate said, ending the call to tend to her brood's emotional needs.

The NYPD detective briefed his captain when she arrived on the scene. "We got two dead Armos and one wounded in the neck" he said, using a typical slur for Armenian nationals, "...apparently shot by the dunce in the backseat."

"We thinkin' Rabiz?" the dour police captain asked, suggesting Armenian mob connections.

"Sure, makes sense. We rustled a translator from a deli down the block, but the shooter's lips are glued tight and he ain't said squat," the detective reported. "He was cursing about his pain when we put him in the bus."

The confusion and urgency morphed into a hostile barrage aimed at Talbot. The lead detective, taking cues from his captain, assaulted Talbot with accusations and blame. "It sure looks to me like you're maybe tied in somehow with these Armos. You owing them money, maybe? After all, you shoved the two guys that got shot into the car." *Obviously, it must be his fault that someone made a mess of trying to snatch him off the street*, the detective thought.

Talbot remained stoic and would not repeat an answer once he had given it; no matter what was shouted at him, he casually, quietly remarked that he had already answered that question. He would not be rattled or rushed. Talbot DeCourcy refused to be intimidated.

The FBI in the person of Special Agent Radisson glared over at DeCourcy, demanding to take jurisdiction in the interest of national security. Agent Palmer assisted him. Talbot smiled at Radisson each time their eyes met. It really irked Radisson: the subject of his search, his prey, was right here almost within arm's reach—but the NYPD would not back down. Talbot was amused that Radisson was here in New York, coincidentally in place and able to respond to the attempted kidnapping, or at least try.

"Agent Radisson, you're going to back off right now. This is an NYPD issue. There's no plausible national security angle here!" The NYPD captain punctuated her words with spittle and a poking finger. "You have no reason to be here, so back off, or I will arrest you right here, right now!"

"We're taking this man into custody for other reasons," Radisson shouted.

Two burly Irish cops from the precinct stepped in and blocked Radisson and Palmer. No mistaking their message—the FBI agents were not coming any closer.

The NYPD Captain answered her phone and instantly stood at attention. "Yes, sir. I understand, sir." As the captain rang off, she looked out to the street. A black SUV pulled up, avoiding the oddly parked radio and command cars. Three men exited the vehicle, two bearing MP5 Heckler & Koch submachine guns. The cops went on instant alert, but the captain signaled the okay to her officers. Everyone parted, making a path for one of the new arrivals who stepped up to DeCourcy with a clipboard. Talbot took it, along with a proffered pen, and signed the document on the clipboard. He peeled off the document and handed it to the police captain, who, in turn, nodded back at Talbot and offered a conciliatory hand. Talbot inclined his head, accepting the gesture in silent acknowledgement, then stepped past the cops and into the recently arrived SUV. The men with weapons followed him into the car, and a wild cacophony of angry voices rose in their wake.

The captain's caller was the New York City Police Commissioner, who had received a video-email showing the attack on Talbot in high definition taken from several security cameras in the surrounding area. A certain federal judge had called in a favor from her friend, the commissioner; and the billionaire, Talbot DeCourcy, agreed to provide a written statement and cooperate fully with any and all investigations.

The certain federal judge had also asked that the NYPD give kind, quiet regards to the FBI—especially Agent Radisson.

Chapter 73

2:00 PM PST - Five days before inauguration

Kidnapping attempts on three children of a federal judge created quite a stir. At DeCourcy Command Center, Gene Artel spent hours on the phone with local and federal law enforcement. He answered questions and encouraged a comprehensive investigation but didn't mention the violent attempt on Kate herself, in compliance with Talbot's strict imperative to keep that information DeCourcy-private. They took care of things on their own turf; moreover, withholding from the Feds would help smoke out the Brotherhood's mole at the FBI.

The Bureau was indignant about the fake federal agents in California and the imposters using Seattle Field Office cars. Phones lit up all over the place; agents were on the move. In combining the investigation of Talbot's attack with those of his children, they were confused by the difference in styles—men posing as federal agents attacking the kids, but Armenian thugs strong-arming Talbot on the street.

The Bureau dispatched dozens of agents in New York, Palo Alto, and Spokane. Frequent memos filtered up to top echelons. Even the Director was regularly read-in on the investigation. In the Hoover Building, one person was paying uncommonly close attention to every detail.

It was time for a phone call. "Carlyle, it's been one spectacular screw-up after another. Where'd you find these clods?" The Brotherhood's FBI source was anxious and angry. "This better not come back on me!"

"How could it? You're clean. We compartmentalize for a reason." Thomas Carlyle sought to keep his legendary temper in check so that he could mollify this pompous FBI asset. "The guys in Florida were mine, and I haven't heard anything out of them since it went down. I presume they're dead. If the Feds had them, you'd know, right?"

"Damn right I would."

"And you would tell me, right?" Carlyle had his doubts about this ambitious informant. "The snatch teams that got caught in Palo Alto and Spokane and New York weren't mine. They belonged to somebody else, so nothing's gonna come back on me *or* you. But I agree—somebody's made a royal mess."

"For what it's worth, all of them have lawyered up, and they haven't said a word to the cops or the FBI during interrogations," the informant said.

That's the only good news this ass of an asset has to offer, Carlyle thought, while he said: "They're pros. We'll plan a way to extract them at the right time. Have you heard anything about the missing team, the one that went after Kate Covington in Spokane?"

"No way! You had a team that didn't get themselves arrested?" He was incredulous. "Trying to take a federal judge…are you guys completely crazy?"

"We needed leverage. Your so-called super agent Radisson has gotten zip on Waldron, and we need her," Carlyle lamented. "But it's obvious. Our missing team in Spokane is like my team that vanished in Florida."

"One thing is clear—this DeCourcy guy doesn't mess around!"

"I'm afraid you're right about that. I'm going to enjoy destroying him more than you know." Carlyle paused, then expelled a heavy breath. "So, two questions remain: what can you do to squeeze DeCourcy, and have you found any link between him and Tarlton?"

"Simple answers, no and no."

"What the hell use *are* you?" Thomas Carlyle ended the call and threw his phone across the room. He knew his asset expected to be named the next FBI director in return for his help. *Fat chance of that!*

Carlyle also knew that because DeCourcy had initiated the uproar that ruined President Cluff's re-election bid, Leon Fuller had tried to marginalize DeCourcy the previous summer by creating phony charges and getting a grand jury started. Leon had also attempted to freeze DeCourcy's assets on some pretext. But Talbot seemed to be coated in Teflon and wriggled out of the traps Leon set, blocking each attempt before it got out of the gate.

Thomas Carlyle harbored his own reason for hating DeCourcy: a clear memory of a humiliating broken arm in a Palo Alto restaurant thirty years ago. Compliments of DeCourcy. In light of the recent defeat of his Florida hit-team, he was never going to underestimate the man again—and would *really* enjoy destroying him.

Chapter 74

January 16

6:00 PM EST - Four days before inauguration

The Brotherhood was frustrated but still confident knowing their larger goals remained on track. True, they had no leverage to bring the assassin's wife out of hiding and silence her, yet nothing she might be privy to had leaked out, causing them to consider that she was not a real threat. The same was not true of Talbot DeCourcy; Roger Burgad and Landan Moss's attempts on the DeCourcy family had failed miserably. He was proving a sore thorn indeed.

As the Brotherhood were gathered in a secret location, John Hancock addressed them: "Brethren, we must keep our minds riveted on our master plan, and we need not be distracted by these little annoyances. They are the expected flotsam and jetsam knocking against the great bow of the New American Ship as we steam through the present sludge to the glorious future. DeCourcy and the others haven't a clue of the force they face. We will wash them away in our wake.

"Individuals in this grand scheme are mere threads of color, not the whole tapestry. We are reweaving the history of our country into a new design of brilliant hues, for, unfortunately, this once great nation has become a worn rag." Hancock spoke with fierce intensity. "We are the agents of America's resurrection. The weakness that is now the United States will be transformed into power of almost inconceivable proportions!" His fevered pitch inspired his band. "Our next steps in the Mexican operation will put enormous pressure on the new president, and she—in her inexperience—will be overwhelmed. You who will be serving in her cabinet will guide the events as they unfold. You will coax her into actions that will alienate her from the entire country, and even average Americans will see that a change must come."

Clapping and a brief smattering of cheers came from the group. "We have designed the New America and soon will implement its government, creating the most fearsome world super power the earth has ever known. The guise of the American nice guy is over. As we demand compliance from other nations, they will beg at our feet. They must fear us in order to honor us. We'll not merely trade and give advantages to partners; we will command and we will take.

"*It is time.* Let us recommit ourselves and our sacred honor to this endeavor—to our great cause. It has been a long time, thirty years, since we last joined in this rite. Now, on the eve of our ascendency, let us again swear loyalty to each other and to our great mission!" The applause was now steady and sustained. His speech was over, and after the toast, conversation resumed.

*   *   *

Forty years earlier, the man calling himself John Hancock had researched cults and secret societies, which provided him with insights that later formed the skeleton of his recruitment plan. His best example in modern times came from Adolf Hitler, who charmed and corrupted intelligent men. John discovered that building extreme loyalty in fanatical devotees was a long process of seduction and testing. He couldn't expect a few speeches and rounds of oath-taking to cement his Brotherhood band with unbreakable bonds.

Hancock led his budding young sociopaths through experiences built on mysticism and escalating levels of depravity. Over time, they sampled and then embraced degrading acts of violence. When Hancock was confident they were ready, he revealed a traitor in their group—an unlucky recruit that had been selected from the beginning to play the Judas role. The others willingly joined in exacting punishment, killing in unison for the first time. This forever bound them together in bloodletting. Soon after, he led them through the first commitment ritual, further sealing their loyalty to each other and the cause.

The second ritual began today.

*   *   *

After much drinking, the Brotherhood stood from their table and entered the chamber prepared for the recommitment ceremony. Candles were arrayed around an otherwise darkened room.

Sufficiently intoxicated, the middle-aged men now possessed enough courage to repeat the sacrifices they had made as young men thirty years before. John Hancock swept his arms before him and revealed four heavily drugged young women tied to low, silk-draped tables. When he sounded a small gong, the men shouted their blood oaths and committed their acts of violence.

When the heinous acts were done, the men washed and went back to the table.

"Brothers, it is time once again for our final recommitment to each other and to our cause. Please open the boxes in front of you."

Hancock spoke as he walked a circuit of the room. Each man solemnly opened his own hand-carved ebony box. Inside eleven of the boxes lay an ivory-handled, curved dagger made of gleaming Damascus steel. Each weapon was individually decorated with intricate carvings reflecting the personality and history of its owner. Hancock came to a stop behind Merritt Angstrom's chair, the last man to join the Brotherhood. He had missed the previous commitment ceremony.

Merritt Angstrom's box contained no dagger. He stared down, perplexed, at a white feather with a gilded quill. Hancock rested his palms on Merritt's shoulders and spoke.

"Merritt was the final brother to join us all those years ago. He has broken bread with us many times, and now he has broken our trust." Merritt stiffened, his face morphing from a mask of solemnity to a rictus of fear. "Merritt has feathered his nest with hundreds of millions of our sacred funds. He has chosen to hedge against us, believing we will fail. Merritt, take your feather—the symbol of your betrayal—and stand."

Merritt Angstrom stood shakily with his white feather and opened his mouth to protest, but his words failed. He turned to face Hancock. The rest of the brothers stood as well, grasping their beloved daggers with smiles of grim determination on their lips.

After the ceremony was complete, the Brotherhood members washed the sticky blood from their hands and sat and drank more wine—some to forget and inwardly deny what they had done—most to celebrate their fervent zeal. All were fanatically committed to their doctrine. No going back for any of them.

Chapter 75

"Seems like the quietest day in a while, Tally," Kate said, her brows raised and her mouth turned up in an ironic smile as they tried to relax on the couch and enjoy the foot-rubbing ritual. "No attempted killings or kidnappings today. How'd we get so lucky?" She closed her eyes and sighed. "Ah, I'm in heaven."

Talbot smiled at her, deciding it was time to switch to her other foot.

"And it's nice having everybody home—nobody shooting at anybody for a change," she mused.

"What's that Kate Hepburn line? 'What family doesn't have its little ups and downs?' At least in our case, we aren't trying to kill each *other*," Talbot responded. "Gene's nailed down the owner of the phone that the snatch-orders came from."

"I tell you I'm in heaven, so you drag me down to hell?" she said, opening her eyes. "Alright, who's the soon-to-be eunuch?" Her rage was still simmering below the surface. "Have they taken him into custody yet?"

"Our people accessed data from the cell towers, and the GPS locators are definitive. It was Roger Burgad's phone, the guy who thinks he's going to be the next secretary of state."

"That S.O.B.! He's a smarmy little snake. What've you got planned for him?"

"He will pay dearly. We've also got evidence that he's been collaborating with David Maxtell, the goon behind Tyson Security. I'll be exacting some serious recompense on that duo—and this is off the record, Your Honor," he said, winking at her. "But I need to wait until things play out with the inauguration."

"How is Madison coping with all this?"

"As well as one could hope, considering the historic implications." Talbot leaned his head back and closed his eyes. "I've been predicting this crisis most of my adult life, but it still feels surreal now that it's here. We're in the middle of a monstrous sea-change."

"Don't blame yourself, darling, just because you practically gave Hancock the blueprint doesn't make it *all* your fault," she teased.

"Yeah, well, I wouldn't have wanted him to blunder around with trial and error, after all."

She looked at him closely. He was so weary. "Still, your pet theory is so right on—our government rebooting every eighty years, especially the consistency of the cycle. But it's a little unfortunate that those detestables are ready to take the helm this time around. I'd like to reboot *them* out of existence." Kate was trying to stay engaged but was beginning to drift into sleepiness.

She listened as Talbot echoed the Fifth Republic thesis he'd recited so many times. "My worry is the escalating severity of the shift—and the slope of factors. It'll make the changes much harder to stabilize." He shook his head. "Hancock is so arrogant. He thinks he can control the outcome, not just kickstart the motor into action. And he's very much mistaken."

"I know, I know. 'No one can predict the future outcome of events once they've begun.'" Kate softly murmured one of Talbot's mantras—as she slid into slumber.

*   *   *

Talbot Tristan Thomas DeCourcy X watched his wife fondly as he slid into memory. The lights were low, and he listened to the winter winds gusting through the ponderosas. He reflected on the major factors and events of his life—how they had led him to this moment in American history.

His colonial ancestors had arrived in Virginia and Maryland in the 1630's. They and the generations following them helped forge the strengths and goodness of this nation. Talbot, coming from a long line of nation builders, was proud of his ancestors and their legacy: the commitment to duty, honor, country. His eyes moistened as he contemplated his heritage—all he had. All he had lost.

He allowed his thoughts to drift back to that pivotal night in July thirty-six years ago. As a fifteen-year-old boy, he had come home around dusk to the family's Idaho wilderness cabin. His muscles ached from five days of strenuous whitewater rafting on the wildest parts of the Selway River with his scout troop, and he was dropped off at the obscure driveway entrance to the DeCourcy land. All was quiet and peaceful. Young Tally felt tired from carrying his heavy pack, but he was contented. Heading home, he rehearsed aloud the Robert Service poem he had learned on the trip: "There are strange things done in the midnight sun by the men who moil for gold…" He planned to spook his little sisters with the ghostly story. "The artic trails have their secret tales that would make your blood run cold…" He walked the nearly mile-long driveway before he had a warning of trouble ahead—with a hundred yards and one sweeping bend in the drive still to go, he heard shouts, screams, and a series of gunshots.

Tally dropped his pack and sprinted ahead. Fifty yards from the cabin where the trees thinned out, he left the driveway and reached a large tree stump and rock—in actuality, a secreted defensive weapons cache. Opening it, he retrieved a tactical-grip Mossberg 12 gauge shotgun and a Colt 1911 model .45 caliber handgun. He continued through the trees, approaching the house as quickly as possible without being seen or heard. The screams gripped him with fear, which he choked down, and relying on his training, he half-circled the house to come up on the side where he wouldn't be seen from the front door or windows. Once close to the house, he raised the weapon and stepped around the corner of the structure to see the front door.

Two men filed out. They saw him at the exact moment he saw them. Twenty-feet away, the men raised their guns, and as a defensive instinct seized Tally, he shot them both in the face. He jumped over the dead gunmen to reach the doorway and look in, his weapon raised. He took in the tableau instantly. His mother lay on her side, a man standing over her aiming a revolver at her head. He saw the man's malevolent grin, the strewn bodies of his sisters, and a dead stranger on the floor. Talbot rapidly shot the semi-auto shotgun twice. At this close range, the impact of the buckshot removed the man's head, spinning it into the kitchen.

Talbot dropped the shotgun and brought up the .45 Colt. He scanned for threats, then rushed to his mother as she rolled onto her back. Wounded in the shoulder and chest, her breathing was ragged and her eyes unfocused. As Tally knelt to lift her head, he noticed his father's body lying half-hidden behind the door. He had been shot through the door itself, and the killers had forced the door open. The blood smear on the floor from his dad's chest wounds graphically demonstrated the sequence.

Talbot's two sisters were dead, single shots through their foreheads. A killer had been holding them by the throat when he pulled the trigger. Talbot could see the massive purple bruises that had formed moments earlier.

His mother, knowing she was dying, lingered just long enough to whisper her love to him. Her last moments on earth were a prayer for her only son, who would be alone and forever scarred by this. Talbot kissed his mother's forehead and softly sang the lullaby she had so often sung to comfort her children when they were small and afraid. *"Hmmm, I want to linger, hmmm, a little longer, hmmm, a little longer here with you. Hmmm, and the years go by..."*

*   *   *

Talbot wept as the memories flooded his mind. The events of that night had altered not only his psyche and identity but the purpose and trajectory of his life. He felt again the sharp pain of loss. Thirty-six years had passed. He rarely allowed these recollections, but tonight he did so in an effort to grasp onto the faith and hope that had rescued him long ago. He was now certain that his current enemy was the same one who had massacred his family back then.

And he had attempted the *same thing* this week.

The Handy Nielson interrogations had produced valuable information, but Talbot's visceral reaction to it made it impossible to review the details intellectually. Handy's boss, Landan Moss, had told Handy about John Hancock ordering the murders of the DeCourcy family when Talbot was a boy. After courting Talbot's father, Thomas DeCourcy, forty years ago, Hancock had asked him to join the Brotherhood as it was then constituted. Thomas refused and actively worked to expose Hancock's scheme. Soon discovering flaws in his original plan, John decided to postpone his New America and began closing down the group. "Closing down" meant eliminating everyone who knew about it.

The young adult Talbot hadn't been aware of his dad's involvement when he met with Hancock thirty years ago, but today he realized that Hancock's appearance back then was no coincidence.

"The Mentor" had been interested in both father and son.

Just as Hancock had claimed, he really had read Talbot's treatise, which revealed to him the missing indicators that would yield the political shift he desired. Hancock very much *wanted* the young Talbot DeCourcy—as he had wanted his father—in his band of founders, but he did not *need* him. He did not *need* anyone.

Talbot, churning with emotions, watched his lovely wife as she slept. He was not a man prone to vengeance, but he was hell-bent on seeing justice meted out on the ersatz John Hancock and his thugs.

"Let's accelerate their entrance to hell," he whispered to Kate.

Chapter 76

January 17

9:30 AM EST - Three days before inauguration

The press pool assembled for the transition committee daily update. With no new disclosures about Tarleton cabinet picks, pundits assumed that the names leaked by Art Messenger before Sarnoff's assassination were still on the roster. Renae Hinckley had conducted the briefings for the last week, and today she fielded the reasonable questions and parried the inane ones.

The briefing room rumbled with surprised murmurs as President-Elect Tarlton stepped into the room for her first daily briefing. She had made a short statement to the press upon her release from the hospital assuring the country she was ready to assume office, and she had delivered her Lincoln Memorial speech eight days earlier—but she hadn't faced the press or public again since.

She decided now was the time for a political bombshell.

The room quieted and Madison began to speak. "For the last seven days, I've been working with my capable transition committee preparing to begin our administration. Unfortunately, we've met with a serious lack of cooperation from the outgoing administration, and although it hasn't been a streamlined process, we're ready to make decisions and act in the best interest of the country at 12:01 PM on January 20th."

Madison *took a breath* and continued evenly, "You should be aware that President Cluff's administration has been negligent and obstructionist in this handover of power. They've violated many decades of tradition and legislation that facilitate the smooth transfer of civil executive authority." The room erupted in crowd noise mixed with shouted questions. "If you'll hold your questions until I'm finished, you'll hear the rest of my statement. I'm disappointed at the bad behavior in the current Cluff White House, and at the close of this briefing, we'll provide press packets—hard copy and e-files—of the information I'm delivering. You'll find memos from Deputy Chief of Staff Leon Fuller instructing agency heads to slow information-flow to Sarnoff's incoming administration, thus making the transition more difficult. Nevertheless, my team is in place, and we won't allow petty political games to hamper us as we move forward. As you may have heard, I am not inclined to wait around!" Laughter arose, reporters recalling Madison's combat record as a heroic pilot rescuing her men against a superior force. Words from her Medal of Honor citation had often been quoted during the presidential campaign: "*...she did not wait for additional assistance but seized the moment of opportunity at great personal peril...*"

"I *take action*, and on January 20th, I will sign an executive order appointing a special prosecutor to investigate whether Mr. Fuller, or anyone working on his behalf, is criminally culpable. Thank you. That's all for today."

Madison was solemn but satisfied; she stepped away from the podium. As the Secret Service escorted her out of the room, reporters stopped shouting questions, grabbed the printed materials at the back of the room, and dashed out to work their spin.

Renae smiled broadly as she walked behind her boss. "That went well," she whispered as they walked back to Madison's office. "Let's see how Cluff plays this one."

Chapter 77

11:30 AM EST - Three days before inauguration

"Everything moves forward, and it will get really dicey from here on out. We can't make mistakes," John Hancock reiterated to his cadre of conspirators. "If Karen Waldron knows too much and comes forward, well, we'll deal with it at that time. My concern over Madison is growing. Her little tirade for the press pool makes me doubt that we'll ever get her to swing into line."

"Then we need to take her out now, before the inauguration," Roger Burgad urged. "We bring back your master assassin, who was supposed to do the job in the first place."

David Maxtell spoke up. "He missed once. He screwed up. I think you overrated him."

"David, we've been over this. It was always a shot prone to a small percentage of error. We needed Madison very close to Wilson in order to make her accidental death plausible. Once the bullet left the gun, we couldn't control the changing positions of their heads. Sarnoff got himself killed by turning to speak to her. He was our useful idiot, but too much of an idiot, as it turns out," Hancock reminded them.

"So, do we need to kill Madison now?" Bertrand Pinkney asked. "According to Roscoe, she's got her own slate of cabinet nominees. If we wait for her to announce her choices, it'll be too late." Bertrand was a chronic equivocator. "Or, on the other hand, an alternative is— we put pressure on her. We tell her that we'll convince the public she was part of the plan to take Sarnoff out from the beginning. Even with limited 'proof,' that kind of scandal could drive her out of office. She'd likely go along with us to keep her presidency. If the blackmail works, we get our cabinet and can go back to the original timeline."

"Let's cut our risks and go with the speaker of the house," Thomas Carlyle chimed in. "Jack Mellon is just as power hungry as any other politician. You know, I think we have enough mud smeared on his ledger to insure his cooperation. And then we can convince the Honorable Speaker Mellon to nominate our VP pick in plenty of time for a Senate confirmation, long before we, uh, eliminate the Speaker-come-President. It's relatively low risk...and maintains the plan we had for Sarnoff after all. We could perhaps even rehabilitate you, Art." Thomas smiled snidely at his friend. "With Madison dead, we'll dispute all her negative claims, and Art goes back into the lineup."

The group rejected the other options and focused on the merits of Thomas Carlyle's suggestion to work with Speaker Mellon. Several members brought up sticking points about this, particularly the very short window of time for the opportunity to act.

"We've got to act right away for this to work," Art added desperately. "No one knows exactly when the Madison team will announce her picks for cabinet posts, and she'll be a much harder target after she becomes president."

"Yeah, let's get our buddy Art off the bench and back into the game," Bertrand Pinkney said, followed by snarky murmurs of "Rah, rah!" He continued dressing his explanation in his best professorial tone: "The succession law, as articulated in the Constitution and the

25th Amendment, is not altogether clear-cut. Certainly, the speaker of the house is next in line to assume the presidency, but a case could be made that there should be a new election, and the wording is ambiguous regarding a sitting officer of the government assuming the role of president."

Eventually, The Brothers concluded that Speaker Mellon would be the best alternative to Tarlton. He couldn't be apprised of the change in batting order ahead of time, but both Leon Fuller and Art Messenger had good working relationships with the top House Honcho. The Brethren felt certain those two could persuade the Speaker to go along with Sarnoff's cabinet picks, and Art, especially, could think of plenty of incentives for the Speaker—some tangible and some subtle innuendo.

Realizing they needed to act in great haste, the group voted on the plan. After a unanimous vote, phone calls went out, putting the plan into immediate action.

Chapter 78

11:00 AM CST - Three days before inauguration

The assassin sat calmly and comfortably in his keyhole sniper-blind seven stories above ground level in a twenty-five-year-old residential tower. He was ready to take the shot. Momentarily, the target would come into view. Moving from right to left, the target was 706 meters away and surrounded by a modest entourage. The elevation difference between the rifle muzzle and the target was only twenty-two meters. Not particularly difficult. The target would be in the zone for several seconds, and the firing solution was excellent. There was no wind, and the air was fairly clear for this city.

The sniper was at peace; he did what he was ordered to do. Missing many years of personal memory, he didn't even know his real name—his superiors had explained to him about an explosion years ago and how it had changed him. Not only was he missing a huge chunk of his own life, but he had no recollection of anyone he'd ever known. Emotional context did not exist for him, and consequently, he lacked a moral compass. All he possessed was his great precision with a rifle and a drive toward duty—to follow orders and complete the mission as assigned. Killing was the job and he was great at it. He was a machine: no emotion, no hint of curiosity, no conscience. His commander had told him only enough of his wartime injury and recovery to help him stay on mission and do the job. He was here and ready. He would kill the target and go back to base, same as all the other missions.

He saw movement at the left edge of his scope apprising him of the target's party heading to the podium area. As the entourage moved into view, he acquired heads and shoulders in his scope's center. His effective range of vision was limited by the nature of the keyhole alignment—his rifle muzzle positioned six feet back from a slight gap of window drapes in the room where he sat. The drapes framed a wedge-shaped view of the target site as he focused the scope on the crowd mounting the stage area. No obstacles impaired the bullet's flight.

The sniper took up the slack on the trigger and breathed out slowly. In a second, he would release a 7.65x55mm bullet from a standard NATO round delivered from his M24 bolt-action sniper rifle. This particular rifle, along with ten other rifles and 2,000 rounds of ammunition, had been stolen two years earlier from a National Guard armory in El Paso, Texas by Mexican cartel thugs. Many of these weapons had consequently been used in numerous killings along the Mexican-U.S. border and were later confiscated by U.S. law enforcement.

The time came. The assassin tracked his target's head. He took the shot. Two seconds later the head of Mexico's young president exploded and showered the dignitaries walking onto the podium platform. The assassin couldn't hear the screaming and shouting from so far away, but through his scope he could see the instant chaos and confusion as people started running or crouching, waving useless arms. No need for a second shot. His first task was completed. He turned around.

Two men stood near the doorway. One was a stocky American with a dull smile; the other was a Mexican criminal badly scared on the left side of his face. The assassin handed the rifle to the scarred man. This was his second task.

"We need to get out of here fast," The American by the door said. The Mexican, a Sinaloa Cartel soldier, walked to the open window and looked down at the panic-stricken crowd in the plaza without attempting to conceal himself.

As the Cartel soldier holding the rifle peered below, the stocky American walked two steps into the room, removed a suppressed handgun from his shoulder holster, and shot once. Without further word the Mexican became their patsy, his head snapping forward as he slumped to the windowsill, and the rifle with his fingerprints clattering to the floor. The assassin and his handler quickly left the room.

They followed their planned escape route—just as they had in Chicago.

Chapter 79

12:03 PM CST - Three days before inauguration

A stringer for the Associated Press sent a text fifteen seconds after the assassin's shot killed the President of Mexico. He was gleeful. *This is like a replay of Chicago two weeks ago. Damn, am I lucky! A front row seat for two assassinations. Pulitzer, here I come,* he thought as he snapped pictures and spoke notes into his recorder.

Mexican federal security agents, wrongly perceiving additional threats, fired more shots—killing or injuring several stampeding onlookers. The story was picked up all around the globe, and dozens of professional stand-up TV reporters raced to airports, hoping to catch the next flight to Mexico City. *This is my kind of action,* the A.P. stringer thought. *Madison Tarlton is old news. A new political killing, and the game is afoot!* "I live for this," he said aloud, echoing the credo of many journalists.

The U.S. Ambassador to Mexico was in tears. A close friend of the young president and his wife, the ambassador collapsed in her office with debilitating grief when she heard the news. Her aids fielded frantic calls from the State Department. Because she was temporarily out of commission and unable to represent the U.S. government in the wake of the shooting, the outgoing secretary of state was thrilled to get one last shot at the limelight before he was out of a job. He was preparing his solemn statement for the television audience within ten minutes of the shooting.

President Cluff was again in the air returning from a lucrative trip to Japan. The trip was billed as "The Last State Visit" but was, in reality, his own personal contract negotiation with the giants of Japanese industry.

Madison's team immediately assembled in the small conference room at the Transition Office, and within fifteen minutes, she gathered the Homeland Security, FBI, and CIA directors together on conference call. The worm had turned, and regardless of their political affiliation, these leaders realized that Madison would be their boss in exactly three days and the crisis rising out of Mexican events hers to manage.

"In seventy-two hours, I'll be responsible for dealing with the fallout from the disaster in Mexico. I expect to be kept up to date on everything, minute by minute. Do we know anything concrete yet?"

"Not yet, but we suspect it was a cartel reprisal against the latest government crackdown on their operations," the CIA director stated. "We'll know more soon. Obviously, we've scrambled everybody in the region and have active liaisons with Mexican counterparts." He did not mention that the Agency had suddenly lost contact with several deeply placed operatives in the cartels and government and that they feared their eyes and ears on the ground had been compromised—either captured or eliminated. If that were so, information was leaking out of Langley.

"The DEA has warned us that the cartels are gearing up for something big, perhaps a push for less interference from Mexican military and law enforcement," the FBI director emphasized. "There are persistent rumors about an unusual level of cooperation between the Sinaloa and other cartels. We have indications that they are bulking up with foreign mercenaries. Unfortunately, follow-up has been spotty and hasn't been a priority in the waning days of the Cluff Administration."

"Thank you for the update. Have you forecasted potential spillover into the U.S. from the cartel activity?" Madison asked.

The director of Homeland Security answered: "If this escalates into a full-on cartel versus Mexican government civil war, we'll see refugees and violence on both sides of the border. Cartel violence will be inordinately gruesome—beheadings and mutilations and such. They won't just kill people; they'll strive to spread as much mass hysteria possible, terrorist style. And we could see affiliated gangs acting inside the U.S., either as sympathetic reactions or as part of the larger plan. I've been up nights for months over this, but I've gotten no support from the president or Congress. And to be truthful, no support is an understatement. The president treats my warnings like I'm a babbling old fool."

The CIA director added, "Of course, we don't have enough data yet. The shooter could just be a single-crazy lighting a match in a gunpowder factory."

Madison responded, "Granted, we don't know much right now, but I won't be sitting idly on this seventy-two hours from now. I respect each of you and want to work closely with you in the coming days. I would like your tenures to transcend the change in administrations, so don't think you need to run off and write your memoirs just yet. I expect all of you to be on my team in three days.

"Now, I'll get out of your way and let you fight your battles. Andie Madsen, as you know, is my personal aid, and she's also still serving on my protection detail. Her clearances will go all the way up. Please assume she's your pipeline to me twenty-four seven. Thank you." Madison ended the conference call, anxious to analyze the news with her staff.

Chapter 80

"Madison, I'm afraid you're correct. This isn't simply the drug cartels and the Mexican government expressing their domestic squabbles," Talbot declared. "We've learned a lot from our interrogations of the captured shooters, and we know that there's bigger action planned for south of the border."

"Such as?" Madison asked.

"We believe their goal is to put pressure on our government's stability, but the Brotherhood hasn't compartmentalized as well as they think they have," Talbot said through his M3 video feed. "The leader of the hit team we took down in Florida has friends who are part of the Brotherhood's mercenaries in Mexico, and they're embedded in the largest cartels. It smells like a carefully planned insurrection and destabilization campaign. And our reluctant informant claims that a member of the Brotherhood—he doesn't know his name—has clustered mercenary bands in excess of 3,000 soldiers."

"Civil war?" Madison asked.

"If so, there's going to be a blood bath among Mexican authorities within a few hours, and then there'll be a retaliation against the cartel leaders...and perhaps the Brotherhood has puppets in place to take over both sides of the conflict." Talbot's voice trailed off as he silently reflected on the gravity of his words.

She pondered for a moment, then: "You're such a cheery guy, Tally. I can always count on you to make my day," she said in a more casual tone than she felt.

"Yes, but I do have your back. We'll work through this together." He was good at reassuring her in difficult times and putting her on secure footing when she needed it.

"If you can keep me alive for a few more days," she said ruefully. "But you've always been there for me, even when I wasn't aware of it."

"Always, Jeemie, always." He sighed heavily.

"Thank you, Tally. You know I love you," she added, smiling through her M3. "And *you're* the one who should be doing this president-thing."

"We've been through plenty. We'll get through this."

"*You're* the one. I'm always along for a safe ride behind your shield."

"Well, my dear, it seems you've picked up a knack for pulling your own weight. I love you, too. Bye for now." Talbot signed off, not allowing himself to descend into the memories that inevitably led to sadness and regret. *We are where we are, and I'm doing everything I can to keep Maddy safe and help her be successful.*

And she did her part very well.

Chapter 81

The Sitting President of the United States, while flying over the Pacific on Airforce One, made a terse statement of sympathy and regret regarding the Mexican President's death. The problems of America's southern neighbor were escalating rapidly: reports flew about Mexican cabinet ministers killed, judges and generals murdered, and large-scale gun battles in cartel strongholds. Street riots erupted all over the country. Mexican police forces were overwhelmed. The military was in chaos. Civil war in Mexico was looking like a real possibility, and The United Nations, prone to dithering, even put Mexico on the agenda for the General Assembly's impotent discussions the following week.

Presidential advisors and pundits called for the National Guard to be federalized and sent to the border. But President Cluff, under advisement from Deputy Chief of Staff Leon Fuller, was taking a wait-and-see approach. Privately, Cluff was thrilled that Madison would inherit such a massive potential disaster. He believed that he could bring Mad Tarlton down in a short time and perhaps be mandated back into office through a new election.

As an outgoing one-term president, Cluff's greatest regret was not the loss of a second term or the endemic corruption among his cronies. (He was sure he had been robbed of reelection, and corruption is normal.) His greatest regret—his worse loss—was that he hadn't taken revenge on Talbot DeCourcy for destroying his presidency. He had stopped short of asking Leon to have Talbot killed. Now, he reflected, he should have done it when he had the chance. *After all, as Commander in Chief, I've ordered soldiers into combat, some of them to their deaths. I've ordered drone strikes to kill terrorists, and*

sure, *sometimes Americans were killed also. Collateral damage is no big deal.*
Terrence Cluff as POTUS was accustomed to ordering death. Secretly
it was his biggest rush. To the public and even to most of his staff, he
presented a gravely concerned demeanor whenever he got the chance
to kill somebody. Indirectly, of course.

He should have taken stronger measures to mitigate the
DeCourcy threat. Both his chief of staff and Leon Fuller had
underestimated DeCourcy's resolve to go all the way to the mat. This
was all Leon's fault. Cluff cheered himself by wondering if he should,
even now, have Leon killed for spite. As he pondered, Cluff realized
he probably wouldn't have made any recent decisions differently. *I
still can't believe I was brought down by such a little thing. I had nothing to
do with it in the first place, anyway.*

*   *   *

Cluff had stood up for his greedy college frat brother, Reggie
Campbell. A corrupt contract administrator, Reggie had been
bleeding defense contractors for payoffs on contract cost overruns,
but he overstepped and got in too deep when he tried to extort a
DeCourcy construction company building top-secret NSA facilities in
the mountains. The company wouldn't go along, and eventually
Reggie tried to cancel the contract and get a new vendor on the job.
He wanted a more pliable construction company, but it was bad luck
for him that the contractor had signed a pay-on-completion rather
than a progress-payment type contract. The DeCourcy company
hadn't billed the government for a single penny, and still holding title
to the land, they were legally all walled up. But Reggie wouldn't let it
go.

The upshot: when Reggie arrived at the job site, he signed,
without reading, a release of liability that included a video-and-audio
recording notice. When he attempted to coerce the DeCourcy

Company, using all the tricks of his trade—threats, blackmail, accusations of malfeasance—his crimes were caught on digital recordings…in high definition and surround sound.

Chapter 82

July 8

1:00 PM EST - Previous summer

Talbot DeCourcy stood in the business entrance of the White House West Wing. At the request of President Terrance Cluff, he was to attend a 1:30 PM meeting. Although he had arrived in plenty of time for processing into the national executive sanctum, an impasse remained: Talbot was without identification of any kind. The uniformed branch of the Secret Service recognized him and knew of his scheduled meeting with POTUS but refused to begin processing.

Talbot remained unflappable and the agents officious when they heard the slap-tapping of high heels moving quickly through the hallway. Linda Liengford was definitely on her way. She arrived red-faced, angry, and fearful. Her boss had ordered her to quickly arrange a face-to-face between DeCourcy and the president, but the whole thing had quickly become a nightmare. It had taken a week to learn the ropes of contacting DeCourcy…and they were knotted, tangled ropes.

She was not allowed to call or message him but must wait two days while nameless administrative assistants in Seattle contacted her

White House superior to run background checks verifying her identity. Eventually they supplied her with a phone number and strict verbal instructions for its use.

The west coast number could only be used within a fifteen minute period—11:30-11:45 AM PST—fourteen days after she had received it. DeCourcy assistants explained that he was highly scheduled and used this method to keep on track. After calling the number, she would be put on hold for up to five minutes. Once she was connected to Mr. DeCourcy, she would have precisely ten minutes to chat and then would hear a thirty-second warning before the line was dropped. Moreover, she was cautioned that if she tried using the number before the specified time, the call-appointment would be cancelled and she would have to start over. Jumping through these hoops made her frustrated and her boss livid.

Deputy Chief of Staff Leon Fuller was not a patient man; all this nonsense to get ahold of one egotistical jerk had upped the heat of his temper. Linda didn't know the subject of the DeCourcy meeting, but it was obviously a high priority in the West Wing. Unfortunately, it apparently was *not* a priority for Mr. Talbot DeCourcy. Leon had forced her to call the Seattle number early, and, of course, it didn't work, causing an additional week's delay to get back on the call-schedule. This, again, didn't sweeten Leon's mood.

Leon then dispatched an aggressive young man to Seattle to see Mr. DeCourcy, but the man didn't come back. Leon received the report that his emissary, after waiting a week-and-a-half, had seen DeCourcy for ten minutes and was now under arrest by both federal and state officers. It seems that he tried to entice DeCourcy, and when that didn't work, he made threats in the name of the White House about tax audits, contract cancellations, etc. He was charged—under Title 18—with using the power of his office to coerce and create the appearance of government sanction. Leon finagled and got the federal charges dropped, but the State of Washington still held the young man as a flight risk, ignoring pressure to drop the charges from the *other* Washington.

This is a humongous headache, thought the extremely high-heeled Linda Liengford as she approached Talbot DeCourcy in the West Wing. She saw a tall, distinguished man who exuded calm confidence. They shook hands stiffly. "Why didn't you bring I.D. to the White House?" she said curtly.

"Did you instruct me to bring I.D.?"

"It's obvious that you need to produce I.D. when you come to the White House," Linda said, almost boiling over now. "Everyone knows that!"

"Do you think I wanted to come to the White House? Isn't it a tenet of this administration that Americans shouldn't be required to show identification when voting or enjoying the other rights and privileges of citizenship?" Talbot asked flatly.

"You're here," she said, wide-eyed at his obtuseness and ignoring the political barb.

"You insisted that I come; it was not my desire that brought me here."

"You said you were available to come, and you're here. But, of course, you need to *prove* that you're Talbot DeCourcy."

"You invited me specifically. I do not need to prove who I am. I'm not seeking an audience with the president. He's seeking an audience with me."

"What?" She was astonished at his arrogance. She worked for the leader of the free world. Who did this jackass think he was? "No one gets in here without I.D. —I work here every day and I have to show my I.D. every time. It's a federal law. You have to show I.D. to get into the Executive Mansion."

"Ah, Miss Liengford, it isn't a federal law. The administrative requirement states that visitors must be properly vetted. I'm sure you are aware that the Prime Minister of Canada came to the White House last month. Did she present identification?"

"Well, no, of course not. She's the Head of State."

"Was she vetted?"

"Of course..." Linda stopped speaking, seeing her flawed logic. She couldn't argue with him.

"Shall I leave, then?"

"No!" she almost shouted. After all the abuse she'd taken from Leon just getting DeCourcy here, she wasn't going to let him go. "Please wait here for a few minutes. I'll be right back," she spun on her tottering heels and slap-tapped back down the short hallway. In a few minutes he heard her returning, and her shrill voice said, "Agent Knight, I'm sorry to drag you down here, but I need your help. Unfortunately, we have a visitor who didn't see fit to bring I.D., and we need him admitted for a very important meeting."

Linda Liengford and Agent Knight arrived together in the secured entrance area. Preston Knight, head of Secret Service White House protection detail, looked at the subject of all the fuss and smiled broadly. "Well, well, Talbot DeCourcy, as I live and breathe! So you're the cause of all the trouble. Why am I not surprised?" He stepped forward and enthusiastically shook Talbot's hand. "Very good to see you again, sir."

"Good to see you, Agent Knight." Talbot smiled, genuinely pleased to see an old friend. Linda, supposing her visitor was an ignorant, arrogant man who was too dull to bring I.D. to the White House, was shocked to witness this companionable greeting. The uniformed agents stood silently at their places.

"Agent Knight, this man didn't bring I.D., and we need to get him in for a scheduled appointment," she repeated herself. "We're losing time."

"Miss Liengford, this is Talbot Tristan Thomas DeCourcy; he never uses I.D. unless he wants to." Preston put his hand on Talbot's shoulder as he spoke. "We have no problem admitting Mr. DeCourcy; he is fully vetted." Preston didn't mention that during his seventeen years assigned to the White House, Talbot had been a frequent visitor and had met with other presidents before his own assignment. He also knew that Talbot DeCourcy hadn't come to the Mansion *once* during the current president's administration.

Linda ushered Talbot into a small waiting area and left without a word. Ten minutes later, another young woman entered the waiting area, introducing herself. "Mr. DeCourcy, Ms. Liengford has other duties, so I'll be your guide for today's schedule. First, I'll be happy to take you on a tour of the White house and then…"

"Wait a moment, please. What do you mean by 'schedule,' and why would you suppose I'm interested in a tour?"

"Um, first-time visitors usually like to see the Executive Mansion while they wait," she answered cheerfully.

"I'm not a first-time visitor, so no tour needed. My meeting is scheduled for 1:30," he said abruptly, not liking this at all. He was suspicious that Ms. Liengford had obfuscated concerning the meeting.

"Oh, I'm certain that Linda filled you in. First we planned a tour, and then a one-hour meeting with Leon Fuller at 2:30. Then, if the president is free, he'll do a walk-by at about 3:30." She rattled off the plan. A walk-by was the way visitors were put in front of the president without an entry in the official record. Clearly, Talbot had been vetted into the White House ostensibly to meet with Leon Fuller; later, the president would happen to walk by and be introduced to the visitor—thus no official record.

"Well then," Talbot said unemotionally. "Ms. Liengford did not explain these plans. She expressly told me that my meeting with POTUS was scheduled for 1:30. It seems she lied; nevertheless, we're done here. I have other appointments this afternoon, and I will, under no circumstance, have a meeting with Mr. Fuller."

"You can't mean that." She noticed Talbot's expression and changed her tack. "Why won't you meet with Leon?"

"In my opinion, Leon Fuller is a deplorable character assassin and an emotionally stunted scumbag bereft of ethics and morals. I will not voluntarily be in the same room with him." With that statement, given for effect, Talbot walked out of the room and headed back to the security entrance. The young lady stood stunned. After a full minute, she regained her presence of mind and ran to find Linda to tell her what happened. Linda, in turn, ran to tell Leon.

Much of the West Wing heard Leon Fuller's reaction.

At the same time, Talbot calmly tossed his visitor's badge to the uniformed guards and strode out the door. They did not try to stop him.

Chapter 83

July 8

"How could you let him leave the West Wing?" Leon Fuller screamed, adding a string of expletives. "It was *your* job to keep him here. You should've had the Secret Service detain him!"

"*Your* name is what drove him out of the building! Apparently, he didn't want a meeting with *you*," Linda responded.

"That's not the way to talk to me—just because you sleep with the president. I'm still your boss!" He paused, and turning to Agent Preston Knight, shouted, "Preston, you need to go after DeCourcy and bring him back. Right now!"

"No, sir, that is not within my job description," Preston answered smoothly.

"You insubordinate ass! You go after him right now or you'll be fired. That's an order!" He was hyperventilating now.

"With all due respect, sir, I work for the director of the Secret Service, not for the deputy chief of staff. Furthermore, if a private citizen wants to leave the premises, we can't stop him. He is not in custody or under arrest," Preston lectured.

"I'll have you fired right now if you don't go after him!" Leon raised his hands and clenched his fists, wanting to strike Preston but restraining himself. Preston walked away without further word.

In full-tirade mode for the rest of the day, Leon's attitude infected the staff and even the president himself. Linda Liengford immediately tried setting another call-appointment with Mr. DeCourcy in the same complicated way as before but, instead, was relegated to negotiating with a DeCourcy administrative assistant in Seattle. Through an arduous two-week process, Ms. Liengford finally achieved a new agreement for the president to meet with Mr. DeCourcy at his Washington State home on August 15th when President Cluff would be on a campaign swing through the Northwest.

The president was sour for days after the failed White House meeting. Secret Service Agent Preston Knight was booted out of the White House, his director bowing to the president's command to get Knight off the detail; but the director wouldn't cave to Leon's childish rant demanding Preston Knight's termination. Instead, Preston was assigned to be head of the opposition candidate's detail protecting Wilson Sarnoff. After seventeen years in the White House, he was out on the street and happy about it. The previous three-and-a-half years had been miserable with Cluff in the big chair.

Soon after his reassignment, Preston received a call from Talbot...and was reassured and amused to learn that Cluff wouldn't be winning re-election.

Chapter 84

August 15

2:50 PM PST - Previous summer

President Cluff's trimmed down motorcade arrived at the Courci Downs Estate in Spokane on a balmy August afternoon, accompanied by Deputy Chief of Staff Leon Fuller and Attorney General Percy Lightfoot. The Secret Service performed their usual protection pattern surrounding the president. They were uneasy about so many DeCourcy security people packing weapons on the grounds, but they couldn't have asked for a better physical layout to protect their principle.

When the Secret Service advance team had come to the estate a few days previously, they were met with uncompromising resistance from Gene Artel. Agent Lamar Beale, in turn, had reacted with belligerence, alienating the DeCourcy household and insisting that all DeCourcy security staff surrender their firearms while POTUS was on site. Gene refused.

"If you feel the president won't be secure under these operating conditions, you are free to recommend that he cancel the visit," Gene said.

Agent Beale blew his cool, and a DeCourcy guard escorted him off the property, depositing him on the public street bordering the six-mile-long DeCourcy parkway. When Beal stepped out of the security vehicle, Deputy Kintson picked him up and escorted him to the downtown federal building. As they drove, Beale's phone rang. The head of presidential detail who had recently replaced Preston Knight was calling.

"You won't believe what's happening here." Beale stopped talking and listened, his face turning a deeper red.

His boss, Liam Cane, said, "Do you even realize that every single one of DeCourcy's security force is either former Secret Service, FBI, or Military Special Forces? And some of them have current security clearances that exceed yours! If your uncooperative attitude craters this meeting, you'll be fired. You got that? POTUS really wants this meeting to happen, but DeCourcy doesn't care either way, so he holds all the cards. You are relieved, starting now, and Andie Madsen is taking over as head of the advance team. Come back to DC, write a long cover-your-ass report, and take up a guard post in the basement for two weeks. Goodbye, Agent Beale." Liam Cane had always been tough but never this brutal. Beale couldn't help thinking that something was going on—something he didn't understand.

On the appointed day of August 15th, the presidential party mounted the steps of Courci Downs, and the DeCourcy children came out for a photo op with POTUS. Gene Artel, the Barbies, and Secret Service Agent Andie Madsen stood by the front door. After posing for photos, President Cluff dropped his campaign-honed smile, replacing it with his poker face. *Time to go inside and get out of the hot sun. I gotta deal with this jerk and get on with the campaign...what a waste of my time.* The leading agents entered first. The president followed with an agent on both sides and behind him, but before the rest of the party could follow, Gene Artel intercepted them.

"Attorney General Lightfoot, please go in; however, Mr. Fuller will need to wait out here."

"What?" Leon said. "Of course I'm going in. President Cluff requested my attendance at this meeting."

"We cannot allow Leon Fuller to enter the house. Mr. DeCourcy was crystal clear on that," Artel said, smiling slightly.

"He's with me," the president stated dismissively as he looked back over his shoulder.

"Your advance team was instructed that Mr. Fuller wouldn't be permitted to attend this meeting. It's only a courtesy to you that Leon is not waiting on the road outside the estate. He's not going in." Gene's smile broadened.

"I *said*, he's with me," the president repeated, walking further into the entry.

"This is not your home, President Cluff. If you insist that this uninvited guest stay with you, then I need to inform you that the meeting will be cancelled and you'll be asked to leave."

"Are you seriously going to defy me, Mr. Artel?" The president used his signature glare, the mean-eyed look that melted the resistance of lesser mortals—especially unimportant senators or ambassadors from "ugly little countries," as he thought of them. Gene continued to smile back without answering. After a few moments, the president continued into the house without a word. He realized the tough negotiating had just begun.

Chapter 85

August 15

3:00 PM PST - Previous summer

The president and attorney general were seated in the lovely parlor of high-ceilings and white classic moldings immediately off the grand foyer. As fifteen-year-old Lydia was serving iced drinks, Kate and Talbot entered. Once the couple was introduced and seated, Talbot turned to the president.

"Welcome to Courci Downs, Mr. President and Attorney General Lightfoot. You asked for this meeting, so I'm happy to have you open the discussion."

"First, Mr. DeCourcy, I must say I am *shocked* that you would walk out on our meeting at the White House. That does not bode well as a good starting point." The president struggled trying not to sound irritated. "And...I'm unhappy that you barred Leon from this meeting." He waited for a response.

"Did you come all the way to Washington State to complain about a cancelled meeting?" Talbot was fluid and calm.

"It disturbs me that you would insult the Office by walking out on me that way."

With the president beginning the negotiation in this manner, Kate and Talbot realized the whole thing was already over and nothing would be accomplished. "Mr. President, your staff intentionally misrepresented the time of the meeting and at least a portion of the purpose. I was otherwise obligated at the later time you actually intended to meet with me. When I realized that Mr. Fuller wanted to spend time softening me up and then you might drop by, I was not interested in that arrangement. I left."

"But that's how we do things. I'm a busy man and Leon is very capable. He would've reasoned things out with you, and we could have easily dispensed with the misunderstanding about Reginald Campbell," the president said with condescending exasperation.

"There is no misunderstanding," Talbot began. "Reginald Campbell attempted to coerce and solicit bribes from the president of a company in which I have a controlling interest. Our legal staff presented this information and lodged a formal complaint to the DOD, the GSA, and the U.S. Attorney for the Southern District of Virginia. Our effort to get this crime investigated and the perpetrator prosecuted was unsatisfactory."

Attorney General Lightfoot broke in: "I reviewed the complaint with the assistance of the proper authorities and determined we had insufficient evidence to move forward with legal action. Of course, Mr. Campbell was removed from his position," he said, trying to steer the conversation. He was extremely smug, with no concept of the dangerous pit he faced—his toes were already dangling over the edge.

"If there was inadequate cause for action, why was he fired?" Justice Kate asked matter-of-factly.

"Fired? No, he was reassigned. This was done to eliminate any taint of inappropriate action," the A.G. responded lightly, minimizing the issue.

"So," the president resumed, "This has ballooned way out of proportion. I came all the way out here to let you know that we care about your issue—want to make things right for you." He smiled, lapsing into his default manipulative manner. "So, how can we help you get over this unfortunate misunderstanding? In other words, tell me what you need to make this little annoyance go away."

"There is no misunderstanding," Talbot repeated. "Reginald Campbell committed a series of federal crimes, and we insist he be properly prosecuted. I'll not accept any more of your attempts to mitigate this 'little annoyance.' And I'll certainly not entertain any more political inducements or financial threats."

"Oh, Talbot, come on. We're all adults here. Let's work this out," said Attorney General Lightfoot.

The president suddenly dropped the friendliness and brought out the gloves. "It's ludicrous to make such a big deal out of a minor judgment error by a small cog in the giant DOD machinery," he said, finishing with expletives.

Kate said, "You understand that I'm speaking as a private citizen for the next few moments and not as a federal appellate court justice." The president blanched at her forceful comment, having forgotten Kate Covington's professional position. "As a stakeholder in DeCourcy enterprises and as a concerned American, I'm appalled at the Justice Department's amateurish handling of this matter. I also don't believe for a moment, Attorney General Lightfoot, that you looked at the digital audio-visual evidence and dismissed our complaint as having no merit. So, I see two possibilities: one is that you didn't look at the evidence and detrimentally relied on your underlings; two is that you are just plain lying."

Lightfoot blurted, "Ms. Covington! I will *not* be spoken to in that manner and be accused…"

"Mr. Attorney General, this is my house, and you came in here lying to our faces. You are a dishonest political hack and a disgrace to your office. As a former U.S. Attorney and litigating prosecutor, I reviewed the evidence provided in the complaint, and I'm telling you, a conviction would be a slam dunk!" Kate nodded her head for emphasis.

"I will *not* be treated…" Lightfoot sputtered again, Kate's worse-cop ploy thoroughly rattling him.

"Percy, shut up!" The president took charge. "DeCourcy, I'm not going to let an insignificant event like this undermine my re-election. So let's come to terms. What do you want? You seem to want Reggie convicted of a crime. Okay, so we'll get him to plead no contest, and he's done. There, will that work?" Cluff had resisted punishing Reggie—they were frat brothers, and Reggie knew too much about Cluff's wild and woolly days; he also knew about things in Cluff's political career that were better left unearthed. Now Cluff was thinking he could placate Reggie with a few million dollars and a presidential pardon. Why hadn't Percy suggested this earlier?

Kate and Talbot saw that President Terrence Cluff, by taking this too personally, was not maintaining the ability to negotiate dispassionately. "Mr. President, what seems such a little thing to you is a great matter of principle to others," Talbot said. "This 'minor judgment error' could have easily been dealt with through normal legal channels months ago, and no one in the press would have paid attention. I assume that your fraternity brother didn't want to get hoisted on a spit. So here we are." The president's eyes widened, shocked that DeCourcy was aware of his relationship with Campbell.

"I'm surprised that you politicians never learn from your predecessors: the cover-up of a crime always creates a larger scandal than the original crime. Do the names Woodward and Bernstein ring a bell?" Kate asked.

"So, to answer your question, no. That will not do," Talbot said adamantly. "If the attorney general had dealt with it legally and properly, it may have been sufficient. But now, more crimes are added to the account. The attorney general has conducted a cover-up."

"Now, see here, DeCourcy. I will not sit here and have you insult me!" Percy exploded. "We are here to work this out, not to be accused."

"Then, Mr. Attorney General, I suggest you make your way to the door. Our folks will see you safely to your vehicle to wait with Leon. The adults will continue to talk." Talbot smiled engagingly.

"Again, DeCourcy, what do you *want*?" The president shouted.

"As I was saying, because of the cover-up, simply punishing Reginald Campbell won't square the account. He should be publicly prosecuted in an expeditious manner, and the attorney general must resign and face prosecution for his role in the cover-up." Talbot calmly laid out terms.

"No way in hell, Talbot," came Cluff's peremptory reply as he looked over at the now impotent attorney general. "I will not let you blow this up into a great big thing. There must be something else," he said, sweat accumulating on his brow.

"But you can't prove your allegations of a cover-up," Percy Lightfoot shot in.

"That's a naïve assumption," Kate interjected.

"We have the original recordings documenting Reginald's crimes, which are clear probative evidence of the cover-up," DeCourcy said. "So, I have no problem presenting our evidence to the court of public opinion."

"There's got to be another Woodward out there looking for a juicy tid-bit like this," Kate added.

Talbot did not reveal that he also possessed an affidavit from the U.S. Attorney for the Southern District of Virginia showing both Percy Lightfoot's role and President Cluff's consent in the cover-up. A direct line of dots connected them.

"You're threating me, DeCourcy? That's a big mistake," Cluff said with menace. "You can't conceive of the wheels that will start to turn."

"No threat. Just stating acceptable terms. Now you have them." Talbot and Kate rose to leave the room.

"This is crazy! This is a tiny, meaningless thing," Cluff said, resorting back to his pacifying tone. "Why all the drama?"

DeCourcy made no response as they reached the door; Cluff erratically switched again to fury: "Talbot, I swear, I'll come down on you and make your life miserable!"

"You and Leon have already tried that. And you'll lose again. And quite possibly, your presidency won't survive your obstinacy."

Cluff knew he wouldn't get this moment back. "How long will you allow me to think about this before you do something rash?" His only remaining move was to stall and push this problem forward until after the election.

"In secunda regula negotiatorum **est**, ut non ostenderet tibi hac vice." Talbot slung a bit of Latin at him. Cluff and Lightfoot looked at each other, perplexed. Talbot turned and repeated himself in English. "The second rule of negotiating: never reveal your real timeline."

Lightfoot couldn't help asking, "What's the first rule?"

"Numquam agere in a plena vesicae. Never negotiate on a full bladder," he chuckled and the DeCourcy couple left the room.

The president and attorney general were left alone, shell-shocked. Secret Service agents entered the room to move their principle back to the motorcade. The meeting was a disaster, and everybody in Cluff's circle would soon pay a nasty price.

*   *   *

On the day Cluff left Courci Downs, he was leading Sarnoff by an 11-point margin in most reliable polls. DeCourcy did nothing for five weeks, and Leon Fuller tried pulling out every Machiavellian trick from his black bag: freezing Talbot's finances, putting pressure on DeCourcy customers through threats and innuendo, and initiating more IRS audits that could burden DeCourcy companies with legal battles for years. But Talbot outmaneuvered him. Day in and day out.

Finally, in the third week of September, the counterattack came. President Cluff was humiliated in the press when everybody in the free world got a front row seat to view the corruption of his administration. He mistakenly doubled down and stood by his attorney general, and although he threw Reggie Campbell under the bus, it wasn't enough. He lost the election by 6 percent in the popular vote and only three votes in the Electoral College.

As a result, Cluff constantly roared insults—many of his staff worried about his irrational mental state. *This is all their fault…Leon screwed up the whole campaign strategy…that cheap, greedy bastard Reggie was so stupid…Percy should've resigned and taken blame for the entire mess.* As he raged, he picked up a heavy bust of Franklin Roosevelt and slammed it, head first, against the Resolute Desk, scratching the desk's historic Morocco leather.

Chapter 86

January 18

12:30 PM EST - Two days before inauguration

The erupting violence in Mexico sent refugees spewing over the U.S border. President Cluff did nothing, so the governors of each bordering state—California, Arizona, New Mexico, and Texas—called out their own National Guard troops. Because the units were not federalized, coordination between the states' forces was chaotic. The 3,000 mercenaries sent by the Brotherhood to aid the cartels fomented hundreds of refugee slayings—with beheadings and other gruesome dismemberments designed to ignite hysteria.

The news outlets were in a feeding frenzy. The U.S. intelligence apparatus and the military, without consulting the outgoing president, raised their alert levels around the globe, while President Cluff hunkered down with Linda Liengford despondently passing his last two days as king of the world.

The Cartel war with Mexico's government was only twenty-four hours old, and the government was already teetering on the verge of collapse. As a result, the Mexican military was on its own and unable to maintain effective civilian control. The Senior General of the Mexican Army, (the key Brotherhood surrogate slotted to become dictator in a coup), was found with two shots to the back of his head—a serious loss for the Brotherhood. They were also foiled by the disappearance of Mexico's constitutional successor to the president, the Secretary of the Interior. Hancock's Cabal had planned to kill him, but he eluded their hit squad and was in hiding. The Brotherhood's mercenaries were still backing the cartel leaders, but the cartels were stepping out of line with the Cabal's marching orders, making their own rules of engagement.

Bad actors around the world noticed that the American President was not on watch, not taking action. ISIS terrorists jumped on the opportunity, destroying two U.S. embassies in small African nations—no one at the State Department or the CIA had been aware that ISIS had fighters in those countries. The U.S. Marines guarding the embassies fought bravely, but thirteen American diplomats and seven Marines were slaughtered before extraction.

Cluff was leaving office in the opening act of Armageddon.

*   *   *

The Brotherhood was dancing a jig—but adjusting their footwork. Roger Burgad's Mexico operation team pivoted rapidly, altering the war plans to meet the current conditions on the ground. Burgad still had connections to a vast network of spies from his former days as CIA's Mexico City Station Chief, and he used those contacts trying to hunt down the Secretary of the Interior.

Because Hancock refused all but face-to-face communications, his right hand man, Landan Moss, was busy shuttling messages between the Mentor and the other Brethren. Moss was the only human who knew Hancock's location, and he maintained the leader's electronic blackout by racing through the Virginia mountains personally delivering verbal reports.

The Brethren were hastening their timetable to meet the imminent deadline of Madison's inauguration—upping the ante before playing their trump card. They were stacking the deck for a whole new game, a game in which John Hancock controlled the mint-new cards for an American political redeal.

As they scurried around set for success, no one in the Brotherhood suspected they were being carefully watched and tracked.

*   *   *

"Go ahead, Eddie." David Maxtell answered his phone.

"Hot damn and kiss my ring, I've got a connection," Eddie Smyth bubbled. "I've found a fiduciary connection between Tarlton and DeCourcy."

"Tell me!" Maxtell pulled to the side of the road. He was driving to meet Hancock and some of the others.

"It's the house...the house that Tarlton bought in Georgetown and that she's been living in since she became the nominee. That's the lead...and the house right behind hers facing the next street over is the connection. I dug into ownership and permit records from four years ago. The same DeCourcy construction company that caused the whole Cluff scandal used to own both houses and remodeled them at the same time. Then they were sold through a land trust to an offshore investment firm."

"What do you think this means?" Maxtell asked.

"There are no house plans on file at the building permit office for either house." Eddie took a breath and launched again: "Madison bought her house from the offshore investment trust, but the other house is still owned by the trust."

"Okay. So how do we know that DeCourcy is in control of the trust or that his company wasn't hired just to remodel the houses?" Maxtell desperately wanted this to be the key he was looking for.

"It's very convoluted, but I'm 99 percent sure that DeCourcy controls that investment group, and I think that the two houses might be physically connected underground. I got that feeling when I looked at the before and after google-satellite images showing the backyards of both houses. I also accessed local traffic and street-lighting cameras. It looks like the Secret Service is using the second house behind hers as a barracks for Tarlton's detail. They must have it set up as a backdoor escape route."

"This is great, Eddie! This means the whole DeCourcy-Tarlton connection is real. DeCourcy is Karen Waldron's lawyer, which means that Madison knows Karen's husband wasn't the shooter. But she's kept her mouth shut. Why, I wonder?" Maxtell was excited—he would be carrying the promethean torch into his meeting with Hancock! And he expected the laurel wreath.

"This is good info, boss. You can rely on it."

"Alright, Eddie. Start looking at images of that second house and find me a spot. You know what I mean. We struck out on her townhouse because it poses problems getting at her. But this other house is a whole new chance for a great insurance plan."

"You got it, chief. I'm on it right now."

.

Chapter 87

2:30 PM EST - Two days before inauguration

Karen Waldron and her new friends, the Lubneskis, were on a private flight heading south to D.C., accompanied by one of Karen's lawyers, Sheila Lance. It would soon be time to come in from the cold and re-emerge in public, but first Talbot would secretly stash her in the penthouse of a D.C. hotel. He had arranged for an unobtrusive, highly reliable security team to protect her in anonymity. Although

Karen was nervous, she had gained complete trust in these people over the last week—especially the Barbies.

While in flight, Sheila Lance called Larry Radisson. "Agent Radisson, this is Attorney Sheila Lance. Do you remember me?"

"Of course, counselor. I couldn't forget you." Radisson perked up and didn't want to show it. But playing it cool was a challenge since he remembered the recent humiliation she'd caused him. "What's on your mind, Ms. Lance?"

"Listen, Larry. If you would still like to have a chat with my client, she's willing to make herself available."

"Really. Why the sudden change of tune? She's been dodging me for over a week." Radisson sensed something different in play.

"Well, since your lame attempt to apprehend her with a material witness warrant was tossed out, perhaps you'll be willing to meet on friendlier terms," she said, all sugar and spice.

"Friendly terms? I can manage that, even if it's against my nature." He played along, choking back biting retorts and attitude. "I can be out in Portland first thing tomorrow."

"Oh, no need; we'll come to you. We'd like to meet in D.C. on, say, the twenty-first? I'm sure the city will be pretty busy on the twentieth." Sheila struck a conciliatory tone.

"Ah, okay. Send me your itinerary so we can meet you at the airport."

"Very kind of you, but no thank you. I'll contact you around 10:00 AM on the twenty-first to explain the meeting place and the conditions of the meeting. Goodbye for now, Agent Radisson."

"Wait, Ms. Lance…" Radisson realized the line was dead. He immediately called Agent Palmer to tell him about the incoming call: "Hey, spool up some phone voodoo, would you? And find out where Sheila's call originated."

Twenty-five minutes later, Palmer reported back, verifying that the call had come from the lawyer's office in Portland. As good as he was at technical wizardry, Palmer was ignorant of two important facts: Sheila had called on her M3 device while flying to Washington D.C.; and Luau was tracking all the phone calls between Palmer and Radisson.

An excited FBI agent called a private number in D.C. and reported on the plans to interview Karen Waldron. Next, he called Thomas Carlyle in New York, leaving a brief message that something *big* was up. His "unofficial" bosses needed to act fast. If they moved too slowly, Karen would get to tell a startling story to the FBI. That wasn't a good option for anybody on his side of the playground. *And it sure as hell wouldn't be good for my Brotherhood bonus plan*, the agent thought as he waited for a response. Carlyle called back in two minutes; he had made a snap decision.

*   *   *

"Can you guarantee it'll be just you and your partner at the meeting representing the FBI?" Thomas Carlyle asked.

"Yeah, we got that covered. Sheila Lance wants a private sit-down."

"Any way to keep your partner away from the meeting?" Carlyle asked, thinking it unlikely.

"Nah, he has to be there. If I try to exclude him, it'll raise too many eyebrows."

"Then you need to control the agenda and keep Waldron from spilling details to the rest of the FBI. If you can't modulate the discussion, you'll need to take everybody out. That means Waldron, the lawyer, and even your do-gooder partner. You understand that?"

"Yeah, no problem. I've been wanting to put a bullet in Larry Radisson's head for about a week now. He's such an insufferable ass," Agent Palmer answered.

Chapter 88

Gene Artel and his staff at Courci Downs conferenced by live feed with chief-geek Luau in Washington D.C. Having set up a telecom data trap, they listened to the Lance-Radisson conversation in real time, then watched their screens as data showed Agent Radisson calling his partner, Palmer, and then calling his direct supervisor. The most interesting calls came next: Palmer first called Thomas Carlyle and then a cell number inside FBI Headquarters. That same cell number also called Carlyle, and Carlyle subsequently called the number belonging to Landan Moss, the Brotherhood's Praetorian Guard ringleader. Puzzle pieces were coming together.

"Chief," Luau said, starting the conference-call discussion.

"Go ahead, Luau," Gene Artel answered.

"Now that we have the numbers, I'll track back the location of the mystery phone, and we should have our FBI mole. Obviously, Palmer is a mole too… but a smaller one… like maybe a vole," Luau began rambling. "I mean…"

"Good, we got that. Great work, Luau. Shoot me the info as soon as it pops," Gene said.

"Good, okay, got it. But I have something else." Luau was just warming up. "I got a ping this morning from one of my watcher-bots sitting on public data stores. Somebody hacked into the D.C. Building Permit Office *and* Land Records *and* G.I.S. data bases. They focused on Madison's townhouse and then poked around until they pulled down data on the house right behind her. I think they've locked up a connection through the remodeler and the trust."

"Okay. Then what?" Gene sat up straighter.

"The same hacker took a look at records for two houses that sit in the same position as the backup house behind Madison's, but two blocks over."

"Who's the hacker?"

"I'm pretty sure it's Eddie Smyth over at Tyson Security. That place is owned by David Maxtell, right?"

"Yes, it is. And now we know Maxtell is a confirmed Brotherhood member."

"Anyway, Eddie Smyth's footprints are pretty obvious, and he doesn't bother erasing his tracks. Very arrogant, if you ask me," Luau said with professional smugness.

"Thank you for the info. Stay on this, and watch for anything else in that neighborhood. Keep me posted. Excellent work, hotshot." Gene ended the conference call with half a smile; the enemy was showing his hand.

He promptly called Talbot in Seattle to fill him in. "Tally, I don't like this. There's only one reason for someone to research the houses two blocks away: they have a direct line-of-sight to the front door of Madison's backup house," Gene said in a tone that disguised his worry.

Talbot was silent for a few moments. "Do you have good images of those houses?"

"Yes. We zoomed in from the roof cameras and found three windows with clear views of the front door of Madison's backup house. We're still clean on views from the front of Madison's own house—no clear sightline from that direction."

"Have you put Garrett Miller and his team on alert?"

"Yes, he's geared up and ready to move. I can have him in Georgetown in four hours."

"Good, get them going and into position." Talbot ran the enemy's strategic options through his head. "Since their plans for

Sarnoff and Madison have been reversed, they're forced to alter their operating theory altogether, and this is one of their backup plans."

"Okay, once Madison is in office, she becomes an almost impossible target," Gene said, speaking as a former deputy director of the Secret Service.

"So, let's think this through from the beginning," Talbot said. "They wanted Cluff to win and then they'd destroy his second term so that Sarnoff could run again next cycle with a landslide victory and a mandate, and because they've been managing his political career for years, they knew they could control him."

"You betcha."

"Giving them a clear field to bring in their form of *The Fifth Republic*," said Talbot.

"But you screwed up *that* whole plan."

"It was my pleasure," Talbot said. "So *plan B* was to kill Maddy. *Plan C was* to control her once she became president-elect and manipulate her into choosing Roscoe or even Messanger as V.P., but we killed Roscoe's chance when we instigated the congressional meltdown, so a Messanger pick would be the only way for *plan C* to work. And I think they're starting to see that Maddy is pretty uncontrollable." Both men laughed.

"Art Messanger would've been a logical V.P. choice because he was Sarnoff's Chief of Staff and then a Brotherhood big boy would be a heartbeat away from the presidency," Gene added.

"So now that Maddy has kicked him to the curb, our friends have to gamble on whether they can still move forward with Madison as president, or if they have to move to *plan D* and take her down before she takes office," Talbot said gravely. "And I bet they're weighing both options."

"Do you think they've already recruited Speaker Mellon, or will they roll the dice on him as the next in line and gamble on him playing their game?"

"I don't know. Speaker Mellon is a born and bred politician. It could go either way with him, but I doubt he'll sneeze at becoming president in one jump."

"What do you think Cluff is doing? Do you think he's involved?"

"I think he's sulking and licking his wounds, or maybe Linda Liengford is. He may be making comeback plans, but I don't think he's an immediate threat. Leon Fuller, though, is in this all the way, and he's always been Cluff's puppet master…" Talbot paused, then continued more intensely: "Let's get Miller and his guys in Georgetown right away to scan for threats."

Chapter 89

10:00 PM EST - Two days before inauguration

Madison Tarlton and her staff spent the entire day writing and rewriting the series of executive orders she planned to sign minutes after taking the oath of office. She had decided on her final list of cabinet appointees and other important department heads after discussing each name with Talbot. The Brotherhood faction was in for a rude awakening when she revealed her choices—*They're not Hancock's homies*, she thought, smiling to herself.

Late in the evening, Madison met with some of the current Military Joint Chiefs of Staff. They made recommendations for the growing conflict along the Mexican border and the escalating terrorist threats in Africa. They also explained active military operations to secure vulnerable U.S. embassies and other areas of strategic American interest. All the Chiefs voiced their support for Madison and their willingness to work constructively with her.

"Gentlemen, thank you. Now this next topic is off the record, and I need your complete candor. No one outside this group will hear a word of what we say next." She paused, making eye contact with each man around the table. "I'm going to ask you a question, and I don't want any nice-nice hedging; you are military leaders, not diplomats. I want frank opinions." She paused again, then continued, "Tell me your opinions on retired General Nathan Basil taking the Secretary of Defense slot." She watched for their reactions because she suspected Basil of Brotherhood leanings. "You know that Sarnoff's team was vetting him."

They looked warily at her. The Chairman spoke up. "Allow me to speak for the group. We discussed this, and we have a consensus. None of us trust him or want to work for him. He covers well, but we consider him a narcissistic snake in the grass with no regard for the wellbeing of our country."

"Please, no sugar coating." Madison smiled at these solemn, powerful men. "Okay, I've got your opinions. Thank you for your time. Let's convene again at 1:30 PM after the inauguration in the West Wing. We'll need to get right to work."

After meeting with the men in uniform, Madison made a few calls. It was still early evening in California and Washington State. First she called Mike Clayborn, her close friend of the last six years while she served as California Governor. Working alongside her as secretary of state, he had often given her sound advice on key decisions; currently, he was California State Attorney General.

"Mike, I'm looking forward to seeing you and Belinda at the festivities on the twentieth. We have seats for you on the stand next to Lucy and my sister-in-law, Janine. This is a big ask on short notice, but I would like you to come work with me again. I need an attorney general I can count on. Are you willing to come on board?"

"That's out of left field. I mean, sitting next to Lucy, that's a big ask," Mike teased. "But about this other thing—don't you think old Bert Pinkney might object a little?"

"Bertrand was Sarnoff's pick, not mine. I need someone like you as top cop."

"Madison, this is a tremendous honor. Normally I would talk to Belinda first, but not this time. Hell, yeah! I'm in."

"Thanks, Mike. I gotta go. See you in the fish bowl."

After her California call, she called Talbot. "It's so good to close out this crazy day with the calm reassurances you'll be giving me." She smiled as she kicked off her shoes and stretched out on her office couch.

"Ah, well then, consider me calm and reassuring." After a pause, "There, that's all I got." He sighed.

Madison stiffened. "Tally, what is it? You never sigh like that over the phone. I get the feeling I'm not going to be calmed or reassured." Talbot was not given to dramatics emphasizing his emotions. He had sighed only once before on the phone that she could remember; it was when he had called to tell her about the Russian Mob attacking him on a Seattle street.

"You're probably not in the clear yet. These Brotherhood clowns may not want you sworn in after all." He spoke in his unflappable business tone, as though communicating that Kate's dry cleaning wasn't ready for pickup.

"Well, you'd better tell me, so I can get some sleep." She mirrored his expressionless tone, taking her cue from him. She was as controlled in dangerous circumstances as he.

"Luau caught Eddie Smyth hacking away at databases other than the transition committee's and gathering data on your townhouse and the backdoor house. He thinks Eddie Smyth and David Maxtell have found a connection between you and me. It follows that if you have to dash out the back, they could be waiting."

"Yeah, hitting me here at night is more logical. In the daytime, when I'm a moving target, the risks and unpredictability levels are higher." She paused to consider. "I sense another shoe about to drop. Let's have it."

"Luau has identified the hacker, Eddie Smyth, as the Brotherhood's script kitty, and he's been focusing on a couple of houses two blocks away from you. They both have a direct line of sight to the front door of the escape hatch."

"Well, isn't this kettle of fish simmering nicely?"

"You bet," Talbot agreed. "Even though you have a very good protection detail, you're still a much softer target now than you will be at noon, day after tomorrow."

"I still don't want to reveal publicly that I was the real target...and still am."

"I understand. I think the logistics are pretty narrow if they're going to make a play. I have a tech-package for Preston Knight to install that'll add extra safety insurance, and I'll have Jason Southwick brief you on it. Okay, you good?"

"Yeah, Tally," she laughed. "Paint a target on my chest and send me in, coach." Madison had faced moment-by-moment threats during combat enough times that her heartrate rose only slightly under stress. *Stay cool under pressure* was her favorite mantra, and she found that focusing on humor and normalcy helped her achieve it.

She returned to routine conversation: "Lucy has been staying with her Aunt Janine until we move into public housing, and that was to accommodate my schedule. But now with all this...thank goodness she'll be out of harm's way."

"Jeemie, once you're sworn in, I'm going to *eliminate* the Brotherhood. But they're going to be like blackberry bushes, and it'll take some doing. It won't happen all at once."

"I'll cover you with executive orders and any pardons you need—free of charge," she said, still searching for humor. After a pause: "We have to destroy this cancer."

"Damn right. We have a lead on several bank accounts we can raid to reduce their war chest. It's probably not all of it, but it'll deeply wound them."

"Good. We'll make it a legal confiscation and use it to fight this war," she said with ironic cheerfulness.

"Good night, Maddy."

"Good night, Tally. Appreciate you."

"Yeah, backatcha."

Chapter 90

January 19

10:00 AM EST - One day before inauguration

Madison took a call from Juan Rodrigo Lazaro Cardenas, Secretary of the Interior of Mexico and successor to the murdered Mexican president. She respected Juan Cardenas and had met with him several times during her terms as California Governor.

"Señora La Presidente Tarlton, I am very happy that you survived the attempt on your life," Cardenas said in his understated way. "Thank you for taking my call."

"Juan, I'm very glad to hear from you. Are you safe?" Madison was surprised—she had received reports Juan was missing. "We feared for your safety."

"Thank you for your concerns, Madison. As you can imagine, it has been very chaotic here. It embarrasses me to tell you that my government is in hiding. Many members of our Congress are dead, and many more are missing. Important judges have been killed. The army is not well-coordinated. The violence has expanded, and we may be facing outright civil war," Juan said wearily. He had slept little since the unrest began soon after the assassination. "For now, I believe I am safe, but that may change. Many of the soldiers protecting me have been killed, and others have deserted in fear. We moved from the capital to a secure hacienda in the mountains. I have not been able to speak to the Mexican people."

"The American government will come to your aid, Juan," Madison said emphatically. "What can we do to help you?"

"I have tried to call your President Cluff and your secretary of state. They will not take my calls. I was told to contact the American Ambassador first," he said angrily. "She is hunkered down behind her embassy walls, crying like a little niña; she cannot help me." Juan was incredulous. "Surely they are aware that I succeed our slain head of state. My country is in chaos and in dire need—but America ignores us!" He exhaled forcefully. "I am trying to get control of the military, but I have not established a safe haven from which to operate."

Madison burned with embarrassment that her government had ignored Mexico's urgent plea for help. "Juan, I fully recognize that you're the legitimate head of your country. The resources of the

United States Government will be at my disposal in twenty-six hours. What do you need me to do?"

"I must speak to the Mexican people to reassure them that their government has not abandoned them to the lobos."

"Juan, are you in a safe enough place to get food and rest?"

"Yes, I think so, as long as I keep my head down like a frightened rabbit," he said bitterly.

"Please, don't blame yourself. Your military commanders know their jobs and should be able to rally their troops soon. I can help you officially tomorrow—and I *will* help you. The might of the United States will stand with you and come to your aid. I'm going to put my assistant on the phone with you while I make another call. I'll get right back to you." Madison handed the call to Andie.

"Señor Cardenas, this is Agent Madsen. May I assume that this call is not completely secure?"

"Señorita Madsen, to be safe, sí. We must assume that this line is not secure."

"Okay, Señor Cardenas…"

"Juan, please."

"Alright, Juan. You may call me Andie. Do you know your exact GPS location?"

"Sí, I do."

"Great. Now can you think of a number, any number that would be significant enough that both you and Madison would know it—a number that we'll understand by you describing how you both know it?"

"Sí, I think so. Let me think about it for a few moments." He paused, then said, "Madison and I spoke over dinner once about an important historical date that is especially meaningful for me. Madison should remember that date. To me, the date is written in day, month, and then year," he stated firmly.

"Okay, Juan. I know that you are probably fatigued, but what I would like you to do is take that date, just the year, and multiply it by forty-two. Then divide that new result by each of the two GPS coordinates of your current location. Make sure you drop the decimal point."

"Okay, I understand, Andie. Give me a few moments to be a school boy again, and I will double-check my sums."

After ten minutes, Madison reentered the conversation. "Juan, thank you for waiting. I have discussed your problem with a trusted friend. He has considerable resources, and some of them are already in your region. He will get additional protection and supplies to you within eight hours. The people coming to you are veterans of American Special Forces, so they know what they're doing. You understand that I am not yet president, so I can't officially conduct foreign policy operations. My friend's people are acting as private citizens, as amigos of Mexico."

"Thank you, Madison. It is good to have a friend who is moving into the White House!" He almost regained his humor. "These men who come should identify themselves by using the name of the appetizer we shared at dinner the last time we met in California." He laughed at his suggestion.

"Alright, Juan. And your recognition code is the food we joked about, and I asked you how yours compared." They both laughed, reliving the pleasant memory. "The men coming to you will bring you a secure means of communication. Someone will monitor that channel continuously until the crisis is over."

"Gracias, my dear friend!" He rang off.

Madison stared thoughtfully at the speaker phone for a few seconds, unaware that both Andie and Renae were watching her expectantly, waiting for an explanation.

Renae intruded on Madison's memories. "What date in history did you and Juan discuss?"

"He would have used June 14, 1800—the date of the Battle of Marengo in Italy," Madison answered. "We were eating Chicken Marengo, which Juan adores. He explained the legend about Napoleon's chef inventing the dish on the day of the battle. He had to use olive oil instead of butter, and tomatoes were a later addition."

"Okay, so what are the call signs and recognition codes?" Andie asked.

"Uh, calamari was the starter, and we had sliced avocados with them. Juan explained that the word 'avocado' comes from the Aztec word for testicle. He was comparing his own manhood to the two enormous fruits on the table when the waitress started slicing. Juan winced at the sight, and we laughed like fools!"

The women laughed at the gruesome image.

"Okay then," Renae said with mock solemnity. "Now that you've conducted foreign policy as a private citizen and violated a major federal law or two, let's move on to some other more constitutionally allowed business."

Chapter 91

Gene Artel gave instructions to Pablo Zedillo, his field team leader in Mexico. All DeCourcy security operators in Mexico and Central America were former Delta Force or Army Rangers, and all were fluent in Spanish. The seventeen-man team protecting DeCourcy personnel and assets throughout the region would now race to the aid of acting Presidente Cardenas. Pablo Zedillo didn't react to the call sign and recognition code; "calamari" and "avocado" worked as well as anything else, but he did smile when Artel shared the background on the avocado choice. That irresistible detail would probably make it into the official history when this episode was eventually recorded. Zedillo could imagine a political cartoon of Juan Rodrigo Lazaro Cardenas and his sliced avocados.

Gene Artel reported to Talbot over video-conference. "Pablo Zedillo and his men are geared up and on their way to augment Cardenas's security force. They'll establish a secure satellite feed and begin broadcasting to the Mexican people as soon as possible."

"What's their ETA?" Talbot asked.

"Five hours from now we should have assets closing in on Cardenas's position. We shortened our original estimate, so it'll be 3:30 PM local time, same as central time to us. They'll go in stealth mode as long as possible. After Pablo's men secure a perimeter, they'll approach Juan at about five-and-a-half hours from now, and that's assuming they have a clean insertion and don't have to fight their way into Fort Apache," Gene said.

"Great. Thank you, Gene. You've got stand-up guys."

"You got that right," Gene smiled into the camera. "We have assets on the way to backfill positions that Pablo and the boys are vacating at DeCourcy facilities in Guadalajara. Signing off."

Talbot called Renae next. "I know Maddy is a busy girl today— last day as a free woman and all, so can you just relay Gene Artel's report? The cavalry is on its way to Juan Cardenas's location, and they'll have boots down in five hours...How are you holding up? We might as well think about *your* new pressures, as well."

Renae laughed, responding, "Ah, well, you know, nobody ever thinks about the hired help. Madison has approved the wording for all the executive orders we've put together. She wants you and Kate to read them over before they're finalized."

"We will. Tell Madison to *breathe*," Talbot said, ending the call. He thought about Jeemie for several minutes. She was about to make the most extraordinary transition of power in U.S. history.

*   *   *

While Kate Covington flew with her children to D.C. for the inauguration, she reviewed Madison's executive orders. Talbot had flown into the city a few hours before and planned to meet with Madison later that day.

Late January in Washington D.C. was always a bleak place, and this year the city was reeling with polar mood swings. Preparations for the inauguration were steaming ahead, and excited anticipation was high—yet many people were somber, still staggering from the shock of Sarnoff's assassination and the serious upheaval in Mexico. Additionally, the intensely heightened security measures created electric jolts of anxiety and fear for many citizens.

The Cluff administration was sputtering to a stop. The last minute work of a peaceful transition was left to the career civil servants because the political appointees had checked out days earlier. Staffers in the West Wing exhibited the same poor sportsmanship as their uber-boss; they vandalized keyboards, prying off the letters that spelled "Madison" and super-gluing them onto desktops. This was the type of dig that characterized one party reluctantly leaving power and the other one entering it. The cabinet secretaries knew they were out and had their "little people" clean their desks out. Some cabinet members had not been to work for weeks.

The press secretary announced that President Cluff had traveled home to Florida for a visit but had come down with a kidney stone and would not make it to the inauguration. Vice-President Johnson would preside over the events instead. Media reporters snickered at the sudden kidney stone ploy and generally agreed that Cluff was sulking…again revealing his inability to pretend good grace.

Chapter 92

2:00 PM - One day before inauguration

Madison Hemsley-Tarlton spent hours in training learning the nuts and bolts of assuming office, which included a demonstration of the nuclear launch-code process. Directly after taking the oath, she would be in control of the code card and constantly a short distance away from the key to the world's greatest destructive power. Renae was also busy during this training session: due to President Cluff's absence, she was able to move most of Madison's office memorabilia into the Oval Office. Always devoted, Renae desired her best friend to feel comfortably at home after the inauguration.

The director of the Secret Service met with Madison to review the changes happening tomorrow, both in White House protocols and in the list of agents comprising her daily protection detail. She insisted that Agent Preston Knight take charge of the detail rather than the individual the director had proposed; she wouldn't allow last summer's dust-up between Deputy Chief of Staff Leon Fuller and Agent Knight to hurt Preston's career. Because the director owed his own appointment to his friendship with Leon Fuller, he likely planned to put Preston out to pasture. She also wanted Jason Southwick to be second in command on the White House detail.

Although this last day before entering office was an extremely busy one, Madison squeezed in a late lunch with her daughter. Lucy was excited about moving into the White House but missed her California friends. Madison promised they would all be invited to the White House for Lucy's next birthday party and Lucy could pay their airfare and hotels by selling some of her stock in mommy's companies.

"Tomorrow is a really big day, sweetheart. We're going to become what people call 'the First Family.' Are you excited about that?"

"Yes, but I wish our family first had a daddy," Lucy smiled. It was the usual pleading of a child for a father figure and a normal family. "But you never date, so how can you find me a new daddy?" she teased.

"What, and share you with a man?" Madison said in mock surprise.

"No, mom. I would have to share *you* with a man."

"Someday, baby, someday," Madison smiled wistfully. "It'll be hard to find anyone who remotely comes close to the great guy your daddy was." She tapped Lucy on the nose.

"Well, Madame President, tomorrow you'll have to try!" They both laughed at the oft-repeated family joke.

Chapter 93

6:00 PM - Eighteen hours before inauguration

Andie Madsen brought a phone to Madison. Pablo Zedillo said, "Ma'am, this is Pablo Zedillo from DeCourcy Security Forces. My team arrived at Cardenas's hacienda thirty minutes ago. All is secure here. Acting Presidente Cardenas is safe, and he's preparing to broadcast to the Mexican people."

"Thank you for your efforts, Pablo," Madison said with relief. "Did you encounter rebels or any other trouble?"

"We had a small dustup with a couple of Humvees full of cartel hombres, but they saw things our way after a pleasant little discussion, ma'am."

"Are they all contained so they can't lead others to President Cardenas?"

"Well, in fact, ma'am, they're all expired due to the intensity of the discussion," Zedillo stated in an unemotional soldier's tone. "Don't worry, we'll keep the *Señor Avocado* safe."

She laughed. "Very good, Pablo. I'm very happy to hear your news. Thank you for your diligence. We're proud of you."

"It's our pleasure to serve the next Madame President of the United States, ma'am. Zedillo out."

Handing the phone back to Andie, Madison said: "Well, that's one little victory in the Mexican Civil War." She smiled.

Chapter 94

Don Verde's five-man team had been surveilling Landan Moss, the leader of the Brotherhood's rapid action force, physically and electronically for several days.

Don Verde reported in to Gene Artel: "Landan Moss has dropped off the grid completely. And he's done this before. He'll drive to a shopping mall and dump his car and then turn off all his electronics."

"What's different about this time, Don?" Artel asked.

"Each time before, he returned to his car in a few hours, and the electronics came back on. But this time it's been over eight hours, and he hasn't come back to the mall in Harrisonburg," Verde said, agitated.

"Okay, so perhaps he's dumped the car for good. Did he make you guys?"

"We don't think so," Don responded. "He may have a bunch of vehicles stashed around."

"Okay. Tow the car and take a look at it. We have a travel pattern emerging from his previous *go dark zones*—he dropped off the grid in Lexington and Charlottesville and now in Harrisonburg. These are large enough cities to hide a nondescript car in and pick up another car and drive to his clandestine meetings with Hancock. Have someone watching to see if he comes back for the car, and we'll keep scanning for a signal that we can identify as his. And you'd better get someone up to his house to keep it staked out in case he comes back without electronics."

"You got it, Chief," Don answered. "So, we have to assume that Hancock is in the mountains somewhere around the points where Landan Moss vanishes each time."

"We'll go back and look at everything in a big circle to see what we can identify. If you find Moss, don't mess around. We can't lose him again. Take him."

"Okay. We're on it." Don Verde rang off and got his team together.

Two hours later, Gene's tech guys got a ping on Landan Moss's cell phone showing it was located near Culpeper, Virginia. Gene called Don Verde back: "Moss is on the move. Hancock must be in or near the Shenandoah National Park, which is a big area. Moss thinks he's being careful by cutting off his electronic emissions, but in reality he's just sketching out the extreme edges of the zone where Hancock's hiding. You're too far away to pick Moss up, so send half your guys after him, and put two more in a plane to get ahead of him. He may be heading home to Alexandria."

"Will do, Gene. I have one guy in Staunton, so he's not too far behind him. And I can rent a plane in Harrisonburg and catch up, too. I have two guys in Manassas staking out Moss's bad-guy-number-five—I'll pull one of them off and tell him to swing out and pick up Moss's trail and follow him if he keeps going north. We need eyes on the vehicle."

"We'll broadcast the GPS location info from his phone every five minutes, and we'll alert you guys if we see any serious deviation from his general vector."

"Okay, thanks. We'll chase this guy down and be ready to grab him," Don Verde answered.

Chapter 95

9:00 PM - Fifteen hours before inauguration

Talbot was worried—if the Brotherhood was going to make a move against Madison before she took office, it would have to be in the next fifteen hours. After that she would be too well protected. But maybe he was wrong. Perhaps the Brotherhood was willing to let her take office and then try to manage her. He didn't really believe that… but he wished it were true.

He checked in with Gene Artel: "What's going on with Landan Moss?"

"Thirty minutes ago we tagged him heading north out of Charlottesville," Gene said, "and the boys are scrambling to get eyeballs on him. We're guessing he's heading for home. Verde is jumping ahead of him by plane, and we put other assets on an intercept course with him," Gene said quickly.

"Very good. So, really, no new guesses on where Hancock is burrowed?"

"The universe is maybe a little smaller for him now, but that still leaves a large area," Gene answered.

"Let me know if anything changes on Moss. I hope the Secret Service is on their game tonight. This is going to be clutch time…"

After ending the call, Talbot called Kate and the kids at the hotel. "I wish we were all together, but I still think it's safer for you and the brood to be in the five star rather than crowded over here with me."

"Do you really think the dirtbags will try something tonight?" Kate asked, tired from the long flight.

"I hope not, but I'm fresh out of omniscience and crystal balls. So, who knows?" He saw this last night as a highly critical time, but not wanting her to worry, he gently added: "Honey, I wish I could come over for a late dinner with you and the kids, but I've got to stay here at the townhouse in the unlikely case that something pops. Sheila Lance will come back to the hotel when she's done with Maddy's business."

"I don't say this to you very often, but please be careful, Tally. See you soon." She ended the call and headed for the shower.

*   *   *

A few hundred feet away from Talbot's townhouse in Georgetown, Secret Service agents on Madison's detail admitted Special Agent Lawrence Radisson into her residence. Wondering why he'd been summoned, he was startled to see Sheila Lance, the attorney from Portland, sitting next to Madison Tarlton. He took a proffered seat opposite Madison. Andie Madsen was the only Secret Service agent remaining in the room.

"Agent Radisson, thank you for coming to meet with me so late in the evening," Madison said with a friendly smile.

"No problem, ma'am. I was curious about the summons, but now I'm really curious, seeing as how this woman is also here." He stared at Sheila as he spoke to Madison. "I mean, what's going on? With all due respect, of course."

"What's going on is this, Agent Radisson. I've brought you and Ms. Lance in for this little chat to clear the air between you two and bring you up to speed on a few things."

"But why you? Tomorrow you'll be the president. I mean, I understand that you were a victim in the shooting, but you really haven't been a party to the investigation and all..."

"Agent Radisson," Madison interrupted, "Why don't you listen for a minute and see if it becomes clear. You have a reputation for being a hard-headed and tenacious agent, but you don't seem to listen very closely sometimes." She stared him down, and he wisely chose not to fight with the woman who would be master of his universe in less than twenty-four hours.

"Yes, ma'am."

"You've been pursuing Karen Waldron for no reason. I understand that you were instructed to do so, but there's really no legitimate reason for chasing her down that pertains to the investigation."

Radisson could not help himself. He opened his mouth to argue.

"I suggest that you listen," Madison said firmly, and his mouth snapped shut. "We're about to tell you some things that will surprise you. You may even find them hard to believe, but I assure you that everything we tell you is completely backed with evidence. The reason I've called *you* here specifically—even though you're a complete jackass when it comes to dealing with people—is that you seem to be honest, and you're not corrupted."

Larry blanched at that.

"I'll vouch for the part about him being a jackass," Sheila piped in.

"Nevertheless, I think you'll be motivated and useful in the coming days," Madison continued. "Sheila's going to explain something to you, and I don't want you to interrupt until she's done."

Sheila began: "When you came to my office in Portland trying to serve a warrant on Ms. Waldron, I assumed you were under orders from on high at the Bureau, but like Madison said, your search for her was unwarranted. You assumed that Karen had additional information about the assassination. The truth is, she did, but not the kind you were expecting. You thought she knew of her husband's plans. But she did not. The information Karen was withholding is that her husband couldn't have shot Wilson Sarnoff." Sheila took a breath.

"That's nuts. Of course Doug Waldron is the shooter!" Radisson blurted.

"No interruptions," Madison reminded.

"No. In fact, Doug Waldron was physically incapable of taking the shot. Karen left Chicago and went to her house in Portland to retrieve the medical records that proved Doug was not the shooter. You pursued her—and you were not the only one. In short, Agent Radisson, Karen Waldron's life is in jeopardy because of her knowledge."

"Let me insert something here," Madison spoke up, "and remind you that everything Sheila is saying has been verified by highly credible sources."

Sheila explained the chain of events occurring after certain individuals learned of Doug Waldron's eye problem, and she revealed the names of all those who were killed to cover up that information: the doctor and his wife, the lawyer, and the FBI agent. She also told Radisson about the attempt on Karen's life in Florida.

"Am I supposed to believe all this? If you had this information, then you were withholding evidence from the proper authorities who were conducting the investigation—meaning us, the FBI," Radisson said, perturbed. "You had a duty to bring this crazy theory to our attention."

"No, Agent Radisson, we didn't. The FBI was well aware of this information before we were," Sheila replied.

"How so?"

"You may have missed a key point while you were half-listening and preparing your rebuttal," Sheila said. "Unrelated to Karen Waldron as a source, someone at high levels in the FBI also knew the same information about Doug Waldron's eye damage. Recall, if you will, that Doctor Robins called a lawyer friend in Seattle, who in turn called an FBI agent in San Diego. That agent then called

FBI Headquarters. Obviously, someone in the FBI clearly understood the implications of the eye problem."

"Then why haven't I or anyone else in the investigation heard about this?" Radisson was fuming.

"Because, dear dense one, the person on the other end of the call in D.C. is a co-conspirator," Sheila said.

"No way. Who do you claim is dirty in the FBI?"

"We didn't know until today," Sheila continued. "I called you to set up the meeting with Karen for day after tomorrow. By calling you, we knew that we would set off a chain of calls, and we tracked those calls, Larry. You called your boss at FBI Headquarters, and you called your partner, Agent Palmer. This is where it gets really informative. Agent Palmer called someone in New York, and then Palmer called a private cell number inside FBI Headquarters. You see, Larry, your slimeball partner is working with the people who are responsible for covering up the truth about Doug Waldron not being the assassin."

"Palmer? You're joking. Not him."

"No jokes here," Sheila said. "This is deadly serious. You were in New York with Palmer, quite coincidentally, when some goons tried to kidnap Talbot DeCourcy. Have you asked yourself why you were there? Someone higher up in the FBI chain wanted Palmer in place to get DeCourcy in case the Armenians couldn't. Also, on the same day, men posing as FBI agents tried to kidnap three DeCourcy children."

"DeCourcy is a rich dude. He must have enemies. I doubt those attempts were connected to Karen Waldron."

"You're very mistaken about that. You didn't hear that Justice Kate Covington was attacked at the same time. And again, the attackers were posing as FBI," Sheila said.

"No, I didn't hear anything about that. And what would Judge Covington have to do with any of this?"

"If you had done a little checking, you'd know that Justice Covington is Talbot DeCourcy's spouse and the mother of the children who were attacked." Sheila saw the effect of her words on Larry. "The attack on Kate was not reported to the FBI, and you can probably imagine why. So, to sum it up—those failed-kidnappers tried on multiple fronts to get DeCourcy to give up Karen Waldron."

"This is unbelievable! Whose number was it at Headquarters?" He was still incredulous, but the investigator in him took over.

"We don't know. The question of the hour is—who else is involved in the FBI? And how many?" Sheila said.

"This is more than far-fetched; it's crazy," he said, his face flushing to its customary red. "I have lots of questions…"

"Save them, Agent Radisson," Madison said. "I want to tell you why you're here. Tomorrow after I'm sworn in, I will sign an executive order naming Sheila Lance as a special prosecutor. She will report to the new attorney general and to me. I'm giving you the opportunity to be the lead special investigator…to follow the trail uphill for us. This will be the most important criminal investigation you'll probably ever lead. Do you want to come on board, knowing that you'll be working for Sheila?"

"I can do that. I don't like half the people I have to work with every day, including Palmer. I can follow Ms. Lance's lead. If what you say is true, this is huge."

"It very much is huge," Madison said.

"One thing. With all due respect, ma'am, I'll have a very hard time working in close proximity to Bertrand Pinckney. I can't stand that guy!"

"Well, I wouldn't worry about that, Larry." Madison smiled. "And I want you to keep quiet about Sheila's appointment; this whole thing needs to be a top-secret investigation. We are on the edge of a political precipice, and we don't want to Jack-an-Jill our way down the hill."

"I got it, but what do I say to my boss?"

"Nothing, yet," Madison said. "By tomorrow afternoon, I'll be having another chat with the director, and I'll lay out the plan. Go home and get some rest. You're going to need it."

As the meeting broke up, Sheila asked Radisson for a ride downtown, which shocked him. She seemed to bear him no ill will. *Maybe she's just amused by me*, and that thought made him smile.

Chapter 96

11:00 PM – Thirteen hours before inauguration

Madison met with Talbot in the underground sitting room halfway between their two townhouses. Her protection detail positioned outside her bedroom door was unaware she had used the secret passage to the hidden complex beneath the two townhouse units.

After Madison and Talbot finished discussing the executive orders that would enable them to go after the men trying to change America's system of government, Talbot said soberly: "Maddy, things might never be the same after 12 noon tomorrow."

"That is profound, dear, but it seems to me like things have been very different for a couple of weeks now."

"Okay, more *different-er* than that," he teased.

"Well, I *agree-er*, then."

"*Okay-er*, then." It was an old game between them, one they hadn't played in a long time. Talbot watched this woman who would not just sashay onto the global stage—this woman could change the world.

"I can't really comprehend all this on a purely human level…" Madison whispered.

He reached for her hands. "You're going to be the change agent for a new version of the American Republic. Hancock should've remembered the old adage, 'be careful what you wish for, you may get it.' And…you know this means we're at war with the Brotherhood until we obliterate them."

"Well, old boy, fighting traitors and stomping out treason is usually a wee bit messy. I suppose it's too late to go back to Silicon Valley and build a few more companies."

"I hesitate bringing up the *destiny* word…but here we are." Noticing her weary face, he added, "I think you ought to get some sleep before you remake the world tomorrow. Goodnight." He kissed her forehead and walked her to the stairs. "Maddy…"

"I know what you are going to say, 'Be prepared. Stay calm and cool.'"

"Yeah, you're right. Once a scout—always annoying."

The sound of his deep baritone voice always comforted her. "No, Tally. Not annoying. But always there. And I love you all the more for it."

Madison returned to her room and thought about their discussion. She changed out of her clothes, put on sweatpants and hooded sweatshirt, and laced up her cross trainers. She zipped her M3 device into her pocket and put a small LED flashlight into the other.

Finally, with Talbot's worries running through her mind, the next President of the United States lay down on her bed covers and drifted off to sleep.

Chapter 97

January 20

3:52 AM - Inauguration Day

Alpha and Bravo units were staged. "Alpha ready to roll, Top," Alpha leader said, checking in with his overwatch spotter.

"Copy that, Alpha. Make sure to check your six."

"Bravo pumped and ready to rock, Top."

"Copy that, Bravo. Hold…on your clock." Overwatch, from his vantage point of the second story window two blocks away, turned and nodded at his sniper to be ready. Then looking through his spotting scope, he commanded over his radio: "Start your roll, Alpha, by the numbers. Bravo, you are holding."

At overwatch's command, a gray, half-ton Chevy pickup started rolling down the street. The headlights were off, and the crew in the truck was tense. This was their real ride. They had driven dozens of practice runs, but this was *it,* and all five crew members were ready to break the back of history. The sentries first saw them a block out from the target. The lack of headlamps gave Alpha a few extra seconds before Secret Service agents manning the barricade knew they were under attack. The man in the Chevy passenger seat leaned out his window and opened up on the guards. The rattle of Kalashnikov rifle fire shattered the overcast night. Three Secret Service agents went down, and the truck rolled through the barrier half a block from Madison's townhouse.

The signature sound of the AKs caused agents at the other end of the block to turn around and face down the street. Agent Lamar Beale, lead agent at the front of Madison Tarlton's house, shouted into his wrist mic: "Incoming tangos from the west. Weapons hot. We're taking fire at the checkpoint. Evac Dolly, backdoor, *move, move, move!*" Even as Beale called out commands, the pickup truck slewed nearly to a stop. Three black clad figures rose from the truck bed and as one raised their RPG-32 Nashab launchers. Practically at point-blank range, they aimed and fired the rockets at the townhouse. The truck began screeching away as soon as the rockets cleared the tubes.

Explosions rocked the night. As the grenades blew out the front of the house, three Secret Service agents at the eastern checkpoint poured automatic gunfire back at the truck. The driver and passenger took multiple rounds, and the truck slowed, drifting to the side of the road. One of the shooters in the back of the truck was killed by explosion-shrapnel blasting back, and the remaining two dropped their launch tubes and unslung their AKs, preparing to shoot. They were cut down by Secret Service agents. But Agent Lamar Beale was breathing his last under a pile of rubble in front of the ruined townhouse.

Inside the house, the structure shook but remained sound. Unknown to the attackers, the townhouse walls were built of 18-inch thick, high-density, reinforced concrete covered by explosion-diffusing carbon-fiber armor. The living room was a mess, but the walls shielding Madison's bedroom were essentially unscathed. Agents Andie Madsen and Jason Southwick responded to Agent Beale's call out and were moving from the kitchen to the bedroom when the grenades hit. The overlapping wall layout protected them from the blast, but the noise was debilitating for a few seconds. When they could hear again, they received word that the men in the truck were terminated.

Andie and Jason swung Madison's door open and rushed toward her. They were surprised to see her, code-named Dolly, up, completely dressed, and ready to go. No time for questions. Together they went through the door and into the kitchen. Jason hit a hidden wall switch, and the lights dropped to safety-red as the floor fell away, exposing a staircase going downward. Madison and the two agents jolted down the stairs and through a spacious, underground tunnel. They followed its path beneath the back garden and sprang up the stairs leading to the house directly behind Madison's.

They were taking Madison out through her escape hatch, or the "backdoor."

Chapter 98

3:55 AM – Inauguration Day

Talbot shot awake at the first sound of Kalashnikov's. A second before the rocket-propelled grenades launched from their tubes, he was racing down his secret stairs. He slapped the hot button on his M4 wristband, and the Command Center at Courci Downs lit up with camera views from Georgetown. Alarms sounded. Gene Artel jumped up from the cot in his office. The night team was already broadcasting a *Max-Gideon-Alert* to all field teams.

"Be advised, Madison is under attack, rifle fire and RPG's. Evac is underway." Talbot heard the report through his earpiece as he ran; he also heard Command Center background commotion three thousand miles away.

Gene came on the air. "Talbot, do you read me?"

"Copy that, Artel. Report." Without pausing, Talbot kept running.

"We show telemetry and audio signatures of three RPG strikes and 137 rifle rounds fired. All agents on the western approach are down. It looks like the eastern-end guards nailed all the tangos. Madison and her minders are in the tunnel. No activity at the backdoor yet."

"Start the sweep on Moss and his slimebags *now*!" Talbot ordered. "We can't wait. No more time to let Moss lead us to Hancock. *Take them down*, and drain the banks." Talbot wanted Landan Moss and his five remaining henchmen in custody *right now*. Garrett Miller and Don Verde's two teams were scattered throughout Virginia, Maryland, and New York. They had located Moss and were maintaining twenty-four-hour surveillance on him and his men. It was time for six snatch and grabs.

"Copy, and affirm that, Tally," Gene responded. "Our guys are on the move."

"Mad-Status?" Talbot asked about Madison as he reached the sitting-room area of his large tunnel.

"Madison, Jason, and Andie have reached the stairs to the backup house. Three agents are on the main floor above them holding defensive cover. The Evac car is coming up on the stoop right now; two agents are getting out and defending."

"Tangos?" Talbot shouted as he ran.

"Clear field so far," Gene responded. "The Barbies are inbound on the suspect house." Meredith and Brian Lubneski were quietly closing in on the house where they thought a sniper was stationed.

Chapter 99

Swirling commotion.

As Madison and her agents emerged from the hidden stairs of the backup house, three more Secret Service agents joined them and formed up around their principle, automatically using their bodies to shield hers. They were in the line-of-fire and knew the blasting outside was coming for them. One agent rushed to the living room and slapped the door switch, causing the steel front door to swing heavily outward. An up-armored, black SUV escape vehicle was parked near the door with engine running—and two agents were outside the car, weapons lifted and facing away from the house. They were ultimate professionals doing the job they had trained for.

From two blocks away, the assassin held his crosshairs on the upper center of the doorframe as he saw it swing open. His spotter, the overwatch commander, clicked his mic to make sure the sniper was focused. "This is it, Bravo boys. Time to roll," he said to the second attack team. The sniper saw his target coming into view—he saw Madison being led by male agents and trailed by a female agent. Although the interior lighting of the doorway was a dim red glow, he clearly viewed the target advancing into his effective range of fire.

Madison and her guards hesitated briefly, then strode toward the opened door as Preston Knight had instructed them to do the previous day. Madison Hemsley-Tarlton's heartrate was elevated but less than the average person's would be. She was the consummate soldier, long-trained to be cool under pressure, and once again, as in so many previous times, the training was paying off.

The sniper held his breath and squeezed the trigger between heartbeats. As the trigger was in mid-travel, the assassin had a fraction of a second of emotion and moral doubt—only the second time in his shooting experience.

The shot was not a perfect firing solution, and although the male agent was in his direct line of fire, it was good enough. The .50 caliber round, capable of penetrating a steel engine block, traveled for one-and-a-quarter seconds before slamming into the first obstacle in its path. The impact of the bullet dropped Jason and Madison to the floor.

A female agent, Hardesty, was on the porch and reacted instantly to the shot. She slammed the front door closed behind her, leaving herself exposed to fire as she shouted into her mic and to the other agents beside the escape car: *"Abort, abort—go, go, go—get out of here!"* She saw a black Chevy pickup truck skidding to a stop on her right. The other Secret Service agents scrambled into their egress vehicle and roared away, escaping the incoming truck. Agent Hardesty dove off the porch and rolled, then came up firing at the black pickup. Three attackers rose from the truck bed and launched RPGs at the backup house. Two of the rockets exploded against the reinforced townhouse wall. At the same time, Agent Hardesty emptied her weapon at the driver and shooters, nailing one shooter in the head. He dropped his launcher while still squeezing the trigger, and his rocket penetrated the truck bed, hitting directly into the fuel tank.

The resulting shrapnel-laced fireball consumed the attackers and most of the truck.

Chapter 100

Talbot ran up the stairs, praying that Madison was safe. His mind raced back to long-buried memories of that other night—the most hideous moment of his life, the night his family was struck down. When young Talbot burst into the cabin and shot the man about to kill his mother, his entire life lurched off course.

*　　*　　*

As he knelt singing to his mother, her tears streamed. She felt the pain of her wounds.

"Tally, you can do this. You've been so extraordinary your whole life." She coughed up blood and had trouble continuing. "Save the baby, please. Always remember I love you, son." She fell back, still alive but too weak to speak again.

Tally, a child prodigy, was blossoming into a brilliantly curious young man—a true polymath. While most boy scouts learned enough first aid to pass requirements, patch a cut, and splint a bone, Talbot read several books on emergency medicine and life-saving procedures, especially those pertaining to childbirth crises and cesarean section, because he was worried his mother would go into early labor far from medical care. He had just read the last book on the way to Idaho that summer.

Wiping his tears, Talbot pulled out his Victorinox Swiss army knife and opened the smallest blade. It was extremely sharp. With a silent prayer and more tears, he said goodbye to his mother. Because she was seconds away from death, he didn't need to be gentle. Speed was paramount, but so was caution. He must cut in the exact place and to the correct depth. In a few moments the baby was out—and the mother's heart was still. Talbot found a cloth to swaddle the baby after cleaning her. The baby howled—and the boy cried out in anguish beside her.

A moan came from behind the door. He suddenly realized his father was not dead, but critically wounded. Gently laying the baby girl on his mother's cooling breast, he rushed to his father and quickly compressed and bound the wounds. With a desperate drive to go for help, he ripped off a closet door, rolled his father onto it, and pulled it like a travois outside to the driveway. He levered it up into the back of the Land Rover, with the door barely closing tight, and after finding a basket to put the baby in, he fired up the engine.

Idaho farm kids were legal drivers at age fourteen. Even though Talbot was a Virginia boy, he had spent summers in Idaho every year and had learned to drive while doing farm work. Now, he drove the Land Rover as fast as he dared, and although he only had five miles to go, he knew every second counted. Because his family was church-going folk, prayer was an everyday part of their lives, and at this moment, Talbot prayed with the greatest fervency of his young life—and without ceasing.

His intense emotions almost overcame him. Although he had uber-genius abilities, they were of little use to him now. He had just held his mother as she died, delivered a baby, and witnessed his murdered sisters. And…he had just killed three men. Taking a human life is an agonizing thing for the normal psyche.

Tally had been trained by serious combat veterans, graduating with flying colors from the courses his Special Forces instructors had tailor-made for him. He'd been to the firing range every week since he was eight. *And all of this* because his father was determined that Talbot could hold his own in any situation—be it combat, survival, or the unusual rigors of complex DeCourcy life.

He reached the long driveway belonging to Dr. Jonas Abernathy, a lifelong friend of his father. Tally honked the horn, slowing to a torturous crawl because of the setting sun's glare in his eyes. The blaring alerted the household, and as Talbot reached the house, Dr. Jonas was on the front steps, his features creased with concern. Seeing the DeCourcy boy leap from the vehicle, he could barely understand the boy's shouted words, but the urgency was obvious. The doctor ran to the car as Tally pulled the back hatch open. The sight was shocking. Dr. Jonas shouted to his wife and college-age son, and after they came running out the door, the men worked to move Tom DeCourcy into the home office.

Kari Abernathy heard a baby crying. She found the newborn on the passenger-side floor—and twenty-plus years of professional cool as a trauma nurse gave way to flooding grief. Her tears cascaded. She realized in an instant what this baby meant: her dear friend Sandra DeCourcy had given birth, and because she wasn't with the baby, she must be dead. Kari brought the child into the house and handed the basket to her daughter. She desperately sought composure as she gathered the necessary items to check the baby's airway and vital signs. She found her alert and healthy. After softly bathing and swaddling her in clean, warm blankets, she placed the baby back in the arms of her daughter, who was sitting near the warm stove.

"Encourage our little girlfriend to suck water from the bottle so she won't get dehydrated," she instructed her daughter as she dashed out to help Jonas.

A tall and lanky rural family practice doctor, Jonas Abernathy made house calls, saw patients at his home clinic, and performed minor surgery at the two hospitals within range of his practice. After he and his son put Tom DeCourcy onto the exam table, Jonas began cutting away the clothing to fully assess injuries. He called to Kari just as she entered the exam room. "Start an IV with normal saline, and monitor his vital signs."

Talbot watched while Doctor Jonas irrigated the blood away to view the damage. "Tally, it looks like three gunshot wounds. Any head trauma?" the doctor asked.

"Not that I know of. Dad was shot through the cabin door. I thought he was dead when I first got home, but then he started moaning," Talbot recited rapidly.

"Okay, son, you did great on these compression bandages. You saved your dad's life. He's lost a lot of blood, but he still has decent vital signs, so hopefully we can save him. I can't promise though, so let's get to it."

The doctor shouted to his son who had gone to the other room: "Ben, bring me whatever gauze and large ABD dressings you can find and more sterile water to irrigate the wounds."

Jonas promptly reverted to the business of battlefield surgery; he was a Viet Nam War army veteran. As Ben entered the room, Jonas instructed, "Go down to the hospital and get me four units of whole blood, type 'O' positive. Take a sheet from my script pad, but don't tell anybody what's going on. This is family-private."

"Okay, dad. I'm outta here," Ben called over his shoulder, racing out of the room. He grabbed keys from the striped-yellow fish key-holder by the back door and hustled to his jeep.

"Kari, you'd better call Leland and get him over here on the quiet," Jonas called to his wife.

Talbot, no longer adrenalized, sat slumped over in the exam chair watching the doctor work. He was moving into full-meltdown mode. Doctor Jonas patted him on the shoulder, saying: "Tally, like I said, you did really great on your dad, and his vital signs are holding stable, so I think there's a good chance he's going to make it."

*   *   *

County Sheriff Leland Davenport arrived at the Abernathy
house an hour later. He'd been at the other end of the county, but
when he received his sister's call and heard the urgency in her voice,
he dropped his work and raced over with flashing lights and
blurpping siren. As he entered the exam room, he gaped at his friend
and distant cousin, Thomas DeCourcy, stretched out on the exam
table.

"How's he do'in, Jonas?"

"He's alive for now. I've plugged the holes, got some blood in
him, and he's sedated. He tried to wake up and fuss," Dr. Jonas said,
scrubbing the blood off his arms as he spoke to his brother-in-law.

The sheriff pulled a chair up close to Tally, a boy he liked and
admired very much. "Tally, can you tell me what the hell happened to
your dad?" Talbot shakily told him the story of coming home: the
shootings, the baby, and driving his dad to Dr. Abernathy's house. He
explained how he had killed three men and that he assumed his
father had killed the fourth man. He sobbed through his words when
he spoke about his mother and sisters.

"Okay, son. This is really crappy, I know." He spoke soothingly.
"We all loved your mom and sisters very much. And we love you and
your dad. Okay, son. You did an amazing thing, and we're as proud
of you as your dad will be when he wakes up. The hurt and pain are
gonna take a long time, but you're gonna make it. I can tell you from
personal experience. And you just keep letting the hurt come out.
Don't bottle it up. Let it come out." Tally slumped forward and
sobbed as the Sherriff cradled him in his arms.

Leland Davenport and Thomas DeCourcy had served together
in Viet Nam in the Seawolves, a navy attack helicopter unit that
supported and supplied Navy SEALs in special operations. Both men
had been wounded in the same battle and had lost many dear friends,
but had survived against the odds—their unit had suffered the

highest casualty rate of any chopper unit in the Viet Nam conflict. They had seen unspeakable suffering, and it had taken numerous years to heal. But they *had* healed over time. Sheriff Davenport knew what he was talking about.

"Look, Tally, I'm gonna go back over to your place to have a look. There's no reason for you to come, and there's no reason to let anybody else hear about this. We don't know if these were the only guys after your dad, and we don't know if this is over."

Tally fell asleep while the Sheriff was gone, and Leland came back after midnight. Although someone had put the boy in a single bed in the next room, he woke up when he heard the adults talking. His father slept in another bed nearby, an IV infusion dripping steadily into his arm. Tally got up and walked slowly to the half-closed door to listen.

He heard Leland speaking to Doctor Jonas and Kari: "Oh, man, it was a bad, bad scene. I don't know how Tally managed to blow those guys away without getting himself hit. He shotgunned three dudes! And then to see those poor girls and watch his mother die like that. It's like some kinda miracle that he could function at all. I mean… he didn't freeze up. He took those bastards on, and then he delivered his baby sister and saved his dad's life. He's something, that kid. But it's all gonna hit him really hard now."

"Oh, yeah. It will. We're gonna have to help him as much as we can. But thankfully, he's one strong young man. He'll make it, I think." Jonas spoke softly. "What about the crime scene?"

"I'm gonna have to process it in the morning, but I'm worried. Tom warned me that he was concerned about some crazy guy who might come after him. He didn't say who, but he did say that the guy had unlimited resources and wouldn't stop till he hurt Tom bad. He asked me and my deputies to be on the lookout for any tough looking strangers. I pried, but that's all he would give me."

"Tom's going to wake up in four or five hours. We'll have to discuss this with him. For now, my niece, Melissa, is nursing the baby. It's the first thing that's brought her out of her depression since she lost her own baby three nights ago," the doctor said, almost overcome with empathy. "So much tragedy lately! Melissa loses both a husband and a baby in the same month, and now this."

Tom DeCourcy awoke and was stunned when he heard the news. Adamant that the killers wouldn't stop if they thought he was still alive, he decided on a difficult course of action. Sheriff Leland and Doctor Jonas—who was also the county coroner—went along with his plan. Their first priority was keeping the remaining DeCourcy family members safe. The law was secondary.

The headless killer would become Tom DeCourcy, as certified by the coroner. The Sheriff would report that one of the four killers had escaped and was wounded, and his vehicle would later be found—with plenty of blood and tissue—in the river. After a thorough search, he would be presumed drowned. And young Talbot, after finding the bodies, would return home to the family estate in Virginia to be lovingly raised by extended family.

Most importantly, Tom DeCourcy would go live near Nevada City, California, where Doctor Jonas's brother, Todd, lived and practiced medicine. Melissa Hemsley would move back to her hometown: Rough and Ready, California. Her father, Doctor Todd Abernathy, would certify the home birth of his baby granddaughter, Madison Hemsley, in Rough and Ready. No one in the Nevada City area had ever met Melissa's husband, so Tom DeCourcy would assume that identity. The death of Melissa's real husband would be erased by Sheriff Leland Davenport and Doctor Jonas Abernathy, the coroner of Idaho County, Idaho.

And with his vast resources, Thomas DeCourcy would be able to tie up any loose secrecy-ends in those two small towns of Idaho and California.

Melissa Hemsley would become the devoted mother of the beautiful baby girl—and the deception would successfully endure for more than three decades.

Chapter 101

4:03 AM *– Eight hours before inauguration*

When Talbot reached the top of the secret stairs, he raced to the front of the backup house and saw Madison lying prone underneath Jason Southwick. After helping Jason up, he lifted his baby sister from the floor, and because she *was* breathing, hugged her until she couldn't. Andie and Jason righted themselves. The grenades hadn't penetrated the house at all; with careful foresight, it had been built as a shield wall.

"Sniper," Andie reported breathlessly. "We were walking to the door when a round hit your decoy package. Its wheels weren't locked, so it came back at us and knocked us over." She was pointing to the tall rack unit on wheels, about the size of a small vending machine, standing two feet inside the front door of the backup house. As Madison and her agents had moved toward the door, several cameras on the unit captured their forms and projected them—as a solid-looking, three-dimensional image—onto a ballistic gel mass within an acrylic shell. These projected images were what the sniper saw. He took his shot, and as the high-velocity projectile blew through the acrylic shell and ballistic gel, it expended its energy against a honeycombed, kevlar force-distributor at the back of the decoy unit. A new model developed by one of DeCourcy's tech companies, the decoy package had performed perfectly—saving Madison's life and those of her protectors.

"Okay, we need another exit." Secret Service Agent Preston Knight boiled into the room and pulled to a stop. "Talbot? What are you doing here?" he said, momentarily at a loss.

"Backing you up, Preston. Let's go," Talbot turned, and taking hold of Madison's hand, headed toward the secret stairs leading to her ruined townhouse. "Follow me quickly, everyone," he added.

"Talbot, wait. Madison's house is toast. There's nothing safe about it," Preston said, perplexed.

"Preston, I've got this covered. Come on."

Preston Knight's objections evaporated. He knew it was wise to trust DeCourcy.

Andie, Jason, and the other agents fell in line. Jason called out for a sit-rep (situation report) and got nothing but a radio squelch and static and then a few garbled words from the agents outside Madison's house.

"Look, the guys out there will get things sorted out and secure the scene, but we've got to secure our principle," Preston instructed his agents. "Whatever Talbot has up his sleeve will probably be what we need."

The group descended into the tunnel, quickly reaching the underground midpoint beneath the backyards of both houses. The agents paused to surround Madison and face outward with weapons drawn. Talbot keyed something on his M3 device, and immediately, a section of the wall slid away, revealing another larger tunnel running perpendicular to them.

Brighter lights illuminated this passage. As they turned and stepped over its threshold, Preston looked to his left and saw *another* tunnel paralleling the original passage between the two houses. This hidden passage allowed Madison to secretly rendezvous with Talbot. Six feet of concrete separated the parallel paths. The newly revealed tunnel ended at another set of stairs. *This is obviously another entrance to Madison's house and probably leads to her bedroom. She could leave her room without us knowing...and probably has,* Preston thought.

He was amused. "Curiouser and curiouser," he exclaimed aloud.

As they traversed through the tunnel toward a door about 200 feet ahead, the portal they had just stepped through slid closed with a whisper. Soon they came to the door, which opened as they approached, revealing a sitting area.

They paused. Madison entered and sat down, inviting them to do the same. "Let's all catch our breath," she said.

"I see you have a few mysteries, Mr. DeCourcy," Preston said dryly. "I think there's even more hidden behind all this than I can guess."

"You're right about that, Agent Knight," Madison replied. "We can take a minute to regroup. We're perfectly safe...for now."

"Okay," Preston said, expelling a deep breath. "There's a lot going on that I'm not privy to, and we can deal with that later. Let's knock out a plan for the next few minutes." He sat down. "Chaos will reign out there. Local cops, FBI, the Service, EMTs...they'll all be pouring into the area. It'll be a zoo, and then there's the added challenge of maintaining the integrity of the crime scene. If we signal out and they think we're in the house, it'll be *crazy palooza*—that's a legal term, by the way," Preston said, smiling.

"Don't worry. I can't *get* a signal out from this underground maze," Jason complained, still trying to reach the teams outside.

"We're completely shielded down here, at least in the frequencies you have access to," Talbot responded. He walked over to a wall and, opening a sliding panel, showed them a large set of displays. Over twenty outside camera views came up on the screens. "Preston, I realize you're in charge here, but let me make a couple of suggestions. Outside is a combat zone, and we don't know if there are more assassins in reserve waiting for Madison to resurface. As I see it, they've fired six RPGs at her house, and who knows how many AK rounds, and at least one fifty-caliber shot directly at her midsection. And they could have even more ammo out there."

"Talbot, I think they've probably shot their wad. But I agree, let's be safe," Preston acknowledged. "It looks like we can observe the action from here."

"But the agents out there are going to assume that Madison is down, and they deserve to know the truth," Andie opined.

Madison spoke up: "Guys, you need to realize that there's a serious political component here as well as an awfully suspicious intelligence leak. Look at the timing of the three coordinated attacks." She took a moment deciding how much to say. "Listen. All of you cannot reveal what I'm about to tell you. Do you understand?" she said forcefully. They nodded, each wondering some version of *how could this get any weirder*? "We've known for some time that Wilson Sarnoff's assassination was part of a conspiracy and wasn't perpetrated by Doug Waldron. There's solid evidence for that, which I'll share with you later when we have more time for Q and A."

As the agents digested Madison's words, Andie said: "Now's as good a time as any to tell you that I already knew about this." They reacted with a mix of expressions. "Don't act like I'm the bad guy here. I'm under confidential requirements. In addition to everything you'll soon learn, the most important thing is that Ms. Tarleton was the actual target of the assassination, not Sarnoff."

"Hey, listen up, folks," Madison said, standing up. "We have under eight hours till I'm really in charge, but it's my life they're after, so I'm taking charge now. Anybody have a problem with that?"

"Maddy, nobody doubts how exactly in charge you've been since the day you became president-elect," Talbot said, smiling.

"I feel awful about the lives lost. We'll mourn them when we have time. And they were killed protecting me—so I feel that very deeply. But we have to deal with the realities as they are right now in order to get the job done." She felt callous even saying these words. "I'm going to assume that the killers still have someone out there, and I don't want them making another attempt. There'll be too many people at risk if there's a follow-up hit."

Talbot cut in, "To make a safe extraction for Madison from this site, we've got to maintain uncertainty about her fate—keep the press and public wondering. We know there are boys and girls in this political sewer we can't trust, so let's operate on a strict need-to-know, and choose our allies carefully. The news outlets will go crazy in a few minutes…I have some ideas."

Chapter 102

5:00 AM - Seven hours before inauguration

At five AM, the Speaker of the House heard the phone ring as he rose out of bed. He read the caller I.D—it was Art Messanger. *Shouldn't be surprised,* he thought.

"Hello Art. It's pretty early, even for you. What's up, future Senator from Ohio?" The Speaker's well-known good humor prevailed even at five in the morning.

"Just turn on the TV. I'll call you back in a few. This is the luckiest day of your life, Jack." Art Messanger rang off.

The Speaker turned on the TV. The breaking news was that the fate of the president-elect was uncertain, but it didn't look good. Reports followed of multiple explosions, many gun shots, and unconfirmed casualties. The FBI and Secret Service weren't forthcoming about details, and investigations were, of course, ongoing. It was the tip of a confusion-iceberg.

Maybe this really is the luckiest day of my life. If things work out, I'll be sworn in as president in about seven hours. "Hot damn!" he said aloud.

Art called back shortly. "So Jack, great news for you, huh? So now let's make a deal, good for today only," he said with giddy excitement.

"She may not be dead, Art," the Speaker said smoothly, calculating his options for the rest of his life.

"What you've *not* heard is that a sniper blew the bitch down with a fifty-caliber slug. She's dead as a rat in a trap. You're going to be sworn in as president!"

"Art, what do you want from me?"

"You're going to need a chief of staff, one that's ready to go with a full slate of cabinet officers pre-selected and a lot of sweet deals already in place."

"I *have* a chief of staff, Art; and I'll probably want to choose some of my own cabinet folks, right?"

"Try this bit of incentive on for size. Do your job. Be very charming and *very* presidential. Show proper concern for the nation, and let me do the hard work. In exchange, I'll keep you popular and productive for the next eight years. Oh, and I'll give you a little number for your very own secret offshore bank account. The current balance is $250,000,000. That's a full quarter billion dollars, my friend. So?"

"When you put it that way, welcome aboard, Mr. Chief of Staff. We'll have a great time running the country together."

Chapter 103

6:00 AM - Six hours before inauguration

The Secret Service agents led Madison through the tunnel to Talbot's townhouse. Agent Preston Knight contacted Deputy Director Liam Cane, cautioning him to keep Madison's status closely guarded, and to leave the director in the dark. Preston knew of Talbot's concern regarding the director's loyalty, who was essentially a Leon Fuller appointee. There were other potential threats out there also—and no way to tell which players in government were controlled by Fuller or Messanger. Consequently, Director Liam Cane was the only one at Headquarters who knew that Madison was safe and secure in an undisclosed location because Preston trusted him implicitly.

The inauguration would proceed whether Madison was there or not. The Constitution allowed for a replacement—in this case the speaker of the house—to take the oath and act as president until such time as the president-elect was qualified and available to take office, meaning until the disability was remedied.

Talbot called Kate to fill her in and reassure her that he and Maddy were safe. He was surprised to hear her crying; it wasn't like her to be emotional over the phone. She was a strong woman who regularly held her emotions in check.

"So much drama," Kate joked through her tears.

"I'll have Gene get in touch with Lucy and Auntie Janine. He'll have them brought to your hotel room," Talbot said in an effort to comfort her.

Reactions from the world at large were rapidly heating up. East coast people called west coast friends, waking them with the horrendous news. Internet images of the carnage outpaced the 24-hour cable news cycle. Photos of tattoos worn by Mexican cartel members—the suspected attackers—shot into the ether. The press and even law enforcement assumed that "The Cartel War" contagion was spreading, infecting Washington D.C.

Since the wellbeing and whereabouts of Madison Hemsley-Tarlton was unknown, the Secret Service descended on the speaker of the house to quadruple his protection detail.

*   *   *

Don Verde's takedown team was sitting on Landan Moss's location: a three-story antebellum farmhouse surrounded by a defunct 350-acre dairy farm in Culpeper County, Virginia. Infrared scanning showed one warm body on the third floor, prone, assumed to be sleeping. The house was just a half-mile from Brandy Station, the site of the Civil War's largest cavalry engagement. General Robert E. Lee had set up his field headquarters at this house, but to show affinity with his men, had slept in a tent under an oak, now two hundred years old.

In the few hours since the attack on Madison, Don Verde had gained six men to reinforce his snatch team. They were ready to go. But Don was concerned they couldn't make a quiet ingress because of the creaking and groaning from the 175-year-old stairs that his four-man team must climb to reach the third floor. Two men hovered at the front door while Don and the three remaining shooters covered the four corners of the house from fifty yards away.

"Red Leader, you mounted?" Don asked quietly over com-units.

"Copy that, Chief. Red Team's ready to hike the stairs."

"One more time, Red Leader—we need this clown alive, but don't let him get a shot at your guys."

"Copy that, Chief. Red is moving." The snatch team entered the house, advancing to the first set of stairs. Instantly, lights glared throughout the house and a claxon sounded.

Three seconds after the breach, Don Verde heard gunshots and saw brilliant flashes coming from the top part of the house.

Red Team, rushing up the stairs, dove to the sides of the broad stairway as bullets rained down on them. The team sprayed massive return fire up at the third-floor landing. Red Leader continued firing short, suppressing bursts while his boys reloaded. When no more gunfire came their way, Red Team flew up the flights.

From the outside, Don Verde saw a window on the third floor burst outward and a coiled rappelling rope drop down. Immediately, a man jumped out headfirst with rifle in hand, shooting randomly as he slid down the rope Australian style. Reaching the ground, Landan Moss flipped over and released his rappelling harness. He dashed toward the woods.

"*Drop your weapon. Drop your weapon!*" Don Verde shouted, running toward Moss from 40 yards out. "Lay on the ground, Moss. Lay on the ground."

Landan Moss swiveled his M16 at Verde and fired a sustained burst. Answering shots fired from the third-floor window and from two other directions on the ground. Moss went down and lay on his side writhing. Verde's men rushed to their target and kicked his weapon away, aiming their rifles down at him. He was bleeding from several wounds, bloody air bubbles bursting at his lips.

"You're done, Moss. You may have a minute or two. Where's Hancock?" Verde spoke softly.

"In the house…" Moss wheezed. "… address for my ex-wife and kids…" He coughed and gurgled on blood and saliva. "You swear… take care of kids… give you John…," Moss was barely understandable.

"We provide for your kids and you give us Hancock?" Verde asked. "Right?"

"Yeah… deal I want." He was fading. Moss was a realist; he knew it was over and the Brotherhood was finished. He'd never been a believer anyway—just a well-paid hireling with a taste for torture and murder.

"Done deal, I swear. Where's Hancock, Moss?" asked Don, inches from Moss's mouth so he could catch his final, garbled words.

"Car… map… red dot." Moss expired.

The Red Team quickly reassembled as Don sent an operative to retrieve the map with Hancock's location. After scanning the map, Don uploaded it to Artel and left two men behind to dispose of Moss and the evidence of the shootout. He then raced off with the rest of his team, who would link up with another DeCourcy team at Harrisonburg on the other side of the Blue Ridge Mountains—to gear up and hunt down Hancock.

Don Verde relished the thought.

Chapter 104

"Well, looks like we finally got it done. How is Mr. Speaker taking the news?" Bertrand Pinkney said to Art Messanger.

"We've got ourselves a new employee, and he'll be president in two hours. Of course, he thinks he has a full term or two to play chief executive."

"Then he'll be upset when we toss him off a cliff." Bert chuckled at the thought. "Politicians are such babies most of the time."

"And so disposable," Art said, while thinking: *I'd like to dispose of this small talk…got other important calls to make. It's always hard to get away from Bert…That's how lawyers are.*

"Alright, Bert. Good chat. But I've got to call Thomas and David."

"Oh, sure. I'll see you on the west Capitol steps for the triumphal entry in two hours, brother."

Without positive confirmation of Madison's death or photos of her bullet-riddled body, Art Messanger felt unsettled. But there was nothing he could do. He made his other calls and rang down to the lobby for his limo. *Time to go schmooze with the people who will be groveling at my feet.* He could visualize the powerfully rich, self-important fools begging favors from him. He was about to make the New America happen—a lot of changes were coming to this country and to the world. He would soon be the master of it all, with John Hancock acting as senior advisor.

The other Brotherhood members assumed they were equal and vital partners in the enterprise. Art and Hancock had privately discussed this many times. Art would be the leader, the *Fifth-Republic President*. A dictator, really. The other guys were important, but they were his supporting cast. As a side benefit, he decided he would track DeCourcy down at some point and watch his beheading. Nice thought. The buzzing intercom interrupted his daydreams.

"Your limo is here, Sir," the doorman announced.

"About time," he said, thinking *Showtime!*

"Welcome, Mr. Messanger. We'll have you to the Capitol VIP entrance very quickly," said Meredith Lubneski, opening the limo door for Arthur Messanger. He was pleasantly surprised to have a statuesque blond as his security on the way to the Inauguration. The male driver also looked movie star-esque.

This will be the last time I travel in anything less than a multi-car motorcade. I'll put in time as chief of staff for a couple of years before I take over. Maybe less. Once Jack Mellon names me as the vice-presidential nominee, well then, Jack is VERY expendable.

"Mr. Messanger," the woman said as he turned to look at her. "I would like to introduce myself."

"I don't care who you are—just get me there on time," Art snapped.

"Ah, well, be that as it may, I'm Meredith Lubneski, and our incredibly handsome driver is Brian, Brian Lubneski. He's my hunky husband."

"So what? I don't care."

"Well, you need to buckle up. Company regulations." Meredith was sweetness and light, very patient, completely professional. Art huffed but buckled up, unaware that he was now tightly bound and couldn't release himself.

"Mr. Messanger, we're going to make a little side trip. Well, that's not *exactly* true. There won't be anything little about this trip. But it will be scenic—for a while."

"What the hell are you talking about? Is this some kind of a joke? I demand you take me to the inauguration without delay!" he shrieked, his Mr. Hyde emerging. This was the Art Messanger everyone knew and loathed.

"Our employer made an alternate appointment for you. Does the phrase 'suspension of habeas corpus' give you a hint?"

"What?" He couldn't process what was happening.

"Our employer, Talbot DeCourcy, has arranged some accommodations for you. And great news! You already know all of your new neighbors—kind of like a cozy little community of treasonous psychopaths."

"You can't kidnap…" his voice dropped off as he noticed the gun in Meredith's hand.

"By the way, nobody ordered me to get you to your new home *alive*. So sit back, relax, and shut the flax-up." She waggled the gun at him. "I'm not really a rough talker. I save my energy for action." She smiled and lightning-quick smashed his face with the gun, and then again a second time. Not very professional, but not deadly either.

While the Barbies transported Art Messanger, Garrett Miller's team successfully captured four additional Brotherhood members, which they dumped at the Quarry for safekeeping. They finished by hustling to Tyson Tech Security and capturing David Maxtell as he was getting ready to leave for D.C.

This last run was the team's fourth trip escorting prisoners to the Quarry since 4:00 AM.

Chapter 105

11:51 AM – Nine minutes before The Oath of Office

The Presidential Inauguration proceeded as scheduled with a stand-in taking the oath. Speaker Jack Mellon was ecstatic to be here for the biggest career upgrade of his life.

Outgoing Vice President Johnson droned on: "…And the terrible attack this morning on President-Elect Tarlton has once again made this transition of power the most unusual in the history of our nation. Today, for the first time, the Speaker of the House of Representatives will take the Oath of Office as Acting President of the United States. Jack Mellon is a man…"

Suddenly there was a commotion, and heads turned to see the source. A procession was coming out of the Capitol Building and down the short flight of stairs. The vice president, confused, halted his speech. Twenty Secret Service agents were leading Madison Hemsley-Tarlton in wedge formation toward the podium. The massive crowd went stone silent for a few beats, then rose up with deafening cheers, shouts, and applause.

As word spread quickly from television commentators and whispers in the crowd, the Marine band struck up "The Marine Hymn." One of their *own* was marching with perfectly erect posture to her place in history. Madison was striking in a navy-blue tailored suit, her dark hair pulled up in a French twist. She was a war hero and the only woman alive to have earned the pale blue ribbon, the Medal of Honor. She had survived two assassination attempts. And now she was here, standing tall, her smile radiant as a lighthouse and her penetrating eyes glancing over the assembled thousands. The roaring crowd would not be silenced for several minutes.

Finally, Madison raised both arms above her head and turned full circle, as if to make eye contact with each person in the audience. After what seemed an eternity, she gestured for the Supreme Court Chief Justice to stand and join her.

It was almost twelve noon. Pulling a tiny Servicemen's Bible from her pocket, she opened it to a marked page, The 23rd Psalm. She handed the book to the Chief Justice and put her left hand on the opened page. She raised her right hand in the ancient symbol of oath taking. The world held its breath. "I do solemnly affirm…" Madison repeated the words of the Oath with tears flooding her gray-blue eyes. When she finished, the cheering resumed as the band played "Ruffles and Flourishes." From Taft Park, a 21-gun salute pierced the air. The band concluded with "Hail to the Chief," and Madison continued to stand at the podium acknowledging the emotional outpouring of her fellow Americans.

She was now President of the United States.

After three more minutes of enthusiastic pandemonium, she inclined her head to the crowd and went to her seat. Singer Julia Howe Lightener, a descendant of the author of "The Battle Hymn of the Republic," walked to the pulpit to sing a moving rendition of the hymn. Following a second vocalist's rendition of "America the Beautiful," everyone joined in singing "The Star-Spangled Banner." As music played and voices sang, Madison discreetly signed thirty-three executive orders, which Renae immediately took back to the Capitol, with several people trailing in her wake. Andie Madsen took a seat next to Speaker Mellon—the same seat designated for the absent Art Messenger. The Speaker looked at Andie as she handed him an M3 device and motioned for him to put the earbud in his ear. He was uncomfortably curious.

Speaker Mellon had been stunned to see Madison this last hour, but now he was sickened to hear his own voice answering the phone and speaking with Art Messanger. The recording was very clear; he could discern every word. He felt faint and went pale as a kabuki dancer.

When the recording concluded, a deep baritone voice said, "Mr. Speaker, you have two paths; please choose one. The first is public humiliation and prosecution. The second is resignation and political retirement. Good luck. You have ten seconds to choose." Jack slumped forward, about to hurl his morning meal.

Speaker Mellon looked over at Andie, who held out an open leather binder with a pen and letter of resignation. He couldn't grasp it all. Everything he'd worked for was over. Returning to trial law was not attractive, but he realized that Art was missing for a reason. This was his time to choose fight or flight. A fast calculator, the Speaker glared as he picked up the pen, and after signing and dating the document, he sat stone-faced, wishing he didn't have to endure the remainder of the program.

Andie turned toward Madison and nodded with a faint smile. Madison did not react.

Chapter 106

Inaugural Address, 12:21 PM EST

"Mr. Vice President, Mr. Chief Justice, and distinguished guests: Thank you for *waiting* for my arrival," she paused, letting the weight of the irony settle upon them.

"My fellow Americans: I stand before you in humility and gratitude as one who has made the sacred commitment to defend our Constitution. I've taken this Oath in the place of recently assassinated Wilson Able Sarnoff. May he rest in peace. The journey to this place in history has not been smooth. There has been violence and subterfuge, but leadership *always* has inherent risks, and I accept the risks and tasks I have been elected to perform." Tremendous applause followed these words.

She continued, "Many Americans believe that our political system is dysfunctional and that the people's business is not getting done efficiently. Many fear that we are too divided and that our current problems will never end. But *I* say: we will overcome each challenge we face."

Talbot was watching the speech alone in his Georgetown home. Tears flowed as he smiled at his little Jeemie. *Dad, if only you could see her today…the great woman you molded.* He looked to the screen at a crowd-reaction shot and saw Leon Fuller, his face creased with unmasked disgust. *Leon, old boy, you're almost alone now…most of your Brotherhood boys gone…and soon you, too.*

The camera shot returned to Madison. "Cowardly terrorists strike at innocents. Enemies of peace flood our youth with drugs and dampen our hope. But *I* say: we will stop the cowards, and we will renew hope in our young."

"The American experiment appears to be in crisis. Deep corruption among elected officials has caused resignations of Senate leaders. Some say that this creates chaos in Congress. But *I* say: the corrupt are chaff; let the whirlwind carry them away. Those who remain in the Senate have a wonderful opportunity to wisely choose new leaders. In keeping with this opportunity to select new leadership, Speaker of the House Jack Mellon, seated here on the platform, has informed me that he has resigned from both the Speaker's Chair and from Congress." A shocked murmur arose from the crowd. "The House will choose new leadership…"

Jack Mellon sat stiffly upright and stony faced. *How could I have been such an asinine fool to follow that bastard, Art Messanger?*

"Since Congress is still in recess, I am filling all vacant cabinet posts. Using recess appointments, we do not need to wait for the Senate to get reorganized and back into session. These officers will instantly have the full authority of their positions. They can serve for up to twenty-two months without Senate confirmation. We will announce all these appointments later today, but I will mention just a few now. I have asked my trusted colleague from California, Michael Clayborn, to serve as Attorney General; Ron Melbourne, the current CIA Director, as Director of National Intelligence; Gene Artel, former Deputy Director of the Secret Service, as Director of Homeland Security; and Roma Joplin, retired Lieutenant General of the Air Force, as Secretary of Defense…" Madison waited for the hubbub to die down. She mentioned no Sarnoff appointees.

Kate Covington sat with Lucy and Aunt Janine. As they watched Madison with bursting pride and love, Lucy squeezed Auntie Kate's hand. Karen Waldron sat beside them, experiencing a wide range of emotions as she witnessed the spectacle. She was honored to be included and gratified that Madison held no ill feelings toward her.

However, one sat among the throng not sharing those positive feelings. Bertrand Pinckney, brewing pernicious plans, briskly schemed his revenge.

"A dire state of emergency exists along our Mexican border. I hereby instruct the new Secretary of Defense and Joint Chiefs of the Military to leave these proceedings and go secure our southern border. Go render assistance to acting President Juan Rodrigo Lazaro Cardenas in stabilizing his country. Our neighbors should not live in chaos and fear, beset by vicious criminal gangs seeking to overthrow the legitimate Mexican government." Roma Joplin and the Joint Chiefs stood as one. The Chiefs turned to their new Commander in Chief and saluted sharply. Secretary Roma Joplin led the way back into the Capitol Building. Thunderous applause followed, and the entire assembly stood in ovation. Americans who had served in uniform swelled with gratitude—at last, a real Commander, a leader who knew the cost and would pay it for the greater good. The true purpose of American power is *the power to serve*. With great sincerity and also a flair for the dramatic, Madison smiled at the reaction of the crowd.

When the cheering subsided, she concluded her address. "When I entered service in the Marine Corp, my father gave me a cherished gift: a marked-up draft of a famous speech signed by the author, with a brief note of gratitude to his friend, my father. The core part of that speech was quoted so many times in my youth that it was deeply embedded in my soul. The great General said:

> *Duty, Honor, Country: Those three hallowed words reverently dictate what you ought to be, what you can be, what you will be. They are your rallying points: to build courage when courage seems to fail; to regain faith when there seems to be little cause for faith; to create hope when hope becomes forlorn.**

I hear the echo of General MacArthur and other great defenders of this nation, and I gladly stand in their shadow. It's time for this Executive Administration to get to work. Thank you for your generous support. I will do my best to serve the American people and to be a good mother to my daughter, Lucy. May God continue to bless our nation, and may God bless the people of the United States of America!"

*General Douglas MacArthur's farewell speech, West Point, New York, May 12, 1962

Chapter 107

8:00 AM - Four hours before inauguration

Garrett Miller and Don Verde's teams joined together at the James Madison University parking lot in Harrisonburg.

"We'll take Highway 33 up through Rawley Springs," Don Verde said, tracing the road on Landan Moss's map as he spoke. "Approximately three miles before the West Virginia line, we'll turn right on this dirt road. No name. Looks like five rugged miles before we hit the end of the road. Moss didn't live long enough to tell me what we're going to find there."

"Satellite shows a structure but not much detail," Garrett Miller added. "I suggest we stop the vehicles two miles before the end of the road and send our guys in three groups."

"Okay. You take your men straight up the road on foot and I'll send two groups up either side so we can surround the house...or cabin...or whatever. With that terrain, we're looking at one-and-a-half to two hours to get everybody in position after we leave the vehicles."

"Right, let's move out," Garrett finished.

The three DeCourcy teams climbed into their SUVs and drove west into the Alleghany Mountains on Rawley Pike. It took them until noon to silently surround the large mountain lodge that backed up against a granite cliff. It had to be the place; nothing else was around for several square miles. Don Verde knew that Madison Hemsley-Tarlton was being sworn in at the same moment his men were poised to hit Hancock's front door.

"Spotter, what've you got?" Verde asked from inside the vehicle a hundred yards down the road.

"I see two potential humans on infrared; it's hard to tell with the fireplace or stove burning so hot," the spotter reported.

Verde called each element of the attack. "Red Team, you ready to breach?"

"Roger that, Chief. Ready to blow through."

"Blue Team, you ready on the north side?"

"Ready, locked and loaded, Chief," Blue Team Leader whispered.

"Miller's Team, you ready on the south?"

"Ready to rumble, Don," Garrett said, excited.

"We're all set, so breach on three. One, two, three—*go, go, go!*" Don shouted.

The three DeCourcy teams hit the cabin door and windows simultaneously, but the entry didn't go so well this time. From his observation post, Don saw the teams attempt to enter.

"Chief, this is Red One. The door is reinforced steel and opens outward. Our battering ram is useless. Setting charges now."

"Copy that, Red One," Don Verde said tersely. *Looks like a bunker. The windows are reinforced too…no entry through them. Surprise is gone…damn it all!*

A single gunshot sounded from inside the house, followed by the blast of the breaching charge blowing the door off its hinges. The spotter kept watch on the perimeter while all three teams were forced to go in through the front door. Moments later came shouts of "Clear. Clear." The men rapidly searched the big house, but there was no sign of Hancock. Don Verde quickly drove to the cabin and entered; a young woman lay crumpled in front of the fireplace, a gunshot wound over her heart.

"Damn!" Garrett exclaimed to Don. "No Hancock anywhere."

"Has to be here somewhere; this girl didn't shoot herself," Don responded. "He wanted no witnesses."

"Chief, I got something in the basement," Red Team Leader called urgently over the com-unit.

"Copy that, Red One. What'd you find?" Don asked.

"You'd better get down here and see for yourself, Chief."

"Okay. On my way." Don hurried down the steep cellar stairs and found two Red Team boys standing over a cleverly concealed trapdoor in the floor. They couldn't rip the door open quickly—it took several precious minutes to locate and disarm a booby trap set to explode. After accomplishing it, they shined lights down the opening.

"I'll be damned. It's a limestone cave," Don said, whistling. "The whole Shenandoah River Valley sits on limestone, and there's a lot of cavern systems. Looks like Mr. Hancock's got himself a private cave escape route—he can't be too far ahead. Let's hustle after him. Be careful, don't get ambushed down there!"

Chapter 108

January 20

2:00 PM

Talbot, meeting with Gene Artel via M3 conference call, began: "I hear our troublemakers are resting comfortably at the Quarry. Be sure to put mints on the pillows."

"Absolutely!" Gene quipped. "And we got quite a haul. But there's bad news. When Don Verde and Garrett Miller hit Hancock's hideaway, it was empty. Moss was telling the truth, but Hancock bugged out before our guys got there. His cabin sits on top of a limestone cave system. Who knew? They followed the tunnel through and found that it exited on the other side of a granite ridgeline. Hancock must've had a vehicle waiting, so our boys had no way to give chase. They had to go back through Hancock's spider hole to reach their cars and then drive twenty-five miles around the mountain just to find the road Mr. Brotherhood escaped on. That gave him over an hour head start."

"Disappointing," Talbot said flatly.

"Yeah, he's on the loose—and no way telling which way he went. On the positive side, we did drain 3.2 billion dollars from his war chest and capture half his Brotherhood."

"So, *Director Artel*, you can use some of your shiny-new, official DHS assets to go after him." Talbot smiled, then changed topics. "What about Madison's sniper? You said the Barbies got him?"

"Boss, the spotter went down hard. Didn't make it out alive, and we have the shooter all bundled up and tucked in at the Quarry. But we have a little, itsy-bitsy problem."

"Are you going to tell me or what? You're dancing, Artel," Talbot teased. He was sure his elated mood couldn't be dampened today.

"The sniper has a severe traumatic brain injury from previous combat, with extensive memory problems. He doesn't know much, not even his real name—just what they call him. He can only keep track of about a week of his life, and then it all resets for him. I sent you his photo."

Talbot opened the photo and stared dumbstruck for a few beats.

"*Damn, Artel. Pandora just hit us in the gut,*" he said, looking at a photo of the assassin and recognizing the face of Marcus Tarlton, long dead husband of his sister, the brand-new President of the United States and the assassin's wife.

Acknowledgements:

There's always a history—a place where things begin. My first computer notes and chapter outlines for *The Assassin's Wife* are dated 4/14/2007, and that was after many undated notebook entries. I dabbled with the story while continuing my career and family life. And then about October 2015, I decided it was time to pound out the finished prose, bringing to printed life the scenes and sequences I had crafted in my mind for years as I traveled and worked.

The result was a draft novel with no outside input. A friend in London, *Andy Mathieson,* suggested he read it and give me comments. I responded, "Okay, but if you hate it, just tell me you didn't have time to read it." He read the draft in two days, was very positive and encouraging, and provided excellent, constructive suggestions. Next, my daughter, *Jenalee Fortner,* read the book and was excited; she added more nuggets of wisdom. My other children, *Daniel, Anna,* and *Ethan,* also encouraged my effort. More acquaintances piled on as willing early readers: *Dave Dickson, Dennis* and *Kari Davenport, Pam Mathieson, Jeff Wallin, Patrick Burch, Jack Kaplan, Susie Hill, Alan Ehlert, Don Hamilton,* and *Lorna St. John.*

Writing is a solitary experience, until it's not! Once others begin reading and coming back with questions and suggestions, it becomes a community effort. The early readers were generous with their time and suggestions, helping make the story better.

My wife, *Lara,* is an astute editor—not shy at all about helping me see when a line is unclear or can be said in a more compelling way. She calls it "decorating the chapters." *Diane Kipp, Christine Geddes, Becky Quick, Marilyn Dickson,* and *Carol Welch* helped polish the book into finished word art. My sincere gratitude goes out to all who have kindly assisted and cheered me on. A special thanks to *Don Hamilton* and his crew at Hamilton Studios for producing an excellent video trailer; to *Mike Dixon* of Rastro Graphics for designing the intriguing cover art; and to two successful authors, *Steve Hanson* and *Cheryl Bradshaw,* for their advice in navigating the writing/publishing business.

To all of you -- Thank You Very Much.
Dan Daines

Dan Daines - is a story teller, a collector of facts and ideas, and a world traveler. His passion for history and continual learning has led him to read thousands of books and to explore many cultures of the world. In addition, because he's also spent decades working in the exciting realms of innovation and advanced technology, he's able to draw from his skills and experiences to create fiction that deals with themes both current and timeless. Dan Daines, father of four, resides in Spokane, Washington with his wife and youngest son.

Contact the author at <u>dan@episode.media</u> or <u>www.dandaines.com</u>

CPSIA information can be obtained
at www.ICGtesting.com
Printed in the USA
LVOW12s2339090617

537622LV00001B/287/P